LORE O DRAGONS
ESSENCE OF A QUEEN

A. KING

Copyright © 2024 A. King

All rights reserved.

No part of this publication may be reproduced, distributed, or transmitted in any form or by any means, including photocopying, recording, AI training, other electronic, or mechanical methods, without the prior written permission of the publisher, except in the case of brief quotations embodied in critical reviews and certain other non-commercial uses permitted by copyright law.

This is a work of fiction. Names, characters, businesses, places, events, locales, and incidents are the products of the author's imagination or are used fictitiously. Any resemblance to actual persons, living or dead, or actual events is purely coincidental.

Our official page: Loreofthedragons.com
The author is on TikTok as missanitaking.

Thank Yous

This second publishing of LOTD Essence of a Queen would not have been possible if I not for all of you;

My mum Amanda for all your help, financially, emotionally, physically and mentally. My friend Remy Fosberg, who from the very start was a rubber wall I could bounce ideas off. The nutty test reader, Aud Helen Raven, who gave me the feedback I needed to keep going. My dear sister, Sylvia King for making such a wonderful web page. Lars Erik Brennvall, thank you for proofreading the manuscript. And Rúni Simonsen; thank you for going over it with a new and different perspective. And to Robert Offerdahl, for taking my scribbles and making a wonderful cover for this book. I don't know what I would have done without your help.

And last but not least, thank God, that you gave me the ability and the imagination to create this story.

*What do you see when you look into a stranger's eyes?
Do you only see what lies on the surface…?*

*Usually we take one look at what is on the outside and dismiss the rest. The clothes are wrong, the hair is strange or the way they speak is not what we are used to.
How many times do we glance at a stranger and in a split second make up our mind as to which box they belong in.
What do we truly know about what hides in the deepest, darkest recesses of the heart?*

Should we look more closely?…

Or are we afraid to reveal the powerful creature that may lie dormant inside…

Ireland year 991 AD
Chapter 1

 The cold light of the full moon reflected off the dragon's silver scales as he glided through the night. His deep bronze eyes scoured the landscape below for something to quench his hunger. Rows of darke spikes, that ran down the length of his slender neck, lay flat as he descended towards a cliff overlooking a pasture. His less than graceful landing created a small landslide of rocks one could hear tumbling down into the darkness below. This once brilliant mind was being replaced with basic instincts. Some memories were still clear, but he could not hold on to them for more than short periods at a time. He had been here before.. No... Yes! He remembered a human, a female? He lost the thoughts again. He whimpered softly as if straining a muscle he had not used in long time. Spreading his leathery wings he dove down into the field with terrified sheep now darting in every direction. It was not his first time feeding here, over the past year he had come to this very field almost every night. The humans from this village had started laying out offerings for him so that he would leave the other fields and livestock alone. Then about six months ago he had found a human tied to a pole when he came to feed. Ah the female. He still

LORE OF THE DRAGONS: ESSENCE OF A QUEEN

remembered the terrified look in her eyes as she cried and begged for her life. He had let her go, but then another instinct had taken over; the primal urge to breed. Most of this was a blurred image, but he knew that soon his life would be over, as his child took its first breath, he would take his last.

Orelaith awoke, her eyes only just opening. It was still dark and quiet in the house. She closed her eyes again, but sleep eluded her. She heard the crackling fire, but other than that, nothing stirred. Something felt wrong. She sat upright. Smoke stung in her nostrils.

"Fire… fire!" she yelled. The pounding of her heart was loud in her ears as she grabbed her clothes and rushed to her mother and father's bed to rouse them. "The house is on fire, we need to get out. Now!" Her brother Conner and his wife scrambled out the door in front of her. Orelaiths mother froze suddenly and stared at her with wide eyes.

"Orelaith, your wedding dress!" She turned and ran back in, shielding her face as the heat became almost unbearable. Orelaith grabbed her arm and pulled her mother over the threshold just as burning debris began crashing down. Safely outside the inferno Orelaith simply stared at the wreckage that had been her home. Just a few hours ago she had been sitting by the hearth with her mother talking about the upcoming wedding. She heard her father and brother scrambling towards the creek behind the barn with buckets in hand and her mother sobbing.

"Look at your dress: it's ruined," her mother said. "How are we going to get a new one ready in time?" Tears were making tracks on her ashen-stained cheeks.

"Oh Ma. It will be fine. We are all alive that is all that matters." Orelaith pushed her long red braid over her shoulder and got up. "I am going to help Pa and Conner. If we can get the fire out quickly maybe we can salvage a few things." The string from the wooden bucket cut into her blistered hands as she grabbed it. She had only taken a few steps when a scream from her mother stopped Orelaith in her tracks. On the edge of the light she saw the two stable boys. Arrows protruding from their backs - dead eyes staring blankly at her. Glenda and her mother rushed to her side. "Northerners! It's the northerners!" her mother's voice was shrill and full of fear. Orlaiths eyes searched the dark for any sign of movement. The roaring of the fire made it hard to hear anything else. For a split second the three of them stood still.

"We need to get out of here now!" Orelaith's mother sounded worried but determined.

"I will go after Pa and Conner. You just get Glenda to safety."Orelaith said. Her mother nodded then they ran, Orelaith towards the back of the house and her mother and Glenda towards the woods. The surrounding darkness in stark contrast to the blazing fire made it hard to see and she had to strain her eyes as she reached the back of the barn. She stumbled and fell, sending a sharp pain up her leg from her ankle. She turned to see what had caused her to falter, but soon wished she had not. The body of her brother lay

LORE OF THE DRAGONS: ESSENCE OF A QUEEN

behind her. The flames from the house reflecting in his dead eyes as they staring out into nothingness, and a small cry of grief escaped her. "Orelaith…" Her father's voice sounded from somewhere down by the creek.

"Pa, where are you?" she whispered as loud as she dared.

"Here…" his voice was weakening. Thorns and rocks cut into her skin as she crawled towards the sound of his voice. He was halfway in the stream, bloody and straining to breathe.

"No! No! No!" Her fingers ached as she started pulling him out of the water. He cried out in agony, baconing her to stop. Her hands were warm and sticky with blood as she gently lay his head in her lap. She tried to find out how badly he was injured, but he stopped her searching hands and smiled through the pain.

"It's too late for me now, Shorty. I need you to stay strong for your mother." Tears streamed down her face.

"Don't say that Pa! We will get help. You will be well again. Ma needs you… I need you." His rough hands gently touched her face.

"My dear child. You must get out of here and take your mother to safety." With some effort he pulled off a leather strap from around his neck. On it, hung a rough crystal, glinting green light splintering in several directions. He pushed the necklace into her hand. "Take this. It's important. And…" He strained against the pain before he continued. He coughed and closed his eyes. When he continued his voice was even more weak and more strained than before. "Promise you will keep it safe…always." Warm blood hit her face as he went into a coughing fit, and then he was still.

"Pa?"she whispered. But he gave no reply. She knew he was gone as she cradled his limp body in her arms. Tears mixed with the blood on her face dripping into his hair. She didn't want to leave him, but the sound of gruff voices yanked her back to the danger she was in. She scrambled frantically into some bushes nearby.

"There are three women on this farm and I have yet to see any of them. Find them! Now!" The rough voice was harsh and angry. She prayed her mother and Glenda had gotten to safety.

Orelaith knew that she would not be able to stay hidden indefinitely. Morning would come, and,

with it, the light of a new day which would reveal her hiding place. She needed to get away from the farm and try to seek help at the McAngus or the O'Tool farm. They were the closest neighbors, at only a day and a half walk away. Her hands were hurting from cuts and bruises and her knees and feet likewise. Her legs were cramped from sitting curled up in the bushes for way too long. She strained for sounds of the outlaws. She heard them laughing and the sounds of the horses being led out of the paddock. They would take anything that was not tied down to sell or use for themselves, including the women. She prayed that they had given up looking for them by now. But before that thought had even left her mind she heard Glenda scream and knew that they had found Glenda and her mother.

LORE OF THE DRAGONS: ESSENCE OF A QUEEN

The men were obviously pleased, hooting and cheering. Then the leaders dark voice cut the fun short.

"There is still one missing. I don't need to tell you what will happen if she gets away and gets help. So save your victory cheer till we are well on our way." She heard the men grumble and start moving. "And you! Stop eating that. We will have enough time once we are away from here." Some discontented grunts followed and she knew they were looking for her again. She saw the silver lining of dawn and knew if she waited any longer it would be too late. She listened carefully, holding her breath. No one seemed to be coming her way just yet. Then she crawled as quietly as she could out from the bushes and down towards the stream. If she could just get there unseen she could swim downstream until she was at a safe distance, then head south east for the McAngus farm and get help. Her fiance, John McAngus, would be there. Her heart was racing as she crawled on her hands and knees down to the embankment and slid into the water. She gasped for air as the cold water covered her body. Slowly she started moving downstream, but stopped when she heard voices and saw lights coming towards her. There was not much to hide her in the stream but she sank down as far as she could and with one hand pulled up some weeds from the bottom of the stream that she draped over her head.

"I heard something from the stream. Could be nothing, but you know Malum. If you are not sure, look again." The other man grumbled.

"He's a bastard." The men stopped and she heard the other one say,

"You better not say that too loud. Last one to call him that had a bad accident."

"What do you mean by accident?"

"He fell onto Malum's sword... in his sleep." The light reached her and she heard the second man saying,

"It's just weeds for God's sake." The first man sighed.

"Better check anyway." Should she bolt and try to outrun them? Probably not a good idea as she was freezing cold and wet and she could barely feel her feet.

There was a splash of water as the first man dropped in followed by an,

"Oh hell no!" as he scrambled out again just as fast. "It's freezing! If she is in the water she will die anyway."

"What is taking you so long?" The rough voice of the leader they called Malum approached.

"Oh, it's nothing. Just thought we saw something in the stream." The heavy footfall of the leader came closer still.

"Where?" The light reached her again and she closed her eyes. There was silence for a second, then the men whispered words she could not make out.

"No, it's nothing. And I don't think she would be stupid enough to get in the water anyway. Let's go, we are almost done here. It's time we move on before anyone sees the smoke from the farm." She held her breath as she heard them walking away. As the darkness surrounded her once more she breathed a sigh of relief, but knew she would have to move quickly if she was going to survive. She was frozen to the core and she had to get out of the water before she passed out. She let herself drift off with the current until she was sure she had left the farm a safe distance behind her. Then at a painstakingly slow pace she climbed out of the water. Knowing she had to warm up quickly she stripped off her wet dress and squeezed out as much water as she could. Then she grabbed handfuls of dry grass and rubbed herself down with it. She got the blood flowing and felt a little warmer, but she knew she was still dangerously chilled. Her dress got the same treatment as her, and she kept grabbing new handfuls of grass until she was certain she had gotten as much water out of it as possible. Then she pulled it over her head and started walking. She had been going for a few hours when the sun was coming up over the hillside. So far no one had come after her and she started to relax a little. As she did, an overpowering feeling of despair came over her. Her father and brother were dead, her mother and Glenda captured, and she was running for her life. She sank to her knees, exhausted and overcome with sadness. *"Do not give up now child. You must keep going for your family."* She looked around. "Who is there?" There was no one in sight, only the trees and bushes. She shook her head. Her father was gone, but these words still woke something in her. What would he think of her if she just gave up? No, she needed to do what needed to be done. Her hand touched something under the dry leaves. It was a long stick that she could use to support herself. She grabbed it, pulled herself up and looked around. The woods were thick here. The sun shone through only in a few places. In full summer there would not be any daylight here at all. The ground was brown and covered in last year's leaves. That was good for her as her bare feet were blistered and sore. A path wound its way through the trees and the sound of the early morning birds twittering followed her as she walked along it. Tears were running down her face again. She was supposed to get married the day after tomorrow, but now everything had changed.

Her father and brother were dead, her home burned to the ground and her mother and Glenda taken away. No! She would not give up! She would find them and she would rebuild the farm her father had built with his own hands. She dried her tears and with determined, yet painful steps, she continued walking towards the McAngus farm and help.

The sun was on its way down before she stopped again. She knew she would not make it there in one day and started setting up camp close to a small stream. There was plenty of firewood around and freshwater. She even found some sprouting herbs down by the stream when she went to clean her sore feet. She tore her apron up in strips, crushed the herbs and bandaged her feet. There was a fallen tree that would do as a place to sleep for the night and she gathered as many of last year's leaves that she could reach. She hesitated before she started the fire. What if the men from last night saw it? But by now she was too cold and the thought of a warm fire was outweighing the fear of being discovered. She dug a small hole and broke up some sticks, then covered them with leaves and stacked some bigger branches on top. She pulled out the spring onions she had found earlier in the day and put them next to her. Her hand bumped into the leather pouch she had tied around her

LORE OF THE DRAGONS: ESSENCE OF A QUEEN

waist. Her mother had given it to her some weeks before. Orelaith ran her fingers over the strange symbols imprinted into the leather. Her mother had told her what the symbols meant. "In your hour of greatest need, call and help will come at great speed". She was in dire need of help now but no one had magically arrived to come to her aid. She had a piece of flint and a small knife in it from a trip earlier that week. It took her a few tries to get the fire going because her fingers were hurting badly from the cold and scratches. It was completely dark now and the warmth from the fire felt like healing on her skin. The spring onions were so good. She had not eaten all day and the strain of last night's events had left her absolutely famished.

The food would give her the strength she needed to get the rest of the way to the McAngus farm in the morning. She laid down in the leaves she had gathered and pulled more over herself. She lay there listening to the crackling from the campfire and the sound of forest animals all around.

Just before she fell asleep she said a quiet prayer for her mother and Glenda and hoped they would be safe… wherever they were.

The boy had seen enough destruction for a lifetime and he had not yet turned fifteen. He slept lightly every night as did everyone in the small village. The black dragon had raided their village so often this past month that they had talked about leaving the land and heading north. His mother had given birth a month ago, and it was about then the intense attacks had started. For a week after Garbhan was born they had not seen the big silver dragon and they thought they had seen the last of the attacks. But it seemed a black dragon had taken his place. Some of the women in the town had said that it was the baby's fault, that he was the result of the silver dragon raping his mother, but his father would not hear of it. Almost a year ago, while his father and he were out, some of the people from the village had tried to sacrifice her to the dragon in hope of stopping the offerings that were taking a toll on them all. But she had gotten away and later that summer she had become pregnant with Conri's baby brother. He had heard his parents argue about who was truly Garbhan's father, but it didn't matter to his father anymore. He loved Conri and Garbhan just as much. Conri looked down on his brother sleeping in the crib. His dark curls were starting to get longer now, and he moved restlessly in his sleep. He had lost three of his uncles and several friends to the dragon's fire, and now it seemed the dragon had come back for more.

"The black dragon is back! Sound the alarm!" Conri jumped up and pulled on his clothes.

"Conri!" his father yelled. "Take your brother and go to the food cellar. You know what to do." Gently he picked up his brother and wrapped him in a sheepskin, then he ran. The alarm bell woke Garbhan but he did not cry. It had become a familiar sound to him already. The dragon swooped low and sent scorching flames raining down on the straw roofs lighting them up like torches. His mother was in charge of the water line that tried to put out the fires, and he saw his father and two uncles arming the huge crossbow on the other side of the field. Several of the other children were already there when he got to the steps leading down into the cellar. He was the last one in and as the oldest in charge of closing it up tightly. Then came the part he hated most, waiting. He wanted to fight this beast like the man he felt he was, but he knew that he was the children's last defense against the monster that now raged outside. He heard the younger children crying quietly in the back. Then the earth shook and outside he heard people screaming. Something was wrong.

Conri handed Garbhan to the oldest of the girls. "Stay here. I need to find out what's going on out there." But when he tried to open the door it would not budge. Conri pushed on it again with a little more force but it only moved an inch. He stopped to listen, but the screams had died away. He felt the urgent need to get out, so he threw his full weight on the door, again and again. Then he broke through. Rubble had fallen across the steps and he had to climb over it to see what had happened. Never before had the devastation been as complete. All the houses were burning and several had been torn down to a pile of stone and burning straw. The women who were supposed to douse the fires were scattered and he saw several dead among the ruins.

"Father!" Conri shouted at the top of his voice. But there was no reply. Some of the village women came running towards the cellar and their children. He started wandering around trying to find his mother and father. He found his uncle Art sitting at the outskirts, next to the burned remains of the crossbow.

"Uncle Art, do you know where my father and mother are?" The man looked up at Conri.

"No... we tried to arm the crossbow, but it was as if the dragon knew what we were doing. Just as we had got it set, it flew over and burned us all. Your father... he was right behind the crossbow as it hit us... I don't know." His uncle put his head in his hands. Conri walked over but could not get too close because of the heat. He realized that his father was probably dead. He started to cry but dried his eyes quickly. Then he set off to see if he could find his mother. By the time dawn was creeping over the hillside he realized he would not find his parents. Most of the village was burned so severely that there were not even any bodies left to bury. He wanted to break down, he wanted to cry, but knew he had to be a man. It was just him and his brother now..

The snap of a branch woke her up that morning. Her heart started racing at once. Had they followed her? Pulling some nearby branches over herself for cover she waited and listened. All she heard was the pounding of her own heart and the early morning birds. It was still twilight dark and her eyes darted back and forth looking for movement. Something was coming down the trail she had walked down last night, but it was still too dark to see what. She curled up to make herself as small and invisible as possible. Closing her eyes she felt like the sound of her pounding heart would point out just where she was. No, she had to find out what was out there. She opened her eyes and stared down the trail only to see two deer eating the spring onions she had left for her breakfast. She sighed in relief, and as she pushed the bushes aside and climbed out from her hiding place she

LORE OF THE DRAGONS: ESSENCE OF A QUEEN

startled the deer so that they took off running. She started laughing as they bolted off with her breakfast. She laughed as if it was the funniest thing in the world. But as she gathered her things the laughter turned to tears. She was exhausted but knew she had to get to McAngus before they left. They would probably be traveling on the main road and she could not do that in case the men that had raided her farm came that way. So if she didn't make haste she would miss them. She took her bearings then started off in the direction of the farm. Her feet still ached but her determination was stronger than the pain. And slowly but surely she came closer and closer to her destination. The McAngus farm was at the edge of the woods she had been walking through these past days and she felt hope rising as she started to recognize the woodlands. She even walked a little faster as her feet pushed her towards safety. She had the wind at her back as she saw the trail that led through the dense forest and up to the farm. A sigh of relief escaped her as she walked the last feet to the opening where the woods stopped and grassland began. Then her heart sank and she stopped dead in her tracks. The farm was burned to the ground. All that remained of the main house was the chimney and some smoldering wall. She fell to her knees and just stared. Her mouth felt dry and she could not quite believe what was right in front of her. There was no movement, no people or beasts to be seen. She felt her stomach turn and discarded what little food she had eaten the night before.

  Her efforts these past two days were all in vain. She had wasted all this time and the last of her strength to get here. Who would help her rescue her mother and Glenda now? She saw movement out of the corner of her eye and turned to see. Whatever it was had gone now, but maybe someone had managed to get away and hide like she had. If so, they would need help as badly as she did. She sat there for a little while gathering her mind and the strength to get up and search the ruins of the once beautiful farm. Pulling herself up and leaning on her staff she limped towards the charred ruins. As she reached the main house she saw the first human remains under the burnt beams. There was not much left to tell who it was, just the black burned shell of arms and legs half buried in the rubble that had once been the home of the wealthiest family in the region. She held her scarf up covering her nose and mouth. There were signs of scavenger birds that had picked at the body. She walked around to the center of the farm only to find Mrs McAngus and their daughter lying dead by the burned down barn. Birds had picked at their faces and other soft parts of their bodies. It sickened her to see them like that and she looked away. The food cellar was untouched by the fire, although the doors were hacked to pieces. With one hand resting on the wooden frame she leaned in and listened. Something was down there.

"Hello! Is there anyone there?" she called into the darkness below. No one replied and now it was silent. "I am not one of the raiders, I won't harm you," she tried. She heard some movement as she put her foot on the first step. "It's OK, I won't hurt you. I am here to help." There was a mad scramble and a small fox almost ran her over on his way out. She fell backwards and saw the terrified little creature running as fast as his little legs would carry him. She felt relieved and disappointed at the same time. No raiders, but no survivors either. After her heart had settled she went into the cellar and looked around. If she was lucky

LORE OF THE DRAGONS: ESSENCE OF A QUEEN

she would find some food that the raiders and the fox had missed. It seemed the fox had eaten some dried meat that the raiders had left behind, but there were some of last year's apples they had not bothered with. The skins were wrinkled and tough, but inside they were still sweet. She ate a few and even found some cheese in the corner behind the crate the apples had been stored in. She gathered what she could find then sat down and considered her options as she chewed on an apple. Staying here would not help her get her mother and Glenda back. No, she needed to find someone that could help ,but first she would bury the dead. And she could look around and see if maybe there were some things she could use. She took another bite of the apple and closed her eyes. Her feet and hands were full of blisters and scratches and caked in dirt. She would need to clean them or she would get sick from it. Sighing, she got up and went outside. It was about midday now, and the bodies would attract birds of prey and other dangerous creatures by dusk, so she needed to bury them before then. She found a shovel and started digging. It was a straining task and she rested often. Her hands and feet burned from the dirt and sweat getting into the wounds. When she felt the hole was deep enough she returned to where Mrs McAngus and young Agnes were lying. Before she came too close, she undid her scarf and tied it over her mouth and nose to keep some of the foul smell out. A few birds had come for lunch, it seemed. She shooed them off before taking a deep breath and walked over to grab Mrs McAngus feet. She leaned backwards and started pulling her towards her final resting place. She was a lot heavier than Orelaith had first thought, and it was wearing on her already exhausted body. She slipped several times in the mud and at one point fell backwards holding nothing but Mrs McAngus' boots in her hands. When she finally managed to get her into the grave, Orelaith sat down and closed her eyes for a moment. She knew she could not rest for long as it had taken her hours to get this far, and she still had the other dozen bodies to drag to the grave. She glanced at the boots she had pulled off and decided that she needed them more than their previous owner. It was a grueling task, but by sundown she had pulled all the dead into the grave. After filling the hole she made a cross above. She had not found her betrothed among the dead, so he could still be alive or he could be the one trapped under the beams in the main house, but she had hoped he had not come to any harm during the attack. Sitting down by the stream she imagined being reunited with him and her mother. She smiled as she washed her sore feet and hands and put on fresh herbs. Then she wrapped them in cloth that she tore from her headscarf. She leaned over the water and looked at her reflection. Dirt streaked her heart shaped face and her high cheekbones were stained with mud. She tried to clean off the worst of it. Her almond shaped green eyes had dark rings under them but there was not much she could do about that.

    She decided to spend the night in the food cellar and head back towards her home the next day. Her dress needed washing as did a cloak she had found, so she set to that task before gathering some dry grass that she carried into the cellar to make a makeshift bed for the night. The cellar was dry and she curled up in the grass to keep warm. Tomorrow she would make her way back to her own home and maybe find her loved ones waiting.

Chapter 2

The next morning she awoke with a feeling of urgency, so she quickly dressed and gathered what little belongings she had. Carefully she looked out of the cellar. It was quiet, too quiet. Something was wrong and she felt the hairs on the back of her neck standing up. Nothing was moving out there, so she cautiously stepped out as her eyes scanned the ruins of the farm. She had only taken a few steps when she heard a sound behind her and she quickly turned around. Strong arms grabbed her and she screamed both in fear and anger. The raiders had found her. "Well well well, what do we have here?" The man called Malum walked up to her and grabbed her chin. "You ran like a rabbit, but no one gets away from me. No one!" She spat in his face and stared at him defiantly. He just smiled back at her and wiped his face. "Oh, we have a feisty one here boys," he said as he looked around at the men smiling. He leaned back in and spoke into her ear. "I am going to have such fun with you." The men close enough to hear laughed at the crude joke. "No one is to touch her. She is mine," he said as he walked over to his horse and mounted. "Bring her to the camp. Tonight we feast and drink." His words brought on a cheer from the men. As he rode off, the two men holding her arms chuckled.

"Ten gold coins he breaks her in tonight." She stared horrified at him.

"Oh, I don't know. He likes to torture them a few days before he does them. So you're on!"

They tied her hands behind her back and walked her over to a waiting horse. The man sitting on it had a scar running from his left eye down to his mouth, dark wavy hair and narrow eyes. She was thrown over the man's legs face down. The man that threw her up grabbed her feet and started running his hands up her legs and under her dress. The others cheered but the rider kicked him in the face sending him flying backwards.

"If Malum says don't touch, you don't touch!" And with that he spurred the horse and they raced off after Malum.

By the time they reached the camp her belly was sore and she felt more than a little nauseous. The camp was set up in a small clearing and tents were erected in straight lines with the largest one a little away from the others. Ten smaller and one large tent in all. It surprised her a little how tidy it seemed. Some men were taking care of the horses and others were making food. A few looked up when they came riding through, but no one spoke. There were men that saluted Malum, but most of them kept to their tasks. As soon as they stopped, two men came running and took hold of the reins of the horses.

"Put her in my tent and make sure she stays there," Malum said to the man with the scar on his face. He nodded and she was flung over his shoulder and carried towards the

LORE OF THE DRAGONS: ESSENCE OF A QUEEN

large tent. She did not see her mother or Glenda anywhere but they might be in one of the tents. The man set her down inside Malum's tent and tied her to one of the two center poles and left. Now that she was alone, she let the tears out. She had no idea why he had chased after her, but the men's crude words still rang in her ears. Just the thought of this evil man touching her made her sick to her stomach. She wanted to run, but even if she got loose there was no way she could get past the men in the camp unseen. So she sank to her knees and tried to rest as much as she could. The rope they had tied her up with was cutting into her wrists and the emotional stress she had been under these last days were wearing on her mind. She needed to stay focused on finding a way out of this.

It was not until it was dark that Malum came to his tent. He stood in the opening with his arms crossed. With the light from the big camp fire behind him she could not see his expression or even his face, and with the sound of the men singing and cheering in the background she could not hear how his breath became heavy. For a while he just stood there staring at her. She looked away so he would not see the fear in her eyes.

"Stumpy! Why is there no light in my tent?" he shouted suddenly, making her jump. A man came running in with an oil lamp.

"I am sorry, very very very sorry," he said while bowing

his way in. As he placed the lamp on a small wooden table, Orelaith noticed he only had one hand.

"And bring me some food and wine. Be quick, or else I might take the other hand," he grinned threateningly as the small man hurried off to do his tasks. He looked back at her and walked in and around her a few times, then sat down in the chair to her right just as the small man returned with the food and wine. After he placed it on the table he backed out of the tent, bowing and scraping. She realized how hungry she was seeing all the food that had been brought in, but she would not beg. She would not let him see her cower so she lifted her head proudly and stared straight ahead.

"So what am I to do with you?" he said almost like a child that has got a new toy and tries to decide what to play first. He picked at his food and ate some pieces of freshly roasted meat. "You almost got away from me because of those idiots out there. Just shows that if you want a job done right you have to do it yourself. Well, my tracker helped a little once I pointed him in the right direction." He poured himself a cup of wine and took a few sips then got up and walked around her again. He crouched down in front of her "I bet you're hungry and some wine will do you good too." He lifted up her thick braid and let it run through his fingers. She stared at him defiantly but that only made him laugh.

"You truly are magnificent. But alas, like a beautiful horse full of fire you must be broken". He got up, walked over to the table and put his cup down. "But that will have to wait. My men expect me to join them for the feast. My pet will be along to keep an eye on you while you eat." And with those words he left her. As soon as he walked out she pulled against her restraints knowing they were just as tight as before. At the verge of panic she wrestled with the ropes which now started to break skin, and she felt trickles of blood running down her hands. She had to get away from this man, but soon realized her efforts were futile. Tears started filling her eyes. She knew she needed to stay strong but everything came crashing down on her all at once. From somewhere deep inside she forced a calm up to the surface. Closing her eyes she visualized her father's strong face and her mother's stubborn posture. And by the time the tent flap opened again she had regained control. It was the scar-faced man who had come at Malum's order. He moved a little like a cat on the prowl, keeping his eyes on her as he walked in and pulled out his big knife. Her eyes followed him until he was directly behind her and out of eyesight. He cut the rope that tied her to the pole, pulled her to her feet and pushed her over to the table and chair. Before he cut the rope that tied her hands together he spoke in her ear

"I will hurt you if you try to run. And if you do make it out I will hunt you down and hurt you more than you ever thought possible." Then he pushed her down onto the chair and put his knife away. "Now eat," he said and then walked over to the tent opening blocking it with his huge frame. She hesitated a little, keeping one eye on him as she rubbed her wrists. Then the hunger took over and she dug into the pile of roasted meat, cheese, bread and fruits that lay before her. Once her initial hunger was stilled she drank some wine and leaned back. Then she looked at the man with the scar. He was very tall with broad shoulders. Like Malum he was dressed in black dyed leather armor . He seemed to be a hard man but did not have the same evil aura as Malum.

"I need to know, is my mother here?" she prayed he

would answer. He just looked at her with a face void of expression. "Please," she begged. "Is she here?" Still he did not reply, but something in his face softened a little. She got up and took a few steps towards him.

"Please, I beg of you. I just need to know if she is…"

"Sit down." His voice was dark and threatening. Quickly she found her seat again. For a little while there was only silence in the tent. She hung her head and twiddled nervously with her belt. No one here would help her.

"There are a few women here, but if the one you are looking for is among them I do not know." Orelaith was so surprised that the sound of his voice startled her. A surge of hope made her bolder.

"She has red hair like mine but it is graying and…" He abruptly cut her off.

"Enough talk. I am here to guard you, not gossip like a woman." Biting her lip she sunk back in the chair. She let her eyes wander around the room to keep from looking at him. The floor of the rectangular tent was covered in animal hides, keeping the cold ground from chilling the tent. Between the two center poles a brazier was set up, but it was not yet lit. On both sides of the table and chair were large wooden chests, some simple, some with elaborate carvings. She guessed these contained the more valuable items he had stolen along with his personal belongings. On the opposite side of the tent was a big pile of sheep skins, probably the bed. The one handed man Malum called Stumpy entered with firewood for the brazier. As he lit it he cast quick glances in her direction. When he left, the man with the scar leaned over and whispered something in his ear. He nodded and left quickly. After a few minutes he returned with a bucket of water and a wash bowl.

"You can clean up now. Malum will be returning shortly." Another man entered with a clean dress, a comb and even a mirror that he set on the table. Then both Stumpy and the other man left. She waited for Scar-face to leave but he just stood there staring at her.

"Well, you don't expect me to change with you here?" she said, trying to sound like her mother. He didn't move an inch, didn't even seem to blink. So she just crossed her arms, lifted her chin and stared back at him. After a little while he sighed and walked out. She heard him shouting for Stumpy and the men talked with low voices. Then he came back in and stood where he had before, staring at her. There were signs of irritation in his eyes. Stumpy entered with a big piece of linen cloth that he started hooking to the ceiling of the tent. There now was a fabric wall that she could go behind. Stumpy left and Scar-face pointed to the fabric wall.

"Now, get to it." She kept her head high and walked in behind it. Stumpy had moved the table and the water back there as well. The water in the bucket was actually warm and it felt so good to just soak her hands in it. There was even a small piece of lavender soap next to the wash basin. She stripped down nervously looking towards the tent opening. She washed down quickly and put on a clean dress. It was all white with broad leather bands around the upper arms. The arms were long and narrow with points going past her hands. She gently cleaned the leather belt she had and fastened it around her waist. Then she picked up the bone comb and unbraided her long hair and combed through it.

While she sat like that, Stumpy came back in with what looked like a cape. He whispered something to Scar-face, then he left.

"Come here," her guard said. She got up and walked slowly around the fabric wall. His eyes widened slightly when he saw her, but he quickly regained his composure. "Hands." She held out her hands and he tied them together.

"Please, let me go," she whispered. For a split second his hands stopped, but then it was over. "Malum wants you at his side," he said as he tightened the rope. He picked up the hooded cape and draped it around her shoulders. She found herself staring into his chest for a second, then he pulled on the rope and halfway dragged her out of the tent.

Chapter 3

It was completely dark outside now. Only the light from the campfires lit up the night. The cape she was wearing covered most of her and with the hood pulled up, her face was covered in darkness. The men they passed cast some glances in their direction but seemed almost afraid to look too closely. Scar-face pulled her along the outskirts of the camp until they came to where most of the men were getting stupid drunk. She saw Malum sitting in a big chair facing the heavily drinking crowd. Her jailer stopped just out of reach of the light from the fire. Malum looked over and nodded. When he got up the crowd quickly grew silent.

"In these past weeks you have been fighting hard, working hard, and killing anything that stood in my way. This land was ripe for the picking, and pick we did!" The men cheered. "And tonight, we will get a little taste of what will come. There is no one that can stand against us, no one that can stop our plundering. And no one got away from us." Malum nodded to Scar-face and she was pulled along behind him. He handed Malum the rope and walked over to his right side.

"So feast, my men. Drink like there is no tomorrow. And

I," he grinned, "will enjoy my little prize as well." He pulled back her hood and the men cheered and hooted. She decided she would not seem to be afraid, so she lifted her chin and stared defiantly at the crowd. He stared at her for a moment then sat down pulling her rope so she stumbled. Some of the men pulled out some musical instruments and started playing. She noticed now that there were some women among them, but they did not seem to be there against their will.

"Sit," Malum commanded and yanked on the rope. She sat down on the sheepskin next to his chair. She noticed that a few men didn't join in with the drinking. Scar-face was one of them. Malum on the other hand was not. But he did not drink like the rest. He watched them and once in awhile whispered to Scarface. He paid her little attention, which she was rather grateful for. It was hours later when Malum got up and handed her rope to Scar-face.

"Take her to my tent and… well, tie her like you did last time. I will be along shortly." She panicked. All the things he had said earlier and the men's crude bet in mind. But there was no opening to get away. As he led her back the way they had come, she knew she had to try something. She stopped and said, "I need to go," which caused Scar-face to turn around.

"The only place you are going is to Malums tent, so come on. Or do I have to carry you again?" She shook her head.

"Not like that. I have to go… relieve myself."

"Oh…" he replied and looked around. "Fine, you can go in the bushes there."

"While you watch?" she replied as if sounding very offended. He looked a little flustered at first, but quickly

LORE OF THE DRAGONS: ESSENCE OF A QUEEN

regained his composure.

"I will turn around but I will not untie you, just so we are clear on that. And before you start arguing with me, I can just drag you to the tent and leave you tied up instead. So take it or leave it." She made her way over to the bush and waited for him to turn around, then slid her hands out of the ropes that were loose after she had worked on them while sitting next to Malum all evening. She started moving as quietly as she could until she could not see his silhouette against the fire, then she ran... straight into Scar-face's chest.

"Do you really think I am that stupid?" he said with that quiet yet intimidating voice. Then he threw her over his shoulder and walked back to the camp and into Malums tent. As he tied her to the pole she felt defeated and tears filled her eyes. Scar-face looked up from what he was doing, his face showing his obvious irritation with her attempt at escape. But when he saw her fear, his expression changed and for a minute she thought she saw compassion in his eyes.

"Don't fight him. He will take what he wants and fighting him will only make him hurt you more," he whispered. Then he got up and walked out. Moments later, Malum walked in. He looked at her and smiled. Not the friendly smile, more like a hungry cat circling a mouse.

"I heard you made a run for it. It made me a little angry I must say." he said as he walked over to the table and poured a cup of wine. "But you are returned to me so I am not upset any more." After taking a sip of his wine he smacked his lips and looked thoughtfully up at the makeshift wall that Stumpy had put up.

"No, I am in a rather good mood, I must say." He pulled a big knife from his belt and walked over to her. "You have such beautiful skin..." his voice a mere whisper in her ear. The cold steel of the knife against her cheek made the hairs on her neck stand up. He must have seen the fear in her eyes because he laughed and cut the rope binding her to the pole. "I would not ruin that pretty face of yours by leaving any marks on it." Stumpy entered with another chair that he placed on the other side of the table. "Take a seat," Malum said as he took off his leather vest. She sat down in the chair and looked at him.

"Why did you hunt me down? I am no threat to you." He sat down in the other chair and poured a cup of wine that he then handed her. "I would accept but my hands are tied," she said, holding up her hands. He put the cup on the table and picked up the knife.

"Come here." There was a certain irritation in his voice when he spoke. For a second she hesitated, then got up and walked around the table. Stopping a few feet from him she saw something in his eyes. Not sure how to respond she set her chin high and held out her hands. He looked at her with that same smile he had when he first entered. Then he got up so quickly it startled her, making her stumble backwards. That only made his grin wider. He grabbed the rope and pulled her close. His breath smelled of wine as he whispered in her ear,

"Don't be so jumpy. It could make me believe you don't really want to be here." Then he cut the rope and sat back down again. She stood still for a moment rubbing her wrists, then returned to her chair and picked up the wine. "You are no threat to me," he said. "But I never leave anyone that might be able to recognize me or any of my men. If someone got away… let's just say it would be bad for business." He looked at her as he sipped his wine.

"Why not kill me then?" she asked and tried not to let her fear shine through. Grinning, he set his cup on the table and leaned over.

"I will take this land and crown myself king. And if you play your cards right you will be my queen." She almost choked on her wine and started coughing. "There, there. I know it's a lot to take in, but you can show your gratitude later." Once she stopped coughing she stared at him. This man was clearly insane.

"What makes you think I would accept your offer?" He got up and walked over to one of the more elaborately carved chests. Opening it displayed gold and silver coins, gems, and jewelry.

"Because I have so much to offer," he said, throwing his arms out to the sides. "And," he said while taking off his shirt, "who can resist me?" His bronze body was toned and firm and his arms muscular. She blushed and looked away. He walked over and put a hand on each armrest of the chair she was sitting in. As he buried his face in her hair he whispered hoarsely,

"You will come to want me, to crave me." A groan slipped from his lips, then he walked back to his chair and sat down. She felt her heart racing and took a sip of wine to settle her nerves. "It's warm here. Take off your cloak," he said as if nothing had happened. She fumbled with the clasp at her neck and couldn't seem to get it open. "Come here and let me help you, it can be tricky." His voice was suddenly soft and almost sweet. This man changed personality so often it made her head spin. He stood up as she came around the table. After opening the clasp he let his hands follow the sides of her body as the cloak fell to the floor. She stiffened as he took a step closer, his hands still resting on her hips. "I think I am done talking for tonight," he groaned. He grabbed her waist and pulled her in the rest of the way. Then he kissed her hard. She tried to turn away but he just grabbed her chin. Once he released her she slapped him across the face.

"How dare you!?" She tried to sound offended, but the fear in her voice was strong. He grabbed her upper arms and held her fast while she squirmed to get loose.

"I dare what I want, and I take what I want!" His voice was full of an untamed rage she had only seen in deranged animals. Then he grabbed the rope he had cut off and re-tied her hands. He strung her up with her arms over her head to the pole facing the chairs. Then he sat down in the chair and looked at her. For a while he was just staring. He took a few sips of his wine and seemed to calm down a little.

"Look what you made me do. You really need to behave. Didn't your parents teach you any manners?" The mention of her parents threw all caution to the wind.

"You killed my father! You have no right to talk about my parents!" He sighed, putting one hand over his eyes.

"There you go again. No respect!" he thundered, slamming his fist into the table which sent the wine and cups crashing to the ground. He got up and started pacing back and forth. His temper was calming, but she knew she had made a fatal error forgetting that she was dealing with a mentally unstable man. Best thing she could do was to feed his ego.

"I am truly sorry for my outburst... your highness. It will not happen again." He stopped his pacing and stared at her while his brain processed her words. Then he grinned widely.

"Apology accepted." He picked up a cup and called for Stumpy to bring more wine. Stumpy came running in with the wine and cleaned up the mess on the floor. Then he left quickly. "See, I am a compassionate and forgiving man." He sipped his wine and looked at her.

"Yes, I see that, your highness," she replied, trying to play the part.

"So if I cut you loose, will you behave?" She nodded and he picked up the knife and reached for the rope. "If not, I will have to punish you, and I really don't want to do that," he whispered menacingly. For the rest of the evening he sat drinking wine and talking of his big plans. She sat quietly sipping her wine and nodding as he talked. As his speech got more and more slurred she relaxed a little. And when he left to relieve himself she looked around for a way she could escape once he had fallen asleep. She felt a sting of disappointment when he came back more composed than he had been when he left. "I do believe it's time to retire, my future queen," he said and held out his hand to her. She did not know what to do. If she took his hand he would expect her to sleep in the same bed as him, but if she refused he would get angry like he had before. She hesitated too long and she saw his eyes narrow.

"Now!" When she still did not react he took hold of her arm and pulled her up. "Remember what I said earlier - I will take whatever I want, and right now I want you." His voice a mere whisper but his tone still threatening.

"Please..." she whispered. "I... please, don't do this." Tears started filling her eyes as she begged him. He laughed and threw her down on the sheepskins.

"Woman, you belong to me and I will do whatever I want with you" he said, straddling her. She struggled to get away, but he grabbed her hands and pinned them behind her head. "I don't mind, just keep fighting me. I like to conquer. It's so much more satisfying if there is a fight to be won." She knew that fighting him would not help but she was not thinking straight at the moment. His weight on top of her prevented her from moving much and made it hard to breathe. He groaned as he kissed her neck while still holding her wrists. Once he let go of her hands she started hitting him but he just laughed at that.

"Still feisty I see. Well, then I will just have to harness you like I do when I break in a wild horse." He grabbed the rope from the side of the makeshift bed, tied her hands together and fastened her to the corner post. Then he lay down next to her grinning.

"You can't win, it's ok. If I am not mistaken..." he whispered hoarsely, "this will be your first time." She closed her eyes and tears ran down the sides of her face. "You will enjoy this, you'll see," he said as he loosened her belt and tossed it to the side. For a moment he just stared at her, then he ran his fingers through her hair, across her chin and down her neck. They felt rough against her skin as he followed the neckline of her dress crossing her breasts. His eyes followed where his fingers traced. Then he pressed himself up against her as his hands traveled down her side to her hips. "You can stop asking about your mother, by the way. She… well, she didn't make it off the farm," he said grinning. She wanted to scream as he pulled up her dress, but she knew no one would come. As he pushed himself inside her she felt only pain, and by the time he was done she was covered in bruises and bites. He rolled off her and fell asleep mere minutes later. It was when she heard him snoring that she really started crying. For the pain, for the humiliation, for the loss of her loved ones and for the total isolation she now felt having lost everything she loved.

Over the next few days he forced himself on her several times. The only times she was let out of the tent were when she had to relieve herself. Scar-face was the one that took her out and guarded her when Malum left. She was dying inside, she didn't even cry anymore. Like a ship drifting on the sea with no one steering it, she washed, drank and relieved herself, but she was not really present. Scar-face noticed. She saw the anger in his eyes escalating every day when he helped her up and bandaged her wrists. His kindness was the only thing that kept her halfway conscious of what was going on around her. One morning after Malum had been especially brutal with her, Scar-face whispered as he cleaned her cuts.

"I can't watch this any more. Today I will try to get you

out of here. Malum will be raiding tonight, so he will not be back until tomorrow morning. As soon as he leaves I will try to get you out of the camp." She looked at him like she didn't quite understand. "You... will help me?" He nodded in reply. Stumpy entered with a bowl of water, and as he left he looked at her and Scar-face.

"I will come after your evening meal. That way no one will notice that you are gone until morning." He finished her bandages and left. The surge of hope she felt made her come alive again. She washed and braided her hair, then put on her belt making sure the pouch her mother had given her was attached. She even took some of the gold coins from Malum's chests and put it in her pouch. She would need some if she actually got away. By the time her last meal of the day arrived she felt more like herself again. But as she ate she realized that she had nowhere to go if she got away. It did dampen her mood but she decided that first of all, she needed to get away from Malum. Then she would hire Scar-face with the gold she took to help her rebuild the farm. After she was done eating she put on the cloak and sat down in the chair and waited. As time went by she started to get worried that he would not come, or worse, that his plan had been discovered. She had blown out the light so the guards outside her tent would think she had gone to sleep. Thus she sat in complete darkness. She had almost given up when she heard something right behind her. The fabric of the tent was cut with a knife and Scar-face whispered for her to come. She climbed out and quietly they made their way into the surrounding forest.

"I have two horses waiting not far away," he whispered". Are you going to be able to walk?" She nodded.

"I think so." But before they got to the horses she had fallen several times, so he had to support her. The pain was making her every step torture, but she smiled knowing they had actually gotten away. But when they reached the horses everything changed. Malum was waiting for them along with five of his men.

"Traitor. Where do you think you are going with my woman!?" His eyes were full of rage.

"Taking someone by force does not make them yours! You don't deserve her. I am sick of having to patch her up every morning after you are done." Scar-face drew his sword. "Let's see if you are as tough when you come up against someone that can actually fight back." The other men had circled up behind them, and two of them grabbed her. Malum pulled his own sword and charged at Scar-face as he screamed in rage. The clang of swords rang through the silence of the night again and again. She saw that Malum was struggling while Scar-face was barely breaking a sweat.

"You have done too much ordering and not enough fighting lately Malum," he mocked. This made Malum scream in rage again and charge. Again their swords met, locking them in a close struggle.

"You will die knowing I am going to punish her severely tonight," Malum growled through his teeth. She didn't see him until it was too late. One of the men sneaked up from behind and stabbed Scar-face in the back several times.

"No!" she screamed and tore away from the men holding her and fell to her knees next to him.

"I am sorry. So sorry…" he whispered. Then his body went limp, and he was gone.

"You are a disappointment," Malum said with a voice full of contempt. "Take her," he said and climbed on his horse. One of the men threw her over his horse and followed behind Malum as they rode back to the camp. Tears were running down her cheeks as they got to Malums tent. Men were posted all around it now, and she was pulled roughly off the horse and into the tent by Malum. "Time to teach you what happens to those that disappoint me," he said and slapped her face sending her to the floor. Then he continued to beat her until his temper was spent.

By that time she lay bleeding on the floor curled up in a ball. He kicked her in the back a few times before he grabbed the bottle on the table and started drinking.

"You are pathetic. I don't even know what I saw in you anymore," he said and grabbed her braid pulling her head up. "You are a waste of my time." She felt his knife on her throat. Her hand bumped the leather pouch at her side and she grabbed hold of it. In her heart and mind she cried out for someone to come to her aid. She truly believed she was going to die, and in one way she almost welcomed it. But the human soul is a strange thing. It will fight for life long after the mind has given up.

Suddenly a thundering voice cut through the night.

"Let the woman go!" The strong voice seemed to come from all around them. Malum hesitated for a split second then let go of her hair. Outside, the camp's usual sounds had stopped and the night was completely silent.

LORE OF THE DRAGONS: ESSENCE OF A QUEEN

"Judgment has come to you all. And now, you will pay the price." Malum grabbed his sword and ran from the tent just as the screams started. She crawled over to the opening of the tent and looked out over the camp. Fire rained down from the night sky and the men were fleeing in panic, Some had even caught fire. She heard Malum's voice over the chaos.

"You damn fools! Stop running around like headless chickens! Come to me!" Most of them ignored him, but a few gathered around him in the middle of the camp.

Back to back they formed a circle, swords all drawn and their eyes darting back and forth searching the surrounding darkness. When all the others were gone or dead, silence fell on the camp again. Only the roar of the burning tents could be heard. She held her breath and waited. It seemed like hours but it could not have been more than a few minutes when all of a sudden a flapping sound like that of a big bird broke the silence. As it came closer she felt the wind pressure of it moving Malum's tent. Then followed a loud thud that shook the ground. She heard the men cursing in disbelief.

"Holy mother of Christ…" She gasped in shock when she turned her head to see what had come. An enormous golden creature was folding its wings around its scaly body. Her mind said run, but she was unable to look away. Several of the men dropped their swords and half of them took off running. It shook its big head and blinked it's big dark eyes. Then with its gaze fixed on the men left standing in the middle of the camp it started moving towards them, circling them. The full moon and the fire from the burning tents reflected in its scales making it look like it glowed. As its muscular body came closer it surprised her how graceful its movements were.

"What do you want, hellspawn?!" Malum screamed at the dragon. It stopped moving and sat down, cocked its head and looked at him.

"I was called," his (she assumed it was a he) voice was quiet and firm. The few men still standing with Malum looked at each other wide-eyed. Fear was in their eyes and one of them dropped his sword and ran into the woods.

"I didn't call you demon! So go! Crawl back to the hellhole you came from!" Malum screamed at the dragon. It laughed and started circling the men again.

"What makes you think I come from hell? And no; you did not call for me. But you are the reason I was called." The men seemed to back away from their leader a little. "You are infected with... evil," the dragon said as it sniffed the air. "The destruction you leave behind you knows no bounds and no one has stopped you from coloring the land red with the blood of your innocent victims. Until now." One of the men had circled behind the dragon and charged him with his sword over his head. A clunk sounded as the man hit the dragon's scales. He turned and just looked at his attacker. "Your men are loyal, but not very bright," the dragon said as he sent a ball of fire after the now fleeing man. A puff of smoke, and both the flame and the man were gone. That resulted in the rest of the men dropping their swords and slowly backing away.

"Not so loyal after all I see," the dragon said casually. "Cowards!" Malum shouted after the men who were now disappearing into the darkness. "What do you want from me? Take whatever you want and I will just leave." At this the dragon smiled threateningly.

"What could you have that I would possibly want? No, the price for what you have done cannot be paid in mere things. I will make sure that no one will die by your hand ever again." Orelaith did not quite see what happened next, but suddenly Malum dropped his sword as the dragon pounced on him. With one clawed foot resting on his chest, Malum's eyes widened and he snapped for air.

"Now…" the dragon whispered. "You will feel what your victims felt, body and mind." Malum's eyes widened if possible even more and every muscle in his body flexed. Then he let out a blood-curdling scream filled with pure horror and fear. When the dragon lifted his paw off him, Malum curled up into a ball. His eyes were blank and he was mumbling incoherently to himself.

The dragon sighed and closed his eyes.

"You can come out now child," he said in a surprisingly soft voice. She backed away from the tent opening. The sound of the dragon moving towards the tent terrified her and she tried to hide behind the chests. She heard the dragon stop and knew he was right outside.

"Why do you hide from me child?" the dragon asked. Maybe if she did not answer he would go away. Then he sighed and the tent was lifted straight up. She found herself face to face with this golden creature. "Ah, there you are," he said, sounding like a father that had found his missing child.

"Please don't kill me," she begged. The dragon sounded puzzled. "Why would I do that?" He cocked his head to the side. Now she was confused.

"You're not going to eat me?" The dragon laughed.

"No, of course not. Whatever gave you that idea?" She relaxed a little

"Burn me..?" The dragon shook his head.

"No child," he said as he laid down and crossed his front paws. "I came because you called." She stood up.

"I called you? How?" He smiled "In your hour of greatest need"… do you know these words?" Her hand went to the small leather pouch.

"That is what it means?" The dragon nodded. "When you in your heart felt the end was near, your emotions became a beacon that drew me to your aid." Orelaith chewed on her lip and thought on it for a moment, then looked up into the dragon's eyes.

"So now what?" The dragon got up and unfolded his wings. "Now you are free to go." She sat down on the wooden chest behind her. "Go where? I have nothing left." Tears fell gently down her face, creating streaks in the dirt on her cheeks. The dragon folded his wings again. "This I had not considered." She covered her face in her hands and cried . "It would have been better if he had killed me…."

"No child, do not say such things. We will find a solution. But I sense your vessel is broken. I will take care of it for you."

LORE OF THE DRAGONS: ESSENCE OF A QUEEN

"Vessel?" Orelaith asked.

"Your body... it's damaged." She looked at her hands and arms covered in bruises and cuts.

"It's fine. It will take some time, but it will heal." The dragon laid down again.

"I can take the pain away now, if you'll permit me to."

She looked up into his big golden eyes and knew somehow that she could trust him. So she got up and nodded. The dragon seemed pleased.

"Good, come a little closer. That is fine. Now close your eyes, child." She hesitated briefly, but decided she had nothing to lose. The dragon gently put his big paw around her back. She started to feel a warm, tingling sensation. It was strange, but not unpleasant. It felt like unseen tendrils of warm light curling around her body. "This may feel a little strange, but it will take away the pain." She felt the sensation building. Then it was as if a thousand stars exploded in her mind. She gasped for air and her eyes flew open. The dragon emitted a rich golden light. His eyes were closed and he seemed to be in deep concentration. She quickly closed her eyes again. As the feeling passed the tendrils of warmth seemed to enter her mind and thoughts.

"Orelaith," the dragon whispered thoughtfully. Flashes of memories passed before her mind's eye, slowing down at certain parts; her loving mother's face as she bandaged Orelaith's knee, the pride in her father's eyes the first time she sat on their horse. The death of her grandmother.

Herself and her brother chasing each other as kids. She

thought she heard the dragon gasp when the image of the gift her father had given her passed before her. When she started to remember the bad things, it was as if memory and emotion were pulled apart. She still remembered, but the feelings were gone. Then slowly the unseen tendrils pulled back and the dragon gently put her down. Her legs felt weak and her knees gave way under her.

"What pain you have endured these past days. You will feel better in a little while, but for now you need rest, and so do I." She nodded at him, all of a sudden feeling very tired.

"And my name is Basilicus." His voice was the last thing she heard before she fell into a deep dreamless sleep.

The dragon stared at this fragile little creature. It amazed him the amount of suffering she had been through in such a short period of time, yet she still fought to stay alive. He couldn't think of a better choice to carry the queen's essence. The kind and gentle nature he had seen when he looked into her memories made him sure she was the one. He had done more than repair her body and emotions. He had stripped away the evil from the life that was growing inside her. Not all of it, but the parts that were tainted he had replaced with parts of himself. It had drained him more than he thought it would, but it would be worth it in the end. He curled around her in a protective circle in case some of the men who had escaped returned. Not that he believed they would. These humans were not suicidal.

Chapter 4

It was early dawn and Orelaith was still fast asleep. Bas was awake and heard the others approaching. "*Quietly,*" he mind sent to them. There were no loud wing flaps or thundering thuds as they landed. Last night had all been for show to scare the evil men so he could save her. He lifted his head and greeted his companions. Seven other dragons had gathered around him, all quite different from one another. One brown, one yellow, one green, one gray, one blue, one dark blue - almost black, and one pearl white. The yellow one was stretching her neck trying to sneak a peek at the girl sleeping.

"*Stop it Solis,*" Bas sent. "*You will all meet her later. But first we need to clean all this up. We don't want anyone to know of our involvement.*" The white dragon nodded.

"*We will find a place to put it. You just rest. But I think we all want to know what you intend to do with her.*" Bas looked at them smiling.

"*I will ask her to come to our home. She has something we have been searching for.*" There was a collective gasp.

"*You don't mean... she has it?*" There was a flash of

lighting in the gray dragon's eyes. Bas nodded. The dragons were ecstatic. The white dragon closed her eyes and what looked like diamonds fell from her eyes.

"*Finally.*" Orelaith stirred and the dragons looked at her wide eyed. Then she grunted and curled up, still sleeping soundly. "*We can talk of this later. But first we, that is you, need to clean this up, then go home and wait for me to return with her. Seeing so many of us at the same time might scare her.*" The others agreed. Almost without any sound they picked up and flew off with every last thing that could reveal there had been a camp here. "*What do you want me to do with this one? He is still alive… sort of,*" the gray dragon asked, standing over Malums curled up body. "*I don't really care Tempest, but don't kill him. He needs to live with all the pain he caused others. Letting him die now would be too easy on him.*" Tempest nodded and flew off with him. A few of them returned, and the green dragon finished up by digging her long talons into the earth and closing her eyes. Everywhere the grass had been trampled or burned now glowed with a rich green color and new grass sprung up instantly. Then she opened her eyes and a satisfied grin appeared on her face as she looked at the result. There was no evidence of anyone ever setting foot here. "*You never cease to amaze me, Serovita. Wonderfully done,*" Bas said and bowed his head in respect. "*Thank you, Bas. My only regret is that I don't get to use my powers much any more.*" They gathered around Bas. "*Thank you all. I will see you tomorrow sometime.*" With that, the other dragons left as quietly as they had arrived.

Orelaith opened her eyes and stared up at a perfect blue

LORE OF THE DRAGONS: ESSENCE OF A QUEEN

sky. For a moment she could not recall where she was. Then the memories of last night's events came crashing down on her like a giant wave. She jumped up and looked around. There was no sign of the camp she had spent the last week in.

"Good morning, child." She spun around and saw the golden dragon looking at her with his big head resting on his front paws. "I trust you rested well?" She nodded.

"Yes, thank you. But how long have I been sleeping? The grass has grown and everything that was here is… gone." Bas sensed her confusion. He smiled at her.

"Not as long as you think. I had a little help cleaning up." Orelaith looked at him,

"I don't understand, who helped? Cleaning up I understand but the grass…? How did the grass grow so quickly?" Bas smiled at her.

"Ok, I will explain. But first you need to eat something to regain your strength." He got up and unfolded his wings. "Do you eat the sea creatures here? I believe you call them fish." She nodded. "Good, I will go get one while you find what you need to prepare it. I won't be long." Then he jumped up in the air and flew off. Her eyes followed him until he disappeared over the trees. So many things had happened the last week, so many bad things. But as she ran through them in her head she felt strangely detached from the events. She still felt sorrow over the loss of her family, but the abuse Malum had put her through was somehow just strangely distant. She felt no fear, no anger, no shame, no pain. No pain! She looked at her arms and hands. There were no marks, no cuts. She took a few careful steps. It didn't hurt! Soon she was running around in the grass laughing. She felt stronger than she had in a long time.

When Bas returned she had made a small camp. He dropped a few fish on the ground and laid down watching her as she prepared the fish.

"So, how did you do it?" she asked once the fish was roasting over the flames. He smiled.

"Well, as I said I had a little help. I am not the only one of my kind here. I have some companions. And while you slept they came and removed the things left behind by these evil men."

She turned the fish on its stick and looked at him.

"But the grass? I must have slept for a month for the grass to grow as much as it has." Bas shook his big head.

"No child, you only slept for one night." She bit her lip as she pondered this.

"But how? How did the grass cover the trodden paths so quickly? There is not a single sign of the big campfire that was in the middle of the camp."

"That..." said Bas and winked at her, "was a little magic done by one of my companions. She has a powerful connection to plants and everything that grows. You could say she convinced the grass it needed to grow a little faster."

LORE OF THE DRAGONS: ESSENCE OF A QUEEN

She seemed satisfied with that explanation, and Bas was glad she was. He didn't really know how Serovita did what she did, just that she did it. "How do you feel, child?" Bas asked her. Orelaith looked up at him. "Confused... but I guess that is normal under the circumstances. Any time I have heard of your kind, they come across as nothing more than mindless beasts. You are... not like that. And you speak so I can understand. You are kind and intelligent. And beautiful." Bas actually blushed and bowed his head.

"Thank you. I must say you are not quite what I expected either. Most humans we have come across do not give us the chance to show what we truly are. Usually when we open our mouths to speak, they scream and start running."

"I do understand them. The stories say that your kind have burned down entire villages and eaten the people who lived there. So if you open your mouth close to them they will think it's to swallow them whole." Orelaith replied with a smile. Bas pulled his head back.

"I would never eat a human. I can't imagine having my food talk back at me. But..." Bas seemed almost embarrassed when he continued. "There are others. I guess its like you humans, not all are good." They sat in silence for a while, both seeming to ponder the things they had learned. Bas studied her as she ate and found her remarkable. He and his companions had not interacted much with these creatures before, but he knew that their lives would change dramatically through this delicate little woman.

"Have you considered what to do?" he asked her.

"Not really. I mean, there's nothing for me to go back to.

My family is gone. My fiancée and his entire family has been wiped out. There is no one left that I care for." Bas was quiet for a while. "Would you consider coming with me?" he said in his soft voice.

She looked up at him.

"Where?"

"To our home. My companions would like to meet you. And you could teach us more about your kind."

"Are your companions like you? I mean, are they nice like you are?" He nodded. She chewed her fish thoughtfully whilst considering the offer. She almost had Bas worried for a moment. Then she looked up with a bright smile.

"Yes, I would like that." Bas let out a breath he didn't even know he was holding.

"Good. We will leave when you are ready." When she was done eating she stood up, put on her cloak and brushed off her dress.

"So which direction?" she asked.

"North," he replied. They started walking but after a few hours it was obvious that Bas was having trouble fitting on the narrow paths they followed. When they stopped for a short lunch, Bas asked her if she trusted him.

"I think so. I mean yes, I believe I do. Why?"

"Well, I need to ask you something, and I am not sure of your reply." She sat upright and put her hands in her lap.

LORE OF THE DRAGONS: ESSENCE OF A QUEEN

"I won't know what I will reply either until I hear your question." She smiled up at him.

"The thing is…" Bas seemed a little uncomfortable. "It's taking a little longer than I had thought to get to where we are going. You see, we tend to fly where we need to go and very rarely walk." Orelaith blushed and looked a little upset. "I am sorry. I am slowing you down and putting you at risk. I understand if you want to leave me here." Bas shook his head.

"No, no, no, I don't want to leave you here. Quite the opposite. Actually…." Now Bas was a little flustered. "What I wanted to ask you… well… would you mind if we flew? I have never had anyone on my back before, and I don't know how you feel about heights." He had been so busy explaining that he hadn't noticed how her face had lit up when he had mentioned flying. When he looked at her again she was beaming.

"You would really take me flying?" she asked as she got up.

"Well, it's just an idea. Of course it's up to you. It's understandable if you don't want to. But we would get there in less than an hour. If we walk, I believe it will take all day, maybe even longer." She clapped her hands and did a little dance.

"I would love to fly with you." Bas was surprised by her sudden display of unbridled joy.

"Oh, that's settled then." He smiled back at her. It astounded Bas how open minded this human was compared to the others he had encountered. Maybe there was hope after all. Bas laid down on his belly and helped her climb up. When she touched his scaly skin he could not help but read her mind. She was surprised it was not at all what she had expected.

"Hold on," he said and gently flapped his wings. He wanted to make sure she would not be pushed off once they were on their way. Then he gently lifted off into the air. As they flew over the treetops she squealed in delight. He sensed no fear in her, only excitement. Down below them rivers and streams, forests and woodlands flew by. Then the ocean appeared ahead of them. Bas flew down to the water so low that she could feel the spray of water on her face as the wind from his wings stirred up the surface.

They followed the coastline for a while, then Bas swerved in over land. Shortly after they flew over a densely wooded area, and Bas swooped lower, landing gently in front of a large cave.

"This is it," he said and helped her down. "It's not much, but it is one of the caves we call home." She looked around nervously.

"Are the others here?"

"They are probably inside." He saw her looking nervously into the darkness beyond the cave opening. "Let me know when you are ready." She took a deep breath and pulled her cloak tight around her shoulders.

"Ready." Bas walked in with her following close behind.

LORE OF THE DRAGONS: ESSENCE OF A QUEEN

The cave was huge with stalactites dripping down from the ceiling and stalagmites growing up from the cave floor. The walls were so far off that she could not see them. As she walked behind Bas she noticed how smooth the floor was. These creatures must have lived here a very long time. There were stone towers coming up from the floor too, but they seemed to be carved somehow. As she peeked into one, she noticed they were hollow. She wrinkled her nose. There was a rather pungent smell coming from the strange towers. Bas turned his big head and looked at her curiosity.

"They are lights." She cocked her head

"Lights?" As he walked over, she backed up a little,

"Let me show you," he said and gently blew a small flame over the top. It lit up like a torch.

"Oh!" exclaimed Orelaith. Then she frowned and walked around it

"But how does it work?"

"Natural gas," Bas answered. Over in the dark corner of the cave came a snigger. Bas huffed, "Not that kind of gas, Luna." He turned back to Orelaith. "You must excuse her, she has a sad sense of humor." Orelaith barely held back a laugh of her own. There seemed to be more to these creatures than she first assumed.

"May I ask how many you are?" She looked up at the big dragon, then quickly added "Your Highness." "I think we have passed the formal stage, child," Bas said with a smile as he sat down. Orelaith winced a little at the toothy smile. It was a bit scary seeing these potential meat hooks up close like that. "To answer your question I need to explain some things first." His voice sounded a little sad. "We used to be many more than we are today. Once we were a great nation, countless in numbers like sand in the sea. And like the sand we were made up of different types of grain. One day burning rocks fell out of our sky and poisoned one third of our nation. Some of the effects were madness, some died and some were infected with what I can only describe to you as evil." Bas looked away. "You must understand, we were unfamiliar to fighting amongst ourselves. And as it spread, the infected overcame the ones still pure. It spread, and no matter what we tried we could not find a cure. Finally our world was all but a ruin, a shadow of what it had once been." He got up and started walking further into the cave as he continued his story, stopping only to puff at the towers he called lights. "Finally, our queen along with the few of us left uninfected decided to burrow deep into the earth and go into hibernation to preserve the last of our kind." He stopped and puffed at another tower. "Our beloved queen divided us into groups of eight. I and seven females made up one of the groups. Anyway, we burrowed down into the earth and made a hollow sphere in the rock." Orelaith looked up at him.

"What do you mean? What's a sear?" Bas shook his head.

"No, child. A sphere is like a round ball." Bas puffed at yet another tower before he continued. "After we had climbed inside we went through the ritual of hibernation.

And that is the last thing any of us remember. That is, until we woke up on this green isle." Orelaith was quiet for a while, but when Bas did not continue she asked, "There was more than one sphere?" Bas looked at her.

"Yes, several thousand." Again he turned quiet and seemed to be remembering his past as his big eyes closed. Orelaith stood still for a while, almost like a child who is told to stand still. She fiddled with her dress and looked at her feet. When he still didn't continue she asked as quietly as she could.

"So… did you ever find any of the other spheres?" When he heard her soft words he opened his eyes. "Yes, we did," he sighed. "But only two more." Bas frowned and shook his head back into the present. "Both were infected. Inside one we found two females, Spero and Postremo. Both dead." He cringed as if it physically hurt. "My brother, Frater, was supposed to be in that sphere."

"Oh!" Orelaith exclaimed. "I am sorry…" As Bas stared out into the early night with distant eyes he continued. "We never did find his body nor the bodies of the other five females from that sphere. For all we know they may still be out there. We have searched but found only rumors." Orelaith frowned. "You stopped looking? Why?"

"Well," Bas continued. "If they are still alive, they are most likely infected. We could not risk being exposed to the sickness." With that Bas fell quiet and moved further in. Orelaith could see more of the cave now that Bas had lit more towers. She would have thought it to be more damp, but it was quite dry. As they approached the back of the cave she saw a wall that had several large compartments, eight in all and in four of them dragons were lying. One brown, one green, one yellow and one white.

"Let me introduce you to the others," Bas said as he sat down in front of the chambers. "This is Vigoratus, our healer." The white dragon lifted her large head and smiled the same toothy smile at Orelaith.

"Hello child." As Vigoratus stepped out of the chamber, Orelaith noticed that she was not just white. The scales that covered most of her body sparkled in the light of the flames like the inside of seashells. She had long talons on her feet like Bas, but unlike him she had no spikes on her neck. Her face was much like a horse, and she had a mane of long white hair all along her neck. She sat down and almost like a cat, she moved her feet around until they were situated just right, then wrapped her long tail around them. Behind Vigoratus the big green dragon climbed out. She was bright emerald green and her skin looked more like leaves on a tree than scales. And like leaves have veins, so did the green dragon.

"This is Serovita. She is the one that made the grass grow in the field where we first met." The green dragon bowed her head in greeting.

"Welcome child." Her voice was like the wind blowing through leaves on a summer day. Behind her both the brown and the yellow dragon stirred. Just as Bas opened his mouth to speak there was a commotion at the entrance and they all turned around. Into the cave came a large blue dragon, running like a big puppy and dripping wet. In her mouth several fish tails were sticking out. She slid sideways and spun on the floor before getting a grip and then came pouncing straight towards them. She screeched to a halt right in front of them and dropped a dozen fish three feet long almost on top of Orelaith. Then she shook like a dog sending sprays of water all over them. Basilicus put his front paw over his eyes and sighed. The other dragons gasped as they got hit by a spray of cold water a second time.

"Aqua!" the yellow dragon exclaimed exasperated. They all glared at the blue dragon.

"What?" She sat down. "I brought lunch," she said with a voice like running water and a big grin on her face displaying rows of pointed teeth. Orelaith found herself holding back a laugh. She looked up at Bas and saw the same thought reflecting in his big golden eyes. Before she knew it they were both laughing out loud.

"Aqua, you'll never grow up," Bas said between the laughs. "And I wouldn't have it any other way."

Just then Aqua noticed Orelaith

"Oh! We have company." She circled Orelaith a few times, occasionally sniffing the air around her. "Bit on the tiny side, ain't she?" Bas laughed,

"No Aqua, in human standards she is actually rather tall." The blue dragon poked her with her nose "Scrawny too, I'd say." She picked up a fish with her mouth. "Herf, fakes dife." she said and dropped a fish as long as Orelaith's arm in front of her. "That will do for a snack for you," she said with a grin. Bas smiled as he shook his head "Aqua, my dear. She will need it cooked . Eating it like that would probably make her rather sick." Aqua huffed.

"Picky too, then." Orelaith noticed a twinkle in the blue dragon's eyes.

"Don't mind her, she is always picking on everyone," the white dragon said and gently nudged Orelaith back. "Oh, my dear child. You are freezing cold!" Vigoratus exclaimed. "Solis! Heat things up in here, but just a little." The yellow dragon, though calling her yellow would be like saying all trees were the same green, stepped forward.

"How warm do you want me to make it, Vig? I mean, we can take both greater heat and cold then it seems these humans can. I wouldn't want to harm her." Solis had yellow and orange scales that looked a little like arrowheads all over her body. She did not have a mane like the white dragon, nor spikes like Bas. All along her neck and back small bumps protruded and they had veins stretching from the top and down.

"Like a summer day," Vigoratus said with a smile. "Not too hot." Solis nodded and unfurled her delicate yellow wings. She walked to the middle of the cave, closed her eyes and stood up. She started pulsating slightly and the light around her grew brighter.

"Shield your eyes, child. She tends to get a little flashy sometimes." Orelaith turned away and closed her eyes. She heard a crackling, pulsating sound followed by a pop, and a wave of warm air flowed over her.

"You can open your eyes now," she heard Basilicus' dark voice say. Orelaith opened her eyes carefully and looked at Solis as she thumped down on all four again. She seemed to be sparkling still, surrounded by a warm glow.

LORE OF THE DRAGONS: ESSENCE OF A QUEEN

"I do hope this is better for you," Solis said, looking at Orelaith.

"Oh yes, thank you very much," Orelaith replied and curtsied.

The brown dragon stepped forward and sat down next to the others.

"This is Terra. She knows all about our history." Terra was more a dark bronze color than brown, but she did have almost black feet, face and tail. Her skin was not covered in scales like the others; they were more like small octagons side by side. She did have the same talons and teeth as the others but they seemed less sharp somehow.

"Hello child," she said, sounding like Orelaith's wise old grandmother. Orelaith curtsied again.

"Hmm… where is Tempest?" Bas asked as he looked around the cave.

"Out somewhere cooking up a storm I would think," said Luna as she came trotting over from her corner. Luna was a dark blue velvet color like a night sky. And like a night sky she was covered in small shiny white spots. She had no scales at all, just smooth snake like skin. Down her neck she had small spikes that curved slightly backwards. And her tail had spikes too, all the way down to the fin-like end . Her eyes looked like big grey moons and she smiled at Orelaith as she introduced herself. "Hiya kiddo, my name is Luna." Orelaith curtsied again.

"Pleased to meet you."

"Bas dear," Vigoratus said. "Have you given any thought to where this child is to sleep? If she will be staying with us permanently she will need a chamber of her own, you know." Bas looked at Vigoratus. "I... well, I hadn't really given it much thought yet..." His complexion turning a shade like copper. "Males... the same all over. Hrmf!" Orelaith stepped forward.

"It's fine, really. I am used to sleeping out in the open."

"Nonsense!" Vigoratus huffed. "You will do no such thing." Then she turned to the Terra. "How quickly can you have a chamber ready for the child?"

"Orelaith," Orelaith said quietly.

"Sorry, what did you say, child?" Vigoratus turned and looked at her.

"My name is Orelaith." She looked up at the big opaque eyes of the white dragon. Vigoratus just stared at her like she didn't quite understand. Then her big white face turned bright pink.

"Oh my, I truly am sorry chil... Orelaith. I can't believe I just did that; that we all did that." She looked around at the others then back at Orelaith. Her eyes narrowed as she set her sight on Bas.

"And you! Why didn't you say anything?" Bas shrugged his shoulders and smiled sheepishly.

"I guess we just aren't used to being around others. And as we have been here longer than the human race, we tend to call you humans children without even thinking about it. I assure you, we mean no offense." Orelaith smiled and put her small hand on Bas' front leg.

LORE OF THE DRAGONS: ESSENCE OF A QUEEN

"It's ok, no offense taken." An awkward silence followed. Then Terra spoke.

"Where do you want the chamber made?" Bas and Vigoratus exchanged glances. Unspoken words seemed to pass between them then Vigoratus nodded and Bas voiced what seemed to be a mutual agreement.

"Between mine and Vig's. Do you think there is enough space." Terra nodded.

"I will start at once."

Bas and Orelaith sat outside the cave looking at the stars. Terra was busy getting her chamber ready. Solis had flown off to get something and been very secretive about it. Serovita was being ordered around by Vigoratus, and Aqua had mumbled something about being hungry, then rushed out of the cave before Vig had got a hold of her. Luna came trotting up behind them.

"I see you got away," smiled Bas.

"Yeah, Vig was looking the other way so I got out before she had me picking up rocks or something. She tends to go a little overboard when she gets in that mood," she winked at Orelaith.

"Why do you think I am sitting out here?" Bas laughed. He turned to Orelaith, "What do you say we go for a night run? We can fly down to the ocean if you like." She clapped her hands in excitement.

"Oh yes, I would love to."

"Care to join us Luna?" Bas asked. She unfolded her bat-like wings.

"Don't mind if I do. Anything to make sure Vig doesn't find me. But the question is if you can keep up with me." And with that she flew off. As Orelaith climbed up on Bas' back she felt his muscles contract.

"Ready?" Bas asked.

"Ready" she replied and wrapped her arms around his neck. Like a spring, he leaped up in the air and shot after Luna like an arrow.

For hours they played in the moonlight; racing, playing hide and seek, or catching a bite to eat. When they finally returned to the cave, Orelaith had fallen asleep on Bas' back.

"Would you lift her from my back Luna?" Bas mind sent so that he wouldn't wake the little human. The dark blue dragon nodded and gently picked up the sleeping girl. She looked down on Orelaith in wonder.

"I think I like this one," Luna sent back to Bas.

"She is quite extraordinary. I am glad she was the one to find our queen's essence," the golden dragon replied.

"And as we can have no children of our own, this seems to be a gift from above." Luna sent and looked at Bas. He leaned in and let their foreheads touch. *"After all this time, I finally see some kind of hope for us. A change is coming."* Together they walked into the cave side by side with Orelaith cradled in the nook of Luna's right front paw.

Chapter 5

When Orelaith woke up the next morning, she felt wonderful. Covered in soft sheepskins, she didn't really want to open her eyes.

"Good morning Orelaith." Vigoratus' motherly voice came from the opening of her chamber. "You, Bas and Luna had a lot of fun last night, I hear," she smiled. Orelaith sat up and rubbed her eyes.

"Oh yes. It was wonderful." She looked around the chamber she was in and gasped. It looked like a royal castle. The walls covered in red tapestries, a chair with elaborately carved patterns and a matching table of hardwood, several chests and a mirror. A mirror! She jumped out of bed.

"Oh Vigoratus," she exclaimed delightedly with tears in her eyes. She opened one of the chests to find an array of beautiful dresses. She pulled the top one out and held it up in front of herself. She had never owned anything so nice before.

"So I take it, you approve?" Vig laughed. Orelaith ran over and hugged her.

"Thank you. It is more than I could ever have dreamed of."

"Oh yes, there is one more thing I want to show you," Vig said and pointed towards the back wall in the chamber. "Pull that aside sweetheart. On each side there are hooks to hold the tapestries back." Orelaith could not believe what she found. Into the rock, Terra had made a bathtub.

"You will have to get the water in from the outside, but only until Terra and Aqua figure out a way to get it some other way. It will only be cold water, but just call one of us and we will gladly heat it for you." Orelaith just stared at it.

"So… do you think it will be ok for you? We had to guess what you like. I just hope we got it right." Bas came walking over and sat down next to Vig.

"*Does she approve?*" he sent to Vig. Orelaith turned with tears in her eyes and just looked at them both.

"*I think she does,*" Vig sent back.

"*Are you sure? She looks like she is going to cry,*" Bas replied when he saw Orelaith's face.

"*I am sure. The tears; it's a human thing that displays two emotions, sadness and great joy. So unless she really hates the colors, we got it right.*" Vig smiled at Bas and held out her paws to Orelaith as she came running over and straight into Vig's embrace.

"Thank you so much, I love it. I just wish my mother and father could have seen it. You would have liked them. I don't know how I can ever repay you for all this kindness." Vig laughed.

"No need, my child. You have already given us so much. Now, have fun going through your things and I will get

LORE OF THE DRAGONS: ESSENCE OF A QUEEN

Aqua to bring you water so you can take a bath." Orelaith turned and walked around her chamber, admiring the things she could now call her own. She found a comb in one of the chests and sat down on the chair and started untangling her hair.

"How come you all are so nice to me?" she asked suddenly.

"Well..." Bas said and laid down. "We made a promise to your forefather we always keep our word. And... you have brought us back something we have been searching for. It was lost to us for a very, very long time."

"You knew my family?! How come I have never heard of it before?"

"The child we met then did not know us as dragons. We made a pact with that child that if the need ever arose we would come to aid."

"But I have nothing of value. The only things left are the two gifts my parents gave me; the leather pouch and this rough green rock," she said and pulled the necklace out from inside her dress. "Oh!" she exclaimed as she saw it glowing. "Why is it glowing? Is it a dragon stone?" Bas smiled. "It's a lot more than that, my child. Remember I told you that we once had a queen who ruled us?" Orelaith nodded. "Well, she didn't go into hibernation like the rest of us. She took all of her memories, emotions and power and poured them into a crystal which was placed inside one of the spheres. When we awakened, it was gone." Orelaith stared at the crystal.

"So all she was is inside. How is that even possible?" Bas

smiled.

"Magic. She was very powerful and mastered all the abilities that we now have spread between us and more. Like all the rulers before her, she was chosen." Orelaith took the necklace off and held it out to Bas.

"You should have it. It belongs to you, after all." He shook his head.

"No, child. It would be an honour if you would be its guardian. At least until the time comes for her to be reborn." Orelaith put the necklace back on.

"How would that happen? I mean, how will she be reborn?"

"That," Bas said with a sigh, "we have not figured out yet. We can not do it ourselves."

"I don't really know how this works, but I am guessing a baby dragon would have to come along and she would be it? Something like that?" Bas smiled at her.

"Something like that. But since we came to this isle, we have been unable to breed. The few times we tried, the female laying the egg died and was reborn in the whelp. It was immensely frustrating for the others watching the process. All of the females here have tried. It takes about twenty-one of your human years for them to be able to handle all the memories again. Can you imagine having to deal with Luna as a whelp? It nearly killed us all," Bas laughed. "Aqua, on the other hand, hasn't changed much at all." Orelaith smiled,

"I like Luna and Aqua. Well, I like them all, I guess. And

I owe you my life. I don't think I will ever be able to repay you for the things you have done for me."

"You already have, Orelaith. I see how the others are enjoying having you here. There is a new spark in their eyes. You have given us one more of the things we had lost. You have given us hope."

Chapter 6

Over the next couple of days, Orelaith settled into her new home. She still cried over the loss of her family, but when it got too much to carry, one of the dragons would seem to know and set her mind on something else. She had gotten to know them all a little, but it was Bas and Luna she spent most of her time with. Terra taught her more of the history of the dragon kind and a little about how her abilities worked. Terra drew the energy for her powers from the earth itself, transforming it and shaping it to do what she wanted. She did not breathe fire like most of the others either, but she could make solid rock melt and shoot it wherever she wanted. Vigoratus was very interested in anything Orelaith could teach her about humans, such as how they lived and what sort of religious beliefs they had. She seemed fascinated about how the family system was built up and asked so many questions Orelaith couldn't answer them all. There was never a dull moment where she wished she had something to do, quite the opposite actually. If she was not learning about the dragons, she was teaching them about humans. She knew more than most girls her age because her mother and father had insisted she was taught about the land she lived in and the people that they shared it with.

LORE OF THE DRAGONS: ESSENCE OF A QUEEN

There was a strange unease in the cave later that day and she asked Bas what was going on.

"We are worried about the last of our group. Tempest, the one you have not met yet, should have returned days ago. She was disposing of the man who hurt you, but she hasn't returned yet. She does tend to go off sometimes. However, she has never been gone for this long before; at least not without letting us know beforehand." Orelaith walked over to Bas and put her delicate little hand on his nose. "Don't worry. I have a feeling she will return soon." Bas looked at her with big, sad eyes.

"I hope so, Orelaith. I truly hope so."

That same night, she was awakened by a loud crashing sound followed by a cry of agony. She jumped out of bed and saw the dragons rushing towards the entrance. As she was about to step out of her chamber, Vig's motherly voice sounded in her head. *"Stay where you are, child. We have to see if it is safe first."* The cave was not as well at night, so she had to strain her eyes to see what was going on. It was a huge grey dragon that had come crashing into the mouth of the cave. She was trying to stand up, but failed miserably. As the others flocked around her it became clear that something was amiss. Tempest (Orelaith guessed as much) was moved to her chamber. Vig shooed the others out of the way and placed her front paws on the grey dragon's head. A white light flowed between them as Vig attempted to heal her. Suddenly, Vig gasped and backed away as her eyes flew open and she cried out, "Infected! She is infected!" The other dragons also backed away slowly and cried out in frustration and despair. Orelaith stepped out of her chamber and walked slowly over to the dragons who were now in the middle of a heated discussion.

"We can't let her suffer, but the risk is too high for me to tend to her as I wish." Vig's voice was soft and sad. Bas was pacing back and forth.

"I agree. We can't risk the last of us, but we can't lose her either. We need to find a way to secure her. If she goes mad or turns on us, it will be the end of our race." Serovita sat down and sighed.

"I could make a gate in front of her chamber, but should she regain her full strength it will not be strong enough to hold her." They all went quiet and seemed to be trying to think of something that could resolve the situation.

"I can do it," Orelaith said quietly. The dragons all turned and looked at her.

"Do what my dear?" Vig asked.

"I can take care of her." They stared at her in silence for a moment, then all spoke at once.

"Oh no, that is not safe."

"She might not be herself."

"It is way too dangerous."

LORE OF THE DRAGONS: ESSENCE OF A QUEEN

"We couldn't risk that."

"I need some lunch." They all stared at Aqua. "What? Thinking makes me hungry." Bas sighed and looked at Orelaith.

"Are you sure? None of us can guarantee your safety. You could get infected or Tempest may attack you." Orelaith nodded and crossed her arms.

"Of course I am sure. I have dealt with big sick creatures before. They are not much different if they can talk back or not. And I do believe I can help her, if not cure her, I can at least make her comfortable." Vig looked at her skeptically then turned to Bas,

"Yes... I believe she can do it. If she has any questions I can assist and guide her." Bas was not really convinced but they had no other options.

"Very well, it is settled then. Orelaith my dear, let us know what you need and we will do what we can. And..." he added. "Once you have started your treatment of Tempest you will need to stay isolated for a few days. We need to make sure this infection does not transfer between our races." Orelaith nodded. "That goes without saying." She turned to Vig "Is there any village or town close by? There are some things I would like to get." Luna scratched her chin.

"Well, there is a rather large settlement not far from here. But it would take your kind a day or so to get there." Aqua's belly rumbled loudly.

"I can take her. We will eat on the way there." Orelaith sat down disappointed.

"No, wait. I have no money to buy what I need." Solis cocked her head to one side.

"Money? Oh yes, you told us how you humans use it to get things. I put a chest with some of that in your chamber. I didn't know what it was for at the time. I just thought it was pretty." Orelaith walked over to her chamber and looked inside. There were about seven chests in there.

"Which one is it?" she asked.

"I think it's the one in the corner there. The one with the pretty pictures on," Solis said and smiled. "I like pretty pictures." Orelaith opened the lid and gasped. It was full to the brim of jewelry and gold and silver coins.

"Do you think there is enough to get what you want? If not, I can take a look at our dump site. I believe there are a lot more like that one, but the chests are not as nicely carved." Orelaith had never seen so much gold before.

"I... I think this is more than enough."

"You will need something to transport what you buy back here, won't you?. Hmm," Vig said thoughtfully.

"I can make a harness to attach to Bas' back?" Serovita suggested.

"Yes, that would work, but she will still need one of the working animals the people use here. A horse I believe they are called. It's not like Bas and Luna can just trot into town with Orelaith on their backs." "Well, actually," Luna said, "we might be able to do just that. I have taken on the form of a horse before." Orelaith stared at Luna.

LORE OF THE DRAGONS: ESSENCE OF A QUEEN

"You can shape-shift?" The dragons chuckled and Bas smiled.

"We all can, my dear, but only for short periods at a time. It takes a lot of energy to do so, but sometimes it is worth it. An entire day and night of sleep will get us back to ourselves again."

"And lots of food," Aqua added with a grin on her face.

"Very well, let's all get busy. The sun will be up in a few hours and you will need to get as close to the town as possible before the sun comes up. We don't want any humans to see us. Everyone knows what to do."

With that they all set off in different directions. Serovita and Bas went outside and Aqua flew off for breakfast with Luna following her. Terra started making bars in front of Tempest's chamber while Vig and Solis helped Orelaith pick out a suitable outfit for the trip. It was important she blend in and carry as much gold as she could, she had to look the part as well. When Orelaith had found and put on the right clothes she sat down and brushed her hair.

"I meant to ask you," she said and looked at Vig, "when Tempest came crashing in, you told me to stay in my chamber." Vig smiled at her.

"Yes, I didn't want you to come to any harm." Orelaith shook her head.

"It's not that. What I mean is… you didn't actually speak the words out loud. I heard you inside my head." Vig and Solis glanced at each other, then Vig explained.

"I thought-sent to you. It is a way we communicate sometimes. It can be done when we are close together but also when we are far apart. I didn't mean to unsettle you, but we didn't yet know what had happened and silence is better in situations like that." Orelaith frowned.

"How does it work? Could I do it?" Vig smiled.

"It's like holding a clear thought in your mind; thinking what you would say but not actually voicing it." *"Like this?"* Orelaith looked at Vig.

"Yes child, just like that." The dragons both smiled.

Chapter 7

Not long after Luna, Bas and Orelaith set off towards the town. It was still dark, but the light on the horizon promised a bright day was not far away. After about half an hour flight they saw the town and came in for a landing far enough away that they could not be seen. In a huge meadow of wildflowers, Orelaith watched in fascination as Luna transformed into a beautiful jet black horse with a long flowing mane and tail. Luna's long talons pulled together into shiny black hooves and Orelaith looked on in amazement as her actual body mass shrunk down.

"*What do you think?*" Luna sent as Orelaith walked around her.

"You are absolutely beautiful, and one of the biggest horses I have ever seen," she laughed.

"*Good thing I got the biggest saddle from our dump site,*" Luna sent. "*But I am not putting that metal thing in my mouth, I can tell you that.*" Orelaith laughed.

"It comes off, and it's not like I will need to use the reins anyway. It's just so the people in the town won't think it strange that a girl can handle a horse like you." Once she was finished, Bas helped her up on Luna's back.

'I will meet you back here at midday. We should be far enough away that we won't run into any humans." They said their goodbyes and went their separate ways.

As they got closer to town an increasing flow of people with carts full of supplies merged on the road ahead of them. They towered over all of them and got their share of long looks. Orelaith had pulled the hood of her gray wool-cloak over her head leaving her face obscured in darkness and Luna was playing her part as a fiery horse, dancing along lifting her knees high. When they got to the gate there were so many people on their way in, that everything had slowed down. Orelaith saw guards on the walls and at the gate. They sent her some curious looks but did not stop them. She had gone to the spring market with her father every year but had never been to a town as big as this. There was so much to take in, not only in sights but in sounds and smells as well.

"*You seem overwhelmed. Is it your first time in a big town?*" Luna sent and voiced a horsey snicker. "*Yes. I must say I am a little nervous. I don't even know where to start looking for what I need. And I feel like someone is watching us.*" Luna shook her head.

"*Don't worry, everyone is watching us. Not every day they see such a beautiful specimen, and I see them looking at you too. I will take us to the trade district. You should find everything you need there.*" Orelaith let Luna walk along and tried enjoying the view, but she couldn't shake the feeling of being followed. Children were running and laughing, people were carrying laundry baskets, guards patrolling, most of them in a hurry to get somewhere. She smelled fresh pastry and roasted meat, smoked fish and strange herbs. And it seemed everyone was shouting out what they had to offer.

"*Stop over by that herb trader.*" Orelaith saw herbs hanging on the wall that she knew she would need. When Luna halted she jumped down and approached the old woman sitting on a stool while bundling up fresh herbs.

"What can I do for you today?" The woman smiled at her, displaying a big gap in her upper jaw where all her front teeth should have been.

"I need healing herbs for a big... eh... bull. He has some gashes and cuts and I am afraid he could be getting sick from them." The woman looked at her skeptically, probably wondering why a young girl of an obviously wealthy family had come alone to the market and not sent a stable-hand or maid to get the goods. Then she shrugged and bunched up a few herbs while instructing Orelaith on how to use them. When Orelaith told her to triple the amount of herbs just to be safe, the woman first raised her bushy eyebrows then handed her the rest and grinned widely as Orelaith put a gold coin in her bony hand. She bit the coin with her molars, then stuffed it quickly into her apron pocket. As they walked from vendor to vendor slowly getting what they needed, Orelaith found herself looking over her shoulder several times. She couldn't rid herself of the uneasy feeling that something dark was lurking just out of sight. She pulled her hood forward cloaking her face in darkness. It was hard to enjoy being able to just ride along on Luna, but she decided it had to be nerves because of being in such a big town for the first time. She did see a few things she wanted for herself and asked Luna if she thought it would be ok if she got them. *"I don't see why you have to ask, it's your gold. If you want to, we can come back when we don't have a pressing matter to attend to. I think you and me could have some fun."* Orelaith smiled and patted Luna's neck.

"I would like that. Right now I just want to get out of here and back to Tempest."

Once she had got everything she needed and a few things she hoped she wouldn't need, they headed for the well so Luna could have a drink before heading out. Orelaith got some lunch for herself and even a few apples that Luna felt a strange craving for.

"I don't know why but they look sooo good to me. And mmm they are! We need to get some more." Luna munched down a dozen apples. Orelaith laughed and stroked her neck. *"There is one thing I would like to do before we go."*

"Oh, what is that?" Luna asked with a mouthful of apple.

"It's on the way out, so just go slow when we get close to the gate and I will tell you when to stop." When they got there, Orelaith climbed off and walked along with Luna behind her. A poor woman with two little children sat begging by the roadside, mostly ignored by the people who passed by. Orelaith stopped and knelt down.

"What is your name, woman?"

LORE OF THE DRAGONS: ESSENCE OF A QUEEN

"Bronoch, my lady."

" Tell me Bronoch; how come you are reduced to begging?"

Orelaith noticed now that this woman was not much older than herself.

"My husband was killed by a band of outlaws half a year ago and his brother took over the farm, forcing me and the children to leave. Now we don't even have a place to stay at night." Orelaith's heart went out to her.

"I want to help you, but you must do most of the work yourself. Take this and spend it well. Feed your kids and get a place to stay. And don't let anyone see how much you have," she said with a low voice and handed her the pouch with the rest of the gold. The girl looked at her in shock and her eyes flowed over with tears.

"I can't take all of this…" she said and tried to hand the pouch back, but Orelaith closed her hand around it.

"I have more than I need for myself, and you need this more than I do. Tonight I will sleep better knowing these wonderful children and you are somewhere warm and safe." She smiled and handed the children an apple each then mounted Luna.

"Thank you my lady," Bronoch said with tears flowing down her dirt stained cheeks. "How can I ever repay you for your kindness?"

"By living a long and happy life." Orelaith smiled and Luna set in motion.

"What is your name my lady so I may thank the lord for you?" the woman said, walking after her.

"Orelaith, my name is Orelaith." she replied as Luna set off in a trot through the gates.

"*That was kind of you,*" Luna sent as she set off in a gallop. "*But did you have to give her all of the apples? She could have gotten a thousand apples with what you gave her.*" Orelaith laughed.

"I will get you more the next time we go to town. I promise."

Bas was waiting for them at the appointed place and they quickly repacked the things Orelaith had bought. Once Luna was back in her true form, Orelaith noticed how much of a toll it had taken on her.

"Eat some of the fish I brought and we will leave," Bas said tenderly. Luna gulped down every last one and flapped her wings a few times.

"Let's go home, the others are waiting."

Chapter 8

Back in one of the town's toughest inns, a man made his way through thugs and whores to a table in the back. Dougal was a big guy and he had acquired a taste for violence after working for the outlaw Malum the last two years. Even among Malums men he was looked upon as worse than most. His hair was short and his eyes were dark brown. He had a crooked nose and lots of scars from more than his fair share of fights. Him being taller than most, people usually moved out of his way. Those who didn't got a well placed fist to help them along. Like most men in his line of work he wore leather armor and carried a short sword at his hip. He took what he wanted, usually at someone else's cost. But today he was working for a man that made him look like a priest in comparison. A large cloaked figure sat hunched over a mug of ale. He looked up when Dougal sat down across from him. There was something odd about his posture but nothing specific one could put a finger on.

"This had better be good Dougal. You have no idea how big an effort it is for me to come here after trying to patch Malum back together. He has worn my patience very thin." Dougal seemed almost nervous; a strange emotion for a man like him.

"You told me to let you know if I saw anything of

interest. Today, I saw the woman from the camp here in town." The hooded figure leaned back and crossed his arms over his chest.

"You better have more than that. If not, I will slowly pick you apart with my bare hands just for dragging me down to this dump." The voiced threat was not empty. Dougal had seen him do that to a man before.

"There is more, of course. She has a green crystal tied around her neck. I do believe it is the one you described. There was something strange about it; when she was leaning over looking at some herbs, it seemed to glow."

This seemed to pique the hooded figure's interest.

"Are you sure it was not just the sun reflecting through it? I need you to be absolutely sure before you answer." Dougal nodded.

"There was no sun where she was standing. It was completely blocked out by the building next to her." Nex leaned forward.

"Next question. What was around her at the very time it glowed? Get this right and I might consider leaving your limbs intact." Dougal seemed thrown by the question.

"Around her? Eh…well, there was a table, a stool and the old hag selling the herbs. And her horse; a big black mare."

The corners of Nex lips curled up into a smile that would have made any wolf proud.

"They have taken on a pet…" he almost whispered. Dougal seemed confused.

"They? Pet? Sorry, but I don't understand." Nex looked at him from under the hood.

"It is not your concern. But I will not rend your body to

pieces today, I am sorry to say." Dougal caught the small bag of gold tossed to him and grinned widely as he felt the weight of it. "You did good today. And…" Nex said as he got up, "let me know the instant she returns." He stabbed Dougal in the chest with a long nailed finger. "The very instant!" As he walked out the temperature seemed to rise in the room and Dougal let out a sigh of relief. Then he smiled, weighing the amount of fun he could have with the gold in his hand.

After unloading the goods, Orelaith started grinding the herbs and mixing the paste for Tempest's wounds. With some last instructions from Vig, Orelaith walked over to Tempest's chamber and stepped inside. There was not a lot of room in there now with the big dragon taking up most of the space, but she managed to lay all the things she needed out behind her. Tempest seemed to be half asleep, but opened her lightning blue eyes and looked at her every once in a while. Orelaith sprinkled the herbs into the bowl of water and stirred it well. Once she seemed satisfied with the mixture, she rinsed out several clothes that she put in a clean bucket.

"I am going to clean your wounds. Just so you know and don't burn me to a cinder, this might sting a little." Stepping a little closer she noticed that even if Tempest seemed half asleep the dragon's big eyes were following her every move.

"Ok… as I said, it might sting, but trust me when I say it will help ease the pain." Their eyes met, and for a second the big dragon just stared at her, then nodded and closed her eyes. Orelaith squeezed the cloth over the big gash in the dragon's right shoulder. A stifled groan after a quick intake of breath was the only indication of how painful it really was.

"You did good." Orelaith smiled encouragingly to Tempest. "The herbs also have a numbing effect, so the next step will be less painful. Now we only have three more to go." Tempest sighed and closed her eyes. Once Orelaith was done cleaning the other deep gashes she gently started washing the dragon's neck, face, feet and shoulders.

"Why are you doing this?" Tempest asked in a whisper sounding like a distant storm.

"No offense, but you are rather dirty. Dirt and wounds can quickly make you even sicker and even stop the healing process altogether," Orelaith replied matter-of-factly. Tempest shook her head.

"No, I mean why would you care for me? I am a dragon after all. Are you not afraid I could suddenly decide to eat you?" Orelaith crossed her arms over her chest.

"First of all you don't eat meat. Secondly, I don't know you, but I will get to be your friend soon, or so I hope. And thirdly, I don't scare as easily as other humans you have met, and I know how to deal with sick creatures, no matter what size and shape." Tempest raised an eyebrow and smiled. "I need to get some clean water, I should not be long. Will you be ok until I get back?" The dragon nodded and smiled to herself as Orelaith left. This tiny creature was quite tough for her size, no wonder Bas had taken to her so quickly. It had not passed by her that the queen's crystal glowed constantly and that some of Queen Primoris' personality was shining through in the girl's eyes. Maybe she would survive

LORE OF THE DRAGONS: ESSENCE OF A QUEEN

this after all.

Over the next week, Tempest seemed to heal at a painstakingly slow rate, but there was some progress. And by now it was clear that Orelaith was not susceptible to the infection, to Bas' big relief. He had become almost as closely attached to her as to his dragon companions and it seemed the others felt the same way. She made them laugh and was like a daughter to all of them. Bas had not yet told anyone of what he had found when he healed her, the tiny life that was growing inside her. He hadn't told Orelaith either, but he wouldn't have to. She would realize it herself soon enough. He was sitting outside the cave when Vig came out.

"Bas my dear, is there something you want to tell me?" She sat down next to him and looked up at the stars.

"Eh… no, not that I can think of." He knew the look she just sent him all too well. He was in trouble and she was not too pleased.

"I just finished examining Orelaith to make sure she was not infected. And do you know what I found?" Bas avoided her piercing gaze.

"She isn't infected, is she?" He knew very well that she was not affected by Tempest's illness.

"No Bas, you know she is not. She is a picture of health and so is her baby." Bas knew it was only a matter of time before Vig found out, but he was unsure if she had figured out yet… what he had done to it.

"Well, I didn't tell her, Vig. She needs to find that out herself. You didn't tell her, did you?" Vig shook her big head, sending her mane flowing in the wind.

"No Bas, I didn't. But I saw something else; something I recognized."

She paused and he knew that she had found him out. She did know he had done something to the little creature.

"Vig… I had to do something. The child had evil intertwined into her very being." Vig's eyes narrowed. "So you replaced it with your own? What were you thinking, Bas? We have no idea how that will affect the development of this new creature. It may not even live after birth and what if Orelaith dies like we do when we try to breed? Did you even think of that? Or worse, what if you die?" Bas cringed under the scolding Vig was dishing out.

"I… I just thought… I couldn't let this wonderful woman have a child with so much of that evil man in her. I know I should have consulted you first, Vig, but you were not there and I felt I had to act immediately." Vig's face softened.

"Oh, Bas… Your heart is bigger than your brain sometimes. We will just have to see, I guess. I will keep a close eye on the baby and on Orelaith." She put her head on his shoulder. "Next time, ask me before you do something as foolish as this." Bas put his head on her shoulder too and sighed,

"I am sorry Vig. And I promise, I will."

Chapter 9

It took an additional month before Tempest was back to her old self and, according to Vig, infection free. The dragons were astounded over her progress and the fact that the infection could be healed at all. They discussed it at length but could not find a reason why Orelaith had succeeded where they had failed so utterly. Tempest had not yet told anyone how she got infected in the first place, but one day she gathered them all around her and told them what had happened. She had flown North for almost a day when she came across a fortress on a cliff by the sea. It seemed like as good a place as any to dump the twisted creature she was carrying. But as she approached she had an escalating feeling of unease. She had dropped the man as close to the fortress as she dared go and turned back.

But she could not out-fly the feeling of unease and soon enough she realized why.

"It was your brother Nex. He overtook me and brought me down. At first I couldn't believe my eyes. Another dragon, one of our own. But he has changed. He is at the last stage of the infection. The darkness has consumed him completely, the kind-hearted dragon we all knew is gone.

For days he taunted me in my weakened state, not letting me leave and scorching me and clawing me. He seemed to wait for the infection to set in." The dragons seemed truly shook up by what Tempest told them and Bas appeared to be in a state of shock. "Finally, he told me to give you a message, Bas; I will find the queen's essence and breed, ridding our race of weakness. And you will join me or I will end your pathetic little life like I would have done with Frater if he hadn't got his sorry ass killed already." Everyone stared at Tempest in shock. Bas hung his head and a single golden droplet fell from his eye. "In one way I am glad he is still alive, but it breaks my heart to hear how he has changed. He is no longer my brother, the brother I knew and loved. And Frater… he is gone." The entire cave seemed to hum with the sadness they all felt and Orelaith rushed over and hugged them one by one. Suddenly the light in the crystal flared and Orelaith was enveloped in its eerie green glow. The dragons gasped and stepped back. Then a familiar voice all too long gone broke the silence.

"My beloved children… finally I can speak to you again. It saddens my heart to see how high a price you have all had to pay in my absence. And I am afraid I can not stay long. But this young woman is the key, and I will be able to pass on my knowledge to this child thanks to you Basilicus. My beloved son, you did right by tampering with the life inside her. It gave me the opening I needed to pass on my abilities, but I will not be joining you as myself. This child will have my wisdom and powers and even most of my memories, but she will have to grow and mature just like we all have. Have patience with the human whelp, she does not know what power she possesses. My time is short. Guard her with your lives, for she is the one that will make it possible for you to survive here on this blue planet. I love you all dearly, farewell…" Then the light died and Orelaith was left curled up in a ball on the stone floor.

LORE OF THE DRAGONS: ESSENCE OF A QUEEN

"Mother..." Bas whispered. They all stared at Orelaith in silent shock and no one moved. Vig was the first to regain her composure.

"Oh my... now that was not at all what I had expected. Blessed is the day we found this child," she said and gently picked up Orelaith's limp body and carried her to her chamber. Solis was right behind her pulsating at an increasingly accelerated rate.

"Oh do calm down, Solis. You are having hot flashes," Vig said, sounding slightly annoyed.

"Sorry Vig, but this is just way too fantastic for me to hold it all in," the yellow dragon said as she bounced about with a wide grin on her face.

"Then I suggest you go for a swim to cool down," Luna said dryly.

"You wouldn't want to harm Orelaith now would you?" Vig asked. Solis shook her head.

"No, you are right. Anyone want to join me?" Aqua raised her paw.

"I'll go. I am getting hungry again from all this excitement." An increasingly joyous feeling was spreading among the dragons now. A few joined Solis and Aqua while the rest gathered outside Orelaith's chamber.

"Who would have thought that this woman would be the solution to our survival?" Vigoratus said with a quiet awe in her voice as she looked at the sleeping woman.

"After being set in our ways since before humans evolved, the time for change is upon us. We have waited so long… so very long for this." Terra ran her talon down the outline of Orelaith's chamber leaving a series of glyphs etched into the stone.

"We need to tell her what is to come. I don't even think she knows that she is carrying a life inside her." Luna voiced what both Bas and Vig was thinking.

"Not yet. Give her the chance to figure it out on her own. When she does, we can tell her," Bas said. The others nodded in agreement. Tempest stayed behind as the others walked away. She owed this little human her life, and she would give it willingly if it came to that. She would do anything to keep her safe.

Over the next month the dragons found it hard to keep the secret and Orelaith sensed that something was different. Not in a bad way, but the dragons seemed to be falling over themselves trying to keep her happy. Solis was having hot flashes all the time and laughed for no apparent reason. Finally Orelaith asked Bas to take her for an evening flight. She needed to know what was going on, so when they landed on a cliff overlooking the moonlit sea she looked at him and voiced her concerns.

"What is going on, Bas?" He avoided her gaze.

"Going on? Nothing is… going on. I have no idea what

LORE OF THE DRAGONS: ESSENCE OF A QUEEN

you mean." She crossed her arms.

"Like now, you won't look at me. Something is going on and I want an answer. Everyone is so overly nice to me and it all changed overnight. Not that you weren't nice before, but you all seem to be a little overprotective and I know you are keeping something from me. There is something that you are not telling me. So out with it Bas." He knew he would have to tell her eventually, but he hoped she had found out about her condition first. Maybe she knew already?

"First, is there something you want to tell me?" he asked and lay down, crossing his front legs much like a cat. Her jaw dropped and she looked at him in shock. Then she closed her mouth and this time she did not meet his gaze.

"I...don't know for sure, but I think... maybe, that Malum left a part of himself behind." Bas saw how it saddened her, but he couldn't understand.

"So you are carrying a new life in you. This should be good news, yet you seem unhappy about it. Why?" She sat down on a rock not far from Bas and looked out over the sea.

"I don't know. My mother and father raised me to believe all life has value. But carrying a part of that evil man... What if I have a boy and he turns out to be just like his father? How can I live with that?" Bas smiled.

"It's not a boy. Do you remember the night I found you?" She nodded in reply. "Do you remember the part where I healed your body and mind?"

"Yes, I remember it well." She turned towards him and smiled weakly.

"Well, I did a little more than repair the damage to you." Orelaith sat up abruptly.

"Oh?" Bas felt a little uncomfortable as he did not know how she would react to what he was about to tell her.

"When I sensed the child inside you, I noticed the dark side of Malum intertwined in her… so I removed it." Orelaith's mouth dropped open again.

"Is that even possible?" She unconsciously moved her hands to her belly. "But will that not leave her incomplete?"

"Here comes the tricky part. It needed to be replaced and I didn't have a human man that I could take the parts from… so I used myself." He held his breath waiting for her to react, but she just sat down and chewed on her lip. It felt like forever before she replied.

"I can't believe you did that." She got up and stood in front of him. " You have no idea how honored I am that you would do that for me," she said and threw her arms around his neck. He let out a sigh of relief and closed his eyes. Then she stepped back.

"Oh! Now I know why the others have been so overprotective. They all know, don't they?" Bas nodded,

"But there is more I need to tell you before we go back." He told her what had happened that night a month ago. Most of the time she sat listening silently and only asked a few questions. When Bas was done talking she sat quietly in deep thought. He rested his head on his front legs and spoke quietly.

"I know it is much to take in, but I hope you understand what this means to us." She looked at him. "I am so… humble. I get to be a part of something so big, so… important. But yet I am torn. There are so many uncertainties to consider in all of this. What will this child be like? Will it be a dragon or a human in appearance? Will she even live?" She got up and walked back and forth. "And for me to give birth to this child… is it even possible? How big are dragon whelps?" Bas understood her concerns,

"I can't answer all your questions, but both Vig and I will monitor the child's progress very closely. If we see anything out of the ordinary you will be the first to know." Orelaith smiled weakly. "I guess that is more than any mother can ask." She straightened up. "Actually, I think everything is going to be just wonderful. And I am not alone because I have my family around me." Bas was touched by her words. "I consider you my family too Orelaith, as do the others." She stroked his forehead.

"I think I am ready to go back home to the others now. And I need to tell them to stop being so protective. They're driving me crazy!" Bas laughed.

"Good luck with that. Vig is going to fight you every step of the way." Orelaith climbed up on his back. "I know, but I can be just as stubborn as her. We will just have to see I guess. Now let's go." Bas flapped his wings and dove off the cliff, skimming the water before setting the course homeward.

Chapter 10

Orelaith stood up to with Vig. After a few days of discussions they came to a compromise that both Vig and Orelaith seemed to agree on. Vig still insisted on examining Orelaith every day, keeping a close eye on the baby's progress. To everyone's relief it seemed the baby developed like a normal human, at least in appearance. It was about two months later when Vig was done with her daily check up that Orelaith heard a tiny voice in her head.

"*Ma-ma…*" Orelaith stared at Vig with wide eyes.

"Did you hear that?" Vig frowned.

"Hear what dear?"

"The… that little… you didn't hear that?!" Vig sat down and cocked her head.

"Whatever are you talking about Orelaith? I didn't hear anything." Orelaith chewed her lip and stared into the air.

"I could have sworn I heard…" she mumbled.

"Orelaith, you are starting to worry me. Now tell me

what you thought you heard," The big white dragon's voice was full of concern.

"I thought I heard a tiny voice in my head say mama... am I going mad here?" Vig gasped

"Did it sound like the way we mind-send?" Orelaith nodded.

"Yes, just like that... oh! You don't think? The baby...?" Vig called Bas over.

"Bas, I think we have missed something. The baby just mind-sent to Orelaith!" She was now grinning from ear to ear.

"Really? Oh, that is wonderful!" Bas said. Orelaith seemed confused.

"It is?" Vig laid down and smiled at Orelaith.

"Oh yes, it means that you get to be her mother and watch her grow up. You see, when we tried to breed after we got here, there was no response when we mind-sent to the whelps. That is because there was no one inside so to speak. As they were hatched the essence, or soul if you like, of the mother was transferred to the whelp. But now it means that your essence won't fully go into the child. She has her own soul." Orelaith sighed in relief.

"That is wonderful news, but that means she has abilities that human children don't have. Human babies don't mind-send to their mothers, Vig." She stroked her belly gently. "And I need to give her a name. We can't keep calling her baby or whelp." The dragons nodded and Bas said,

"Even if it is Queen Primoris reborn, in one way I believe that this child deserves her own name. Have you thought of one yet?" Orelaith nodded.

"Yes, Rionach. It means queenly and I thought that would be a fitting name for her." By now the others had gathered around them and they all smiled approvingly.

"Yes, I believe that is perfect." Vig smiled.

"Now, I need to take another look at her. And not just the outside of her. I need to see what is on the inside." Orelaith sat down on the white dragon's hand, then Vig closed her eyes and sent her warm tendrils in through Orelaith's belly.

"Hmm, that's remarkable. She looks so human on the outside but yet…she seems to be developing a second skeleton inside her own . I am not quite sure but I think that means she can switch between dragon and human form without needing time to recover. And…" Vig frowned "she seems to have – oh!" Vig opened her eyes. "She pushed me out!" Bas laughed.

"Not even born yet and she's already standing up to you." Vig sent Bas a stern look.

"You can laugh now, but what about when she starts blowing fire? Or decides she wants to go explore the outside before she is mature enough to realize the dangers?" Bas was still grinning.

"Oh will you relax Vig? There is no need to worry about what may happen. We will just take one day at a time. This is new ground to us all, and we have no idea what we will have to deal with, but when that time comes we will find a way." Vig lightened up a little.

"You are enjoying this, aren't you?" Bas nodded vigorously, sending them all into new round of roaring laughter.

That evening, Luna and Tempest took Orelaith out on a night flight. Since the attack on Tempest they had started traveling in pairs for safety reasons. No other dragons had been seen since, but Vig said, "Better safe than sorry." They flew down to the sea to check on Aqua and Bas who were out catching fish. When they landed on the high cliff, Tempest decided to join Bas and Aqua, leaving Luna and Orelaith to watch as they played tag in the water. Luna laid down next to her.

"You want to go back to town tomorrow? You can get some things for the baby." Orelaith smiled

"I would like that. It won't be long before I get too big to go riding, and I do need to get some things for when Rionach is born. I'd also like to see how Bronoch is doing."

"Who?" asked Luna.

"The woman I gave the gold to on our way out of town last time. The one with the two children?" Orelaith said and tucked a unruly lock of hair behind her ear.

Luna looked on as Bas shot a ball of flame after Aqua who dove under water just in time.

"Oh yes, the one you gave all the apples to. I liked the apples," Luna said and smacked her tongue.

"We can get some more this time. But we still have to get a yes from Vig," Orelaith said and chewed on her lip.

"Do we have to? She can be such a stick in the mud." Luna looked hopefully at Orelaith.

"Oh Luna, you know she is only that way because she cares deeply for us. And if we go without telling her we will have to face her when we get back." Luna sighed.

"Yeah, there's that."

But Vig surprised them both when they told her of their plans.

"I think that sounds like a wonderful idea." She smiled widely. Luna looked at Orelaith then back to Vig.

"Really?" Vig walked around them.

"Oh yes, there are so many things that a baby needs. Well, human babies at least. And you might as well get them now before you start getting too big to travel. It's not like you can send any of us, we wouldn't know the first thing about what to get." Luna grinned.

"Ok, we better be off to bed then. I want us to get an early start. I will bring you some apples, Vig, they are really great." Vig smiled.

"That's ok, I will get some myself." Luna stopped grinning.

"You're going with us?"

"Of course I am. What did you think?" Vig said and headed for her chamber. Luna sighed and closed her eyes.

"I knew there was a catch." Orelaith just laughed as she walked to her chamber.

"It's ok Luna. We might see a different side to Vig and actually have lots of fun."

"Vig doesn't have another side," Luna said sourly. Vig's voice sounded through the cave.

"I heard that!"

Chapter 11

Before the sun rose the next morning, Orelaith set off towards town with Vig, Tempest and Luna. Tempest would stay at the landing site and make sure they had plenty of fish ready for when they came back. Vig was still not sure if she should go as a horse or a human. "Well, if I go as a horse I can't buy anything, but if I go as a human I don't have a horse to ride." Luna was already saddled up and waiting.

"I don't really care what you go as Vig, as long as you make your mind up sometime today." Orelaith was wondering what Vig would look like as a human, but the white dragon had a point, they could not both go riding in on Luna.

"Why don't you go as a horse and I will get what you want. You just have to thought send to me and tell me what you would like." Vig frowned then sighed.

"Very well, horse it is." She changed much in the same manner as Luna and though she was a little smaller she was just as magnificent. Orelaith started putting a saddle on her that they had brought. After endless loosening and tightening Vig seemed moderately pleased about how it felt and looked. Orelaith mounted Luna and they headed for the town.

It was a little too warm to justify a hooded cloak, so Orelaith had chosen the least elaborate dress she could find; a blue dress with only a few embroideries along the neckline. She had braided her hair in a long, thick braid that hung down her back and she wore no jewels besides the crystal and that was tucked inside her dress. As they came trotting up to the gates two children came running up to them.

"*Who are they?*" Vig asked.

"*I have no idea Vig,*" Orelaith replied and stared at them as they came closer.

"You came back! You came back!" At first Orelaith didn't recognize them, but then it dawned on her. These were Bronoch's little girl and boy. They had clean, beautiful clothes on and their little rosy cheeks had filled out. She smiled at them.

"Well hello there. I am glad to see you two. How is your mother doing? Bronoch, wasn't it?" She explained to Vig who they were.

"*Oh, they are so sweet.*" Vig sent back.

"*You should have seen them before,*" Luna added. "*You did a good thing for them, Orelaith.*" They followed them in through the gates.

"She goes by Saoirse now. We have our own home and she has a tailor shop in the trade district. Oh, she is going to be so happy to see you," the little girl said.

"And we have five sheep now," the little boy added proudly.

Orelaith was astounded at how much the children had blossomed. The last time she had seen them they just stared at her with their big sad eyes. The change made her feel grateful that she had had the privilege of being a contributor in that transformation.

"Would you take me to her?" Orelaith asked.

"Oh yes! She is going to be so happy to see you!" the little girl said, clapping her hands in excitement.

"Maybe you want to sit on the big white horse?" Orelaith asked. "If it's ok with you Vig?" she quickly sent to Vig who gave her an approving nod. Their jaws dropped and the children looked at each other with wide open eyes for a second. Then started jumping up and down with big grins on their faces.

"Oh can we?" Orelaith laughed.

"I wouldn't have asked if you couldn't." She glanced over at Vig. "*Would you kneel down so they can get up?*" Vig nodded her head and gently knelt down.

"Oh she is so beautiful." The little girl stroked Vig's neck.

"What is her name?"

"Her name is Vigoratus but I call her Vig for short," Orelaith said and watched as the children climbed up on Vig's back. Gently Vig got up and the little boy put his arms around his big sister's waist. "Now show me where to go."

LORE OF THE DRAGONS: ESSENCE OF A QUEEN

On their way through the town Vig was humming to herself. She found these little humans absolutely adorable and couldn't wait until Orelaith had her baby. It was going to be such a wonderful change for them all to have a child in their midst. She was fascinated over their little hands and feet and the little girl stroked her neck and played with her mane all the way to where they were going.

"It's over there. Mummy!" The little girl pointed at a stone building with a woman sitting outside cleaning a batch of wool in a big wood tub. She looked up, shielding her eyes from the bright sunlight with one hand.. As she recognized Orelaith she jumped up and put her hands up to her face staring at them as they stopped outside her shop.

"Mummy! She let us ride Vig all the way from the gate. Isn't she beautiful?" The girl was all smiles.

"I like the black one. She looks so strong," the boy added. Luna stuck her tongue out at Vig.

"I have prayed you would return so I could thank you and show you what you have done for my family," the woman spoke through her tears. Vig knelt down and the children jumped off.

"I am sorry I have not been able to get back sooner, but I have had pressing matters that needed my full attention at home," Orelaith said and slid off Luna's back. The woman embraced her.

"Thank you. Thank you so much." Orelaith smiled.

"Enough tears, you must tell me all that has happened." She turned to the children and knelt down.

"Do you think you can get some apples and some water for Vig and Luna? I think they are probably both thirsty and hungry after the long ride here." She put a few silver coins in each hand. "And get something nice for yourselves at the same time." The children nodded and ran off in a hurry. Orelaith stared after them for a while then turned to Bronoch and took her hands.

"You look wonderful. It warms my heart immensely to see you again. Your children say you changed your name. It's Saoirse now then?" Saoirse nodded.

"Yes, I left my old life behind and decided I would take a more fitting name. It means freedom. Let me get some tea and we will sit and I can tell you all about what has happened." She ran inside and brought out an extra chair and a table then went back inside to make some tea. Meanwhile Orelaith walked in and looked at the clothes she had made.

"These are beautiful! And you make them all yourself?" Saoirse popped her head out from the back room.

"Yes, I have my own sheep that I get the wool from, and now I even get other types of cloth from traders that come to town." Not long after she came out with two cups and they sat down outside. Saoirse was just a big smile as she told all about what had happened since Orelaith had given her the bag of gold. At first she had been worried that people would think she had stolen it, so she had taken the children out of town and cleaned themselves up before returning. She had gotten some simple clothing for them all, then they had rented a room at an inn. She had put a small amount of gold and silver coins in another bag and used that to pay. She talked of how the next few days she had started forming a plan of how she could best use the remaining gold to build a life for them. The old man who used to run the only tailoring shop in town had died a few years back and no one had taken his place. When she inquired about it, she found that the building was for sale so she jumped at the opportunity. Soon she had a successful shop and made more than enough to support her family. She had told people about her angelic benefactor but they had not believed her and they had slandered her in the town. Orelaith saw two women staring at them as they walked by the shop then they put their heads together and whispered. The children had returned with lots of apples and a bucket of water for Luna and Vig, who were enjoying all the attention the little ones were giving them.

"But enough about me, I don't really know anything about you." Vig's ears twitched.

"*Be careful about what you tell her. Make something up if you like, but be sure to stay as close to the truth as possible without revealing what we are.*" Orelaith took a sip of her tea.

"Well… I don't know where to start. I live quite far away, so that is why I can't come here so often. My mother and father have passed away and I now live with my… husband and his seven… sisters." She glanced at Saoirse who was smiling and nodding.

"How did you meet your husband? Was he your knight in shining armor who saved you from a monstrous dragon?" she said and laughed. Orelaith choked on her tea and Vig neighed as if she was laughing.

"Not exactly, but I do owe him my life."

"Oh, how romantic. What does he look like? Is he big and strong?" Orelaith smiled. "Yes, he is bigger and stronger than any man I have met. He is golden and has big copper coloured eyes. And he is kind and gentle for his size. But I guess he shares a few traits with most men." Orelaith laughed.

"A very accurate description if I may say so," Vig sent to her.

"He sounds wonderful. But how come he lets you go all this way alone? There are many dangerous things that can happen to a woman traveling alone."

"Oh, he knows I am safe with Luna and Vig. They are almost like guard dogs if they think I am in danger of any kind," Orelaith said and winked.

"And we breathe fire too." Luna sent followed by a chuckle.

Saoirse glanced nervously towards the children playing on the ground around Luna and Vig's feet.

"Maybe the children shouldn't be playing around them." Orelaith put her hand on Saoirse's arm.

"They are perfectly safe. Luna and Vig love children and would never hurt them." She seemed to relax and sipped her tea.

LORE OF THE DRAGONS: ESSENCE OF A QUEEN

"It is so wonderful to see you again. I have prayed and thanked the lord for you every day since I first met you by the gate. But what brings you to town today?" Orelaith smiled.

"I am expecting my first born, so I wanted to come get some things before I got too big to travel."

"Oh what wonderful news! Do let me help you. I have been through this twice before after all, so I know what you will need."

Orelaith and Saoirse spent the day finding everything she needed, and some things she didn't need but were too cute to pass up. It was so nice to just be a girl and giggle and spend time with a woman not much older than herself and a friendship grew between them. It was late afternoon by the time Orelaith and Saoirse sat down again outside the tailor shop.

"I have had so much fun today. Thank you for taking the time to help me, Saoirse." She looked at Luna and Vig. "But I am afraid it is time for me to return home. Luna and Vig will need to rest after such a long trip, and I don't want my... husband to worry." Saoirse took her hand

"Oh I wish you didn't have to go."

"I wish I could stay a little longer and I hope I will be able to come back soon. Maybe then I can stay a few days." She didn't think she would be back until after little Rionach was born.

"Oh that would be fantastic!"

"Well, I will have to ask my husband of course," Orelaith said and glanced at Vig. She snickered and bit into another apple that the little girl had given her.

"*Your 'husband' will probably not approve and I am not sure I do either. But we will just have to see, it may be possible.*" Vig's voice sounded amused in Orelaith's head.

"Oh, of course. You could send me word, and I will get everything ready." Orelaith got up and hugged Saoirse.

"We must be off. Do take good care of yourself and these beautiful children." The children ran over and hugged her too and she gave them a gold coin each.

"And you two, help your mother." Then she climbed up on Luna's back and waved goodbye as she rode off.

Chapter 12

They had just gotten out of sight of the town when they met a dark haired young boy carrying a baby on his back.

"*Ba-da!*" Rionach's voice sounded excited, and Orelaith felt her moving for the very first time.

"Hello there. Where are you heading, young man?" Orelaith asked him. His dark brown, almost black eyes looked up at her and she saw a deep pain in them.

"I am going to the town to look for work." Orelaith jumped off Luna.

"Where are your parents?" He looked at his shoes and spoke in a whisper

"Dead."

"I am sorry to hear that… And who is this little one on your back?" He straightened up.

"It's my brother, Garbhan. I take good care of him." He swung his brother around to the front.

"And what is your name?" Orelaith smiled at him.

"Conri, milady." Rionach was cooing away inside and Orelaith looked at Vig.

"*Can you hear that?*" She looked back at Conri.

"My name is Orelaith and I have a friend in town who might be able to help you find a job, and she will give you a place to stay too. Have you been traveling far?" She saw he was not much younger than herself, maybe three or four years.

"A while, since springtime," he replied. She noticed now how worn out his clothes were.

"That is quite a long time, but I see you have been taking very good care of your brother." She walked over to the saddlebags on Luna's back. "I know how hard it must be. I lost all of my family recently too. So please accept this small token from one that knows how you feel. I am a wealthy woman now and I want to help," she said and handed him the rest of the gold she had with her. She saw his eyes tear up a little, but he quickly wiped his eyes.

"I… I don't know if I can take this." Orelaith smiled and quickly climbed up on Luna's back.

"If not for yourself, at least take it for your brother's sake." He looked up at her.

"I will take it for his sake." Luna and Vig were moving restlessly and seemed uneasy.

"When you get to town, find the tailoring shop and tell the proprietor that Orelaith sent you. Saoirse is a good woman who knows how hard life can be. I will come back someday and see you and your brother." She waved goodbye and Luna started trotting away. Conri watched them go then turned and walked towards the town.

LORE OF THE DRAGONS: ESSENCE OF A QUEEN

"What is the matter with all of you?" Orelaith said when they got back to the landing site. "Rionach was making all sorts of sounds and both of you were so jumpy and restless I had a hard time hanging on the last bit of the way." Vig and Luna gulped down the fish quickly after transforming back to their true shape.

"Not here child. We will talk when we get back." Orelaith started to protest.

"Can't you just tell me what's –" Luna was the one to cut her off to Orelaith's surprise.

"For once, Vig is right. We can talk when we get back home." Tempest didn't even raise an eyebrow and within minutes they were flying home in silence. Once they got back they all gathered outside Orelaith's chamber and Vig spoke.

"My dear Orelaith, I didn't mean to be abrupt with you. But under the circumstances I felt a need to get out of there before we spoke. As a human you could not feel what me and Luna and even little Rionach felt." She laid down. "There was another dragon present somewhere near us. Rionach was the first one to sense it, but soon it became strong enough that Luna and I felt it too." Orelaith stared at Vig then she frowned. "But Rionach didn't seem afraid, quite the opposite actually. She was laughing and cooing and I felt what she felt, excited and happy." Bas laid down next to Orelaith and she sat down on his front paw.

"That is strange… maybe there was no threat to any of you," he said thoughtfully.

"Maybe not, but with Nex out there we have to be careful." Even Solis nodded at that.

"When did you start feeling the presence?" Terra asked in her old grandmother's tone. "Let me see… it was not inside the city. I think it was when we stopped to talk to that young man. Conri I believe his name was. He had a baby on his back, his little brother he said. What did he call him?" Vig said thoughtfully. "Garbhan," Orelaith filled in.

"Maybe Nex was hunting him," Serovita suggested.

"I will have to go over all the facts and see what I can come up with," Terra said and walked off. Aqua was not talking about food for once and headed for her chamber to sleep.

"You two need to get some sleep," Bas said and looked at Luna and Vig. "You probably stayed way too long out of your true form and will be out for days." Orelaith walked over to Vig and gave her a big hug.

"I am sorry I didn't understand, Vig. I know you were just being cautious." The big white dragon hugged her back.

"It's ok, I understand my dear child. It's hard that you are left out of certain things. I guess I will talk to you more in a couple of days when I am back to my old self again."

"I wish you didn't get so affected by the shape-shifting."

LORE OF THE DRAGONS: ESSENCE OF A QUEEN

Suddenly, an intense humming started, and within a few seconds there was a loud pop that actually knocked the dragons over. Orelaith was the source of it all and seemed shocked but otherwise unaffected.

"What was that?" Aqua popped her head out of her chamber. Vig got up on shaky feet

"I don't know, but I feel a little different. It's as if all my life-force is restored and I am not tired at all."

"*Ga-ga-buuu.*" All the dragons looked up.

"What was that?" Solis exclaimed in surprise. "Was that…"

Vig walked over to Orelaith

"I believe it was. Orelaith, did you feel anything? Anything at all?"

Orelaith rubbed her belly and whispered,

"I… yes… when I said that I wished you did not get so affected by the shape-shifting, it was like she felt the same way. That was when the humming started." Vig looked at Orelaith.

"May I see if everything is ok with Rionach?" Orelaith nodded and Vig gently put her big paw around her. She sent out her tendrils of light and warmth and closed her eyes.

"She seems just fine. Let me see if there are still any traces left of what she did." Vig frowned in concentration as she tried to find the frail ends of magic that usually were left behind after big changes.

"Oh! I have something here but it is very complicated. Amazing... She seems to have...no... she can't have..." Vig opened her eyes and looked at Bas. "We need to talk. Outside. Now." Turning to Orelaith she said, "Don't worry, Rionach is fine. She has done something to us and I need to discuss it with him first before I am sure. Just get some rest my child. You look like you need it." Orelaith nodded. She did feel rather tired after the long trip. Vig walked out with Bas right behind her and Orelaith crawled into bed.

"Vig, what did you find?" he said and sat down.

"Something amazing, but before I tell you I want to examine you to be sure. If I am right, this means more to our race than you could ever imagine."

Bas nodded and she put her paws on his golden chest. As the tendrils reached into his very core, Vig frowned and then gasped.

"She did it! I can't believe it, but she found a way!" Bas felt a little nervous.

"Did what? What did you find?" She pulled the tendrils back and opened her eyes.

"She found a way to fuse human essence with ours. Not only that, but the part of us that the infection attacks... are gone!" Bas looked at her with wide open eyes.

"But... I don't feel any different. And you don't look any different." Vig laughed and flapped her beautiful white wings lifting her front paws off the ground.

"She did it while hardly changing anything about us. It's

like we didn't lose any essence, we just gained more. Oh Bas, do you understand what this means?" Her eyes almost glowed with excitement. Bas raised an eyebrow.

"Not really, but it doesn't matter as long as you do." Vig landed on all four again.

"It means we can no longer be infected, and shape-shifting is not going to drain our energy. We can take on any form for as long as we please without worrying about how it will affect us. You see, the human essence mixed with ours makes it possible for us to draw what we need from the sun and the earth, even in human form. No more worrying about what the future will bring as these humans spread out, we can hide among them." She frowned. "I need to make sure all the other have gone through the same change. Bas, be a dear and send them out to me one by one."

Chapter 13

When Orelaith woke up the next morning she felt truly rested. She didn't even open her eyes but just stretched out like a cat under the soft animal skins.

"Orelaith my dear…" At the sound of Vig's voice she sat up. She could not believe what she saw; around her bed were seven women. At first she was shocked, then curious, then astounded as she realized who these women were.

"Vig?" The white haired woman sitting on her bedside smiled and nodded. She took Orelaith's hands in hers.

"Rionach did something fantastic last night. It is hard to explain, but we will never have to rest for long periods after taking another form." Orelaith looked at the others. All of them were incredibly beautiful. She recognized them one by one as she studied them. Luna with her long black hair and big gray eyes, Solis with long flowing yellow curls. She saw Terra and Serovita in brown and green dresses, both with brown, waist-long hair. Tempest wore a grey dress, and her eyes were a sparkling blue like that of a lightning flash. And Aqua…she was the only one of them who didn't seem to feel comfortable in human form. She was pulling on the bright blue dress and blowing her blue-black hair out of her eyes. Orelaith noticed that they all had certain things in common; the high cheekbones, the slender bodies and a timelessness in their faces that made it hard to pinpoint how old they were.

"You... you're human. All of you." She looked around. "But where is Bas?" Vig let out a little giggle.

"He was a little embarrassed. We didn't have any men's clothing and I couldn't get him to put on a dress, so he went to the dump-site to see what he could find. He should be back soon."

"I am back..." At the sound of Bas' voice they all turned towards the entrance. "You have no idea how hard it is to find clothes for a man of my size." He was only wearing pants, but they only stretched to a little under the knee. Bas' human body was tall, muscular and a dark bronze color. His hair was a blond, rich golden color and reached all the way to his waist with not so much as a slight wave in it. The high cheekbones and timelessness was apparent in his face as the others, but he had more of a rugged handsomeness about him.

"We really need to get you some new clothes. Those pants are more than just a little too small." Vig chuckled. Bas looked rather uncomfortable and his cheeks turned a shade of pink. Orelaith climbed out of bed and walked up to him.

"It's not that bad," she said and stroked his cheek.

"Yes it is," Luna said and burst out in an infectious laughter. Bas caught a glimpse of himself in Orelaith's mirror.

"I look ridiculous!" Then he started laughing too. "Can you picture me walking into town dressed like this? I am used to sending people running but not laughing as they go." He swooped Orelaith up in his arms. "My Lady, I seem to be in a bit of a difficult situation here. I need to go to town to get some clothes, but I can't go to town until I get some new clothes. What do you suggest I do?" She put her arms around his neck.

"You could turn into a mouse and I could put you in my pocket. That would still leave the problem of getting you measured." He laughed and looked into her eyes.

"Well, at least you could say you have a dragon in your pocket." She looked back into his bronze coloured eyes but suddenly seemed to be at loss for words. As the others silently walked away smiling, she realized she was in the arms of a half naked man wearing only her nightgown. Bas sensed it and he put her down.

"What is wrong?" he said and walked in and sat down on the chair with one leg hanging over the armrest. She quickly climbed back onto the bed and smiled at him.

"Oh, it's nothing." Bas raised an eyebrow,

"Orelaith my dear, don't tell me it's nothing. You forget I have got to know you quite well. Is it my appearance? Don't you like this human form?" I like it just a little too much, Orelaith thought.

"No, it's not that. You look very handsome. I guess it's the nakedness. It doesn't seem… appropriate." Bas laughed.

"But I am wearing more now than I have since you met

me the first time. And you have been riding on my back several times without me being covered up in any way so why should it bother you to be in my arms when I am more clothed than ever before?" Orelaith blushed. She hadn't ever thought of it that way before.

"I know, but it is different somehow. Don't ask me to explain." He walked over and sat down on the bed next to her.

"I won't. But promise me one thing; don't let this change the way we are together. I still want to go flying with you." She nodded and smiled at him. He was still Bas the golden dragon, and she loved him dearly. He touched her face and smiled. "There is one more thing. Don't ask me to wear pants in dragon form. I think it will be hard enough to find pants in this form." She laughed.

"I would like to see the tailor that had the nerves to take the measurements." Bas fell laughing back on the bed.

"Yeah, but he would be a wealthy man if he could pull it off." She laid down on her elbows next to him. "Oh yes, there would be naked sheep all over this side of the land." She looked at him and started to pull away, feeling she was too close again. He smiled and looked up into her eyes.

"You're doing it again." She blushed and said, "I know…" He held out his arms to her.

"Put your head on my chest and close your eyes, just for a little while." She hesitated but realized she would have to overcome this feeling if they were ever going to keep what they had.

"Listen…" he sent to her. "My heart still beats the same.

Just relax and picture us flying over the sea." As they lay like that, a sweet smell filled the chamber, almost like a meadow full of spring flowers.

Chapter 14

Over the next few days, Orelaith taught them how to act in human form. Most of them seemed to enjoy it, but Aqua would go off as soon as she could. Several times they found her dress outside the cave where she had dropped it as she had flown off to frolic in the sea. Orelaith went with her and Bas down to the sea that night and asked her what was going on.

"I just don't like being human, the clothes are tight and the hair! It's always getting in my face. As I am now I feel free and comfortable. Nothing constricting me and you must admit, you humans are rather frail and weak."

Orelaith laughed.

"I guess, and I do understand. But I think I can help you with the clothes and the hair at least. But you don't have to stay in human form if you don't want to. It's only so you can hide from people who fear you." Aqua nodded. "I would like that, and I know… I just feel like I am the only one who doesn't like being human. The others seem so comfortable in that shape." Bas laughed.

"Don't be too sure about that. Terra and Serovita don't

much like it either, but they know how important it is that we are able to be seen as humans if the situation forces us. We share this planet with them, and as much as they have spread out over just the last five centuries, who knows how long it will be before there no longer is anywhere we can hide in our true form." Aqua frowned.

"You mean we might have to change on a more permanent basis?"

"There are things you may like as a human," Orelaith said with a smile.

"Like what?" She glanced over at Bas then back.

"The food. You will need less to feel full and there are a lot more different foods you haven't tried." This seemed to pique Aqua's interest.

"What kind of food?" Orelaith grinned and knew she was on the right track.

"Apple pie, sweet cheese, tender roasted lamb and wonderful flavored soups." The big blue dragon squinted at her.

"I know what fish tastes like and I like that, but I don't know anything about the food you just mentioned." Orelaith put her hand on Aqua's shoulder. "Then why don't you come with me the next time I go to town and you can try it all. If you don't like it there, you just leave and come back here." Aqua thought of it for a while then nodded.

"Ok, I will do that. But if I don't like it I can just leave, right?" Orelaith nodded and Bas sent her an approving smile.

LORE OF THE DRAGONS: ESSENCE OF A QUEEN

They decided to go to the town a few weeks later. Only a few went as humans, Luna and Vig agreed to take horse shape again along with Serovita, Tempest and Terra. Orelaith had made some clothes for Bas out of the animal skins in her room so he could travel as her husband. Solis and Aqua would come along as Bas' sisters. Once they had all taken on the shape of their choice they started towards the town. Solis was riding on Tempest, now a big grey mare with darker spots on her back, and she seemed to be enjoying herself immensely. Orelaith looked over at Bas riding on Terra who was now a beautiful brown mare with darker legs, head, mane and tail. He was dressed in brown leather pants and boots with a loose white wool tunic. His hair was tied back with a leather strap and he seemed at ease. He smiled at her and she realized how much she was enjoying this. Vig came trotting up next to her.

"*This is nice. All of us went on a trip together. We haven't done this in a very long time.*"

"Why not?" Orelaith asked.

"*I don't really know. We just haven't.*" Vig replied and tossed her head back sending her long mane flowing in the wind. Luna huffed.

"*Next time, I get to ride instead of being ridden.*"

As they approached the gates, Saoirse's children came running towards them. They greeted Orelaith and stroked Vig and Luna, but they seemed sceptical of the others. Vig let them climb up on her back and they chattered without stop as they rode towards Saoirse's tailoring shop. People stopped to stare as they passed through the town.

"Don't talk to anyone and try not to look at anyone in specific. That is what they would expect of our kind of people," she sent to them all.

"Our kind of people?" Bas sent back.

"Wealthy people," Orelaith replied and stopped outside the tailoring shop.

"Orelaith! I didn't expect you back until after the baby was born." Saoirse came running out of the shop. She stopped when she saw Bas and the others. "Oh, you brought company." Orelaith climbed off and hugged her.

"Yes, this is my husband Basilicus and his sisters Solis and Aqua." Bas smiled and nodded, Solis waved and smiled and Aqua nodded quickly.

"I wish you had sent word that you were coming so I could have made arrangements," Saoirse said with a frown.

"We didn't even know we were coming until last night. You see, we had a bit of an accident and we need your

LORE OF THE DRAGONS: ESSENCE OF A QUEEN

assistance. But let's have some tea first," Orelaith said and winked at Saoirse.

"Oh I would love to help you. Tell me what I can do," Saoirse said. The others dismounted as Orelaith walked into the shop with her friend.

"My husband had a slight problem with his clothes; they all caught on fire. Could you make some new ones for him?" Saoirse cast a glance at Bas over her shoulder and giggled. "I have just finished a load of wool and linen cloth, so I think I might have enough. You said he was tall but oh my, I have never seen a man so big. Is he just as well proportioned all over?" She spoke almost in a whisper and giggled again.

"Oh Saoirse." Orelaith blushed. "It wouldn't be very ladylike of me to talk of such things." Then she giggled as well. The children had run off as soon as they had arrived and returned with apples and water for the "horses", then went indoors with Bas, Solis and Aqua, asking all sorts of awkward questions like most children do. Not long after, they were sitting on Bas' and Solis' laps. Orelaith had sent them what to answer when they seemed stuck, and Aqua was learning clapping games from the little girl. Bas sent Orelaith glances and smiled when she looked in his direction.

"So I am your husband? I like that," he sent when Saoirse went to get some more tea. Orelaith blushed.

"Well, I had to come up with a believable story the last time I was here, you know that." She took a sip of her tea and watched as Solis and Aqua were entertained by the children.

"But what did she mean when she asked if I was well proportioned all over?" Orelaith broke into a coughing fit as the tea went down the wrong way, but she soon regained herself and smiled at Saoirse as she came out with some food and more tea.

"Are you ok?" she said and sent her a worried look. Orelaith nodded.

"Well... she ah... was wondering if ALL parts of you are as big as... well, the rest of you."

"She wanted to know if you're hung like a dragon," Luna sent with an amused undertone.

"Oh... Oh!" Bas looked surprised. "I don't know, maybe you could see if I am later, Orelaith." Orelaith turned a bright red and felt more than a little warm.

"I don't think that will be necessary, Bas. I assume you are evenly sized all over."

Aqua had now noticed the food and pulled her chair over to the table.

They spent the rest of the day walking around the trade district looking at all the things offered there. Solis had a band of men following her, offering to help carry her things. Likewise with Aqua, but she practically ignored them and focused on tasting all the different foods she came across. Bas took Orelaith's hand at one point and she looked at him in surprise. "We are supposed to be man and wife, are we not? Relax and have fun with this." She smiled at him. "I will try." As the day turned into afternoon she found herself almost wishing the illusion was true. A faint smell of wild flowers followed them as they walked through the town back to Saoirse's shop.

"I am stuffed!" Aqua said with a content smile on her lips as she slumped down in a chair.

"You shouldn't have eaten so much." Bas laughed. "But I guess there is nothing as too much food for you." Aqua shook her head and took Orelaith's hand.

"You were right and I want to say thank you. Humans seem to have the ability to taste different things than us. There actually are some upsides to being in this shape."

"And the skin is so much more sensitive to touch," Bas added with a cheeky grin.

"Oh yes! And the people here are so sweet and helpful," Solis said and clapped her hands. Orelaith made a mental note to explain a few things about what made the men fall all over her at a later time. Saoirse came out with a customer then sat down with them as the customer walked off casting long glances at them all.

"Where are the horses?" she asked.

"Oh I let the children take them out to a field outside town so they could run a little. I hope you don't mind," Bas said.

"Will they be safe?" Saoirse sounded a little concerned.

"Oh yes, perfectly safe. These are specially trained horses," Bas said and winked at her, making her giggle. Then she turned to Orelaith.

"I have arranged for you to have three rooms at my house. I have a maid now who cares for the baby and tends to the house. She came by earlier with little Garbhan, and I told her we were having overnight guests, so she hurried home to get everything set up." Orelaith smiled at the thought of Conri and his baby brother.

"How were they doing? I hope it was ok to send them to you. They seemed so lost when I met them, and I knew that it would be good for you to have some help from Conri." Saoirse smiled.

"I feel privileged to be able to give a little back after all you have done for me. Conri has been such wonderful help with the sheep. And beautiful little Garbhan, he is a joy to be around. He sleeps all night and is growing so fast." Orelaith smiled, happy that things had turned out so well.

"I can't wait to see them both."

Chapter 15

After Saoirse had closed up her shop they headed out of the gates and followed a narrow path to a small farm just east of town. They found the children in a field right before they came to the farm. Both curled up and half asleep in the afternoon sun; the little girl with Vig and the little boy with Tempest. But at the promise of dinner they came running with the horses trailing after them. As they stopped outside the house Conri came out and smiled at Orelaith. "My lady, I heard you had returned." He looked so different, his sunken cheeks had filled out and the pain in his eyes was only a bad memory. He bowed but she gave him a big hug instead. "I am glad to see you again. And you look like you are happy here, are you?" she said and held him out at arm's length. He nodded.

"Yes, we both are."

"And where is your sweet little brother?" Orelaith said and looked around. An older woman with gray streaks in her hair came out of the house drying her hands on the front of her dress.

"I just put him down for a nap, so he should be out for a

while." She walked up and curtsied to Orelaith and Bas who had come up next to her. "It is a pleasure to finally meet you, lady Orelaith. Saoirse has told me all about how you came as an angel and helped her turn her life around." Orelaith laughed.

"Comparing me to an angel is a bit much. Besides, she was the one who did the work. I just helped with the material to get things started." The old woman smiled and looked at Saoirse.

"So modest too… I like her already! Dinner's almost finished. Conri, would you show them to their rooms?" He nodded and walked ahead of them into the house. After a wonderful meal, where Aqua had overeaten again, they sat around talking. The old lady and Saoirse cleared the table and were setting out cups and tea when little Garbhan started crying upstairs. Orelaith saw that it affected Bas, Solis and Aqua alike. They glanced nervously at each other.

"What is it?" Orelaith sent.

"I am not sure, but there is another dragon close by. We can feel it strongly," Bas replied and looked around.

"It's getting stronger," Aqua added as she got up and looked out the window.

"Here is the little darling. My, did he wake up happy." Orelaith heard Rionach cooing and laughing inside and she looked at Bas.

"Can you hear her?" He nodded and smiled at Saoirse as she sat down with little Garbhan.

"He is a big boy. How old is he now?"

"He was born in springtime," Conri said. *"I have a*

LORE OF THE DRAGONS: ESSENCE OF A QUEEN

theory, but I need to run it by Vig first," Bas sent to them.

"He doesn't really like strangers, though. It took a few weeks before he would even let me and Bridget hold him without setting him off in a crying frenzy," Saoirse said and sat him up on her lap facing the others. His little deep bronze coloured eyes looked around at them, then focused on Bas and he stretched his chubby little arms out to him. "Ba-ba!"

"Oh my! I think he likes you," Saoirse said and looked at Bas. "Do you want to hold him?" Bas nodded and set little Garbhan on his knee. "That is amazing. You must have a special touch with children," Bridget said and smiled. And for the rest of the evening Garbhan refused to let anyone else hold him. He clung to Bas' arms and would protest loudly if someone tried to move him. Conri seemed equally astounded by his little brother's behavior. Besides his brother, Garbhan was only mildly interested in Aqua and Solis, and he smiled and laughed at Orelaith. He completely ignored everyone else. He fell asleep in Bas' arms, and Conri showed him to the crib where Bas laid him down for the night.

"I am going to go check on the horses. Sisters, would you join me?" Bas got up and looked at Solis and Aqua.

"Do you want me to come?" Orelaith asked Bas.

"No, I will fill you in later. We are sharing a bed tonight, remember? Just make an excuse to stay here." She looked up at him.

"Do you mind if I stay here and talk with Saoirse and Bridget? I am feeling a little tired." He smiled back at her and stroked her hair.

"Of course I don't mind, my dear. You just rest. We will be back shortly." Once he was out the door, Saoirse turned to Orelaith.

"Oh my, you have such a dreamy husband. Does he have an unmarried brothers?" Orelaith laughed.

"He does, actually. However, they got separated a very long time ago, and he doesn't know where any of them are." Saoirse sighed.

"What a shame, I would have loved to meet them." Bridget chuckled and picked up her knitting from a basket next to her chair.

"She has had many suitors, but she keeps turning them away. I say she is just too picky." Orelaith picked up her cup and took a sip.

"Where did Conri go?"

"He has turned in for the night. He sleeps in a bed next to his brothers crib. When he first got here, he didn't leave his brother's side for the first two weeks. Even when he did chores around the farm he would put little Garbhan on his back. He is a wonderful boy with a high sense of responsibility. I think it is all the dreadful things he went through even before his parents died." Orelaith realized she didn't know that much about him.

"He never told me what had happened to his parents." Saoirse looked at her. "A dragon killed them."

Chapter 16

Outside, Bas and the others were gathered in the stables.

"I think I might know what is going on, why we keep feeling the presence of a dragon and still can't see one," Bas said.

"We felt it too, even out here." Vig stomped her feet. *"But this time I analyzed the presence. There was no... bad feeling, to put it that way. Could it be that we have found a dragon who is not infected?"* Solis clapped her hands.

"Oh, tell her, Bas!" Bas sent Solis a stern look.

"I am not completely sure yet, but I believe I know where this presence is emanating from." Luna tossed her head back and stomped her feet.

"Out with it Bas, the damn suspense is killing me!"

"You both remember the boy you met the last time you were here? When you felt the presence for the first time?"

"All too well. It was the first time we have felt any such presence at all since we came to this place," Vig replied.

"Do you also remember the human baby?" Bas added.

"Yes… but what has that got to do with it?" Vig was starting to get slightly annoyed, it seemed. Bas noticed, so he came to the point.

"I believe that child is a human dragon hybrid."

"Are you sure?" Vig asked. Bas nodded.

"And I think I know who it is." Five pairs of horse ears pointed towards him.

"How could you know that?" Terra asked. *"We have never been able to feel who, just the emotion of the one we feel."* Bas smiled.

"Exactly. And that is how I believe I know who it is. You see, this child would not leave my arms all evening and he was mind sending the words Ba-Ba. Only I would know what that means because that is what my youngest brother called me when we were still whelps." He sat down on a wooden box, "But to be completely sure, I need you to compare our essences. Vig, you are the only one of us who still has that ability." Vig snorted,

"I can't do it in this form. I need to lay my paws or hands on him physically."

"What if me, Aqua, Tempest and Vig went back tomorrow and swapped? Then they can come back as humans." Solis suggested. Bas smiled.

"That is a good idea, Solis."

"Yeah, how did you come up with it?" Luna teased.

"But my dear Bas, there is one thing you need to think

LORE OF THE DRAGONS: ESSENCE OF A QUEEN

about. If we find out this child is your long lost brother, what then? You can't just steal him away." Vig pointed out. Bas seemed a little downhearted at first but he got up and smiled.

"We will decide what to do about that later, but now I think we have reason to be happy. We have found one of our own."

The house was dark by the time Bas and the other two came back in. Only the hearth was alight and they went to their assigned chambers to get some rest. Bas stopped outside the room where Bridget, Conri and little Garbhan slept and let his mind wander into the space behind the closed door. He found little Garbhan sleeping soundly so he walked to his and Orelaith's room and stepped inside.

"Bas…?" Orelaith sat up in the big bed.

"Yes, it's me." he whispered back. He quickly undressed and climbed into the bed wearing a pair of linen pants that Saoirse had made for him.

"What is going on? Did you figure out why Rionach is acting so strange?" He nodded and pulled her close.

"Yes, we believe that Garbhan is my brother Frater reborn in human form." Orelaith gasped. "How is that even possible?"

"I don't know, to be sure Vig, Tempest, Aqua and Solis are going to leave tomorrow, swap, and come back in a few days. Vig needs to be in human form to examine him since we doubt that dragons are going to be accepted around here." Orelaith decided to focus on what Bas had told her, which was hard to do with his arms around her.

"You have no idea how badly the dragons would be taken around here..." Then she told him what had happened to Conri's and Garbhan's parents.

"Nex... it must be him. This does change some things but we still have found my brother. We should get some rest. Even after what Rionach did, it's still tiresome to be in this form," he said and stroked her hair back and looked into her eyes. "I had fun today. I think I like being your husband." She was glad the room was dark. That way he didn't see how pink her cheeks turned. The way she felt about Bas was changing. Even though she knew he was not human, at least not all human, she liked the idea of being his wife.

"I did too." Bas stretched and his feet pushed against the end of the bed. "There is one thing that I would change though. The size of the bed," he said and laughed. As they fell asleep that night, the sweet smell of wild flowers filled the room and she dreamt of flying over meadows with Bas.

When she woke up the next morning, Bas had already gone down to breakfast. She got up and took her time getting dressed before she walked down to join the others. Saoirse had set out a wonderful meal and everyone was sitting around the table. Conri was sitting next to Bas and little Garbhan was chewing on a piece of bread.

"Good morning, sleepyhead." Solis smiled and made room for her next to Bas.

LORE OF THE DRAGONS: ESSENCE OF A QUEEN

"You should have woken me up, my dear," she said and looked at Bas. "Oh!" She felt little Rionach moving around in her belly.

"Oh, is she kicking?" Saoirse asked, grinning widely.

"Yes, it feels like she is jumping around in there." Orelaith laughed.

"Saoirse, me and Aqua will be heading home today. And we want to thank you so much for letting us stay here with you. We will be meeting our two other sisters about half way so they should be here tomorrow morning." Solis smiled.

"I hope that is not too much trouble for you, Saoirse?" Bas added. "My sisters, Luna and Vigoratus, were eager to meet you too, but someone had to stay behind and take care of some things that could not wait. They should be finished with their business now. Also we were unsure if there would be enough room for us all.." Saoirse smiled.

"Yes, my home is not made for so many. Of course it is fine. I would love to meet them."

"Isn't that the name of the horses you came here on?" the little boy asked curiously. Bas laughed. "Very well observed. All our horses are named after my sisters. And that is because they kind of look like them and have the same kind of temperament."

"Close call and good save." Solis laughed.

"You all have some remarkable names," Bridget said as she sipped her tea.

"Well, our father was a very well read man. He studied the church's language and he picked out the names for us from their meaning," Bas said and smiled. "It did cause us a few fights, but we carry our names proudly." Bridget blushed a little.

"Oh, I did not mean any offense. I just have not heard of them before." Orelaith was grateful she had taken the time to teach them so much about humans and how they lived and interacted.

"No offense taken, Bridget." Bas smiled warmly at her. Surprisingly, she started giggling like a little girl and got up.

"I will make some lunch for you to take with you on the long ride," she said, then walked off to get things ready. After Solis, Aqua, Luna and Vig had left, Orelaith went with Saoirse to her shop to help out and to spend some time with her.

The next morning, just as the sun came over the surrounding hillside, Vig and Luna came riding in on Aqua and Solis. They looked a little like the goddesses of day and night. Luna with her long black hair, a black dress with a silver belt and matching embroideries on her neckline was riding in on Aqua who was a dark bluish gray, and Vig with her long white hair and matching white dress riding in on Solis who was now a yellow mare. Conri was already up and as they stopped in front of the stable he stared with his mouth open.

LORE OF THE DRAGONS: ESSENCE OF A QUEEN

"You must be Conri," Vig said and smiled. He nodded and took hold of the reins as they dismounted. "I guess the others are still sleeping?" Vig asked. He nodded again.

"Cat got your tongue, boy?" Luna teased and winked at him.

"No my lady....I..eh.. I didn't expect you so early, that's all." Luna grabbed her saddlebags off Aqua's back.

"We know you will take very good care of the horses, our sisters said so." He bowed and said, "Thank you my lady, I do my best and these horses are just as magnificent as the ones your sisters left on, although I found myself favoring the beautiful black mare and the even tempered white one. Breeding them would be magnificent." Luna laughed, while at Vigs apparent perturbation . Conri was confused. "Did I say anything wrong?" Luna just smiled at him.

"Oh no my boy, you didn't. But you just made my day." She pinched his cheek and walked off following Vig to the house.

Bridget was up making breakfast for the house when Vig walked in.

"You must be Bridget. I am Basilicus' sister, Vigoratus, and this is Luna." Bridget curtsied.

"My Ladies."

"Oh there is no need for formalities. I will help you get things set up for breakfast. It will make me feel useful."Vig said and smiled. Luna sat down on the chair and watched as Vig and Bridget fussed around preparing the morning meal. Soon the others came down and joined them. After a hearty breakfast that stretched out so long that Saoirse had to rush off to open her shop, Vig picked up little Garbhan ,who was crawling around on the floor. He looked at her skeptically at first, but soon smiled and made happy baby sounds.

"I need to examine him. Is there any way you can get the others outside for a little bit, Orelaith?" Orelaith stretched and said,

"I want to go for a little walk. Bridget, would you come with me and keep me company? I would love to get some tips from a woman with your life knowledge about children and all the things I may expect in the time to come." Bridget seemed astounded but flattered by the unusual request.

"Well, yes I have raised five children so I know a thing or two that would be helpful for you to know. But I have to clean the house. I wouldn't want Saoirse to think I was not earning my keep." Orelaith smiled.

"Oh, let me worry about her. Besides, I don't think she will mind. And we won't be that long." Bridget seemed a little torn.

"But what about the children?"

"I think we can find a way to entertain them until you come back. What do you think children, you want to go for a ride? And you can show me the best place to go fishing around here," Luna said with a smile.

"Oh yes! But do you know how to fish?" the little boy asked and looked skeptically at Luna. "Yes I do, I once caught a fish as long as you" Luna replied and winked at him. *"Not with a fishing rod. And it was not one, but more like a mouthful,"* Bas teased.

"But first we need to help Bridget clear the table," Vig said and got up. "And don't worry about Garbhan. I think the little guy has taken a shine to me." Once the others had left, Bas sat Garbhan on his lap and Vig moved her chair so she was sitting opposite him.

"Garbhan my dear, look at me." His little dark curls bounced as he turned his head towards Vig. "I want you to know what we are going to do here so you don't get scared. If you are who we think you are, you will understand." He looked up at Bas who smiled at him then back at Vig and smiled a toothless smile. "Here we go my dear," Vig said and took his little hands in hers. She closed her eyes and sent her tendrils of light towards Garbhan. To her and Bas' surprise he sent out his own tendrils grabbing on to Vig's and pulled her in. "Oh! He is strong. I don't think I could pull back now even if I tried. I may need your assistance if he does not let go after we are done." She relaxed and let him pull her in. "I see what he is trying to show me. It seems… ah! He did a little of what you did with Orelaith to make the human and the dragon essence compatible. But he… hmm that is strange. Garbhans mother was not pregnant at the time. He made his essence more human, then did it the old fashioned way."

"What do you mean?" Bas asked.

"This child is pretty much human, but with all the abilities and powers your brother had. I can't be absolutely sure because he is the one showing me what he wants me to know. I am surprised he has not done anything out of the ordinary yet." Bas smiled.

"So it is my brother?" Vig nodded and said,

"Yes, that is the one thing I am positive of. I need you to let me go now sweetie. Bas, give me your hand. I am going to need a little assistance." She drew on Bas' powers making her tendrils expand to double the size, and now had no problem letting go. She opened her eyes and smiled at little Garbhan. "Now then, that didn't hurt you one little bit, now did it?" His bronze coloured eyes looked at her with far more wisdom than there should be in a child of his age. Then he yawned and rubbed his little eyes.

"I think it's time for someone's nap," Bas said and got up cradling Garbhan in his arms. "I am going to put him to bed, then we can talk more."

Vig was sipping some cold tea when he came back and sat down.

"So you are sure? Is it Frater reborn?" Vig nodded and put her cup on the table.

"Yes, I am. But there are some things you need to know. The way he… changed his essence to make it compatible with human essence is remarkable. Sadly, Frater is not going to be able to take on dragon form ever again, but he will develop other abilities that will be considered divine." Bas leaned back in his chair.

"What kind of abilities are we talking about here?" Vig frowned.

"I am not completely sure, but it will most likely be things that will keep him safe. Maybe extreme speed at short bursts and stalking quietly. The basic predator instincts will probably be strong in him. Along with the powers he already seems to have, he will be a force to be reckoned with."

"But how soon will he begin to use these abilities?" Bas asked.

"Hard to say really, but I do believe that it will follow his development. When he learns to walk he will start getting fast, and as he starts to develop an intellect he will be able to process information at an alarming pace," Vig said and leaned forward. "There is something we can do to… slow down the process so he will appear to be just like other children." Bas frowned.

"You mean suppress his abilities? But won't that leave him vulnerable? He won't be able to protect himself…" Vig laughed.

"Bas my dear, that is what caretakers are for. Human children depend on someone to care for them closely and guide them." Bas got up and looked out the window.

"But he is not human, at least not all human, anyway."

"Listen Bas," Vig said as she walked up and put her hand on his shoulder. "As much as we want to take him home, I don't think taking him away from his brother and Saoirse will be the right thing to do." Bas sighed.

"What if I lose him again? We have searched for so long without so much as a trace of another of our kind. And now that we have found my brother, my brother, Vig, I am supposed to leave him in the care of someone else? How can you expect me to go along with that?" Vig turned him around and looked into his eyes.

"Because it's the right thing to do." He closed his eyes.

"I know… but sometimes, just sometimes, I would like to do what I want to do, not what I know is right." Vig gently stroked his cheek.

"But you won't, because you always do what's right no matter the cost to yourself." He embraced Vig and gave her a big hug.

"If I stray, I always have you to make me see the right way." She held him at arms length.

"I will do it now, while he is sleeping. That way he won't fight me and I can do it alone." Bas nodded and Vig left him standing by the window.

Chapter 17

Orelaith was chatting away with Bridget as they walked on the path to the outskirts of the woods. She actually felt like she was learning a lot about children and what to do when they had tummy aches or when they were teething. There was so much information that she could use, or could have used that is, if she was having a human baby. She decided there probably were enough similarities that she would need some of it at least.

"We better turn back now," Bridget said. "It's almost time for lunch and I want to send Conri into town with some food for Saoirse, she always forgets to eat." Orelaith smiled and nodded.

"Yes, she seems the type to get occupied with things." As they turned and started walking back Orelaith glanced into the woods and saw someone dart behind a tree. Rionach made whining sounds in Orelaith's head and she knew that they were in danger. She grabbed hold of Bridget's arm and whispered to her,

"When I say so, start running. Don't stop and don't look back until you get home." Bridget stiffened and started looking around.

"What is it my lady?"

"Don't look around! Just pretend everything is normal. But when I say run, you go as fast as you can. Do you understand?" Bridget nodded and kept walking. They still had quite a way to go before they could even see the farm, and she knew that whoever was stalking them would attack before they got that close. When they got to the place where the path led away from the forest, Orelaith stopped and stretched her back. She smiled and whispered to Bridget,

"Go ahead of me, but when I call and tell you to wait, you run." She picked up a staff to lean on and waited until Bridget was about ten paces ahead of her. "Wait for me, Bridget!" she shouted and Bridget took off running. Sure enough, four men jumped out of the woods, two behind her and two between her and Bridget.

"Run Bridget, run!" she shouted. The two men behind her came at her and she directed a well placed hit at the tallest man's groin. He buckled over and cursed. She had used a staff to guard the sheep many times growing up, but had never had any real use for it before now. She managed to trip up the other man and took off running as fast as a woman in her condition could.

"Stop her!" the man she had tripped up shouted to the two men ahead of her. They had not caught up with Bridget yet, and now they stopped and came at her instead. She saw Bridget glance over her shoulder but she kept going. All four men closed on her now and she stopped and tossed her stick aside.

"What do you want from me? I have nothing of value," she said and put her hands out to the sides. The tallest one

LORE OF THE DRAGONS: ESSENCE OF A QUEEN

came walking up behind her. He seemed to be the leader of this gang of men.

"I should kill you for that, but I need you alive and unharmed." He grabbed her arm. "The man who ordered us to get you makes us seem like angels in comparison. Now, let's go! He is not a patient man."

Bas was still looking out the window when he saw Bridget's terrified face as she came running up the path to the farm. Vig came back in just as she burst through the door.

"Where is Orelaith?" Bas grabbed her arms as panic set in.

"Four men... they... came from the woods. She... she told me to run... just down the path." He dropped her arms and ran out the door.

"Careful Bas. Run into the woods before you change form. I will be right behind you," Vig sent and hurriedly gave Bridget instructions before running after Bas. She saw him take off down the path and she ran to the stables.

"Conri! Go take care of Bridget. Now boy!" Without hesitation, he ran to the house. Vig opened the doors wide and let the others out telling them quickly what had happened. Just as they came out, Luna came back with the children and sent them inside when she saw something was wrong. Vig quickly told her what had happened, and they took off after Bas into the woods. Seconds later, eight dragons burst out on the other side chasing down the men who were about to have a very bad day.

Orelaith walked as slowly as she could, pretending to trip and taking her time getting up. The men took off from the path and headed down an animal trail that wound its way through the dense forest. She knew Bas and the others would come chasing after her as soon as Bridget got to the farm and told them what had happened.

"Stop dragging your feet woman. It's not going to do you any good. Even if your man comes after you he can't fight off all four of us." She almost laughed. They obviously had no idea who they were dealing with. "What the hell are you smiling about?" Orelaith looked at him and then nodded towards the end of the trail they were heading down. He turned and saw Luna and Vig walking towards them in human form. They still looked like the goddesses of day and night. A gentle wind blew their hair back and added to the effect.

"And just what do you think you're doing?" Vig said. Orelaith had never seen her so angry.

"Get out of our way women, this is none of your concern" the tallest man said and took a threatening step towards them. Luna took two steps forward accepting his challenge.

"None of our concern? I should turn you into a rat and

step on your neck!" His eyes wavered a little, then he pulled himself together.

"And what are you two little women going to do? We outnumber you, so just step aside and maybe we won't hurt you." Vig laughed.

"Outnumber us? But little boy, how do you figure that?" And from all sides the other five stepped out in human form. "As far as I can see, you are the ones that are outnumbered." He licked his lips nervously then laughed. "Still, what are you pretty little girls going to do about it?" Tempest came up on his left side, her eyes flashing in anger.

"What are we going to do about it?" Thunder sounded overhead and the wind started blowing wildly around them. The men holding on to Orelaith's arms let go and stepped away from her. They all started closing in on the men, slowly walking towards them. Serovita knelt down and put one hand on the ground, sending ripples of roots curling up around the men's ankles pinning them down. Bas came flying in straight above them and crashed down through the trees, still in dragon form. Vig pulled Orelaith out of the way and whispered,

"Are you alright?" Orelaith nodded but kept her eyes fixed on Bas now circling the four men. "Don't kill them. They are only following orders from someone else." Bas looked over at her. "How can you ask me not to hurt them? They tried to take you away from me."Orelaith smiled and replied,

"No one can ever take me away from you. I didn't say you couldn't hurt them, just don't kill them." He turned back to the men.

"Who sent you!?" His voice thundered through their very souls.

"I don't know his name! Please don't kill me..." one of them begged. The tall man seemed more composed than the others. "You have no idea what he will do with us if we don't bring her back. You might as well kill us now. If you burn us slowly, it would be considered kind compared to what he will put us through if we return empty handed."

"Nex! It has to be him." Terra looked at Vig.

"I already know who sent you, and I want you to send him a message from me. If he ever comes near my Orelaith again, I will find him and slowly tear him limb from limb, leaving nothing but a wet spot where he used to be. And," Bas continued, "If I ever see any of you again, I will deal with you like I dealt with Malum." They stared at him.

"It was you at the camp?" The utter fear was clear to read in the tall man's eyes. Bas walked over to Orelaith and Vig and curled protectively around them. Serovita released the men and they ran head over heels down the trail. Once they were out of sight, Bas returned to human shape and embraced Orelaith. The others gathered around them and Vig checked if Rionach was ok, as she had been very quiet through the incident.

"That was way too close. We have been lulled into a false sense of security and this is the result." There were still small flashes of tiny blue lightning jumping off her body as Tempest spoke.

"I agree," Vig said. "We are not as safe here as we thought. And we are putting the humans we surround ourselves with at risk. Poor Bridget almost fell over dead as she came bursting in the door. And if she had not gotten away from those men she would have been dead." Bas was holding on to Orelaith and did not seem to be ready to let go any time soon.

"Now, Orelaith, I want you to go back with Luna and the others. Bas and I have something to talk about." Luna took hold of Orelaith's hand and the others returned to their horse shape. Reluctantly, Bas let go of Orelaith and she climbed up on Tempest's back. Bas stared longingly after them as they rode off.

"Bas... do you understand what is going on with you and Orelaith?" Vig said softly and placed her hand on his shoulder. He looked down at her and said,

"What do you mean? I swore to my mother that I would keep her safe, we all did." Vig smiled and touched his cheek.

"Yes we did, but that is not what I'm talking about. You seem to be bonding with her." Bas looked a little confused.

"Haven't we all? In such short a time she has spellbound us all and I feel she is part of us now."

"Oh my dear Bas, it seems you are in denial." Vig smiled at him and sat down on a nearby rock.

"I... I don't understand. I don't think I'm any closer to her than any of you." She crossed her arms

"Then tell me this: what was the first thought that came to mind when you heard what had happened?" He frowned and said

"I was afraid of losing her and little Rionach, of course. Just the thought of someone trying to take her away from me… or hurt her, made my blood boil inside." Vig nodded knowingly.

"And the scent? Is that just because you feel responsible for her and the whelp?"

"Scent? What scent?" He fumbled with his tunic and then crossed his arms. Vig shook her head and sighed.

"The scent that follows you wherever you are close to her. You know very well that is how we dragons know when we have found a mate for life." The air seemed to go out of him and he sat down next to Vig.

"I… I didn't think… but as you say it, I know it is true." He looked into Vig's eyes. "How is it even possible?" Vig laughed and said,

"Haven't we seen enough impossible things lately to stop being surprised when they do happen to us? But we both know this is not going to be easy. She is human, and her lifespan is only a fraction of ours. How will you deal with her death? Don't look at me like that, we both know you will live long after she is gone." He got up and looked towards the farm.

"I don't want to think about it, Vig."

"One more thing," Vig said. "Does she know how you feel about her? And does she feel the same way about you?" He shrugged.

"I don't know, Vig. We haven't exactly talked about it."

LORE OF THE DRAGONS: ESSENCE OF A QUEEN

Vig locked her arm in his and started walking back towards the farm.

"I did not ask you all these questions to get answers, Bas. It was so that you would realize what I already knew. Just keep them in mind and see if maybe you can get some answers."

"I'm not sure I want them answered. There have been so many changes happening lately, both good and bad. Right now I just want to go flying with Orelaith and forget everything else." The rest of the way back to the farm, they walked in silence.

Later that evening after the children were all tucked into their beds they sat around the table drinking tea and talking. Orelaith was not hurt but Bridget was more shaken by this than she was.

"It's ok Bridget. Because you did as I asked, Bas and his sisters got there before they were able to hurt me." Bridget smiled bravely but she was shaking and feeling a little sick.

"Oh but I should have stayed and defended you." Orelaith shook her head.

"No, we would both be dead now if you hadn't listened to me. You did the right thing." Bridget nodded and said

"If you say so my lady."

"Don't feel like you did something wrong. None of us think so," Bas said and knelt down in front of Bridget This seemed like the ghost that she needed to let it go.

"Really? Well, I did as she said… and you are not upset with me?" Bas shook his head and smiled.

"No, quite the opposite. If you had not come back and told me, Orelaith would be lost to us now." Luna came out with little Garbhan on her arm.

"Someone is awake." She smiled and handed him to Bridget.

"Will they be back? And if so, what do we do?" Conri asked and looked at Bas.

"I don't believe they will be back. We gave them quite a scare," Bas said and laughed, but in his heart he was still unsure. Conri seemed to sense it but said nothing.

In the evening, when Saoirse came home, they told her what had happened.

"Oh dear! How are you doing now, Orelaith?" Orelaith smiled at her.

"I'm fine, thank you for asking. But I was not afraid. I knew my Bas would not let anything happen to me. And besides, I have been through worse."

"Worse than almost being kidnapped by rough outlaws? Whatever can be worse than that?" Saoirse said and looked at her with wide open eyes.

LORE OF THE DRAGONS: ESSENCE OF A QUEEN

"That is a story I can tell you some other time," Orelaith said and got up. "But I'm a little tired, so I think I will head off to bed now. It is time for us to head home tomorrow and I know I will need a good night's sleep before the long journey."

"I think we all had more than enough excitement for one day," Vig said. "I believe I will follow Orelaith's example and retire for the night. Luna, are you coming?"

"I wasn't planning to," Luna said and raised one eyebrow.

"Well, I think you should. So get a move on." Luna and Vig walked upstairs following Orelaith. Bas went outside with Conri to check on the horses before they too called it a night.

Saoirse and Bridget started tidying up after their evening meal.

"They sure are a strange family," Bridget said as she stacked up the cups.

"Yes, but you will never find kinder and more caring people. I owe Orelaith my life. If she had not helped me when she did…"

"Oh Saoirse, I didn't mean it in a bad way. It's just… Well, I believe there is more to them than meets the eye. You didn't see how they all acted as one when they found out Orelaith was in danger. Maybe they have some special bond because they are closely related or something." Saoirse frowned.

"Maybe they had a very strict father, maybe they have had to fight off raiders or something. But it really doesn't matter to me why they are the way they are. As far as I am concerned, they are all saints."

"But what do you really know about them, Saoirse? Aren't you even a little curious?" Bridget didn't want to let it go, but Saoirse faced her and put her hands on the older woman's shoulders.

"Bridget... I'm sure if Orelaith or the others wanted us to know they would tell us. It is not our place or right to ask any more than they wish for us to know. Maybe they are angels that come here to do good, maybe they have reasons beyond our understanding to hide much about who they truly are or where they come from. Whatever the reason, I am not going to dig for information about them. They have done nothing but good to me and my family, and I will not repay that with distrust because I don't know what their father's name is or where they grew up. Do you understand?" Bridget hung her head and blushed slightly.

"Yes, Saoirse." Saoirse hugged the older woman and said,

"Oh Bridget, I'm sorry if I seem harsh, but I believe it is important for them to keep their secrets. You do understand that, right?" Bridget nodded and smiled at Saoirse.

"I'm sorry, I'm just a nosy old lady. And I should probably get to bed before I let it get the better of me and start listening at doors or something like that." They laughed and finished up the rest before heading to bed.

Chapter 18

Orelaith woke up when Bas climbed into bed with her. She had gotten so used to it by now that she no longer shied away from physical contact.

"Orelaith?" His voice was like a gentle whisper in her mind. "Are you awake?" She turned to face him.

"Yes, is there anything wrong?" The room was dark aside from the moonlight coming in through the window.

"No, nothing wrong. I just wanted to ask you how you are. I'm the only one who truly knows what you have been through, and I was a little worried that it would be more upsetting because of that." She frowned.

"You know, it should have terrified me, but I was not afraid. I knew you would let no harm come to me." He gently stroked an unruly curl away from her face.

"I will never let anyone harm you ever again, and I swear, I will protect you with my life." Orelaith folded her hands under her head.

"But why? Why would you, one of the most powerful

creatures there is, do that for me, a common farmer's daughter?" He tried to think of what to say, but decided to be truthful with her, at least partially.

"I have come to care deeply for you, and every day you amaze me with your kind and gentle nature. And you are carrying my daughter, in a way..." She hadn't thought of it that way before.

"Well, that is true... I don't know how you dragons... eh... function. But we never... I mean... it's not like we...oh you know what I mean." She felt her cheeks blushing in the dark.

"Mated? No, we didn't." There was an amused tone to his voice as it sounded in her mind. "Do you want to?" he asked, making her sure that the room they were in would surely have a pink light if she dared open her eyes.

"Bas! I have told you how we humans live our lives. We don't... mate with anyone we are not married to. That was how I was raised anyway." He laughed quietly.

"But am I not your husband, then? Wouldn't that mean in human standards that we are married?" She sat up.

"But we aren't really married. We are just pretending. We humans are only supposed to give ourselves to one another for life and if anyone finds out that we are not truly married... Well, it's just not appropriate for a woman to share a bed with a man."

"Relax Orelaith, I'm only teasing you. I would never do anything that you wouldn't consent to. We both know I'm more than just a man, and I bet the same rules don't apply to sharing your bed with a dragon. Lay down and put your head on my chest and just listen to my heart." She put her head on his chest and sighed. It was hard to think of him as Basilicus the golden dragon when he was in his human form. He looked and felt just like a human man, and he smelled like wild flowers. He had such a wonderful personality about him in both forms, and his human form was just as beautiful as his dragon form. He had lived with seven females of his own race for longer than she could imagine, but he had not taken one of them to be his own. Maybe dragons didn't have a life partner like humans did...

"Bas, do dragons marry?"

"No, not like you humans do anyway. But we do bond to one mate for life and for us dragons that is a very long time." She frowned.

"Have you bonded to someone?"

"No, I never did." Until now, he thought.

"But why not? You have lived with seven wonderful and beautiful females for all these years. Surely one of them would have been a good mate for you." He sighed.

"It doesn't work that way, Orelaith. A dragon only bonds once in their entire life, to only one. And if they never meet they will never bond to anyone." Orelaith seemed surprised.

"You mean that there is only one mate out there for you? And if you don't meet her you will live alone for your whole life?" He nodded.

"Something like that, yes."

"That is so sad. How do you even know that you have

found the right one?" Orelaith asked.

"It's complicated. Usually they both know instantly. But sometimes only one of them knows," Bas said and sighed. "And sometimes, very rarely, none of them know." He thought of their situation and knew that if she asked any more questions, she might realize what was going on. "But what do they do then? I mean… they have to find out somehow, right?" If she had smelled the scent he released when he was close to her, she would realize what was going on, and if she did not approve he was doomed to spend his life without a mate.

"A female will know before the male knows." Orelaith frowned.

"How?" He tried to laugh it off.

"Why this sudden interest in how we dragon's bond?" Orelaith thought about her answer and realized that she felt a sting of jealousy at the thought of Bas finding a dragon mate.

"Oh, I don't know. I guess I'm just curious," she lied. He felt she hesitated before she answered and a small ray of hope lit up his heart.

"Well… When a dragon male starts bonding he may not even know, but he will start emitting fermions that are appealing to the female."

"Fermions?" She had never heard that word before.

"It's like a pleasant smell that that specific female likes, and she will know he is the mate she is bonded to." He almost held his breath waiting for her to realize that he was doing that constantly around her, but she just sighed and laid her head on his chest again, and not long after she seemed to be asleep. He hoped in one way that she never figured out how he felt about her. The fear of being rejected was getting to him. He decided to just enjoy the time they had here at the farm living the illusion of mates.

The next day after breakfast they started packing up all the clothes that Saoirse had made for them, and Orelaith had even got a small bag of baby clothes that Saoirse had made for little Rionach. As they said their goodbyes, Garbhan was crying and would not be comforted. He kept stretching his little arms out for Bas and it was obvious that it affected Bas too.

"He sure has taken to you," Bridget said and handed the baby to his brother Conri. That seemed to silence the worst of the crying, but he was still whimpering quietly. Saoirse was crying and hugging them all.

"When will you be back again?" Orelaith smiled sadly at her.

"Probably not until after the baby is born, and even then it will be a while until she gets strong enough to travel. Maybe in the springtime…" Saoirse hugged her again.

"Oh… that is so long. I will miss you so much."

"And I will miss you too. You have become so dear to me and I value our friendship a lot." Bridget came running with a bundle of food.

"I made something for you to enjoy on your trip back. I wouldn't want you to miss my cooking," she said with a smile and handed the bundle to Vig.

"Oh, thank you Bridget. You have been a great help to us these days, making our stay here so pleasant." The old woman blushed under the praise and curtsied. Conri pulled Bas aside.

"Do you really think the men will stay away?" Bas put his hand on the young boy's shoulder.

"I don't believe they will be back, but I know you will take care of the women and children here if they do return." Conri seemed to swell with pride of being considered the man of the farm and he nodded. Bas looked at Garbhan and smiled.

"Take good care of this little man here too. He is a very special child and I see a great future for him."

"I will lay my life down before I let anyone harm him," Conri said and stood, if possible, even straighter. Bas took Garbhan into his arms and they walked slowly towards the others.

"I don't know if you can hear me anymore brother, but these are good people who will care for you well until I see you again. So do not cry, I will return." Garbhan did not reply but seemed to calm down and stopped whimpering. Saoirse's children followed them almost to the main road leading from the town and out, waving until they disappeared behind a curve in the road.

Chapter 19

The four men almost crawled into the large dark room. They were afraid, and with good reason. The man sitting on the throne-like chair was cloaked and shrouded in shadow. The sound of their boots bounced off the wall as they walked down the middle of the candlelit room. They stopped short of the steps going up to the platform where the cloaked man was sitting perfectly still. An uncomfortable silence followed as they waited for him to speak. He started tapping with his long fingernails on the golden ball he was resting his arm on. Still, he kept silent, and it was almost worse than if he had shouted at them. Finally he got up and stood at the top of the steps looking down on them. "I already know you failed, and I must say I am a little impressed that you pathetic little creatures had the courage to come here and tell me in person that you did. His voice sounded like metal chains being dragged over a stone floor. Burning eyes were hidden in the shadow of the hood he was wearing, but they knew he followed their every move.

"Explain yourselves." The tall man took a step forward.

"Your highness Nex," he said and knelt down. "We found out where she was staying and waited for a time when she was separated from the others, but this stupid old woman she was with made a run for it and got away from us. So we decided to hurry back with her instead of going after the old hag. The girl kept slowing us down, falling and walking slowly. Suddenly these women appeared around us, blocking our path. And these were no ordinary women, they were witches! They used their magic against us so we were paralysed, and as if that was not enough, this huge golden dragon appeared."

"Basilicus…" The hooded man's knuckles whitened as he clenched his fists.

"We were outnumbered and we don't know any magic so we decided it was best to get back and tell you as quickly as possible rather than try to get hold of her again."

"I don't understand how it is possible for four men to fail in getting one little girl to move along without her being able to slow you down. It just proves your incompetence." One of the other men spoke almost in a whisper.

"But your highness, she was pregnant and we couldn't just –"

"Pregnant?! No!" he shouted in rage and rushed down the platform and grabbed hold of the man that had spoken. "She can't be! It will ruin my plans!" He grabbed hold of the man's throat, slowly strangling him. Blood was running down Nex's arm as he dug his long nails into the soft flesh of the man's neck. Soon the man stopped squirming and fell to the floor as Nex dropped him, his face frozen in a mask of terror and his eyes staring into nothingness. Nex walked slowly up the steps, his temper spent it seemed. He licked some of the blood off his fingers before he sat down in the chair.

LORE OF THE DRAGONS: ESSENCE OF A QUEEN

"So... anyone have more bad news for me? No? None of you?" But the men knew better than to answer. "Find out where she is now and do not come back until you can give me the answer I want, or you will suffer a far worse fate than that one." None of the three men moved. "Do I have to finish off one more of you before you do as I say?!" Nex shouted threateningly. The men scrambled out of the room as fast as their feet could carry them. "Pathetic little creatures," Nex said, his voice dripping with contempt. Dougal stepped out of a dark corner as the door slammed shut behind the men.

"You should have sent me. I would not have failed you." Nex waved towards the body on the floor.

"Drain me a few cups and get rid of the rest. He is leaving a stain on my floor." Dougal grabbed two silver goblets off a table behind the throne and pulled out his knife. He stabbed the knife into the dead man's neck right below the nail marks left by Nex and filled the goblets. He walked back and handed one to his master and put the other on the small table which he moved so it sat next to the throne. Then he threw the limp body over his shoulder and carried it out of the room.

"I think I will keep him. He is not so bad, for a pathetic human that is." A red haired woman in a bronze coloured dress came gliding into the room. She had tell-tale high cheekbones and a timeless face. Her eyes were a strange blue, almost white, and she sniffed the air with a disapproving frown on her face.

"As far as I am concerned they are just pests that are necessary to keep around for food. And they do smell dreadfully."

"Inanis my dear, care for a drink? It's fresh." The woman smiled, displaying perfectly white teeth with slightly longer corner teeth.

"Always such a perfect host." She took the silver goblet and sipped it as she walked around the throne. "I must say, even if I despise humans, these bodies do have their benefits. Tastes are stronger, touch is enhanced and the feeling of dismembering a body up close and personal is ecstatic." He smiled at her.

"Yes indeed. And however that happened, I am pleased it no longer drains us to stay in this shape." The man pulled back his hood, revealing long and straight raven black hair, his eyes a deep copper, almost red. He also had the high cheekbones and timeless face, but even in its perfection there was something distorted about it, something evil.

"You heard how these miserable little creatures failed?" She nodded and took another sip of her goblet leaving a dark red stain on her lips.

"Yes, but it was almost expected. They mess up even the simplest tasks."

"And you heard what that cursed brother of mine has done now?" Nex almost spat out the words, the hate for his brother apparent.

"Yes… but I considered it while I waited, it may not be all bad. A human is an easier target than a dragon, and this child may be almost powerless after it's born." Inanis sat down on the top step.

"All we need to do is lure them out of their cave or wherever they are hiding and strike while they are away." Nex frowned.

"You forget Inanis, that we don't know where their den is, and after those idiots failed to capture her for me, they are more alert and cautious than ever before." He sipped his blood and closed his eyes. "Remind me to dismember them the next time they show up here."

Chapter 20

As the full force of the winter storms blasted the barren landscape, Orelaith could no longer get around as she had before. No more night flights with Bas or Luna, but they found other ways to spend their time. The dragons did use human form, but most of their time was spent as dragons. Orelaith taught Vig all she knew about what to expect when the day came for Rionach's birth. Vig made her aware that things might not progress in the same manner as human births.

"We dragons lay eggs, we don't give birth like you humans do. But that I think… we can be sure… that is not going to happen to you. She seems to be growing and developing just like a human child, at least as far as I know." Orelaith laughed.

"That is all I can hope for, I guess. As long as you are there with me, I will feel safe." Vig smiled back at her.

"I am learning all the time, and that is a strange thing for me. I could not care for you more even if you were my own child, and I will not leave your side for a second if you don't want me to." Orelaith hugged her.

"I wanted to ask you something Vig…" She had some

LORE OF THE DRAGONS: ESSENCE OF A QUEEN

questions she did not want to ask Bas.

"Yes my dear. What is it?" Vig said and put her hands in her lap.

"Well… there is one thing I am wondering about." Orelaith got up and walked to the entrance to her chamber and looked out. The other dragons had all gone out to gather food. "The night after the men attacked me, Bas and I were talking about how you dragons live… and how you choose a mate." She turned to Vig and saw her smiling.

"Yes, and what is it you want to know my dear?" Orelaith sat down next to Vig again.

"He told me that you only bond with one mate for life. That there is only one mate out there for each of you. Not several to choose from but only one specific dragon for each of you." Vig nodded and said.

"That's correct."

"He also told me a bit of how you find that special one, but then he stopped answering me, almost seeming to avoid the question. Did I do wrong by asking?"

"No, my child, you did nothing wrong. What was the question that he seemed to avoid?" Vig said knowing very well why he had acted that way.

"There was not a specific question that he didn't answer, but he seemed uncomfortable so I let it go. I have never seen him like that before and it was rather… strange." Vig laughed.

"Males are strange in general. Bas less than most I think,

but yes, it is a touchy thing for him to talk about. He never did find a mate, and he was still quite young when our nation was destroyed. Now... Well, there aren't as many of us around, and I think we all have given up on finding that special one to share a bond with. They are probably gone now anyway, dead or infected and surely too far away for us to reach."

"That is dreadful! I can't even imagine what that would feel like. Although..." She paused and looked at her hands. "Maybe I can. It's not like I will ever find a man who can meet the standards that I have seen in Bas. I will only be measuring them up against him and every one will fall short." Vig wanted so badly to tell her, but she didn't. Best they figure it out on their own.

"Bas is an amazing dragon and he keeps his wonderful being in human form as well," she said. Orelaith smiled at Vig.

"Yes, he is amazing," Orelaith said and fell silent. She had a distant dreamy look in her eyes, and Vig saw that Orelaith cared as much for Bas as he did for her. She frowned, this human/dragon relationship was out of the ordinary. But then again, their lives had changed so much since Orelaith came to them.

"You care deeply for him, don't you?" Vig asked. Orelaith blushed slightly.

"Yes, I do. But we are not even the same race, so it can't be like that. I mean, I loved spending time at the farm pretending to be his wife, or mate if you like, but I don't think it would work out in reality... could it?" Vig sensed hope in her voice and knew that Orelaith had already bonded to Bas. She knew that there would be so many things they would have to confront, but there was no changing a bond, what was done was done.

"I don't know how it would work my dear. It has never happened before. There is so much to consider; for one, the difference in lifespan. Dragons live for an extremely long time. Human lifespans are only a fraction of that of a dragon. That would mean that a dragon would spend most of his life alone, and to tell you the truth, dragons usually die when they lose their mate." Orelaith chewed on her lip and seemed to be in deep thought. Vig stroked her hair. "Even if you humans do not live as long, it seems you live it so fully. Don't worry about it now Orelaith, you have other things that need your attention," she said and smilingly placed her hands on Orelaith's belly.

"You are right." Orelaith smiled back at Vig. "Rionach will soon be with us and I will have enough to think about then."

The others came back and Serovita popped her head into Orelaith's chamber. "Hello Orelaith," the green dragon said with her flowing voice. "I brought you something." She lifted in a cradle made of one solid piece of wood.

"Oh Serovita, its beautiful!" Orelaith rocked it and ran her fingers slowly over the smooth wood. Along the outside there were what looked like carvings, but not like any that could be made with a knife. It was eight dragons circling around a human woman. "It is our family crest. One that will follow us from now on." Orelaith got up and walked to the entrance of her chamber.

"It's the same marks as Terra made around my chamber opening." The big green dragon nodded and said.

"Yes it is." Bas came trotting over in his dragon form.

"That is really wonderful, Serovita. As always you create such beauty."

"Oh!" Orelaith felt a pain in her back. Vig's eyes narrowed.

"Are you feeling ok, Orelaith?"

"Yes, I think so. Just a muscle spasm…" Orelaith said and sat down on the bed.

"Let me take a quick look to be sure my dear," Vig said and placed her hands on Orelaith's back.

"It can't be the baby, it's not due for another full moon cycle," Bas said with a concerned voice.

"It is and it's not," Vig said and opened her eyes. "It is her body adjusting to what is to come and testing the muscles you could say. It will be ten times stronger when the time comes." Vig explained. Orelaith's eyes widened.

"Ten times stronger? Then that?"

"Oh, don't worry my dear. I will be able to help with the pain when it gets to that point. But just remember, I cannot take it all away, as that would disrupt the natural order of

LORE OF THE DRAGONS: ESSENCE OF A QUEEN

things. The muscle spasms help drive the child out. Your hips are already making room for the baby to pass through," Vig said and took Orelaith's hand.

"How do you know so much about human birth already?" Serovita asked and cocked her head to one side.

"I can see inside the body, remember? Some things Orelaith told me, and then I just put two and two together to figure out the entire process. And it did help that I have witnessed a few births in the closest villages since we found out Orelaith was expecting."

Bas sent her a stern look.

"You never told us that you have had contact with humans like that. Have you been sneaking out? Alone?!" Vig sent him the look and put her hands in her lap.

"Really Bas… If you are worried about exposing our whereabouts to anyone, you should know I have taken all the precautions to make sure no one could find out where we live. And…" she added, "You do want me to find out how I can best assist Orelaith when she is giving birth, don't you?" Bas nodded.

"But next time Vig, please let me know when you decide to go out like that and one of us can go with you. After everything that has happened we do need to be very careful."

"I agree, and if it was not for the fact that it is critical to Orelaith that I find out as much as I could, I would not have taken the risk." Solis came over in her human form and sat down next to Orelaith.

"Oh it shouldn't be long. I can't wait until we have our own little baby among us. It is going to be wonderful!" Tempest had joined them and was leaning up against the door in her human form.

"It's not going to be all wonderful, Solis. Children of any kind are more than a handful for their mothers. And we have no idea what challenges we will meet with a human/dragon hybrid." Serovita sighed.

"We can only wait and see..."

Chapter 21

Orelaith had convinced Vig to let Bas take her on a short flight. She had of course been secured so excessively that she could hardly move, but that was one of Vig's conditions for letting her go. And Bas had been so careful that she felt like she was sitting on a bed and not out in the open on his back. The other condition was that Vig went with them. She was constantly asking Orelaith how she was feeling, but Orelaith didn't mind as long as she got out of the cave. Bas landed gently outside the cave, and Vig helped her dismount.

"See? I'm fine, Vig. And the baby is fine too. You really need to stop worrying."

"Better to be safe than sorry, my dear," Vig said with her usual motherly tone.

"Yes, Vig. But don't worry so much. I know it's only because you care for me and Rionach, but I can't sit still any longer. I feel like I'm slowly going insane from doing nothing." She gave Vig a quick hug and walked inside. Bas laughed.

"She should try to hibernate for four months with you snoring in the next chamber, now that would drive her insane." Vig glared at Bas.

"I don't snore, I merely have a breathing problem. The air in the cave gets rather stuffy after a few weeks of Aqua slowly digesting her food."

"Why do you think I am always the first one out in the spring?" Bas winked at her and walked into the cave. "But I still say you snore like a thunderstorm."

"Oh, do be quiet, Bas. Like you are any better." Vig laughed and followed.

Orelaith had unbundled herself and was sitting in her chamber when they came back in. Vig stopped Bas.

"I was meant to ask you, where did you go last night? And don't try to give me a look like that. I know you went out and you were gone for several hours." Bas sat down.

"I just went for a little flight to clear my head," he said innocently. Vig's eyes narrowed.

"And just where did you go flying?"

"Oh, nowhere special. North…" Vig circled him.

"How far north are we talking here?" Bas was a dreadful liar, and he knew that when Vig had gotten a whiff of something she did not let it go.

"Eh… I don't know." " Her eyes widened.

"You went to check on Garbhan, didn't you? After telling

me off for going out on my own you turn around and do the very same thing? Shame on you Bas!"

"Nothing happened. I just flew over and landed out of sight. I just had to make sure that he was doing ok."

"That is beside the point, Bas, and you know it! At least I didn't go anywhere close to danger, but you… you had to go land right in the middle of it! What were you thinking?"

"Vig?" Orelaith said softly, but Vig was too busy yelling at Bas.

"So do you think the rules should not apply to you?" she said and sat down facing Bas.

"Vig?" Orelaith said a little louder. Vig didn't turn around, she was too occupied glaring at Bas. "What is it Orelaith?"

"I think you should stop that," Orelaith said and took one step closer.

"He did something that could put us all in danger. And I am not done yet," Vig said.

"That may be right, but I think you should check on Rionach all the same." Orelaith was quite insistent now. Vig turned quickly and saw Orelaith standing in a puddle of water and said,

"Oh! What happened?" Orelaith said,

"I think my water broke. And the pain in my back just got really strong." Bas' transgression was soon forgotten as it dawned on Vig what was happening.

"It's started!" She quickly transformed and ran over to Orelaith whose knees buckled under the pain.

"What has started?" Bas seemed a little confused.

"The baby is coming, silly. Go get the others." Vig started sounding a bit annoyed now. It took a second for him to realize what was happening, then he rushed off to tell the others.

"Just go lay down, my dear, and let me take a look." Vig helped Orelaith to the bed and lifted her feet up.

"Is it supposed to hurt like this?" Orelaith said through clenched teeth as another contraction set in.

"I am afraid it is quite normal, and it will get progressively worse," Vig said as she closed her eyes and sent her tendrils forth to check. "Yes… it has definitely started. Here, let me do something to lessen the pain." Orelaith felt the tendrils warming her back and curl around her belly. She sighed in relief as the worst of the pain let up. Luna came flying into the cave and transformed practically in mid-air, then came running into the chamber and knelt down next to the bed.

"How are you feeling, kiddo?" she almost whispered and took Orelaith's hand.

"Oh, I could be better, but Vig says it's completely normal. She has taken the edge off the pain, so it's not so bad anymore." Orelaith smiled weakly. Tempest arrived in almost in the same manner as Luna and sat down at the end of the bed.

"It's going to be fine. You are in the best hands here, Vig is the best healer I know."

"Yes, she is," Bas said and entered the chamber in his human form. "How are you feeling, my dear?" He asked and sat down at the head-end of the bed so Orelaith could put her head in his lap.

"I am not quite at my best, but it's better now that you are here," she replied and smiled at him. "How long is it going to be?" Bas said and looked at Vig.

"Not too long. I think, but I have seen some of these births go on full nights so it's anyone's guess." Vig said. The others came in one after the other and found somewhere to sit and soon they were all gathered around her. The contractions got stronger and stronger as time went on, and as the morning light came in through the cave opening, Rionach let out her first cry.

"Oh my!" Solis covered her ears. "Are they always that loud?" Vig laughed.

"Yes, and it's a good sign that they can breathe properly. Go make yourself useful and warm me some water, Solis. And Tempest, bring me a wet cloth so I can clean her up." Once she was washed and dried and Orelaith had held her for a while, Vig asked Bas if he would take Rionach for a little walk so she could tend to Orelaith and repair the damage birth had caused her. The others followed him out while arguing about who would get to hold her next.

"You humans are truly amazing. All this harm you take

from giving birth and you usually have more than one. I must say you did very well Orelaith. So frail, yet so strong," Vig said and sent out her healing tendrils. Orelaith was feeling much better already, and soon Bas was back with little Rionach. She looked at her little girl tucked in next to her, dark copper coloured curls surrounding plump cheeks. She was sleeping soundly, and Bas stroked Orelaith's hair as he looked down on Rionach.

"She is amazing," he whispered softly.

"Yes, she is. And she looks… normal." Orelaith stroked Rionach's tiny little fingers.

"What did you expect, a tail and wings?" Luna laughed.

"I didn't know what to expect to tell you the truth. She is part dragon after all." But Rionach was not all human, they knew that. In the months and years that followed they would find out just how hard it would be to raise a dragon/human hybrid.

Chapter 22

Rionach was growing faster than an average human, and at the age of two she was already talking and running around like a five year old child. Orelaith had not dared to take her to see Saoirse because of the rapid growth and the dragon qualities she had displayed already from birth. It was hard to explain how Rionach could breathe fire and move things by pure will, not to mention that she shape-shifted and flew off sometimes. Orelaith had gone to town with only Luna escorting her. Saoirse had complained and wanted to see her, saying it was hard to make clothes for a child when she couldn't take her measurements. But when Orelaith had said that Rionach was sick and that was why she could not come, Saoirse had settled. Little Garbhan was also growing fast, and it surprised Orelaith to see he was just as big as Rionach. He had not displayed any behavior out of the ordinary, so the magical restraints seemed to be holding. Bas was pleased to hear that, and he said he would come along the next time and see him for himself. They finally decided to go there for a few days right before Rionach's third birthday.

"I will restrict her abilities like I did with Garbhan, so we won't give poor Bridget a shock." Vig said as she was discussing the trip with Bas and Orelaith.

"You can do that?" Orelaith asked, knowing Garbhan was nowhere near as powerful as Rionach. "I will do it tonight after she has gone to sleep. That is the only time I can possibly succeed." Bas nodded and said,

"She has grown exceedingly more powerful than I could have imagined. I think we should leave the binding on even after we come back… it is getting more and more dangerous the older she gets. Last week she almost flew out of the cave in dragon form. If it had not been for Luna grabbing her tail as she flew by, we could have lost her. She is getting increasingly fearless. I am just worried that if we don't take drastic measures now, it will be too late."

"I agree. I have to ask her permission when I am examining her. If she doesn't like what I'm doing, she throws me out." Orelaith had said nothing yet, but she sighed in relief when they had made that decision.

"I'm glad I'm not the only one to see it. I am her mother, but I don't know what to do when she shifts and flies off. It's not like I can fly after her. And I can not depend on having you here all the time in case she does just that." Orelaith looked at Vig. "And I want her to learn how to read and write." Bas looked thoughtful and said,

"You mean putting her in one of those schools? With other children?" Orelaith nodded and smiled.

"Not yet, of course. She is still too young." Orelaith got up and walked around her chamber.

"She needs to be around other children to learn how to interact with others. Don't get me wrong, we love living here with you all. It's just that…"

"You need to be around humans too, I understand." Vig said and smiled at Orelaith. "Although we look human, we are not and we can probably never understand some things." Orelaith had tears in her eyes.

"I love you all so deeply, and I feel like I am being ungrateful."

"Nonsense!" Vig huffed. "It is us that have not been understanding." She took Orelaith's hands. "We will find a way. Now I will go and get all the things I need ready before tomorrow's trip." She gave Orelaith a quick hug before she walked out.

Bas had gone very quiet, staring at nothing with glazed eyes.

"Bas...? Are you ok?" Orelaith spoke softly.

"Hmm? Oh... yes, I was just thinking," Bas focused on her.

"What about?" she asked and sat down on the bed next to him.

"About what you said to Vig. I thought you were content here..." She took his hands in hers.

"Oh Bas, I am. That is not what it's about. I can't imagine a life without you and the others. It's just... I miss having a friend to talk to."

"You can always talk to me. I hope you think of me as your friend." Bas looked a little disappointed. Orelaith got up again and walked around the chamber.

"I keep saying the wrong things. It's not that I don't think of you as a friend, you are just much more than that. I mean a girlfriend that I can talk to about silly things and… all the things I guess girls talk about." Bas smiled at her.

"You think of me as more than a friend?" She blushed.

"Well… I mean, you are sort of Rionach's father. But that's not what we were talking about, and it's not just for me. When Rionach grows up, I want her to have friends her own age. Someone to play with and share little secrets with. I want her to go to the dances at mid summer and fall in love maybe." Bas came up behind her and put his hands on her shoulders.

"I don't know why these things are so important to you, but if they are important to you, they are important to me. We will figure out a way to make it possible for you to live in both worlds." She turned around and looked up into his eyes.

"You mean that?" Bas nodded and said,

"I do. But first I want you to go flying with me. Luna and Tempest will be back with Rionach soon, but I thought we could go after she is asleep. What do you say?"

"I would love to." Orelaith locked her arm in his, and they walked out of the cave to wait for their little one to return.

Chapter 23

"Mama!" Rionach came running towards Orelaith, her copper curls bouncing off her shoulders.

"I saw the ocean! It's soooo big and Aqua was there diving in the water and she caught a whole mouthful of fish this big!" she said and held out her little arms as far as she could.

"That's wonderful my darling." Orelaith knelt down and hugged her.

"Did you eat anything?"

"Yes mother, I had a whole fish, all by myself." Bas laughed.

"I bet you did. You are such a big girl." Luna came strolling in with a grin on her face.

"She is getting really fast." Tempest followed close behind, but she only sent Luna a tired glare before turning towards her chamber.

"I am going to get some sleep."

"I think you tired out Tempest and Luna, sweetheart. You might want to slow down a little or she won't take you out again." Bas said with a smile and picked her up.

"But now, it's someone's bedtime."

"Oh daddy, do I have to? I am not tired at all." Rionach let out a big yawn.

"I see that… still, we are going on a long journey tomorrow, so you need to get some sleep," Bas said. Orelaith kissed her cheek, then followed Bas to tuck her in.

Vig came up behind Luna and they watched as Bas and Orelaith knelt down next to Rionach's little bed.

"Is he ever going to make a move?" Luna said and sighed.

"Probably not. They both care so deeply for each other, but they are equally fearful of hurting the other," Vig said and cocked her head.

"Orelaith doesn't know how to feel. And I do understand. It would be like me bonding to a mortal man, I guess." Luna laughed and said,

"You would never do that, you are too much of a prude."

"I am not… I'm just wise enough to know that it would never work out."

"Yeah, right. Keep telling yourself that." Luna winked at her then sauntered off. Vig glared after her, then walked quietly over to Orelaith's chamber just as Bas came out.

LORE OF THE DRAGONS: ESSENCE OF A QUEEN

"Don't go just yet, I may need your assistance with what I am about to do. Garbhan was strong enough. Rionach… well, she may prove to be ten times as powerful." Bas nodded and said,

"She just fell asleep, so she should be easier to handle. Just tell me what you need." Orelaith came out and spoke softly to Vig.

"Tell me, this is not going to hurt her, is it?" Vig smiled.

"Of course not. I would never do anything to harm her in any way. I am merely cutting her off from magic and from her ability to shapeshift." Orelaith frowned.

"Explain it to me step by step so I can understand exactly what you are going to do." Vig knew that she was worried, so she took the time to go over it with her.

"To make it bearable to her, I will first lock away parts of her memory. All the parts where she has been in dragon form or used magic will be shrouded, and she will not recall them any more. Then I will make a series of tendrils where I bind the very source of her powers with complicated knots. This should prevent her from using any kind of magic. There will need to be a set time limit on it, so it will unravel if any harm should come to the one who makes the knots. At least that is how we dealt with dragons who misused their powers before the big flame rain. I will set the minimum amount of time we use. These knots are so complicated that I must make sure I don't do anything that I am not completely sure I know."

"She won't remember any of it?" Orelaith asked.

"Well, I will only put up a thin wall. It may dissolve if she claws at it." Vig said.

"And then she would remember... everything?" Orelaith said and frowned .Vig nodded.

"She won't be too happy with us if she remembers, but once she gets older, she will understand." They stood in silence, all in deep thought, it seemed. Vig was the first one to snap out of it.

"Are we ready?" she said and looked from one to the other. They both nodded and gathered around Rionach's crib. Vig gently put one hand on Rionach's copper curls and the other on her chest.

"Bas, rest your hand on my shoulder and be ready for me to draw on you when and if I need it." Orelaith took Rionach's little hand and looked on as Vig started weaving her tendrils into complicated knots. They could not be so much seen as felt, at least not by Orelaith, but Bas seemed to be able to see them because he frowned and whispered,

"Vig... this is really complicated. Are you sure you know what you are doing?" She didn't answer, just shushed him and kept on with what she was doing.

"Now, when I cast it over her I will need your help to seal it off. If not, it will unravel and this will all be for nothing. Be ready... now." Bas hesitated and Vig fell backwards landing on her behind. She looked at Bas.

"You can not hesitate, Bas. If I had not been prepared that you just might do that, I would have been caught in my own net and none of you would have been able to remove it."

She was whispering, but there was a serious tone in her voice.

"Bas, you need to go get Luna and Tempest. Together they are almost as strong as you are."

"I'm sorry, Vig. I think maybe I don't fully agree about doing this even though I know it's the right thing to do. I will go get them." Bas got up and walked out with his head down.

"Go after him and comfort him. He did nothing wrong, but it is as he said. He doesn't fully agree, so he will hesitate every time." Orelaith hugged Vig quickly and walked after Bas. She passed Luna and Tempest on her way and found Bas in his chamber in dragon form. He was curled up and looked at her when she came in.

"Are you ok?" she asked and sat down on his front paw.

"Yes. I'm just upset with myself for what I almost did." She stroked his big, golden head.

"But Bas, you didn't do it, so just forget about it. Vig is not harmed, and she understands how you feel." He let out a sigh.

"I still feel bad about it." She smiled at him.

"Let's go on that flight you promised me. It will take your mind off everything." The corners of his mouth curled up in a soft smile.

"Yes, let's do that."

Chapter 24

Blood was trickling down the front of his robe as he walked back to his throne and sat down.

"Dougal, I made another mess! Come clean it up," Nex demanded. Dougal entered and closed the doors behind him. Three bodies lay scattered in front of the steps leading up to where Nex was sitting.

"I am guessing they didn't bring good news?" Dougal said and pulled out his knife.

"No. Where do you find these incompetent men? Surely there must be someone with half a brain in their heads you can hire," Nex said. Dougal drained an entire jug of blood from the men on the floor which he placed on the small table next to the throne.

"I have said you can send me… I know I can find out where she is. It's been almost three years now since we last saw her, and we have sent spies out to every corner of this land. Give me the chance to prove that I can find her. I know I will not fail you." Nex poured himself a cup, leaned back and sighed.

LORE OF THE DRAGONS: ESSENCE OF A QUEEN

"Maybe I should let you try… but I would hate to have to train another personal slave should you fail. You have become such a loyal pet to me." He sipped his blood and frowned thoughtfully. "Very well, I will let you go. But only for a while, then you come back here and report to me." Inanis came gliding into the room in a bright red dress. "I see you dined without me." She pulled out a handkerchief and held it up over her nose. "You really need to wash your food before you bite down, the way they smell has got to be an indication they have gone bad," she said.

"Inanis, my dear, it was not my intention to start without you. But these incompetent fools brought me bad news, and you know how I hate not getting what I want." She sniffed at Dougal as she passed him.

"At least this one takes a bath once a week." Dougal bowed before her.

"You are most kind, Lady Inanis." She glanced at him, then turned her attention to Nex.

"So, no news of where they are yet?"

"No. I have searched this wretched isle end to end and still found nothing. I am beginning to think they have left it altogether," he said and sighed.

"I doubt it. You have just not searched in the right places." Her voice full of unconcealed arrogance. "And… if you insist on sending these pathetic little parasites, you will not get the result you crave."

"I'm sending Dougal on a few days trip to see what he can dig up." She looked at Dougal.

"And how is he any better than the rest? The only difference I can perceive is that he smells a little less putrid." Nex got up and walked slowly down the steps, cup in one hand and the other behind his back.

"My dear Inanis, must you display your ignorance so openly?" He squinted his eyes amusedly. "Most humans are a worthless waste of space, I will give you that. But they are not all that different from us. Granted, we are far superior to them, but we have bad eggs in our midst as well, such as my brother. And I know how you despise that white one. What was her name again…" Inanis glared at him and replied

"Vigoratus…" Her voice sounded so venomous as she uttered the name, it was almost like acid could be seen dripping from her full, red lips.

"Ah, yes; Vigoratus. The royal healer and the queen's best friend." Nex grinned wickedly, knowing how much merely mentioning the white dragon enraged Inanis.

"Self-righteous, annoying, do-gooder… I hate her!" Her whispering voice filled with the utmost contempt. Nex laughed.

"There, there Inanis. Maybe you will be able to put your lovely hands around her neck some day and change her white face to a more becoming blue."

He turned his attention to Dougal standing at the bottom of the steps. "So, do you actually have a plan, or are you hoping the child will just fall out of the sky and into your arms? If not, I can just tear you apart right now and save us both some grief." Dougal smiled just enough that Nex saw it.

LORE OF THE DRAGONS: ESSENCE OF A QUEEN

"Of course I have a plan, your highness. I am not a fool like these simpletons." Inanis raised her perfect eyebrows in disdain and glanced at him.

"Oh, really? Well, let's hear it then. The suspense is killing me…" The sarcasm in Nex's voice was obvious. Dougal took a step forward.

"You remember where this woman was last spotted? Well, I have found out this wasn't just a one time thing. Every so often this woman comes back to see the tailor in the town, and she stays with her for an entire day before she rides off again. It is clear to me that they have become friends. All I have to do is either get the tailor to talk, or simply wait for this red haired woman to return. One way or the other I should be able to get my hands on either some useful information or the mother of the child you want. The downside is it may take more than a few days…" Nex frowned at him, and for a few seconds said nothing. Then Nex got up.

"Very well, you can go. On one condition…" He put his hand on Inanis' shoulder. "You take Inanis with you." Inanis swung around and stared at Nex with her mouth open.

"You have got to be joking! You expect me to go with this… this human?" He slightly raised one eyebrow.

"I not only expect it; I demand it." Inanis crossed her arms and put her chin up in defiance. And with her back turned to Nex she huffed.

"I will do no such thing! I am not one of your pet's, Nex." There was no small amount of contempt in her voice. In one quick move, Nex had turned her around and lifted her up by her throat, his eyes narrow and his voice low and threatening,

"You forget your place, Inanis. I am still a royal prince, and I will be king as soon as my brother and this baby are out of the way. And if I say you go out with Dougal, that is what you are going to do. Do you understand?" He hissed the words out through clenched teeth. She stared at him wide-eyed and gasped for breath as his fingers cut off her air supply, but she managed to nod. Nex dropped her then walked up and sat down on his throne again.

"And you are taking one more with you. I need to see if I have patched him up well enough."

"Oh? You really think he is ready, your highness?" Dougal said and poured a cup of blood, before handing it to Inanis who stood sulking next to the throne. She looked at the cup and without even a disdainful look she took it and swallowed its contents hungrily.

"I do believe he is, but only a test in the field will prove that. He was no more than a blabbering pile of discarded waste when I found him, so he has come a long way. However, you must keep a close eye on him. He may crumble quickly if he relapses, and I would so hate for all my work to be for nothing." Nex had regained his usual icy, calm composure.

Dougal bowed.

"Yes, your highness. When may I leave?"

"See, Inanis? Even this human knows how to address me. This trip will do you good, you may actually learn something." Nex looked at her over his cup as he took a sip. She glared back at him, but said nothing. Nex turned his attention back to Dougal. "You may leave in the morning. Use the rest of the evening and night to get everything ready." Dougal nodded and picked up one of the bodies on the floor and carried it out.

"You can go and make sure the other member of your party is ready for the trip," Nex was expecting protests, but surprisingly enough, Inanis just nodded.

"Where is this… human?" she asked.

"You will find him in the west wing. Talk to one of the maids and you will be shown the way." Nex smiled.

"And what is this pathetic little creature's name?" she asked as she set her cup on the table. "Malum. His name is Malum."

Chapter 25

Orelaith stood on the edge of a high cliff looking out over the perfectly still ocean. A full moon was reflecting on the mirror surface creating a golden road leading out into the horizon. Bas walked up from behind and embraced her.

"Its beautiful, don't you think?" Leaning her head back against his chest, she couldn't think of any other place she would rather be.

"Yes… it looks so magical." He buried his face in her copper curls and the smell of lavender filled his nostrils.

"Your hair smells good." She giggled and replied,

"I'm glad you like it. You smell like wild-flowers… Is that one of the soaps you got from town?" He laughed.

"No, it's all you're doing." She turned and looked at him.

"I smell like wild-flowers?" Turning away from her he took a few steps and cursed himself for speaking before thinking.

"Orelaith… there is something I need to tell you.

LORE OF THE DRAGONS: ESSENCE OF A QUEEN

Something I have been keeping from you for quite a while now." His voice was soft and there was an unfamiliar nervousness to it.

"What do you mean?" she asked carefully, not knowing if she even wanted an answer.

"I should have talked to you about it before, but at first I wasn't completely certain about what was happening..." Bas continued but avoided her eyes. "I was worried you would look at me differently if I told you that you might actually find it ridiculous, find... me... ridiculous. And in the worst case, you would even leave me and go live in the town..." She felt her heartbeat quickening as she looked at his broad back.

"Bas... What on earth are you talking about? I would never leave you." She walked up and placed her hand on his shoulder.

"I have tried to reason myself out of this, saying it is not right, but I cannot. It is a feeling so strong, it can no longer be caged, tamed or denied." He turned and she looked into his dark bronze eyes. It shocked her to see so much savage passion in them, it made her take a step back.

"Bas, you're scaring me. Please, just tell me what is going on with you..." He turned away when he saw her reaction,

"I would never hurt you, I would sooner die. Look into your heart and you will know that is true." As he spoke, she felt almost ashamed for reacting the way she had.

"I know that, Bas. But please... tell me... it can not be as bad as you think it is." He sighed deeply and said.

"I… I love you…" She stood frozen, his words echoing in her head along with all the things Vig had told her about how dragons bond to each other for life. He turned and looked at her as if expecting to be laughed at. When she did not return his gaze or even move, his shoulders dropped and he looked at his feet.

"I understand if you are repulsed by this. If that is how you feel, I promise to never speak of it again." He looked up at her moonlight face, and to his surprise saw tears in her eyes. She turned her head and stared at him,

"Oh Bas…" she walked over and took his hands in hers. "I am not repulsed and I do not find you ridiculous. How could I when I feel the same way about you… I was afraid to tell you for the same reasons you just gave me. But I realize now that it is pointless to suppress these feelings any more. Whatever challenges we will have to face, it will be worth it. And I am truly honored that you have chosen me, a simple human…" He stood there just looking at her as if the words were not quite sinking in.

"You… you feel… the same way about me?" She smiled as he wiped a tear off her cheek.

"Yes. Like you, I tried to deny it. But I can no longer hide how I feel about you, not even from myself." He smiled and knelt down before her.

"I had no idea how greatly you would touch our lives when I heard your call for help that night so long ago. You have brought this dragon to his knees." She stepped closer and kissed the top of his head.

LORE OF THE DRAGONS: ESSENCE OF A QUEEN

"I am the happiest girl in all the world…" She laughed, "Not many girls can say that her man takes her flying at night." He got up and pulled close, holding her tightly as he whispered in her ear, "I want to take you on a different flight tonight…" Then he kissed her so passionately she thought she was going to pass out from the pure pleasure. She sighed and let herself fall into his embrace. Golden tendrils flowed around them, bound them tightly together and lifted them off the ground. It was as if her soul and his were pulled out of their bodies and blended together. They were not two any more, but one soul with two bodies. It scared her a little, but his voice whispered soft reassurances in her head and she relaxed. This was how the dragons bonded, the reason why they usually didn't outlive each other. When one was taken away, the other was left with half a soul. Every part of her tingled as they touched the ground again. Slowly, she opened her eyes and saw him smiling at her. He stroked her cheek and whispered softly to her: "My carus…"

When they walked back into the cave they found Tempest and Luna in front of Bas's chamber tending to Vig who was sitting down on the chair from Orelaith's chamber. She seemed shaken and had her eyes closed. Orelaith rushed over.

"Vig! What happened? Are you ok?" Vig opened her eyes and seemed to pull herself together. "Yes, yes, I'm fine. And Rionach is sleeping soundly in her crib," she added when she saw Orelaith cast a worried glance towards her own chamber.

"What happened?" Bas asked and knelt down in front of Vig. She looked at him and frowned, then looked at Orelaith in the same manner. "You two look different somehow…

and you feel different too." Bas covered a smile behind a new question.

"Did this happen when you tried to restrict Rionach's abilities?" Vig huffed.

"I said I'm fine. Rionach woke up before I could cast the tendril-net over her, and we had a bit of a tugging match going on for a while. She was not scared, Orelaith. I think she actually enjoyed it, as if we were playing a game. I did manage to tie a few knots, so she can't use her abilities or shape-shift for at least a few days. Doing that drained me so much, I could not even walk on my own accord once we were done." She took hold of Bas' hand.

"Bas, she is even more powerful than your mother was at her peak. It is absolutely amazing. Considering she is still a child, I can't even imagine what she will be like once she reaches maturity." Bas frowned.

"Could we do a full circle maybe?"

"We can try, but it will only be done if she will let us. Orelaith, you will have to talk to her in the morning. She can easily unravel the bindings I have placed on her. Ask her to leave it alone and explain how important it is that she does not speak of dragons or where we live."

"I will. She does listen when I tell her," she said and took Vig's hand.

"What…" Vig's eyes widened and she stared at Orelaith. "You are different. It's as if… no, it cannot be. Unless…" She turned to Bas who was grinning widely at her.

"It was about time," Vig said. She got up and gave Bas a big hug. Solis came strolling over in her yellow dress.

"What about time?" Tempest was even smiling now and hugged Orelaith.

"Congratulations, that is wonderful news." Solis looked from one to the other.

"What news?" Luna grinned and released Bas from a hug,

"You could not have picked a better one." Solis was almost frantic now.

"Will someone tell me what happened?!" Vig took hold of her hands.

"Solis, you need to calm down before you start having hot flashes. I will tell you. Bas and Orelaith have bonded to each other." Solis lit up in a bright smile.

"Really? Oh, that is wonderful news!" She let go of Vig's hands and embraced Orelaith. "I am so, so happy. A royal bonding, it's a once in a lifetime experience!" She let go of Orelaith and gave Bas a big hug too. "I have to go tell the others." She clapped her hands and ran off.

"I expect you won't need two chambers any more," Luna said and winked at Orelaith.

"That is entirely up to Orelaith, but I would like to stay with her for the night," Bas said and took Orelaith's hand.

"I think that can be arranged…" she smiled back at him. Soon the others came over to congratulate them, and they all stayed up talking about the trip and how they would deal with Rionach on her first trip to the outside world.

Chapter 26

Rionach had sulked most of the way from the cave to the landing site but as soon as they started riding towards the town she forgot all about it and was pointing and laughing at houses and people they passed along the way. Orelaith had a long talk with her before they left about what she could not under any circumstances mention. If she understood how important it was, they would just have to wait and see. Luna was on Tempest, Vig on Terra, Bas was riding Serovita and little Rionach was sitting on Solis with Orelaith. Aqua was following behind with their luggage, but she kept stopping to take a mouthful of grass.

"I never knew grass was this tasty… and mmm… these clover flowers are so so sweet."

"Aqua, will you stop eating? It's going to take us twice as long to get to the farm if you don't get a move on," Tempest said and stomped her feet. Aqua put her ears back.

"Fine, but if I starve to death before we get there, it's your fault."

"I don't think you are in any danger of starving, Aqua. You have enough reserves on your butt to last you a year in

LORE OF THE DRAGONS: ESSENCE OF A QUEEN

hibernation." Luna chuckled.

"I do not!" Aqua trotted past Tempest.

"From this angle you do…" Tempest laughed.

"I'm still faster than you." There was a challenging tone in Aqua's words, and Tempest and Aqua set off at full speed with Luna laughing loudly as they disappeared around a bend in the road.

"Mama?" Rionach's emerald green eyes looked up at Orelaith.

"Yes sweetheart, what is it?" She smiled back.

"Are the bad humans going to come back and try to take you away again?" Her voice appeared concerned but not fearful. Orelaith was at first at a loss for words, shocked her daughter actually remembered the attack.

"Eh.. I didn't know that you remembered that, but no, I don't think they will. And even if they do return, daddy will chase them away like he did the last time." Rionach smiled and leaned back against Orelaith.

"He scared them, didn't he?"

"He sure did," Orelaith said and hugged her little girl.

"If they do come anyway, mama, can I use my magic then?"

"No my dear. If anything happens, you must let your father or the others deal with it. You are still too young. Besides, if someone else see what you do, they will be angry and may try to hurt us. We talked about that this morning, Rionach. It is too dangerous," Orelaith said just as they came around the trees and saw the town. Rionach's jaw dropped.

"Is that the town? Oh, look at all the people! And the horses! And look, other little humans like me!" She clapped her little hands together and laughed as Saoirse's children came running towards them.

"Orelaith! Luna came racing into the farm, so we wanted to come and meet you" The little girl was all smiles.

"Oh my, how you have grown." Vig laughed. "And who is this handsome young boy with you? He is way too big to be your little brother," she teased.

"But it is me. Mama says I need to stop growing though, or I will be too big for my bed soon," the boy said. Rionach was quietly watching them as they ran next to the horses. The little girl glanced up at her every once in a while and smiled, but she said nothing.

When they got to the small farm, Bridget came out and greeted them.

"It is so good to see you again. And this must be the little princess Rionach. You sure are big for your age. And what wonderful curls you have." Rionach smiled.

"Thank you. I have the same curls as mama. And I have a new dress, isn't it pretty?" She swirled around, showing off the beautiful blue fabric. Bridget smiled.

LORE OF THE DRAGONS: ESSENCE OF A QUEEN

"Yes, it is very pretty." Bas looked around.

"Where is Conri? I thought he would have been here to greet us." Bridget seemed a little bothered and paused before answering.

"He is not here. You see, a few months ago, he and Saoirse went to the port town to make some inquiries about opening a tailoring shop there. He met one of his uncles who had left when he was still very young, and he invited Conri to come live with him and his wife. So when they got back he packed up everything and took Garbhan with him. He told me to give you his most heartfelt thanks for everything you have done for him, Orelaith. He also said he was very sorry he couldn't wait for your return, but his uncle was expecting him back at the port town and he had to hurry back."

"Do not let her see how much this is upsetting you. Outwardly this boy should mean nothing to you, they do not know Garbhan is your brother. Tread very carefully." Vig's tone was one of concern. Bas was straining to keep his face from revealing just how this affected him.

"Oh, I am so happy for him, but yet so sad that our paths have gone in different directions. I do hope we meet him again soon. Did he say where his uncle lived?" Orelaith asked quickly so Bas didn't have to.

"No, I'm afraid not, but maybe Saoirse knows. She should be home soon." Bridget gave her a quick smile. "I will go make your rooms ready. Children, will you run into town and let your mother know Orelaith and her family are here?" Then she turned and walked inside to get everything ready.

"Oh Bas, I am so sorry." Orelaith took his hand.

"I... I will be fine. Just give me a little time to get over the shock," he said and walked off towards the woods. Orelaith stared after him and Vig put her hand on Orelaith's shoulder.

"Don't worry, he will be back to his old self again in no time. As for Garbhan, we will find him. It's only a matter of when, not how."

Later that evening, they all sat around the table eating one of Bridget's wonderful meals. Bas was quiet and appeared to be drifting off into deep thought most of the time. Orelaith felt his pain and knew he was still distraught about Garbhan and Conri leaving. The only times he smiled were when Rionach distracted him with questions or when she wanted to show him something. "Conri was so torn about leaving, but he could not pass up the opportunity to go live with family, and his uncle seemed like a very nice man. He told me that he and his wife could not have children of their own so they would raise Conri and Garbhan as their sons. He did tell me to thank you for all you have done for them, and said he would never forget your kindness. Who knows where they would have been if you had not stopped and helped him when he first came to this town." Saoirse sighed. "I was very sad to see him go, he has been such a great help around the farm." Orelaith smiled.

"You will find someone to help you, I am sure of it. And I am glad Conri found his family, I lost mine but I gained a new one when I met Bas." He smiled at her and mind-sent "Thank you." Orelaith picked up Rionach.

"I think it's way past your bedtime young lady. Say goodnight to everyone."

"Aww mama, do I have to go to bed? I am not tired…" She stifled a yawn.

"It's been a long day and you can play more tomorrow." Rionach reluctantly waved goodnight to them all and Orelaith walked upstairs with her. Bridget had taken Saoirse's little girl up when Orelaith came back down. "I've been meaning to ask you Saoirse, does this town have a place where I can buy some land?" Bas asked.

"I am not sure but I would think you would have to talk to the local king about that. I bought this farm off the family that owned it," Saoirse replied. "Are you thinking about buying some land close by?" Bas shook his head.

"No. I want to expand my land, and I want to do so correctly. My family has lived on our farm for a very long time so I am not sure how they acquired it. I will go into town tomorrow and find out." He seemed to have lightened up now and winked at Orelaith.

"You never told me that you were planning that, but I think it's a wonderful idea."

"Yes… I believe it is time to move out of our cave and into a proper home. The cave is a wonderful home for us dragons, but not for us as humans. It's time we made the change complete." They made plans for the next day before turning in for the night.

Chapter 27

In the morning, Orelaith went into town with Saoirse and Bas while Vig stayed at the farm with the children. A little while later, Luna went to town with Bridget to help her get some supplies for the next couple of days. The children showed Vig and Rionach how they tended to the sheep and the other animals around the farm. Rionach was fascinated and took in everything like a sponge. There were so many new things to see and learn. As Vig watched the children play she realized that Rionach needed to be with other humans. She was missing out on so many things living the way they had up until now. She discussed this with Luna and Bas when they returned to the farm later that day. Bas shared his plans with them about building a castle over the cave making it possible to hide it and for them to still spend time in dragon form when they felt the need to.

"I like it. I was just watching Rionach play, and it is my opinion that she needs to be around other humans. She hardly knows how to play with others her own age, Bas." Bas nodded and said.

"After the castle is built, we will hire some of the locals to work for us. I know we could do the work ourselves, but I

LORE OF THE DRAGONS: ESSENCE OF A QUEEN

want us to help some of the poor families that live around there."

"I agree and if we did not hire some help there would be talk about how we get everything done." Vig nodded thoughtfully.

"And we do have to find some horses that look just like us... in case Saoirse comes to visit," Luna said and snickered.

"I think I can help with that..." Serovita added as she came walking over. They all turned and looked at her.

"What do you mean?" She took a mouthful of the green grass and looked at them.

"Well, I haven't quite figured it out yet but I do believe that I can make animals grow in the same manner that I do plants... but I cannot do it alone. I will need Vig to help me with them as I'm not as familiar with animals as I am with plants. I have done it once to a fish... but that was mostly by accident." Vig leaned forward and asked,

"And it didn't seem to harm it?"

"No, it just grew to double its size and then swam off." Vig frowned thoughtfully.

"We would need to test it out together so I can see exactly what it does to the animal physically."

"You need to stop talking about that now, at least out loud. Bridget is going to think you are mad." Bas nodded towards the main house as the old housekeeper came out with some tea for them.

"I thought you might want something to drink before I start with dinner," she smiled and put the tray on the ground.

"Were the children any trouble while I was gone?" she asked Vig.

"Oh no, not at all. They truly are wonderful and Saoirse's little girl has been so sweet to Rionach all day. Saoirse and you must be so proud of them both." Bridget actually blushed.

"Yes, we are. Saoirse is a good mother and I just follow her example. Now, if you will excuse me, I need to start with dinner."Bridget said and walked off. Vig smiled then got up,

"I think I will take Serovita here for a short ride before dinner." Bas looked at her and laughed. "You just have to try it out, don't you?"

"Well… yes. You know I can't resist a chance to learn more about our powers." Bas smiled at her, knowing very well she could not.

"Do you want us to come along?" Vig jumped up on Serovita's back.

"No need for that, we won't be long," she replied and rode off into the woods.

Orelaith had helped out in Saoirse's shop all morning. She wanted to go and get a present for Rionach before they went back to the farm for the evening so she went to a shop they had passed on the way in that morning. The outside wall of the tinker shop was covered with different things for sale as was the ground on each side of the door. Wooden spoons, cartwheels, broomsticks and fishing rods hung on the wall along with other strange things Orelaith didn't even know what they were. On the ground stood several cauldrons and chairs and even a beautifully carved crib. On a box to the left sat a little old man with wild gray hair and a nicely trimmed beard. His clothes were covered in wood chips from his ongoing wood carving and he looked up and smiled as Orelaith stopped in front of him.

"Good afternoon, milady. What can I do for you today?" He had an infectious smile, and Orelaith found herself smiling back at him.

"I have been looking for presents for three children and I wanted to see what you had in your shop." He got up and brushed off his clothes and said,

"I think I have some things they may like." He went inside and came out with a box of wooden toys; a horse with a tiny cart, a dog, a pig and even a small house with tiny furniture. He had two little dolls with what looked like horse hair stuck to their heads. The craftsmanship was outstanding and she smiled and picked up one of the two dolls.

"You have made these yourself?" she said as she studied the little hands and feet. He swelled with pride as he nodded.

"Yes milady."

"How much do you want for it?" He scratched his beard.

"Oh a few coppers would do." She shook her head.

"No, I mean for all of it." His eyes widened.

"All of them?" She nodded again and smiled at him.

"And how quickly can you make another set of animals and a little house? I will pay you five gold for all this, and if you make me another set just like it I will give you five more gold. Is that fair enough?" She knew she was overpaying for it but she didn't mind, knowing the children would be thrilled. The man's eyes widened and his jaw dropped.

"Five gold?"

"And another five if you can make an extra set for me. Do we have a deal?" She smiled at him. He nodded slowly, still staring at her. "I believe that good craftsmanship should be rewarded equal to the quality of the work done, and these pieces are absolutely amazing. Do you know where the tailor Saoirse lives?"

"Eh… yes. I mean, I do," he answered and straightened up. "Good. Can you have them delivered there when you are done?"

"Yes of course, milady." She counted out five gold from her little pouch and handed them to the old man who was still in shock from receiving more in one day than he had gotten for an entire month.

"I will just take three things with me now so that the children get a little something tonight." She picked up the two dolls and the horse, put them in the large pocket inside her cape, then said goodbye. He bowed and promised he would start the work right away.

On her way back to Saoirse's shop she bumped into a tall, hooded woman in a black cloak. Her face was mostly shrouded in shadow. Only glowing light blue eyes scowled at Orelaith.

"Look where you are going woman." Orelaith stared transfixed into the woman's eyes and stuttered out an apology. The woman grabbed her wrist and to Orelaith's horror black tendrils, unseen but not unfelt, stretched towards her. Both of them seemed equally surprised when Orelaith pushed back at the snakelike tendrils with her own golden ones and sent the woman stumbling backwards. She stared at Orelaith in disbelief.

"Impossible…" she hissed. Orelaith mumbled out another apology and hurried off. What had just happened? Had she just done that? She needed to talk to Vig about it as soon as they got back to the farm.

Saoirse was just closing up when Orelaith returned. If she saw how shook up Orelaith was, she said nothing about it.

"Just in time," Saoirse smiled when she saw Orelaith.

"I'm just about done and starving. Let's hurry back so we can have some of Bridget's stew." Orelaith put on a smile for her friend and said,

"That sounds wonderful. Oh, and I have gotten a little something for the children." She showed the three things she had gotten to Saoirse.

"Oh! Those are wonderful and I know the children will be so happy. Where did you get them?" "At that strange old shop that has everything. The wood carver, you know him?" Saoirse studied the little dolls.

"Yes, but I had no idea he made things like this…" Orelaith kept a sharp eye out for the scary woman in the black cape, but didn't see her at all on their way back.

After dinner, when they were all sitting around with full bellies, Orelaith went upstairs and got the three wooden toys for the children. The little girls clapped their hands and laughed when she pulled out the two little dolls and handed them one each. Saoirse's son looked a little downhearted and thought he was not getting anything. "I got you a little something too, but you are probably such a big boy you don't like toys any more, do you?" He nodded and looked at her expectantly. "I'm not that big yet…" They all laughed and Orelaith handed him the little horse and cart. The usually solemn boy lit up in the brightest smile she had seen on his face since the first time she had met him.

"Thank you so much. I promise I will take very good care of it." When the children were in bed, Orelaith asked Vig and Bas to join her for a little walk outside to get some fresh air.

"I have something I need to tell you," Orelaith said with a soft voice once they stopped outside the stable.

"What is it?" Bas said, concerned when he saw how serious she was.

"Well… I bumped into a strange woman today in the town." Vig frowned.

"What do you mean, strange how?"

"She was wearing a hooded cloak, so I couldn't see her properly, but when I bumped into her she grabbed my wrist and sent out tendrils towards me. They were not like yours, full of light and warmth, but black and twisted like snakes crawling towards me."

"Black tendrils?" Vig said, shocked.

"I have only seen them one place before, but surely it can't be what I think it is?" She looked at Bas who had pulled Orelaith into his arms.

"You could've been harmed. I should've been there with you." The self condemning tone to his voice pained Orelaith.

"But in a way you were, because what happened next shocked me as much as it shocked this woman." They glanced at each other then both looked at her. When she had told them what happened Vig frowned and said.

"How is that even possible? You are all human. As far as I know, only dragons possess that type of magic." She looked at Bas who had a thoughtful smile on his face,

"I think I know... Vig, you and I know that the bonding ritual is secret and only known by the couples that have experienced it for themselves, right?" Vig nodded.

"Yes, that is correct. But where are you going with this Bas? Surely that has nothing to do with it?" Bas winked at her.

"It has everything to do with it. Orelaith," he said and turned to her.

"Do I have your permission to tell Vig what happened the night we bonded? Well... not all of it of course," he added when he saw Orelaith's cheeks turn a shade of pink. She nodded and Bas shared the knowledge that no single dragon had ever had insight to before. Vig sat in silence, only interrupting to ask a few questions.

"First of all, let me say how honored I am that you would let me get an insight into your bonding. I will keep this to myself."

"We know you will, Vig," Bas said.

"I would like to do a deep examination of you, Orelaith, if you would give your consent." Orelaith sat down in the chair next to her and felt Vig's familiar tendrils gently prodding her. They seemed to pierce every part of her, even down to her very core. It felt like being outside when a rainless thunderstorm was right overhead. The hairs on her neck and arms stood up as Vig searched her body and mind. "I think I know what has happened. There are good news and bad news here." Vig opened her eyes and looked at them. "Your bonding has given you some of our dragon aspects, like slow deterioration of your body. This means you will not grow old as quickly as other humans. And you will have some magic like we dragons have too," she said and smiled. Bas smiled and hugged Orelaith, happy that some of the problems they thought they would be facing were no longer an issue.

"And the bad news?" Orelaith asked.

"You have the same curse now that we dragon's carry. You will die and be reborn if you two do decide Rionach should have a sister or brother."

"That is not so bad. We just won't have any more children." Bas smiled at Orelaith.

"But what kind of powers do I have? And how do I control them? I mean, I don't want to harm anyone because I accidentally use these… powers without any form of control," Orelaith asked, visibly concerned.

"We can practice some of it, but your true gift only you will recognize." Vig got up. "But not tonight. There has been more than enough excitement for one day, and I feel that a good night's sleep will do us all good."

"But who is this woman? Is she a dragon? Or maybe a sorceress?" For Orelaith, that was one of the more important questions. If there was more than one evil dragon in human form, she wanted to know.

"Oh, I know it is a dragon, and I think I know who it is. I would know her in dragon form, but as you have only seen her in human form there is no way of being certain." "Who is it you think it is then?" Bas asked curiously. Vig's face was solemn when she replied, "I only know of one dragon with blue eyes like that, and she was not unkind but a little self-centred. She must have been infected in the sphere…" Vig was almost talking to herself and forgetting what the question was.

"Who?" Bas asked as Vig went quiet while she remembered a time long since passed.

"Her name is Inanis."

Orelaith could not sleep that night. Her head was overfilled with so many different thoughts, it was hard to keep them all straight. Bas was fast asleep next to her, grunting every once in a while and moving in his sleep. It stung her heart when she thought of how her father would have looked at him. She missed him so much. And her mother, how she would have loved them all, at least their human forms… but their dragon forms? She smiled to herself picturing her mother telling Aqua to wipe her feet before she entered the cave, or her and Vig discussing recipes. Orelaith's mother had always taught her not to judge by appearances, but by the heart. She believed that after the initial shock, Orelaith's mother would have come to love them like she did. But she would never really know. Her family was gone now, but she did have a new family and a daughter. A wonderful, beautiful daughter… that could turn into a small golden dragon. It wasn't quite the life she had pictured she would have, but one thing was certain. It was not boring.

Chapter 28

Over the next few days, they saw neither the strange woman nor the men who had tried to kidnap Orelaith three years earlier. Vig and Serovita had made some remarkable discoveries in their trials to change the shape and age of creatures. There were quite a few strange animals running around the woods surrounding the town. There had been sightings of all white rabbits, giant beetles and a few oversized squirrels. Luna had spent most of her time with Rionach, who was not too happy about being left out of the testing because she was too young.

"But I want to learn too," she sulked. But Bas and Orelaith had been rock firm when it came to anything that involved magic of any kind.

"Not yet sweetheart, maybe when you get a little older." If they had to go into town, she had been told the same thing. When Saoirse's children had run off to tend to the sheep or go to town with lunch for their mother, Rionach had whined, wanting to go with them.

"It's not fair. I am a big girl too, mama. And I'm already good at magic, so I can take care of them." Orelaith had felt bad for her, but even though she knew her daughter was stronger and smarter than any child her age, she was still a child.

"You will have to figure something out soon," Luna said two days later. "She complains for a long time whenever you leave her behind. I do try to keep her occupied; taking her fishing, riding or berry-picking, but as soon as we get back she starts sulking again."

"I know… but what can we do? She is only three years old," Orelaith had replied, not knowing what to do. "And we need to head to the king of the land around our home to buy the deed so we can start building," she added.

"Maybe keeping her from her powers altogether is not a good idea," Vig said thoughtfully. "She may use her powers when we are not looking, just because we keep her from using them at all. Serovita and I will keep a close eye on her while you are gone, and we can let her observe us trying to change the animals. She really is remarkably clever. Who knows, she might be able to think of something we have not." Bas and Orelaith gave their consent and made plans to leave the next day.

Luna, Tempest and Terra had gone with Orelaith and Bas to see the king. They would fly over at night to locate his whereabouts, then land at the closest uninhabited field, spend the rest of the night there, then ride in by first light carrying the gold and some gifts. Terra would fly back to the cave and wait for them to return with the deed to the land. She would then start working at building their new home and the others would return to the farm where Rionach, Vig, Solis, Serovita and Aqua were waiting. But first, they had to convince the king to sell them the land they wanted.

Orelaith and Bas had made some inquiries about this king and the things they found were not promising. It was said he was a conceited man and not very likely to part with anything he considered his. But they had, under the pretense of being nobles from far away, acquired an invitation to a feast at his castle the next evening. Orelaith had insisted they return to their cave so that she could find an elaborate dress for the occasion, and she picked out some of the finer clothes Saoirse had made for Bas.

"We have to look the part. He must believe that we are a wealthy lord and lady, and certainly won't believe that if we come in ordinary wool clothing," she had said when Bas complained. Now they were standing in the waiting room outside the great hall of the castle. Orelaith looked like a queen in her dark blue, shiny silk dress. She had a golden belt around her waist and jewelry in her hair in the form of a blue droplet gem on her forehead. A matching hooded blue-black cape covered her delicate frame, and her face was hidden from the guards as they were announced to enter the big hall. "Lord Basilicus Le Dragon and her Ladyship Orelaith!" Orelaith took a deep breath and let Bas guide her to their appointed seats. Surprisingly, they were seated next to the king. The other guests politely nodded to them and they nodded back.

A.KING

"His royal highness Cathal Mac Conchobair Mac Taidg!" The doors opened and the king came walking in smiling to his guests. He sat down in his seat and nodded acknowledging to his guests. He glanced curiously at Bas and Orelaith during the meal but did not speak to them until the fruits were placed on the table.

"So what brings a distant lord and lady so far from your own land?" he inquired as he picked through the fruits on his plate.

"Your highness, to be truthful we are looking for a new place to settle down. Our own land has been ravaged by war for so long that there is nothing left for us there," Bas replied as if it pained him greatly.

"Oh really? Where exactly are you from?" The king leaned closer, obviously interested.

"It is far, on the other side of the ocean. We have long searched for a new place to call home and to bring all of our enormous resources in submission under a new king." This statement brought a smile to the king's face.

"Well, this land is the best in all of our beloved green isle. The land is rich and the king is a fair man when it comes to taxes," he said and winked at Bas.

"But it depends on how big a piece of land a man like yourself would require... and where it would be located of course."

"Of course, and we have found a place that would suit our needs within your land." Orelaith noticed how greed flashed in the king's eyes as Bas spoke. She had to praise his skills at playing a wealthy lord, the king swallowed the bait like a hungry fish.

"Good. We can talk more about this in the morning. Who knows, you may be one of my subjects come noon tomorrow." The rest of the evening, they were entertained by jesters and songs, good food and interesting conversations. The king had insisted they stay at the castle that night and had prepared a room for them. When they retired, Bas had kissed Orelaith and had left her in the room to go and tell Luna and Tempest the news.

"I won't be long . Just go to bed and I will be back shortly."

Orelaith had never seen such a beautiful room, and the bed, the bed was so big and the pillows so soft. Orelaith laughed when she thought of what the king would think of them if he had known that she was a humble farmer's daughter and Bas was really a dragon. Nobility were strange that way; throw in a title and you got entirely different treatment. She climbed into the big bed and sighed contentedly as she pulled the duvet up to her chin. Not long after, she was sound asleep dreaming of her family being with her.

Chapter 29

In the morning, Bas had gone alone to talk to the king and it was noon by the time he returned with the deed to the land around their cave.

"He drove a hard bargain and I had to pretend that he had set a price that was almost too high. But we actually have the amount with us that he is asking." Bas chuckled. "You should have seen his greedy little eyes when I agreed to that sum. We will be paying him taxes too, but only a small amount." He picked Orelaith up and swung her around.

"That is good news. But how long will it take to get the castle built?" she asked when he put her down. "I will talk to Terra when we get back and find out if she needs any help." Orelaith sat down in the chair next to the window and looked out over the busy courtyard.

"I want to travel around with you and Vig to find the people to come work for us. There are so many people we can help now that we have our own land." Bas nodded and sat down next to her. "Oh, before I forget, if anyone asks why we're traveling alone, we aren't really. Our people and the rest of the family are waiting, or so I said, at about half a day's ride away." Orelaith saw a little girl with her mother crossing the courtyard and realized how much she missed Rionach and the others.

"Can we leave now then? I miss Rionach and the others."

"Yes." Bas took her hand across the table. "I want to leave as soon as we can, so why don't you start packing up and I will let Luna and Tempest know that we will be going soon."

After they had paid their respects to the king they headed back to the cave where Terra was waiting. Terra said that she would need Serovita to come help with some things, so they decided to all head back to Saoirse's farm. When asked what kind of help Serovita would be, Terra had just smiled and said that it was a surprise. Saoirse had been overjoyed that Orelaith and Rionach would be staying for a few more weeks along with most of the others. Luna and Bas had gone off with Serovita and Terra. The man from the shop had been by with the toys, much to the children's delight, and Rionach and little Blathnat spent a lot of time playing with the dolls. Orelaith saw how her daughter would observe Blathnat and copy her way of playing. It warmed her heart to see how close the two little girls had become even though Blathnat was about seven years older, at least in physical year's. Mentally, Rionach was almost as old it seemed, and she looked more like a five year old than a three year old. When Saoirse had commented on it, Orelaith had laughed it away saying she probably took after her father and would probably be just as tall. Over the next weeks they enjoyed each other's company and even went to church on Sundays. Orelaith made a few contributions which the local abbot seemed to be more than happy to accept. She talked with him about the possibility of opening a school for some of the town's children. He said he would look into it but she knew he didn't really think it was a good idea, so Orelaith hoped that the church closest to her home would be more open to it. Tomorrow, they would be heading back home. Orelaith was happy about going home but would miss Bridget, Saoirse and her children. She longed for more freedom to go where she wished. Although they had not seen the strange woman or any other suspicious people around during their stay, Bas would not let her go off on her own as long as they were visiting.

"I know you can take care of yourself, my love, but I would never forgive myself if anything happened to you," Bas had said when she mentioned it. "Once we get back home it will be different. I talked to Vig and we think we know who is behind this. After Tempest's attack we know that Nex is still alive. He has obviously set himself up with people that do his bidding. Whether or not they've figured out that he is a dragon is hard to know."

"He is your brother, isn't he? Can't you talk to him? Surely he doesn't want conflict with his own family?" Orelaith asked.

"To him I am no more than a hindrance that stands between him and the dragon throne. He wants to harness the powers Rionach possesses for himself." Bas sighed. "He was always striving to be better than me and Frater. I think it was because he was the youngest whelp. The infection made his competitiveness for me and Frater turn to hate. It saddens me to say, but he is not my brother any more. The brother I knew died when he became infected." She hugged him.

"I am sorry, Bas. I thought that maybe when Rionach changed the very structure of your essence, it would remove the infection from the other dragons too. I mean, it seems they can stay in human form for as long as they wish, just like you." Bas shook his head,

"I talked to Vig about that, but she believes that the infection has run so deep in the infected that it has become part of their personality. It more or less defines who they are." Orelaith sighed and put her head on his chest. "I'm glad that I have you in my life. It makes the pain over the loss of my brothers lessen a little," Bas said and pulled her closer. Orelaith lay silent for a while listening to Bas' slow and steady breath. Tomorrow they would be heading home, not to a cave but to a castle.

As the sun rose that morning, they were all packing their things. It amazed Orelaith how much they had acquired in only three short weeks. Even Vig had accumulated more than five bags worth of assorted clutter.

"We will have to take the cart this time just to get all the things you have bought home." Bas laughed as he watched Vig stacking bag upon bag on Solis' back.

"I think we might have to." Vig sighed and started taking the bags back off.

"Thank goodness…" Solis sent. *"I may be stronger than a horse, but those bags are so uncomfortable."* Once they had hitched up the cart to Solis and packed all their things in the back, it was time for goodbyes. There were tears and smiles but also promises of seeing each other again soon. Even the children seemed more than a little upset when they waved goodbye. "Mama, I will miss them, why can't they come live with us? Then we never have to say goodbye again." Orelaith smiled and wiped away a tear from Rionach's cheek.

"I'm afraid they would not understand what we truly are. It may change our friendship." She looked up at Orelaith.

"But why? We are still the same, mama. You said it's what's on the inside that counts."

"I know sweetheart, and it's true. But humans are fearful of things they do not know or understand, so they think it must be evil. But who knows, maybe one day we can tell them. For now, we need to keep it a secret so we don't scare them." Rionach put her head in Orelaith's lap and soon drifted off to sleep.

Chapter 30

It was midday by the time they approached their home. Orelaith gasped in astonishment as she looked upon the most magnificent castle she had ever seen. The walls were light grey, almost white, and with the sun reflecting off the beautiful stone it looked like it glowed. A large rampart with walkways surrounded the castle and several towers loomed over the main structure. A moat surrounded the outer embankments and white roses climbed up the walls of the inner bailey. A road cut through the landscape all the way up to a drawbridge that was the only entry. They glided over it and found they could not see the entrance to the cave at all.

"I must say she has outdone herself this time," Vig called over. Orelaith and Rionach looked down in silent wonder.

"Yes." Bas smiled. "It's almost as good as the work her mother did back home." Bas circled downwards followed by the others and landed in the huge bailey where Serovita and Terra were waiting.

"Welcome back," Terra greeted them.

"Amazing work, Terra. You truly are a master at what you do." Vig gave her a big hug.

"Oh! It's so beautiful," Rionach was turning around and around looking up at the towers. "Careful or you will get dizzy." Luna winked when she passed her on her way up the steps to the doors of the main building.

"I see you have had a hand in this too, Serovita," Bas said and nodded towards the dragon shapes on the doors.

"Oh, just a little out here," Serovita replied and smiled at him. Terra picked up a now quite dizzy Rionach.

"Do you want to see your room?" Rionach's eyes widened.

"I have my own room now?" They all laughed and followed Terra and Rionach in through the big wooden doors.

"I have made a big room in the middle for you two, and the little one has the room next to it," Terra said and sat Rionach down. On their door was the symbol that Serovita had put on Rionach's crib, eight dragons and a woman in the middle. Orelaith ran her fingers across the shapes.

"It's beautiful…" she almost whispered.

"You have yet to see the room." Terra winked and opened the big double doors. Orelaith gasped when she saw it. Smooth stone floors stretched throughout the two rooms that made up their quarters. Two chairs were placed below a big window, and next to them was a door that led out to a big open porch overlooking the valley below. Bright red curtains hung on each side of the open door. Bas followed her in as she walked slowly through the first room. She turned and saw the big bed with velvet bedding and curtains at each of the four bedposts. Big fluffy pillows and soft linen sheets made Orelaith sigh at the thought of curling up there. Like her chamber, there was a bath built into the wall, but now they had engineered a means to draw water from below.

"It was not as hard as we thought but I am not going to bore you with the details. So... what do you think?" Orelaith turned and looked at her with tears in her eyes. For a moment, Terra seemed confused, thinking Orelaith did not like it.

"I love it! I have never seen such a magnificent room in all my life and I can't believe it is my home. Thank you, Terra, thank you so much..." Orelaith threw her arms around Terra who at first was a little surprised then smiled warmly.

"You are most welcome, child. It has been so much fun to use my powers for more than just little things again."

"I bet it has, but where did you get all the fabrics? Surely you could not have made the pillows and sheets ?" Bas said and ran his hand over the velvet covers.

"Actually... Serovita has come up with a way to harvest fabric from plants but they were not used here. We had to go to the trading port in the east to find a few things we were missing." Bas frowned at her.

"That could have been dangerous. You should have waited for us to return to do that."

"I am twice your elder, young whelp, and I do believe I can take care of myself," Terra huffed, sounding a little like Vig. Orelaith wandered the room and opened a big wooden closet only to find all her dresses hung neatly in a row.

"Bas, I have set up a vault in the cave beneath us. And the entrance is in a hidden room with nine hallways leading from each of our rooms. Here, let me show you." She walked over to the wall next to the bed and pulled the red tapestry aside. At first there did not seem to be anything there but she stepped on a specific stone in the floor and the doorway appeared. It slid silently open revealing a dark hallway behind it.

"Sweet…" Bas grinned.

"It gets better," said a voice from inside the darkness. Two big eyes glowed in the darkness within and Luna stepped into the room. She turned and faced the dark hallway and blew a small blue flame into her hand. It floated above her palm.

"See that small ledge that runs along the wall on either side?" Bas nodded. "Now watch this," she said and gently blew the flame from her hand towards the ledge where it lit up and followed the hallway, creating a flowing light that ran down into the darkness on both sides.

"That is pretty good. Natural gas?" Terra shook her head.

"No, it's oil. It burns for a very long time. See above the ledge there is another shelf? It folds down and kills the flame."

"Mama! Papa! You have to come see my room." Rionach pulled on Orelaith and dragged her off.

"We can look at that later. It seems right now I have important business to attend to." Bas laughed as he walked after Orelaith and Rionach.

After they had spent the rest of the day exploring the castle, all of them gathered in a large room at the top of one of the towers. Rionach was fast asleep in Orelaith's lap as they sat by a round stone table with nine big wooden chairs. Red tapestries hung in various places on the stone walls and shelves covered the rest. Big windows were facing towards the valley below as did a large balcony big enough for them to land on in dragon form.

"If we are going to do this right we will need a council chamber, and I thought this would do. From here we will have access from the air and we can discuss any matter that need attending to." Terra nodded to Vig.

"Yes, I must say this is an excellent choice, Terra, and may I congratulate both you and Serovita for the exquisite work you have done here. It is more than one could ever expect. I believe you both are in dire need of some long overdue rest. We will see to it that you get a few weeks worth of sleep." She looked around at the others who all nodded in agreement.

"There are a few things we need to share with you all now that we are gathered again." Vig told them all about the woman Orelaith had run into in the town. She also told them about Orelaith's change. This brought smiles to all their faces, knowing she would be with them for a long time. She told them about her theory that Nex was behind the attacks on Orelaith at the farm some years back and they decided they would need to look into where he could be located. Then came a list Vig had made up of all the things she believed they would need to run this castle like any other. That included everything and anything: candles, people, cooking pots, a set of plates with their seal on; the list went on and on. Bas looked around at the others and found Luna dozing and Aqua looking cranky due to lack of food.

"Vig, my dear, I think we need to continue this discussion tomorrow. We could all do with some food and a good night's sleep right about now." Aqua jumped up and scuttled to the veranda doors.

"Last one to the ocean is a rotten fish!" With that she ran out the doors and jumped, transformed in mid-air and headed for the west coast. Solis, Tempest, Serovita and Luna followed moments after. Vig sat down.

"Sorry I went on forever, Bas, but I see how much needs to be done before we can start helping the people around here."

"Around here? The closest farm can't even see the castle in daylight. We will need to start hiring people pretty soon if we want to get crops planted before it's too late," Bas said and stroked an unruly curl away from Rionach's face.

"Don't you worry about the crops, Serovita will take care of that." Vig frowned.

"But we do need some smaller homes like Saoirse's along the outer wall because the people who come here will need a place to live."

"I agree, but now I believe it's time for me to retire." Orelaith got up, cradling Rionach in her arms.

"Tomorrow, we can start writing a list of all the things we will need and decide when, how, and where we can get them." She nodded to Terra and Vig, kissed Bas then left the room. Vig sighed. "So we will need pens, ink and paper too then…"

Chapter 31

By midsummer they had over fifty families living within the castle. After Terra had rested enough to start working again, she had expanded the outer walls so they could fit almost eighty small homes inside the walls. Orelaith, Bas and Vig had travelled the surrounding land and hand-picked the people they thought would gain most from coming to live with them. Farmers, maids, cooks, stable-hands and they even found a blacksmith. Word had gotten around about them and people had started coming by themselves now.

Serovita and Vig had learned how to make animals grow larger and even how to change their looks. The stables now contained eight beautiful horses named after each of the dragons they looked like, but riding them proved a different matter altogether as Vig found out on her first attempt. She had come marching up the steps with dirty clothes and her hair tangled, mumbling to herself,

"Damn animals…" so they all had to learn how to use their powers to control the beasts. Orelaith had always known how to ride, so she was excused. Rionach was still too young and was told so repeatedly by all of them. This had made her moody and sulky and she was constantly testing her limits, asking to do things that she was far too young to be doing. Orelaith had gotten so tired of her constant nagging that Bas said he would take her to see Saoirse and they could all ride back together.

"We will have to ride all the way there. How long do you think that will take?" she had asked Bas that evening as they all sat down to eat.

"A little over a day, I believe, if we don't make any stops."

"I think I know a way to shorten that, but only for one of the ways. You will have to find your way back on your own," Vig said and picked up her silver goblet.

"I don't see how that could be done, but please, do share," Bas said and leaned forward.

"All I have to do is put the horses into a deep sleep, then you just pick them up and fly there. I will show you how to wake them up again. That way you can just ride in like we usually do. But make sure you follow a road this time so you will know how to head back. It will seem strange to Saoirse if you don't know exactly how to get back." Bas rubbed his chin thoughtfully.

"It sure would save us a lot of time…"

"I want to come, papa," Rionach whined.

"No sweetheart, this time we are going to bring them back here so they can see your room." Orelaith looked at her daughter and stroked her hand.

"I never get to do anything fun! It's not fair! You always say I'm too young. I'm not like other children and you know it! It's just not fair!" Rionach stormed out of the room. Orelaith got up to follow her, but Bas took her hand.

LORE OF THE DRAGONS: ESSENCE OF A QUEEN

"Let her figure this one out on her own. She is right on some points; she's not like other children her age, but that doesn't change the fact she is only a small child in body if not in mind." Orelaith sat down, visibly upset.

"I know… but I don't know how to treat her; as a child or as a teenager, which is more the way she is acting these days."

"I think you are doing a wonderful job with her, Orelaith. She has most of your endearing qualities. She is kind and selfless, well… most of the time, and she has a gentle mind that does not exclude others based on appearance. And she is a really fast learner. She can replicate any of my tendril knots after seeing them only once."

"You need to be careful with that," Luna said and poured another glass of wine. "I saw her growing a toad to twice its size the other day and she turned it bright pink. Poor frog was rather confused." Vig frowned.

"That's not good. She has been told not to try any of this on her own. It is way too big a risk for a little girl. If it backfired, there is no telling what could happen."

"Can't you just reverse it? I mean… if she does happen to do something to herself, can you undo it?" Bas asked. Vig shook her head.

"It doesn't work that way. Once the change is made, I seal it off so nothing can unravel the knots." Orelaith got up and said "I am going to go see to her. With her powers and as upset as she is now, I think it's best she is not alone." Vig nodded.

"I agree, and I will come with you. Maybe I can explain

to her how dangerous it can be to tamper with things. She is just too young." But when they got to her room, she was gone.

They started to search the castle; every room and every walkway. Luna and Tempest flew off to search outside the castle while Bas and Orelaith walked down through the houses in the lower city.

"Rionach! Where are you?" Bas mind sent as loudly as he could. But no matter how intensely they searched, she was nowhere to be found.

"We will find her, don't worry. But it seems she doesn't want to be found right now," Vig said and placed a hand on Bas' shoulder.

"I want to look one more place," Orelaith said and got up. Bas was about to follow her, but she stopped him. "Stay here with the others, Bas. I want to talk to her alone if you don't mind." She left the others in the counsell chamber and found her way to the hidden hallway leading down into the cave below. As she suspected, it was already lit. She was almost at the bottom when she heard the soft crying coming from her old chamber. It was darker down here, but she made her way quickly there.

"Rionach? Is this where you have been hiding, my dear? We have been so worried. Come, let's go tell the others that you are safe."

LORE OF THE DRAGONS: ESSENCE OF A QUEEN

"No, mama… we can't," a woman's voice answered. Orelaith took a step back. This was not her sweet little girl's voice.

"Who is there?" Orelaith demanded. "Step into the light so I can see you." A beautiful, red haired girl stepped forward. Her shoulders were slanting and her head hanging down. "Who are you? And how did you get in here?" The girl looked up at her with big green eyes brimming with tears,

"It's me, mama. It's Rionach." Orelaith stared at the girl not being able to fathom who or what she was looking at. "Mama… don't you recognize me?" the girl cried. "I did something stupid, mama… and now I can't undo it… please don't be angry with me…" Then it dawned on Orelaith what had happened. She threw her arms around the girl.

"Oh sweetheart, I'm not angry with you. But you should not have done this. It can not be undone, my dear." Rionach just hugged her mother and cried.

"I am so sorry… so sorry." They sat down on the bed and Orelaith held her daughter until the crying ceased.

"We will have to change your entire wardrobe now. You know that, right?" Orelaith smiled softly at Rionach who nodded. "Let's go to mine and papa's room and find you a dress that fits you." Orelaith took her hand, and together they walked up through the hallway to Orelaith and Bas' room in search of a dress that fit Rionach now. Afterwards, Rionach would have to face the others and show them what she had done to herself.

The others were still in the counseling chamber when Orelaith returned. "Did you find her?" Bas got up and walked towards her. Orelaith nodded and hugged him. "You'll probably want to sit down for this…" "She is not harmed, is she?" Bas said, the panic in his eyes and voice were touchingly apparent. "No, she is not harmed. But…" Orelaith took a deep breath. "She is not the same little girl who ran out from dinner in a temper tantrum." They all looked at her, obviously confused.

"What do you mean? What has happened to her?" Vig asked, but Orelaith noticed something in her eyes that told her that Vig already suspected what had happened.

"Remember we talked earlier about how she had changed the size and colour of a frog?" "Yes…" Orelaith walked around the table and put her hands on Bas' shoulders.

"Well… she did what we feared the most. She used it on herself." There was a collective gasp and Vig turned an even whiter shade than usual. Bas turned abruptly and stared at her.

"She did what? How… is she ok?"

"As far as I can tell she is a perfectly normal… sixteen year-old."

"Sixteen? But she is only three! How could she? Of all the thoughtless things… What was she thinking?" Bas was frantic now and Orelaith had to push him down into the

LORE OF THE DRAGONS: ESSENCE OF A QUEEN

chair to keep him from leaving the room.

"Now you listen to me, your royal highness Basilicus. You will do as I say in this matter. She was hiding when I found her because she was afraid of what you and the others would say and do when you found out. She was scared and upset. I promised her I would talk to you first before she came up here to make sure you won't lose your temper with her. And you will not! You will be understanding and forgiving. After all, she is your daughter and you love her." Tendrils of light flowed from Orelaith to Bas and curled around his heart, pulling away the anger and fear that was consuming him at this moment. Bas gasped, but soon his face became composed. He sighed and closed his eyes.

"Thank you…" he whispered.

"That, my dear Orelaith, is your true power," Vig sent to her and smiled. She seemed calm after receiving news like this.

"I should have known she would do something like this. Her mind is developing at an alarmingly faster rate than her body, as is her powers." Luna was smiling.

"I think it's wonderful news. It proves how powerful she truly is. And what a queen she will be! Soon, she will be able to remove the binding your mother put on us so we would not overpopulate this planet."

"One thing at a time," Vig said. "First I need to make sure that she is healthy and that she did not do any harm to herself in the process." Orelaith nodded in agreement.

"But first I think she better come in and let you see her

for yourselves. Sweetheart, you can come in now." The doors opened and with her head bowed, Rionach walked into the room. She was wearing Orelaith's blue dress and her long copper hair flowed down her back.

"I… I am sorry, papa. I didn't think things through. Please don't be angry with me." Her voice was barely a whisper. Bas got up and walked over.

"Oh sweetheart… I could never be angry with you. At least not for very long." He embraced her and kissed her forehead.

"Does that mean she can come with me when I go fishing now?" Aqua smiled and said. They all laughed. Terra frowned.

"There is one thing we need to know now, though."

"And what is that?" Bas smiled.

"How are we going to explain this to Saoirse when she comes to visit?"

Chapter 32

Malum was feeling more like his old self again. The slow process of stripping away the memories of all his victims was almost at an end. He still had nightmares about the golden dragon returning to judge him, but Nex had said he would soon take care of that too. He looked at himself in the mirror and found more than a few grey hairs scattering his temples, but he was still a handsome man. He had started training and doing some physical work around the castle to keep himself in shape. It still angered him that the woman had been taken away from him, but Nex had told him she would be his to play with again soon.

"You are up…" the arrogant voice of Inanis sounded behind him. He turned and saw her looking at him. Now, that was a woman to lust for. He knew he annoyed her, and it made him want her even more. She was a woman, at least in appearance, of incredible power. He wanted to harness that power, wanted to own it. He grinned at her.

"You had to come in here this early? What is the excuse to see me this time?" Her eyes flashed with anger.

"Trust me, I would be happy to find an excuse to be anywhere else, but Nex wants you in the throne room.

Now!" She quickly walked out and slammed the door behind her. Dougal must have returned from his trip south. He quickly dressed and hurried off to meet his master.

"Ah, there you are," Nex said as Malum entered the room.

"I came as quickly as I got word that you requested my presence, your highness." Malum bowed deeply before the throne where Nex was sitting. He saw Dougal standing at his right side and Inanis was over by the window looking out as she sipped from a silver goblet.

"Dougal was just reporting some rather interesting information he came by on his latest trip. Do fill him in, Dougal." Nex leaned back in his chair and smiled. It had to be good news then, or there would be bodies on the floor by now.

"There are rumors of a new lord in King Cathal Mac Conchobair's kingdom. He has bought a big piece of land and built a castle almost as big as the kings. He lives there with seven beautiful sisters and his equally beautiful wife. His name is Basilicus and his wife's name is Orelaith."

"You finally found them. I must say, excellent work." Malum was pleased but did not like the way Dougal had somehow become his superior in rank.

"They also have a daughter, but as of yet no-one has seen her. She has been kept away from the people, so no one knows how old she is or even what she looks like." Dougal refilled Nex's goblet before he continued. "They have been taking in the poor families in the surrounding lands and hiring workers to help out with different tasks. Every family that has come to live there praise them for their kindness and will not hear a bad word about them. They have been very smart in this concern."

LORE OF THE DRAGONS: ESSENCE OF A QUEEN

"He always does that, helping the weak. Only means he is going to end up with weak people working for him," Nex huffed.

"I believe that it should be easy to get close to them. And that way lure the child away from the others so she can be taken to you, your highness."

"And how do you propose that it should be done?" Malum asked with an annoyed tone.

"Through the tailor, Saoirse," Dougal replied and smiled.

"I am listening…" Nex took another sip from his goblet and looked at him expectantly.

"The young boy who used to work for her is no longer there, and she does need help around the farm, so I will go offer my services for a meal a day. Times are hard, so it's a believable enough story. If I have your permission of course…" Dougal said and bowed.

"You do. Report back once a week. Inanis, you can help clean him up so he doesn't look like a thug." She sighed and placed her goblet on the table.

"Really? Can't he even do that for himself?"

"Are you testing my patience again, Inanis? Think… Do you really want to do that?" Nex was smiling, but she knew better than to interpret that for friendliness.

"Very well… come on then, you pathetic little bug," she said as she turned abruptly and walked towards the door. Dougal winked at Malum as he passed him and whispered,

"I guess I will get some alone time with the lady Inanis…" Malum glared back at him. He needed to get his mind sorted before Dougal became too comfortable as his superior.

"I have another task for you, but first I will take care of the last few memories my cursed brother left in your mind." Malum clenched his jaw as Nex's black tendrils stretched towards him. He had been through this many times before and knew very well how painful it could be. The tendrils physically lifted him off the ground as they pierced his body and mind. A strangled cry of pain escaped his lips as they reached his mind. The last thing he saw was Nex's sadistic grin as he probed his mind with the snakelike tendrils. Then it all went black and he fell to the floor.

Dougal wasn't really listening to Inanis as she rattled on about everyone and everything she despised. He watched her as she picked up some wool clothing and threw it at him. A creature like her was everything a man like him could want. She was power, beauty and evil all wrapped into one.

"Are you listening? I said, put the clothes on! You can not go around in leather armour if you are supposed to be a farmer who has lost everything." He bowed and started pulling off his clothes. For a second, he thought he saw a glint of interest in Inanis' eyes as she looked at him stripping down.

"Do you see anything you like?" He grinned as she stared at him.

LORE OF THE DRAGONS: ESSENCE OF A QUEEN

"No, absolutely not," she replied and looked away quickly, but not before he had noticed her blushing slightly. He pulled on the brown wool-pants and slowly walked over to her.

"Whenever you want to learn more about the way we humans function, I am at your disposal, Lady Inanis. I could show you things you probably have not experienced before. Who knows… you might enjoy it," he half whispered in her ear. She turned back from the window and looked at him.

"If I want to know how you function, I can rip you open and look inside." The very fact that she could actually do that made him want her even more. She ran a long fingernail down his chest and a trickle of blood followed in its wake. When he did not react with fear, she frowned at him.

"You are a strange creature. Most of your kind would have been terrified just knowing who I truly am, but you… you like to play with fire. You enjoy the pain; it even seems to excite you. I may want to take you up on that offer…" Her piercing blue eyes curiously gazed into his brown ones. Then she pushed him to the side, "But not now. Nex is expecting you to leave for the farm. You have work to do." She walked to the door and stopped.

"Make sure this woman hires you. And lose that grin on your face; it is not one of your best features." He bowed as she turned and left his chambers.

The young man knelt down and ran his hands over the huge footprint in the mud.

"It's a dragon, there is no doubt about that. How long ago did you say it was here?" The nervous farmer fiddled with his hat.

"T-two days or so. It killed all my sheep and it torched the fields on the other side of the river. I didn't actually see it with my own eyes, but I thought it best to call you anyway."

"You did the right thing. I just wish you had sent for me earlier," the young man said as he got up and brushed the dirt off his hands.

"You look a bit on the young side. Are you sure you know what you are doing?" The farmer's wife asked as she looked at him skeptically. If he had a piece of silver for every time he heard that…

"This is not my first dragon hunt Mrs, nor will it be my last." He pulled a leather strap containing three large dragon teeth from inside his black leather armor. "I am not the dragon's tooth fairy…" He grinned. "And…" He looked over their shoulders and saw a big stocky man who was approaching them. "I do not work alone." They turned as the man reached them. He nodded quickly to the couple then turned his attention to the young man.

"What did you find, Conri?"

"It's not the biggest one I have hunted, probably another female. The bad news is, she has a two day head start on us. And you, Uncle? Did you find anything that might help us?" The older man had almost shaved his head completely, leaving only a very short, gray stubble on his head and face.

"This is the first time this valley has been attacked, so I'm guessing it's just passing through. Or it could be that it has just arrived and decided to settle down." Conri nodded and turned to the farmer.

"We will need a few sheep as bait and food and drink for tonight. Have it brought out here. Dragons are creatures of habit; if it is still in the valley, it will return here tonight." The farmer nodded and grabbed his wife's arm, pulling her along before she could protest. The two men watched as the couple walked off arguing.

"They always protest to begin with, but once the dragon is dead they cheer and can't hand over their gold fast enough," the older man said with a grin on his face.

"I don't do this for the gold, Uncle. You know that." Conri looked at him.

"I know, but it does help motivate me." His uncle laughed and started laying out several cloth covered bundles on the ground. Conri asked,

"Do you have all the herbs you need? I would hate to have a dragon only half asleep when I am sneaking up on it, like the first one I killed. Just as I was about to plunge my sword into his eye, he woke up and scorched my pants, and the back of my hair looked like I had been arguing with a barber," Conri said and pulled out his sword and started sharpening it. His uncle laughed.

"Yes, I remember. It looks better the way it is now, short like mine. No chance of it being scorched off."

"At least I'm not grey like you," Conri replied and laughed.

"I seem to have all I need here. You did remember to bring the cauldron?" his uncle asked.

"It's hanging on the saddlebag. I will go get it while you start the fire." They set about their tasks, and as nightfall came they had everything prepared. Now all they had to do was wait.

Conri had first watch and glanced at his uncle snoring away next to him. He turned eighteen last month. His aunt had wanted him to find a girl and settle down with her on his uncle's farm, but Conri didn't care much for the girls his aunt had tried to match him with. Sure they were pretty, and some even good cooks, but he had more important things to do. Well… one thing especially: hunt down and kill the dragons that were responsible for killing his parents and making him and Garbhan orphans. He had yet to see a big black male, but as far as he was concerned they were all evil. He had killed three dragons now, all female, and already had more gold than he knew what to do with. His uncle no longer had to run the farm himself as they could afford to hire as many men to do the work as they needed. Garbhan was growing more than was normal and now looked more like seven than almost five. He talked and acted so grown up for his age. Conri was grateful to his aunt for taking them in and raising Garbhan as her own. Not that he had forgotten the debt he owed to the beautiful red haired Lady Orelaith. One day he would repay her for the kindness she had shown him and his brother. And Saoirse and Bridget who had taken them in on a word from Orelaith. He remembered them fondly. He smiled at the thought of how lost he had been when Orelaith had met him just outside the town. So much had happened since the summer he left to go live with his uncle and aunt. He had been trained to use all kinds of weapons, to fight with his bare hands and hide in plain sight. His first dragon had given him such pleasure to kill that his uncle had to pull him off the creature long after it was dead. Again and again he had stabbed it, anywhere the blade would penetrate. He still remembered how its blood had burned in his eyes and the way the taste had lingered in his mouth for days. His eyesight and his reflexes had become stronger and faster after that. If it was because of the dragon blood he was unsure, but it was well needed in his hunt for these evil creatures. The first dragon's death cry… it sounded so human, it had been the cause of his nightmares since. He stacked up the fire again and leaned back letting his eyes search the darkness for any movement.

He dozed off for a moment. When the sound of the distressed sheep woke him up, he jumped up and grabbed his sword.

"Uncle, we have company…" The older man was on his feet with his sword drawn before Conri was done speaking.

"I hear it but I can't see it yet." Conri kicked sand over the campfire, putting it out.

"Let your eyes get used to the dark first. Do you think it took the bait?" he whispered as they both moved slowly towards the field where they had tied up the sheep.

"If it has, it should start feeling drowsy soon, but no jumping on its head until we are sure it is really out cold," his uncle warned him.

"Would I do such a thing? Never!" Conri pretended he was utterly shocked.

"You would and you have, but not tonight. I have a bad feeling about this one," his uncle replied as they stalked closer to the sheep.

The dragon had eaten two of the sheep by now and was starting to feel the effects of the sedatives Conri's uncle had laced the sheep's fur with. Its feet were unsteady and it was shaking its big head as if dazed. Then it fell over and struggled to get up, but it was all in vain. The more it struggled, the quicker the drug took effect. Soon it lay completely unmoving. Only its panting breath showed it was still alive. Conri started running and jumped just as the dragon raised his head.

"Conri! No!" his uncle called out distracting the dragon that sent a scorching flame past Conri hitting his uncle straight on. He burst into flames and let out an agonizing scream before falling to the ground. Conri plunged his sword deep into the creature's left eye and cried out.

"Uncle!" The dragon twitched in it's final death throes then collapsed. Conri tore off his cloak and threw it over his uncle's burning back to put out the flames. He rolled his uncle over and to his amazement found that his uncle's face was not burned, it was mostly his back and the back of his head.

"Uncle?" Conri whispered as he checked to see if he was still breathing.

"I'm not… dead yet." His uncle coughed. The young dragon slayer pulled out a water-skin and held it up to his uncle's mouth.

"Here, have some water." After a few sips, his uncle sighed and laid on his side.

"How are you feeling?" Conri asked him while he rolled

LORE OF THE DRAGONS: ESSENCE OF A QUEEN

up his cloak to put under his uncle's head.

"Medium rare." He laughed. "No, Conri, I'm just joking with you. I feel fine. Actually, I think I will go for a walk." Conri sighed in relief.

"Damn it, Uncle, you had me scared for a while there." Smoke was still coming off his uncle's back.

"No need to worry boy. I am as tough as they come. It's more like a bad sunburn."

"A sunburn, huh? You just got liquid dragon fire shot straight at you! It's a little worse than a damn sunburn." His uncle leaned up on his elbow.

"Go grab our gear and make us a new fire down here. I don't feel like moving much."

When he returned with the horses and their gear, his uncle was already sitting up and had cleared a place for a campfire.

"What took you so long?" he said and grinned.

"I had to clean up your mess first," Conri replied and threw him his backpack. Then he went off to find some firewood. When he returned, his uncle had pulled out most of the things in his pack and was still searching for something.

"What are you looking for?" Conri asked as he started stacking up the wood for a fire.

"I got a special plant from a man who had been to the

holy land. He said it did wonders for burns, but I can't seem to find it now." He poured out the rest of the contents in his bag and sorted through them. "Ah, there it is." He picked up a small piece of cloth and gently unwrapped it. It contained a strange green plant with hard pointy leaves. "This is supposed to be the best thing against burns, but I have never tried it. Let's see if it can do some magic." He broke off a leaf, squeezed a white liquid into his hand and rubbed it gently on the back of his head.

Later, when they sat drinking their tea, Conri glanced over at the dead dragon. It's purple scales reflected the light of the campfire. A set of almost white spikes ran down its neck and back, and at the tip of its tail was what looked like a cudgel.

"You better start hacking off some of those spikes and get another tooth for your chain before the locals arrive." Conri nodded and pulled out his knife to start the grueling task of butchering the huge creature. As the light of a new day came creeping into the valley, Conri torched what remained of the dragon. A new tooth was hanging on the strap around his neck, and the extra horse was weighed down by the parts they had harvested off the dragon. Conri glanced at his uncle who was sleeping next to the campfire. It could have gone a lot worse than it did. If his uncle had been killed, he would never have forgiven himself. Once they got paid for this job, he would head south to follow a rumor of dragons seen there. But this time he would go alone. All he had to do now was convince his uncle to let him.

Chapter 33

"I don't know any other way to approach this. I say we let Saoirse in on our secret," Orelaith said and put her hand around her cup.

"We have no idea what kind of reaction we will get from her. She may be fine with it once the initial shock has passed, but Bridget is another matter altogether. There is something about that woman that tells me she is more than just a simple maid." Vig shook her head.

"But how can we tell Saoirse and not tell Bridget? She will most likely be coming with Saoirse to see us. She may be old, but she is not blind. She can see Rionach is not a child any more. How can we explain that without telling her who we are?" Tempest got up and walked around while she was talking.

"What if we say it was a sorcerer who did it? At least that way we will be pointing all attention away from ourselves," Terra said and looked at Bas. Vig rubbed her chin.

"That may very well work. None of the people in our town know her as our daughter, not even the maids at the castle itself. Yes, I think that is a great idea." Bas looked around at the others. "Do we all agree?" He got a collective "Yes" from the others. "It is settled then. But the story of how it happened has to be clear too."

"I could probably come up with something." Terra smiled. "I am, after all, the keeper of our history."

After Vig had examined Rionach, she came to the conclusion that Rionach was physically and mentally an adult. The queen's memories had caught up with her and she had the intellect to challenge Vig in any discussion.

"It's remarkable how comfortable she is as an adult. One would have thought she would find the transition from toddler to young woman harder, but that is where the queen's powers close the gap," Vig said thoughtfully. Bas smiled and said,

"She is amazing. Only a few weeks ago, she was just this sweet little bundle of smiles and copper curls. And now… she is a beautiful young woman, wise beyond her years." Orelaith seemed thoughtful and Bas put his hand on hers. "What is it my dear? You seem to be miles away." Orelaith smiled weakly at him.

"I just remembered something my mother said. I didn't think much of it at the time, but now it has become more true to me than it ever was to her."

"And what was that?" he asked softly.

"Turn your back for a short time, and your children are all grown up. I just feel like I have been cheated somehow.

LORE OF THE DRAGONS: ESSENCE OF A QUEEN

There are so many things that I will never share with her, and things that I will have to tell her years before I thought I would. Is it the same way with you dragons? I mean, when are you considered to be adults?" Serovita smiled and said, "From a whelp hatches to the day it is considered to be a young adult is a mere hundred years or so. You must remember that our kind can easily become thousands of years old." Orelaith raised an eyebrow.

"Thousands of years? Easy? I have actually never thought of that before. And how long till you are considered to be... eh, mature enough to... have whelps?" Vig nodded.

"I have considered this too, Orelaith. I know what you are thinking about, and I do believe we... That is, you need to have a talk with your daughter. The young men who work in the castle are falling all over themselves trying to please her. She ignores them, of course," Vig quickly added when she saw Bas' reaction. "But I still think it is time you explained a few things to her." "We still don't know if she will take after you or her father when it comes to finding a mate. Until she is able to remove the binding the queen put on us, it will be fatal for her to conceive a child," Terra added.

"Mama!" Rionach burst into the counseling chamber. "Oh, you are all here." She blushed a little as they all looked at her in surprise.

"I have made a new discovery." She smiled and knelt down at her mother's side. She was smiling widely and took her mother's hand.

"Oh sweetheart, you really shouldn't be trying out things without Vig there to guide you. We talked about that."

"I know and I didn't, I promise. I was just trying out my ability to shift to dragon form, and that is when it happened. But I think it's better if I show you, since you are all here." Vig was frowning at her, obviously not too pleased. Rionach got up and walked over to the open part of the room.

"Now remember, I have only done this once, so I am not sure if it will work again, but here goes…" She closed her eyes in deep concentration and stretched out her arms. They all gasped as her delicate golden wings slowly unfolded from her back. When she spread them out, they almost touched the walls on both sides. She opened her eyes and smiled widely at them.

"Isn't it amazing? I had no idea I could do this!" Vig got up and walked around her.

"Intriguing. How did you… oh, never mind. It is truly remarkable how you can control the transformation in such a manner." They all seemed impressed over her new discovery, but Orelaith was concerned.

"You must promise me you will never do that so anyone can see." Rionach nodded.

"Of course, mama, you know I wouldn't. But isn't it wonderful?" Orelaith sighed and smiled at her.

"Yes it is, my dear." Vig was examining Rionach's back where the wings were protruding from her skin.

"Can you fold them up just as easily?" She nodded and folded them up so quickly it was hard to see how she did it.

"Can I go fishing with Aqua and Tempest tonight then?"

LORE OF THE DRAGONS: ESSENCE OF A QUEEN

Rionach asked hopefully and looked from her mother to her father. Orelaith turned and looked at Bas.

"What do you think, my dear?" Bas drummed his fingers on the table.

"If I say yes… it is on one condition; we all go together." Rionach ran over and hugged him.

"Oh papa, thank you. It is going to be so much fun!"

"And one more thing, you will let Vig do a thorough examination of you." He added.

"Of course papa," Rionach replied and pulled Vig off with her. Aqua was smiling widely and Luna likewise.

"Oh, it is going to be so much fun!" Solis was clapping her hands.

"This is going to be an interesting night…" Terra sighed.

Saoirse was just closing her shop when a man approached her.

"Excuse me milady, but do you know where a man could find work around here?" She turned and saw a man dressed in worn down wool clothing. His dark hair was cut close to his scalp and he seemed to be limping a little. He did not meet her eyes, so she took him for a servant of some kind.

"What kind of work are you looking for?" she asked and locked the door behind her.

"I was a farmer before the raiders burned it down along with my family, so any kind of hard labor I can do." He was tall and looked strong, so Saoirse was a little skeptical.

"How long ago was this?" she asked.

"About three months, but I found work on the neighboring farm until a few weeks ago. He had to let me go then because his son got married and they would have another mouth to feed. I have traveled south since then, finding work wherever I could." He fiddled with his scarf and Saoirse was reminded of how Orelaith had helped her when she was in a similar situation.

"I might know of someone looking for a farmhand. The pay is low and the work is hard, but you do get a dry place to sleep and several meals a day. Are you interested?"

"Oh yes, milady. I haven't seen a full meal in weeks. Who is it I need to talk to?" She smiled at him.

"You're already talking to her. I lost my farmhand a while back and have not found anyone to replace him, until now. I am heading back to the farm, so you can grab those bundles over there and follow me." The man bowed and seemed almost in tears.

"Oh thank you, milady, thank you so much. I will work really hard." Saoirse put her hand on his shoulder.

"There are a few things first. My name is Saoirse, so please stop calling me lady. It is only a few years ago that I was in your shoes, so no need for titles. There may be some catching up to do as I have been spending most of my time working in the shop, and only the children and my maid have been tending to the farm."

"I will catch up quickly, my la… Saoirse." He smiled at her.

"We better get you some new clothes too. I wouldn't want people to think I don't take care of my workers," she said and looked at his shirt that had several rips in it.

"You are most kind, my la…Saoirse." They walked in silence for a while and Saoirse nodded at a few people they passed on their way towards the gates.

"I completely forgot to ask," Saoirse said as they approached the farm, "What name do you go by?" He smiled, and for the first time since they met, he looked her in the eye. "My name is Dougal."

Over the next few weeks, Rionach became the talk of the castle. Her kindness and friendly nature won the hearts of everyone living within the walls. Orelaith was getting used to having a teenage daughter, but worried about Rionach not understanding the danger of leading on the men who were currently falling all over themselves trying to gain attention points with her. When Orelaith took it up with her, Rionach just laughed.

"Oh mama, I know what they are after, but trust me when

I say they will be getting nothing from me. You forget I have the queen's memories and even some of yours. I know what most human men think when they are around me. Their thoughts are so easy to read, it's like picking leaves in the autumn wind." Orelaith frowned.

"You can actually read their thoughts? I did not know that was one of your abilities. Does Vig know you can do this?" Rionach winked at her mother.

"No, and I would like it to stay that way. I have gotten out of a lot of trouble with her because of it." Orelaith crossed her arms.

"I bet you have. But sweetheart, she needs to know so she can chart the powers you possess and teach you how to control them." Rionach's shoulders dropped and she looked at her mother with big puppy eyes.

"Oh mama, do we have to tell her? She is going to know when I haven't done my homework." She pouted. "And now that Saoirse is coming to visit soon, I don't want to be stuck doing homework all day." Orelaith looked at her daughter strictly, but she soon crumbled under her pleading gaze.

"Oh, very well. But only for a few days after they have arrived. Then you will tell Vig that you have discovered something new." Rionach smiled widely and gave her mother a quick hug.

"I promise I will tell her then." She turned and ran towards the door.

"Where are you going now?" Orelaith shouted after her.

LORE OF THE DRAGONS: ESSENCE OF A QUEEN

"Riding with Luna and Solis. See you at dinner, mama," she called back. Then she was gone. Orelaith picked up some clothes from her bed and started putting them away in her closet. Her daughter had just told her she could read minds, and Orelaith wasn't all that shocked. She laughed to herself. Most mothers would have been utterly terrified by that kind of news. She now realized how wonderfully strange her life had become.

Bridget was not too pleased with Saoirse's choice to take on Dougal as a farmhand. There was just something about him she did not trust. He was a good worker and knew his way around animals and farm equipment, so he probably had some experience from farm work, but the scars on his hands and face were not the kind you got from working the land or tending to livestock. She knew he was keeping secrets from them, maybe because she had some secrets of her own. The way he would smile when he thought no one saw him or how he would sneak out some nights and not come back before dawn. She had mentioned it once to Saoirse, but she had just laughed and said that Bridget had to stop worrying and that it was just her imagination. So she had said no more but kept her eye on him at all times. The children didn't like him much either. She suspected he beat the animals when no one was looking because as soon as he came near them, they shied away from him. He had been with them three weeks when they got word that Orelaith and Bas would be coming to see them. She wondered what they would make of Dougal. Bas should be able to see who he really was. If not, she would just have to make him see.

Orelaith, Bas, Vig and Serovita were gathered in a moonlit clearing a short ride from the castle. They had already packed their things on the black and the white mare.

"Are you sure this will work, Vig?" Orelaith asked, concerned about the horses. "I would hate to scare them if they wake up in mid-flight. They could panic and hurt themselves or us."

"No, that won't happen. I will tie off the knot so that it will need to be opened to undo it. Bas, you need to pay close attention to what I am doing when I cast the web of tendrils. Are you ready?" Bas nodded and put his hand on Vig's shoulder. Serovita placed a hand on her other shoulder and Vig placed one hand on each horse's nose and closed her eyes. Within seconds, both the horses were asleep on their feet. "You saw what I did. Do you think you can undo it?" Vig asked Bas.

"Yes, it is a reasonably simple knot. I shouldn't have any problems."

"Then off you go." Vig gave Orelaith a quick hug then shifted to dragon form. "And remember what I said about scouting out a route back. You don't want to let on that you don't usually travel by land." Vig flapped her delicate white wings.

"Noted," Bas said and transformed quickly, helped Orelaith up on his back and picked up the horses with his front paws.

"See you in a few days," Orelaith said and waved goodbye as Bas flapped his wings and flew off through the night.

They landed in the meadow they always used and Bas gently set the horses down. Orelaith jumped off and checked on them.

"They seem to be fine, but I guess we won't know for certain until you have undone the knots. They weren't too heavy for you, were they?" She looked over at him as he pulled on a shirt.

"No, I could easily have carried another two," he said and winked at her. She laughed.

"Not unless you grew another set of paws." He grabbed her waist and pulled her close.

"Oh, what I could do with another set of paws." He laughed in her ear.

"Bas! Not now. We need to wake these poor horses." She giggled. He reluctantly released her and gently undid the knots that kept the horses asleep. First one and then the other. Orelaith used her newfound ability to soothe their frantic minds, and soon the horses were grazing happily in the field around them. She watched them and smiled, happy to know they had not suffered from the trip. She turned and saw Bas stalking around her with a grin on his lips.

"Bas... what are you doing?"

"Stalking a fair lady all alone in the woods. A dragon has got her scent and is getting ready to pounce on its unsuspecting prey." She laughed.

"Oh no! What is a poor lady to do?" She walked backwards, putting some space between them.

"Run..." he whispered and crouched down. She laughed, but only got about three strides before he pounced and knocked her over. They tumbled around in the long grass, laughing. Soon they lay still under the big full moon and he stroked away a curl of red hair from her face.

"Are you happy, my carus?" he said and looked into her eyes.

"Very much so. Things have not transpired as I would ever have imagined they could, but one thing is certain: life with you is never boring." She smiled back at him. "But what does carus mean? This is the second time you have called me that... What language is it? Dragon... ish?"

"Dragon-ish?" He laughed. "Yes, it is. The correct term would be dragoul, or tongue of dragons. As for the word's meaning, it means beloved, or something like that. It's hard to find a good word in your tongue to describe it without losing some of its meaning." She rested her head on his chest, and together, they watched the sun slowly coming up over the surrounding hills.

Chapter 34

"They are here! Mother! Orelaith and Bas are coming!" Blathnat came running into the house with her brother Faolàn right behind her. Saoirse smiled.

"Wonderful. Go find Bridget and tell her they have arrived." She wiped her hands on her apron and walked out the door. Dougal came out from the barn and stared at them as they came trotting down the road to the farm. Orelaith jumped off her horse and embraced Saoirse,

"It's so good to see you again, my dear friend. I hope all is well with you and the children?" Saoirse smiled at her.

"It is. My shop is going so well I have had to hire an apprentice to keep up with demand. And as you can see, the children are growing like weeds." She smiled at Bas as he climbed the steps and gave her a big hug.

"Saoirse, it is good to see you again. And where is Bridget hiding? We have brought her a little something as thanks for all the times she has taken so good care of us here."

"She went to town to buy some food for our dinner tonight. The children just ran into town to help her carry the goods back and let her know you have arrived." Dougal came strolling over and nodded to them.

"You must be Orelaith and Basilicus. Saoirse speaks so highly of you both. It is thanks to you that she took me in. What you did for her, milady… you are such a kind person." Orelaith smiled quickly.

"Thank you, but most of the work to get where she is today is all on her. She worked so hard and it paid off." There was something familiar about him, but she could not recall where she had seen him before.

"I don't like him for some reason. I can't put my finger on it, but I don't think he can be trusted," Bas sent to her.

"What a welcome sight!" Bridget and the children came walking down the road leading to the house.

"Bridget, it is wonderful to see you again. You are well, I hope?" Orelaith said and smiled at her.

"Oh, well enough for my age, I guess. A few aches and pains, but that comes from hard work I am proud to say." The children ran past them into the house with a few things they had carried for Bridget. "Well, I better get on with the lunch. It won't cook itself," she said. She patted Bas on his shoulder and walked into the house.

"I will take care of the horses for you," Dougal said and took hold of the reins.

"I will come with you. These horses are specially trained and need a certain treatment." Bas said and followed Dougal to the stables while Orelaith walked into the house with Saoirse and Bridget.

LORE OF THE DRAGONS: ESSENCE OF A QUEEN

"Is there any chance you can take some time off from the shop for a few days or so?" Orelaith asked as they sat around the dinner table that evening.

"I think so. My new apprentice is doing excellent work, and she has proven to be a reliable person. She has a room above the shop and opens it every morning. She would be so proud if I gave her a chance to prove herself like that, and I would love to spend some time with you while you are here." Saoirse smiled. Dougal got up and asked.

"I was wondering if it's ok that I take a trip into town, if there is nothing else you need me for tonight? I met an old friend who wanted to catch up."

"Of course, Dougal. You have been working so hard, some time off is well deserved." He got up and bid them all a goodnight before he left.

"We had something else in mind than just staying here at the farm…" Bas winked at her. Saoirse looked at him and asked.

"What do you mean?" Orelaith took her hands and smiled.

"How would you like to come and stay with us at our home for a few days?" Saoirse's jaw dropped and the kids started jumping up and down. She looked at Bridget then back at Orelaith.

"Really? But what about the children and Bridget?"

"They are coming too, of course. What do you say Bridget? Would you like to come and inspect our kitchens to see if they are good enough?" Bridget nodded and replied,

"I would be honored, but what about the animals? They will need to be taken care of." Bas smiled,

"I have some men from our home coming to take care of them. It was already arranged before we left as we didn't know you had hired a farmhand, but he can probably show them what to do once they arrive." Saoirse gave Orelaith a quick hug.

"I have to talk to my apprentice and I want to take some clothes and oh… but we don't have any horses." Bas laughed.

"Relax, Saoirse. Transport has been arranged, so no need to worry about that. And we don't leave until my men get here, so we probably won't be leaving until tomorrow afternoon at the earliest." Bridget got up.

"I better get to bed now. I have a hundred things to take care of in the morning if we are going on a long trip. And children, you need to go to bed too. We have a long trip ahead of us, and you will need to help me tomorrow." Blathnat and Faolàn complained, but knew better than to argue with Bridget, so they marched off to bed.

"Oh Orelaith, I am so looking forward to this. It's going to be wonderful to see all your sisters again, Bas. And little Rionach, she must have gotten so big since the last time I saw her."

LORE OF THE DRAGONS: ESSENCE OF A QUEEN

"Oh, you have no idea." Orelaith sighed.

"About that… there is something we need to tell you," Bas said and leaned forward. "You know how we haven't talked much about our home or about our family? There is a reason for that. For as long as I can remember, our family has been under a curse. It has not affected us for centuries, but a few weeks ago, something happened." Bas picked up his cup and sipped some tea.

"I knew something was going on, but I had no idea… You can trust me to keep this to myself," Saoirse said and squeezed Orelaith's hand.

"I know you will. That is one of the reasons we have decided to let you in on our secret." Bas smiled at her.

"I will not go into details, but as I said, something happened a few weeks back that affected Rionach. Since she was a baby, she has grown faster than most children, and she spoke full sentences already when she was two. Now it seems her body has caught up with her mind. I don't really know how to put this, but she now looks like she is sixteen, not three." Bas and Orelaith looked at Saoirse waiting for her reaction. First she frowned, then looked at them both as if they were joking, but as their words sunk in, her jaw dropped.

"Really? But how can she… that's impossible, isn't it?" Orelaith smiled softly.

"That was my reaction too at first. But there's no denying that she is no longer a little girl, but a young woman. She shows no signs of being a child in a woman's body.

Although a little immature at times, she has a greater intellect than most adults I know." Saoirse shook her head.

"This... must have been so hard on you both. However have you been able to handle this? You poor people." She embraced Orelaith and pulled Bas into the hug as well.

"We are used to things that are out of the ordinary, but this was strange even for us." Orelaith held her friend out at arm's length. "We were a little worried how you would react, but I see our fear was misplaced."

"We wanted to tell you first, but it is obvious we need to tell Bridget and the children too. Do you have any idea how they will react?"

"I don't know how the children will react. You will have to find that out when you tell them," Bridget said and stepped into the room. "As for me..." The old woman walked around them with an expressionless face. They all stared at her as she sat down in the chair next to Bas. She looked from one to the other while she poured herself a cup of tea. After taking a few sips she put her cup down.

"I have known all along that you were more than you let on. I may look old, but with years comes wisdom. If this information fell into the wrong hands, it would prove disastrous to everyone involved." There was a sharpness in her eyes that none of them had seen before. "I want you to know, of all the people you could have granted insight into your secret, Saoirse and I are the ones you can truly trust to keep it." Orelaith sighed in relief and smiled.

"Thank you, Bridget. It means a lot to us."

LORE OF THE DRAGONS: ESSENCE OF A QUEEN

"Oh I know a thing or two about keeping a secret, so don't you worry, your faith in me is not misplaced." The old woman smiled and picked up her cup again.

"I thought you were heading to bed." Bas winked at her.

"I was, but I remembered something I wanted to talk to you two about. Especially you, Bas." Saoirse looked at her and was about to say something, but Bridget stopped her.

"I know what you are going to say, but let an old woman speak her mind." She turned to Bas. "It concerns this new farmhand, Dougal." She told them what she had observed, how the animals were afraid of him, how the children kept away from him and all the scars on his body that she did not believe came from farm work. "I just do not trust him. After the attack on Lady Orelaith some years back, I have been much more distrustful of strangers, and he's not what he says he's. I would bet my life on it." Saoirse huffed.

"Bridget, really, I have not seen any of the things you mentioned. Given I am not here most days so I can't be certain. Maybe he has a few secrets, but we all know that having secrets does not mean you are a bad person." Bas frowned.

"I am sorry, Saoirse, but I must agree with Bridget on this one. He does not have a kind hand with animals, that much was clear when he tended to the horses. And I saw some of the scars you are talking about, Bridget. You are right. They don't come from working on a farm, but from battle. He may have lived on a farm as a child, but that was a long time ago. He's a soldier now and has been for a long time." Bridget got one of her I told you so looks on her face as she picked up her tea and took a sip.

"What should I do? I can't just turn him out..." Saoirse said.

"I have thought of that. Right now, do nothing. Wait until you get back from your visit to make any decision. As for the animals, my men will take good care of them and we will not leave until they arrive," Bas said as he looked at her. "Do you think you can do that without letting him know what is going on?" Orelaith squeezed Saoirse's hand. She nodded and smiled nervously.

"I think so. But I better stay away from him all the same."

"Now, we have a trip to plan for..." Bridget said and smiled at them.

Dougal hurried through the muddy streets to his meeting with Inanis. He finally had some news for Nex and was hoping that he would soon have mucked out his last stall. Smelling like a farm animal was not scoring him any points with the local wenches, and he wanted out as soon as possible. No one moved out of his way when he entered the inn either. How he hated this assignment. At the usual table in the back sat the cloaked figure of the Lady Inanis. He slid in on the seat across from hers.

"Give me the news you have for Nex, and be quick about it. This place stinks worse than a servant's armpit, and I

LORE OF THE DRAGONS: ESSENCE OF A QUEEN

want to leave before it settles in my clothes," she said in her usual scornful tone of voice.

"Milady Inanis, how good it is to see you again." He slapped a barmaid's behind and ordered a jug of ale.

"The Lady Orelaith and Lord Basilicus arrived at the farm this morning. They asked Saoirse to take a few days off."

"Only the two of them?" Inanis asked.

"Yes, and the black and the white mares they came on." She frowned.

"What of the child?" He shrugged and tossed a coin to the barmaid who handed him his ale.

"I don't think she will be coming this time. I will keep an eye on them and let you know when they get ready to leave. Then all we have to do is follow them back."

Inanis got up, being careful not to touch anything.

"If that is all, I will head back to Nex and let him know what is going on. I can be reached again sometime tomorrow." As she passed him, he grabbed her wrist.

"Why don't you stay and have a few drinks with me? There's no rush getting the news to Nex. It's not like they are going anywhere." She stared at him.

"Do you have something wrong with your hearing? I said I want to get out of here quickly. And I would never so much as touch anything in this place, let alone drink any of the sewage they serve here. And..." She snatched back her wrist. "You forget your place, pest. Touch me like that again, and you will be in need of new arms." He put his hands up defensively.

"Point taken. My humblest apologies, Lady Inanis. For a moment, I was blinded by your beauty. It will not happen again."

"It better not." She glared at him then hurried out of the inn. He stared after her, smiling. She would be his someday. Or more likely, he would be hers.

The following day seemed like a mad hurry to get everything ready for their trip. Dougal had come back as they were eating breakfast. He looked like he had been sleeping in a ditch. The inn had taken most of his gold in drink, and he smelled like an old drunk. He had excused himself and gone straight to his room. Saoirse was glad he did; that way, at least she wouldn't have to deal with him.

Bas' men had arrived around midday, and Bridget had shown them what needed to be done around the farm. Bas had gotten four more horses for Bridget, Saoirse and her children, and after lunch they were already packed for the journey to the castle. Saoirse had gone into town with Bas to talk to her apprentice and also to pick up some clothes. Bas had also acquired a horse specifically so the animals wouldn't be straining under the weight of all the things Bridget had made up her mind they needed. "You know, we will get there tomorrow, and we do have food at home," Bas said and smiled at Bridget. She glanced at him over her shoulder as she stuffed another bag of food in the saddlebags.

"One should never travel on an empty stomach. And I know how these children eat, the appetites of grown men they have. There is nothing worse than a hungry child." She took a step back with her hands on her hips. "I know what I'm doing here." She looked in a saddlebag and saw there was still some room in it to fit another cheese.

"If you decide to bring any more things than you already have, we will be in need of another horse." Bas laughed.

"Bridget, we don't need any more things now. I brought some gold, so if we need any more things, we can get them on the way there," Saoirse said and fastened the cape around Blathnat's shoulders.

"There. I do believe we are all ready," she said and put her arms around both her children.

"Just going to run over a few things with the men and we will be off," Bas said and walked over to the four men standing outside the stable.

Dougal came out and stared at them as they mounted up.

"Milady Saoirse, I didn't know that you were heading out. May I inquire how long you will be gone?" She tightened the reins but did not look at him.

"Oh, I'm not sure, but maybe as long as a week. My apprentice will be taking care of the shop and Lord Basilicus has arranged that these four men will be taking care of the animals."

"Oh... so you won't be needing my work then?" Dougal smiled at her.

"And where do you go on this much deserved vacation?" Saoirse looked up and sent him a quick smile.

"The Lady Orelaith and Lord Basilicus have invited us to come visit them for a few days."

"That sounds wonderful. It seems Lord Basilicus has thought of everything. I was hoping to get some days off to go see my friend and his family. He's traveling back today and wanted me to go with him. I didn't think I would be able to go, but now it seems I am not needed here." Dougal needed to think quickly. He had to get a horse and follow them so he could finally get their location and tell Nex where they lived.

"How nice for you. By all means, do go stay with your friend. And here..." She pulled out a small pouch and tossed it to Dougal. "This should cover your wages and then some."

"Milady, that is most gracious of you. I bid you all a safe journey." Bas started off and the others followed behind. Dougal hurried towards the town to see if Inanis had returned and to get his armor and weapons from the room he had in the inn. He needed to hurry if he was to catch up with them.

Chapter 35

The forest was near impenetrable where Conri had made himself a camp for the night. He wore a thick animal hide as a cloak and had made a nice big campfire, so he was not cold. A wild rabbit was turning on a spit over the flames and he was sipping some warm tea that his aunt had insisted he take with him. His uncle had not been too happy about him going off on his own, but he had injured his leg worse than he had first thought on their last dragon hunt. Conri had unpacked the bags containing the herbs that his uncle used, and he carefully followed the instructions his uncle had given him on how to prepare the drug that would take down a dragon. There had been a few dragon sightings in this area, but they differed from any of the other sightings he had heard of. Of all the sightings rumored here, there was no mention of any attacks on livestock or people, not one single attack on any farm or crops. It seemed strange to him, as if these dragons were more like protectors than carnivorous attackers destroying everything in their way like the others he had encountered. But as far as he was concerned there was no difference between them. The only good dragon was a dead one. It still made him shiver when he thought of the night the big black dragon had made him and his brother orphans. He swore then that he would kill every dragon he could find until they were nothing more than scary tales to tell badly behaved children. The mixtures were finished and he wrapped them up in separate bags, one dose in each. Once he was satisfied, he carefully washed his hands, not wanting to knock himself out because of carelessness. He stuffed the portioned bags back into his pack and sat down. The rabbit was done and he peeled off a large chunk of meat and ate in silence. He almost choked on his food when a cry sounded over his head, and he looked up just as the silhouette of a dragon passed in front of the full moon. Quickly he stomped out the fire and grabbed his sword. He kept his eyes to the sky and headed in the direction the beast had flown. His feet did not trip over the countless roots as he ran, and his eyes could see through the darkness better than any other man. Bathing in dragon's blood has some benefits, it seems. He slowed down and listened, but the dragon appeared to be gone now. He was fast, but not fast enough to keep up with a dragon in flight, so he turned back. As he did, he saw the moon reflecting on a lake through the trees and decided to move his camp closer so his horse could drink. He figured he'd need to clean up a little too. Being on the road like this had made him smell ripe enough to send anyone fleeing. He took his bearings and not long after he returned with his gear and horse. Once the horse had had its fill of water, he stripped down and waded into the water. The water was not as cold as he had thought. He let himself sink into the dark silence below. The moon was visible from under the surface and he kicked off from the soft sand, sending himself gliding up through the water. He swam towards the shore and stopped when the water was about waist deep. It felt good to be out on the road again, and he liked being on his own. Not that his uncle was hard to be around, quite the opposite actually. His cheery disposition and constant chatter made it hard for him to think dark thoughts, but sometimes he just needed to be silent and have only the sounds of nature around him. His horse neighed and moved restlessly.

"What is it, old girl? Do you sense something?" He started towards the bank. He more felt it than heard it, something was there with them. The water splashed behind him and he turned quickly, but saw only ripples in the water a few feet away. If something was lurking in the deep, his best chance was to stay completely still. But what came out of the water right next to him was the last thing he had expected.

"Is everything ready for tomorrow?" Vig asked Solis, who was humming to herself as she picked through her food.

"Oh yes, Serovita made some beautiful new furniture for the three rooms that Terra made. And I flew into town and got some new bedspreads and picked some flowers to put in the rooms." "How much do you think they told Saoirse and Bridget?" Tempest asked.

"I really don't know. But we must tread carefully until we find out. Aqua," Vig said and sent her a stern look. "You need to stop eating with your hands. We do have knives and spoons, you know." Aqua picked up a piece of fish with her left hand and waved it around while she talked.

"And why do I have to use those, those… things? It's easier to just pick it up with my hands. I really don't see the point."

"We have to keep up the appearance of being ladies, and ladies do not eat with their hands, Aqua. Besides, you don't have to get your hands dirty or greasy if you use the knife and spoon." Luna picked up a piece of bread and tossed it past Vig to Aqua.

"Luna! You are not helping." Vig turned her head and glared at Luna who was sitting with her feet on the table.

"You need to loosen up a little, Vig. It's only us here, so no one can judge us for eating like pigs. Toss me a piece of fish, Aqua."

"Don't you dare, Aqua! If she wants it, she can ask nicely." A big piece of fried fish hit Vig in the face, slowly slid down her cheek, then dropped down on the table. Everyone froze and stared wide-eyed at Vig. Her face was turning bright red and they all knew an explosion of words was imminent. Everyone waited in silence; all that is, except Luna who started laughing so hard that she almost fell off her chair. Vig grabbed the fish that had hit her in the face and threw it full force at Aqua who ducked just in time sending it past her and hitting Tempest square in the face. You could have heard a pin drop as Tempest slowly got up and wiped her face off. Then she picked up a fist full of greens and threw them at Vig, hitting Terra, Serovita and Luna. "Food-fight!" Luna shouted and they all started throwing whatever they could get their hands on at each other. After a little while they ran out of things to throw but by now they were all laughing out loud.

"Wait a minute, where is Rionach?" Vig asked and looked around.

LORE OF THE DRAGONS: ESSENCE OF A QUEEN

"Oh she just flew off to have a dip in the small lake in the woods to the east." Solis smiled and wiped some fish off her face.

"Ah that is fine, she should be ok there. It's pretty secluded and I don't think she will get into any trouble there…"

The young woman stared at him with her big green eyes. Slowly she walked around him, her long red hair clinging to her breast. Conri just stared at her as she circled him, too shocked to speak or even move. He felt a little exposed but then again so was she. But that did not seem to bother her as she looked at him curiously. She was the most beautiful woman he had ever laid eyes on and he stared in awe at her waist long hair and silky smooth skin when she stopped right in front of him. Who was she? A woodland goddess? The full moon reflected off her skin, hair and eyes and gave her an eerie glow. She was almost as tall as he was, with a fine muscle toned body, so fine in fact that he could find nothing wrong, she was almost too perfect.

"Who are you?" she demanded to know. The tone of voice she used, indicated she was of high birth or at least used to commanding people. Maybe she was a goddess…

"I… I am Conri of the northern lands." he replied weakly and she circled him again. For some strange reason he felt like he was being hunted. He did not like that feeling.

"And who are you?" he said with a strong and equally demanding tone. The look she sent him made him physically cringe. There was pure power, flashing in her green eyes. She did not answer him but instead seemed to be studying the scars that criss crossed his chest, back, and arms as she continually circled him. She stopped in front of him and gently touched the large scar that had been inflicted on him by the first dragon he killed. "So broken," she whispered. He felt a tingling sensation as she traced the length of the scar with her finger. He could not take his eyes off her face, with the high cheekbones, the big green eyes and the pink, full lips. Damn! He needed to snap out of it. He reached for her wrist, but before he knew what had happened, he was on his back in the water with her hand being the one thing holding his head above water. He gasped and squirmed but found he had no control whatsoever.

"Stop fighting me." He heard her words, but her lips did not move. Who or what was she? She moved further out in the lake, gently pulling him with her until the water reached her shoulders. She let go of his neck and he put his feet down. She was standing right in front of him now, staring at him. He must have blinked because suddenly she had her arms around him, both palms placed firmly on his back as she looked into his eyes.

"Close your eyes, Conri of the northern lands," she whispered. He held his breath as she came in close like that. He had not had time for women before, and the emotions he was feeling now were more than just a little overpowering. "Close your eyes…" As he found himself reluctantly complying to her words, golden tendrils of light and warmth ensnared him, curling around his entire body. Like being wrapped in a warm soft blanket after freezing rain, he felt his skin prickling. And then she kissed him. It was as if the golden tendrils went through his chest and out through his back, through his skin on all sides and exploded in every pore. It would be wrong to say everything went black; it was

LORE OF THE DRAGONS: ESSENCE OF A QUEEN

more like everything went golden.

His head fell backwards and he went limp in her arms, so she gently pulled him towards the shore where his camp was. He was too heavy for an ordinary girl to carry out of the water, but then again, Rionach was no ordinary girl. Laying him down on his cloak, she stacked up some wood for a campfire, then glanced at him and smiled. His chest was rising and falling slowly as he slept. She blew a small flame into the fire and it lit up, making the wood crackle. Running her hand over his chest, she smiled, pleased with her own work. The scars were gone and he seemed to be whole again, at least on the outside. She had sensed so much pain in him, though. His mind was emotionally damaged, but she dared not tamper with it. Not feeling she truly mastered that skill yet, she was worried she would do more harm than good. He was a little chilled, so she used her dragon breath to gently heat him up. It was getting pretty easy to control the strength of the heat now. She studied his face, there was something about him that appeared familiar. It could be he was the man she had been dreaming about. He was so... beautiful. Not like the men in the castle, with their weak minds and lust infested psyches. Not that she had been unaware of how her closeness to him in the water had made him feel, but this was different. He was different from them in so many ways, as if there was some dragon in him. It had pulled her in, almost overwhelmed her. She watched him sleep for a few hours, studying him and storing mental images in her mind. She gathered some wood and stacked the fire a few times. She knew it was getting late but couldn't tear herself away. Suddenly, a cry sounded overhead and she looked up through the trees. Luna was out looking for her. She leaned over and gently kissed his lips,

"I will return tomorrow. Wait for me." Then she wrapped the cloak around him and walked away.

"What have you been up to? Vig was about to have a fit when you weren't back after dinner," Luna asked as they flew side by side back to the castle.

"Not much, just having a quick swim in the lake," Rionach called back.

"Just a quick swim, huh?" Luna grinned widely at her. "The fact that a quick swim took you a few hours wouldn't happen to have anything to do with a certain young handsome man, would it?" She chuckled and looked at Rionach. She blushed, turning the golden scales in her face a deep copper.

"I have no idea what you are talking about…" Luna burst out laughing.

"You really are a terrible liar, kiddo. We both know who I'm talking about, but you can relax, I won't tell your mother or father of your little date. Or the others for that matter. But I thought you would want someone who you could talk to about the new things you are feeling." Luna winked at her. They landed on the porch outside the counseling room, and Rionach shifted and picked up her dress from the banister.

"I had no intention of staying so long. At first I was just

curious, but as I got close, I saw how broken he was. I only took care of the outside scars, but his mind and heart... oh Luna, he carries so much pain and emotional hurt inside, it's a wonder he's still able to function," she said as she pulled the dress over her head. Luna frowned.

"You should probably ask Vig a hypothetical question about restoring a human mind that has been scarred by bad memories. But be prepared, she is going to talk for hours. You should do that in the morning before your lessons." Rionach sighed.

"You're probably right about that, she does tend to go on forever when you ask her a simple question." They walked in through the open doors and down the stairs on their way to the kitchen.

"I had the cook set some food away for you. I thought you would be hungry when you got back," Luna said as they walked into the kitchen. Rionach sat quietly as she ate, obviously in deep thought. Luna smiled as she watched her, knowing very well what she was thinking about.

"You like him, don't you?" she asked.

"He seemed ok, I guess. I felt sorry for him mostly." Rionach said without looking up from her food.

"I think you are forgetting who you're talking to, kiddo. I was the first one to see the love growing between your mother and father. I know that it is more than just pity you feel for this young man. So why don't you just tell me what you find so fascinating about him. You can have your pick out of all the young men in the castle, so why this one? What sets him apart from the rest?" Rionach blushed a little. There was no point in hiding her fascination with the young man from Luna, as it appeared she already knew.

"I don't quite know. I could feel him as I flew over his camp and noticed he was running below me trying to keep up. So I dove down into the lake and waited for him to catch up so I could take a closer look at him. I don't know why, but I felt like he was pulling me in with invisible strings and as he… stripped off and walked into the lake, I could barely hold myself back. I have never seen so… much of a man before, and I found it immensely alluring. I just wanted to touch his skin to see what it felt like, but the strange feeling was almost overwhelming once I got that close. It was as if someone else was partially taking control over my mind. I saw how scared his body was. Some of them must have almost killed him. I just wanted to fix it, so I embraced him and let my tendrils find the broken parts and repair them." Luna grinned widely.

"You embraced him? In the water? Naked?" Rionach nodded, sending Luna into a roaring laughter. "The poor boy. And you incapacitated him with your tendrils, I assume?"

Rionach blushed.

"Not exactly."

"Then what did you do? When I flew over, he was passed out on his cloak wearing nothing more than on the day he was born…" Luna was looking at her expectantly, still grinning.

"I… well, I kissed him, then he kind of… passed out." Luna leaned back and put her hands behind her head.

"Oh kiddo, you got it bad." Rionach stared horrified at her.

"Got what? What are you talking about?" Luna leaned in and smiled at her.

"You are in love, kiddo. And I'm guessing the young man has got it as bad as you. Are you going to see him again?" Rionach was smiling softly and staring at nothing, her mind somewhere else completely. "Rionach?" Luna spoke softly and touched her arm.

"Huh? Oh! Well, I was planning on going back tomorrow night. Do you think he will still be there?" Luna nodded.

"I do, but you need to be careful. You are still young and have yet to be with a man intimately. It can be a wonderful thing, but you know we can not bear offspring. It is always fatal." Rionach blushed.

"I have no intentions of going that far!" Luna shook her head.

"No respectable young girl ever does. But you are more than that, you are part dragon. All our primal instincts are intensified. Just look at Aqua and her food obsession. If she did not have a heightened metabolism, she wouldn't fit through the door to her room. All I'm saying is to think before you act. Can you do that for me?" Luna looked into her eyes and she nodded.

"But you are going to have a problem getting out tomorrow night. Your mother and father are coming home with their guests, remember?"

"Oh no! How am I going to get out?" Rionach looked at Luna with wide eyes. Luna saw the desperation in Rionach's eyes.

"I think I can come up with something. Just be prepared for when I set my plan in motion." Rionach threw her arms around Luna's neck.

"Oh, thank you, Luna. You are the best!"

Slowly, Conri came to himself again. He felt a little disoriented and lay completely still next to the fire. What had happened to him? He sat up and looked around. His bags were there, his horse was tied up to a tree and the fire was lit. He remembered following the dragon, finding the lake, getting his stuff then taking a swim in the water. Then what? He felt dizzy and still a little groggy. Getting up, he found his clothes where he had left them and pulled on his pants. He looked out over the lake when suddenly, the memories started coming back. The beautiful woman, she had come out of nowhere. She had circled him like a beast hunting its prey and she had touched his scar. His hand went to his chest, but much to his surprise there was no scar. He looked down at his hands searching for all the other scars, but couldn't find them. All of his old wounds were erased as if they had never been there. He disbelievingly shook his head. Had she done that? Remembering how she had embraced him, he closed his eyes and sighed as he smiled slightly. Never before had he been that close to a woman. He had just not had the interest or time. And she was the most beautiful woman he had ever seen. When he remembered her kiss, a soft groan escaped him. That was the last thing he remembered except… Had she said she would come back, or was that just a dream? He walked back and sat down on his cape. There were still things he could not understand. How could a delicate woman have lifted him all the way from the water to the camp? That was not possible… was it? And if by some chance she had gotten him up to his camp… oh god! He had been naked and if she had… he blushed. Best not to think of that. He stacked up the fire and laid down next to it. Tomorrow, everything would make more sense. At least he hoped so…

Chapter 36

The children were up with the sun, running about and playing in the stream they had camped next to. Orelaith heard them laughing and smiled sadly.

"Once Rionach gets full control of her powers, she should be able to remove the curse. Then we can have a string of children of our own," Bas said as if he knew what she was thinking.

"I know. I am just a little sad that I will not be able to see a normal process of growth in her as with other children. But I can not blame her for wanting to be older. She almost has more knowledge in her mind than she is able to handle. And she must have felt like an adult trapped in the body of a child." Orelaith sighed and sat up.

"Good morning to you two. I trust you slept as poorly as we did," Bridget said and looked up from her cooking. Bas laughed.

"The ground can be unforgiving, but it's going to be worth it to eat some of your breakfast out in the open." Bridget chuckled.

"Your flattery will get you first serving, Lord Basilicus. It is almost done, so why don't you all go clean up." Saoirse called the children over and they headed down to the stream to wash up before eating.

Soon they were on their horses again, closing in on their destination. Bas had almost taken a few wrong turns, but now they were on the new road leading up to the castle. As they came out of the dense woods, the castle came into view.

"Is that it?" Blathnat and Faolàn gawked.

"Home sweet home." Bas nodded at them. Saoirse was still sitting on the horse with her mouth open.

"Oh my! I never thought… it's huge!" Bridget didn't seem surprised at all and was just smiling as they approached the big gate. They rode through the lower part of the castle grounds and stopped in the big bailey in the back.

"Saoirse and Bridget, it is so good to see you." Vig came down the stone steps to greet them. "And will you look at the two of you," she said and helped Blathnat and Faolàn off their horses. "I can't believe how big you are now." Aqua, Terra, Tempest, Solis and Serovita came out and greeted them too.

"Where is Rionach and Luna?" Orelaith asked Vig quietly.

"Rionach was worried you had not told our guests about her yet, so she wanted to make sure before she came out."

"They have been told. And I must say they have been

more understanding than I ever would have hoped for." Orelaith smiled at Saoirse as she whispered to Vig.

"You can come out now, Sweetheart. They know you are not as they remembered you," Orelaith called out to her in her mind, looking up at the big wooden doors to the keep. Luna emerged in a long, dark blue, almost black dress and was pulling on Rionach's hand.

"There you are, my darling," Bas said and ran up the steps and gave her a big hug. Saoirse turned and gasped as she saw her. Rionach wore a white dress adorned with an intricate pattern of deep blue around the neck and sleeves, and her long red hair was flowing freely down her back. She glanced shyly at their guests over Bas' shoulder.

"Have you been behaving while we were gone?" Bas asked, holding her out at arms length.

"Yes Papa, I did. But Vig and the others had a food fight in the main hall last night." She grinned and looked at Vig. Bas laughed loudly when he saw Vig's cheeks turn pink.

"I did not start that!" Luna came walking down the steps and winked at Vig,

"No, but you sure did finish it," she said.

"Rionach, sweetheart, come to me." Orelaith held out her hand. Her daughter came down the stairs and gave her mother a big hug.

"Did you have a pleasant trip, mama? It was not too cold for you last night, was it?" Orelaith stroked her cheek and smiled.

"No, my darling. Your father kept me warm." She took her daughter's hand and walked over to Saoirse and Bridget "You remember these two wonderful ladies, don't you?" Rionach curtsied.

"Yes, I do. It is good to see you both again." Saoirse stared at her with wide eyes for a moment then blushed slightly, embarrassed at herself.

"You look so beautiful, Rionach; just like your mother." Bridget was frowning.

"Remarkable. Absolutely remarkable," she said.

"Well, let's not all stand here. Lunch is being prepared, and we need to show our honoured guests to their rooms before then. Serovita? The rooms are ready, yes?" Vig said and started walking up the steps holding little Blathnat and Faolàn's hands.

"They are, Vig." They all followed Serovita inside as the stable-hands came to take the horses away.

Conri lay looking up at the trees. He tried to figure out whether or not what he remembered from last night had really happened. His hand went to his chest again, touching the spot where the long scar had been. Something had happened, but he was unsure of exactly what. He had packed up all his things hours ago, but for some reason it didn't feel right to leave. He got up and walked down to the lake's edge. Tracing the delicate footprint, he knew that the woman had been there, but where had she gone? If she had been a fairy, there would have been no trace of her, no marks on the ground where she had come out of the water. No, he needed to stay here in case she returned. He needed some answers. But if he was to stay, he needed some food, so he grabbed his bow and walked into the woods to go hunting.

It was already dark at dinnertime, and Rionach was getting restless. She needed to come up with a good enough excuse to leave so that no one would question why. She could not say she was feeling sick, because that would only make Vig give her an examination. And if she said she needed to study, her mother or father would come check on her later. Luna had noticed and winked at her. "Just follow my lead." Then she turned to Orelaith.

"I think I will take a short ride. It is such a beautiful moon this evening, and I hear it calling me."

"Isn't it a bit late for a ride?" Bridget looked at her and frowned.

"Our mother named her Luna for a reason, Bridget" Bas said, "She thrives when the moon is full like this. Besides, she is well equipped to take care of herself. All my sisters and I have been through extensive weapons training." Bridget smiled at him.

"I see. But still, she should not go alone."

"I will go with her. I have some plants I want to study that supposedly only bloom at a full moon." Rionach smiled. Orelaith looked at her suspiciously.

"I was hoping you would spend some time with the children."

"Oh mama, can't I go with Luna? She promised she would teach me some flying tricks. Please?" Rionach used her big puppy-eyed expression on her mother. As always, Orelaith eventually gave in.

"I think that's a good idea. But don't stay too late, and for goodness sake, put some warmer clothes on."

"Thank you mama, I will." She gave her mother a kiss on the cheek and hurried after Luna.

Conri was half asleep on his cape. The hunt and a full belly had tired him out. Still, he caught himself looking around any time he heard even the smallest sound. He re-stacked the fire, then laid down again and closed his eyes. Running the images of the woman over in his head, he smiled to himself and started fantasizing about her.

"Conri of the northern lands. You are still here…" He pictured her wading out of the water like he had seen her last night. The moon reflecting off her skin and the water dripping off her...

"You must be having some pleasant dreams by the look of the smile on your lips." He jumped up and grabbed his sword. A woman's voice came from somewhere close by.

"Show yourself," he demanded, turning towards where the voice came from.

"Why the sword raised?" The voice sounded behind him and he turned quickly.

"I don't like being toyed with, woman. Come out where I can see you." Laughter sounded to his right and he turned towards it.

"Why should I come out? A man with a sword pointing towards you is hardly an invitation to be seen." Again the voice had moved behind him.

"No man puts his sword away before he knows there is no threat. If you want me to put it away, you will have to come out and make me." The woman laughed.

"You think I am a threat? You are the one with the sword." The way she moved around was making him dizzy.

"And you are the one hiding in the darkness" he said and turned around only to find himself inches from her face, inside his sword arm. She grabbed it and twisted it out of his grip in one swift move, then tossed it into the lake, but not for one second did she lose eye contact with him.

"I don't much like being commanded," she whispered. He reached for her arms, but somehow he ended up on his knees in front of her. "Not very welcoming, are you?" she said and took hold of his chin, locking her gaze with his. "Luckily for you, I am in a good mood today," she whispered. His horse neighed and she looked over. In one quick move he swept her feet out from under her then pounced, pinning her down with the weight of his body and his hands on her wrists.

"Who are you?" he asked. She squirmed and stared at him defiantly.

"Why should I tell you, Conri of the northern lands?" He looked down at her red hair sparkling in the light from the fire and her emerald green eyes staring into his. God, she was beautiful. He felt an overpowering urge to kiss her. She closed her eyes for a second and arched her body to push him off. A groan slipped over his lips. He knew he had to let her up soon, or else he would be unable to hide his raging emotions.

"You obviously know who I am; but who are you? Tell me, and I will let go of you," he said.

"I must say, I much more enjoyed our meeting last night," she said as her lips curled up in a smile. That was it. He could resist no more and kissed her. To his surprise, she kissed him back as hungrily as he kissed her. She wrapped her arms around his neck and his hands slid down her arms to her waist, over her hips and down her thigh. The emotions were overpowering and he gasped for breath as she moved her hands to his bare back. He kissed her neck and buried his face in her hair. What was he doing? She could be a witch seducing him, using magic to wake the lust in him. He lifted his head and looked into her eyes. No, she was no witch. He kissed her again and let his hand follow her body up from her thigh, feeling her skin through the fabric of her dress. He pushed her arms up behind her head again, and she did not resist him. Slowly, he slid down off her and pulled her up on her knees. He took hold of her face and kissed her, then looked into her eyes. "I want you, more than I have ever wanted anything before. But I would never force myself on you," he whispered. "If you are unsure, then walk away now. If you let me continue, I may not be able to control myself any more." She stared at him for a second, her hand touching his cheek, then she leaned in and kissed him again.

Bas was getting restless. He glanced at the door more and more often and seemed distracted. "What is it, my love?" Orelaith whispered.

"Rionach and Luna should have been back by now. I had some troubling news when I went to check on the horses right after dinner. When I entered the stable, one of the stable-hands was talking about a young dragon slayer who had arrived in the area. I know they were exaggerating, but he has killed at least four of my kind that I know of, and now he has come here in search of more kills." Orelaith looked around at the others who were drinking and talking with their guests.

"Have you told the others? They need to know." Bas shook his head and said,

"I did not want to upset them tonight. Solis for one would not be able to hide her emotions very well. I was planning on gathering them all in the counsell chamber once our guests had retired for the night." Orelaith put her hand on his arm.

"Did you know these dragons personally?" Bas looked at her and shook his head.

"No, but I know they were all infected with madness. I believe they all came from the same sphere as my brother Frater." Now Orelaith started glancing at the door every time it opened.

"Bas, I want you to go and find her. Make some excuse and I will make sure they all stay here until you get back." He nodded and got up.

"My dear guests, I need to go and check on something. I will be back soon." He smiled, kissed Orelaith and left the room.

"Where is he going?" Vig sent her a curious look.

"He's just worried about Rionach and Luna. He wants us to meet him in the counseling chamber once Saoirse and Bridget have retired." Orelaith smiled at Vig who frowned back at her.

"What is going on, Orelaith? Normally he would not be as worried as to go out looking for them."

"I promised not to say. This is news he wants to share with you himself," Orelaith said and turned her attention to their guests.

Chapter 37

The light from the fire was getting low, but Conri did not care as he lay still with his arm around the red haired woman. She sighed contentedly as he gently stroked her arm.

"You still have not told me your name," he whispered and softly kissed her neck. She turned towards him.

"Should I?" She smiled at him.

"I think it's only fair I know the name of the woman who has stolen my heart." She looked away and said.

"You have my heart too, Conri of the northern lands. But it is very… complicated. My family is not like any other family I know of. I would not want you to get dragged into it. If my father found out about us, he would kill you." He turned her face towards him.

"I don't care. I want to be with you forever. Let him come…" A cry sounded overhead, and they both looked up as a sleek black dragon flew by.

"Your father is coming. Hurry!" Luna sent to her. Rionach jumped up.

"I must go." She swiftly pulled on her dress.

"Don't worry, I can protect you from that beast up there." Conri pulled her close. She looked into his eyes for a second, then gave him a quick kiss and ran into the woods. Just before she was out of sight, she stopped and shouted over her shoulder.

"My name is Rionach, Conri of the northern lands." He stared after her.

"I will wait for you here until you return, Rionach!"

⁂

"Just in time. Your father is only a short distance away." Luna looked at Rionach. "Did you enjoy yourself? Oh my! You really must have. You're blushing!" Luna laughed.

"I did something I probably shouldn't have, Luna. I…that is, we…" Rionach tried to find the words, but Luna just winked at her and said,

"I understand. Don't worry about it, dragons are very… passionate. You were never in control of what happened tonight. But I don't think you should tell your father about that yet. To him, you are still just a little whelp, and way too young to be finding a mate."

"But I am not! He forgets who I am. I have memories going back to before he was even an egg!"

"Here he comes. We can talk about this later."

⁂

LORE OF THE DRAGONS: ESSENCE OF A QUEEN

Bas flew towards them and swung around, following them back to the castle.

"I wanted to see how you were doing. It's getting a little late. Did you have fun?" Rionach nodded and Luna laughed.

"You bet we did. She has some crazy skills, Bas. You don't even want to know how she can use that sleek body of hers." Rionach stared horrified at Luna. Bas just laughed and said,

"I'd bet. You wouldn't happen to have seen signs of a camp out here? It would be a single young man." Luna shook her head.

"Nope, I saw nothing. Why?" They landed on the porch outside the counseling chamber.

"He can be dangerous to us, so if you see him, stay clear. Ok?" They nodded.

"Why is he dangerous, Papa?" Rionach asked as they walked into the chamber. Bas poured himself a glass of wine.

"He's a dragon slayer." Rionach felt her knees go weak under her, but Luna caught her before she fell. Bas still had his back turned, so he did not see how she turned pale.

"Keep it together, kiddo. Now is not the time."

"I am going to take Rionach to bed and I will come back, Bas."

"Yes, I feel a little tired, papa." Rionach managed, and walked over to him and kissed him on the cheek.

"Sleep well, my darling. I will see you in the morning. And don't worry about the dragon slayer, he will not get his hands on you."

"*He already has…*" Luna sent to Rionach as they walked down the stairs. "*All over her actually…*" Luna chuckled.

"How can you joke with that?! He's a dragon slayer! Oh my god! He must never find out who I am." Rionach said as they got to her chamber.

"He might stop doing what he does if he finds out, did you think of that?" Luna said and helped her into bed.

"He kills our kind, Luna. I should have known when I felt the darkness in him. He would not hesitate to kill me in my dragon form, I am sure of it." So many things made sense now, the scars, the sword and even the comment about protecting her when Luna flew over.

"I don't even know if I want to go see him again," she said as Luna tucked her in. Luna smiled softly at her.

"I think you will. If what you share with him is true, nothing, not even the fact that he's a dragon slayer will be able to keep you apart. But now, you need to sleep. I need to get to the counseling chamber to meet the others and hear what your father has in mind for the dragon slayer." Luna kissed Rionach's forehead and walked out.

The others were all there when Luna walked into the counseling chamber and took her place by the round table.

"What is this all about, Bas?" Vig said and looked at him

LORE OF THE DRAGONS: ESSENCE OF A QUEEN

seriously.

"I have had some troubling news that concerns us all. A man who can be a threat to us." He got up and walked around as he repeated what he had overheard in the stables. They listened to him silently as he told them of the dragons he had already killed and that he now had come to the area to hunt them.

"What do we know about this young man?" Vig asked when Bas was finished. "Surely something must have triggered such hate for our kind for him to travel so far to hunt us down."

"I don't know." Bas said and frowned.

"But I do." They all stared at the open door and found Bridget standing there with her arms crossed.

"Bridget? What brings you up here so late? We are kind of in the middle of something here that only concerns our family," Bas said and did not quite know what to do or say. How long had she been standing there? And how much had she heard?

"I think you need to let us deal with this privately, Bridget." She just looked at him and walked into the room.

"Oh relax, young prince. I already know who and what you are. And this matter concerns me as much as it concerns you." She sent him a stern look and took a seat. The others stared at each other in total confusion.

"I beg your pardon? What is it you think you know?" Vig huffed and stared angrily at Bridget.

"I know you are all dragons, well, besides you Orelaith.

You are only part dragon. And I know you are Prince Basilicus, the oldest of three brothers and king in right even if not crowned yet. And Vigoratus, you still are an uptight stick in the mud, I see." Luna held back a snicker.

"And you Luna, always the rebel. You haven't changed a bit," Bridget said and winked at her. Vig was staring wide-eyed at her, as were most of the others.

"Who are you, and how do you know so much about us?" Vig almost whispered. Bridget smiled and looked around the room.

"Let me see…" Her eyes stopped on Terra, and to the others surprise, they saw she was smiling knowingly. "I see you have guessed, my dear. What about the rest of you? No one?" She looked up at Bas. "Not even you? Well, let me do this," she said and threw out sparkling white tendrils, unraveling a web around herself. They all gasped as her appearance changed and they could feel her true nature. She was a dragon in human form! She pulled back her tendrils, and now they saw a young woman with all the colors of the rainbow in her waist long hair. The same tell-tale high cheekbones and timeless face stared at them.

"Now then… anyone want to take a wild guess?" Vig approached her slowly.

"I know of only one dragon who could cast that kind of a knot ." Tears were brimming in her eyes as she took the woman's hands. "Opulentia… is it truly you?" The woman nodded and stroked away a tear that had found its way down Vig's cheek.

"You need to stop that. Otherwise I might think you are actually glad to see me." The others all swarmed around her,

LORE OF THE DRAGONS: ESSENCE OF A QUEEN

hugging her, overjoyed to see her. Orelaith pulled Bas aside.

"Who is she?" Bas was crying as he looked into her eyes. "She is my aunt, my mother's twin sister and surpassed only by my mother, the most powerful dragon to ever live."

Over the course of the night, Opulentia told them how she had shielded herself from the others in her sphere who were infected, and how she barely escaped once they crashed in the ocean outside the north-east coast. First she had traveled east to the isle there and after several years finding no sign of others had returned some years back. The first dragon she had run into was Nex. She had already camouflaged herself so he had not sensed her presence. After that she had been very careful, even changing how she looked in human form. She had long ago worked out how to stay in that form without the long rest that usually followed. When she sensed Luna that first time she had been careful and followed them at a distance. When Saoirse later had been looking for someone to help her with the children, Opulentia had jumped at the opportunity. The rest they all knew.

"But now I will answer the question that you first asked, Vig and the reason I revealed myself at this time. The young man… you asked what could have triggered such a hate, that he would hunt down and kill dragons. The young man is someone you all know… Do you remember young Conri, the boy who is half brother to Frater?" Bas nodded and closed his eyes.

"It all makes sense then. A dragon killed his parents, that is where his hate comes from." Solis, who had been silent most of the night, suddenly spoke up.

"But that is not fair! We are nothing like the infected. They are evil, killing and hunting like beasts. How can he compare us to them? We did not kill his family."

"No, we did not, but he doesn't know that. In his eyes, we are all monsters that need to be wiped out. I think the best thing to do is to stay clear of him and in human form until he leaves this area." Luna sat and looked thoughtfully at Opulentia as she spoke, but said nothing. She knew very well that Conri would not be leaving any time soon. But she kept that to herself.

The next day, Opulentia was back to being Bridget, taking care of the children and doing what she had all along. The others were walking around smiling and spending time with her and Saoirse. They had decided to keep it a secret from Rionach until they could figure out how to keep Opulentia with them on a more permanent basis. After dinner that evening, Rionach excused herself and said she would retire for the evening, sending Luna a glance as she left.

"She seems so preoccupied. Do you know what is troubling her?" Orelaith asked Luna as they walked towards their chambers for the night.

LORE OF THE DRAGONS: ESSENCE OF A QUEEN

"Oh, I think the young dragon slayer is one of her main concerns. I think it came as a shock to find a man like that so close." Always keep your lies as close to truths as possible, Luna thought to herself.

"I am going to check on her before I head to bed. Maybe she needs someone to talk to." Orelaith said and stopped outside Rionach's door. She opened it quietly and saw that it was dark. "Rionach? Are you awake, sweetheart?" she whispered. There was no reply, but Orelaith heard her sighing in her sleep, so she closed the door and went to her own room to get some much needed sleep.

Rionach lay still as she heard her mother close the door. Now she had all night to spend with Conri, but she was unsure of what to think of him now that she knew what he was. She knew now why he had smelled like a dragon; it was from the dragons he had killed. Did she even want to be with a man like that? A man who killed out of hate? She just had to make sure he did not find out who she really was. She waited for a while, then jumped out of bed and walked to the small porch outside her room. It was a little small, but she could just fit there in her dragon form. For a little while, she stood there not knowing if she should go or not. But she could almost feel how invisible strings pulled her towards him. She had to go, so she climbed up on the ledge and jumped off, transformed in mid-air and flew silently towards the young dragon slayer's camp.

Rionach had not returned tonight as he would have thought, and he was getting restless. What if he had been wrong about her? Had she gotten what she wanted from him last night and didn't plan to return? No… he knew she would be back. Maybe something had happened to her? During the day, he had explored the land around his camp and found there was nothing out there but a few small farms a few hours away. She had always come and left on foot, and he had not found any sign of a horse close by. She had to be a mystical creature of some kind, but she looked like a woman, smelled like a woman and felt like a woman. He closed his eyes and sighed as he ran the images of last night over in his head. There was something about her, he just could not put his finger on it yet.

"Are you dreaming again? You have the same silly smile on your lips as you did when I found you last night." He jumped up and found her standing on the other side of the campfire. "Rionach! I almost thought you wouldn't return." He started walking round the fire to embrace her, but she moved away from him.

"I know why you are here," she said and stared at him. "You are a dragon slayer." There was something about how she said those words that should have made him understand that she did not approve, but he was blind to that. All he could see was her.

"Yes I am. The only one to take down more than one

dragon and… would you stand still?" She was moving around the fire as he moved towards her.

"It is hard to talk with your lips on mine… and I needed to know if you are the dragon slayer that was rumored to be in the area." She looked down into the fire, and suddenly he was holding her.

"We can talk later," his voice whispered in her ear as he pulled her down on to his cloak.

Bas could not sleep. He tossed and turned as Orelaith lay still beside him. Rionach's behavior last night had made him concerned that there was something he was not seeing. He got up and walked to the window. What if she had gone out despite his rule that they all had to stay in at night? She was always doing things she should not and usually she did not get into more trouble than they could get her out of, but the dragon slayer was a different matter. He could actually kill her. Just the thought of that sent shivers down his back. Bas looked over at Orelaith sleeping soundly in their bed. He would just go and check on his little whelp and return before Orelaith woke up. Quietly, he walked out of the room and closed the door behind him. But when he entered Rionach's room and saw the bed empty and the door to her porch open, he felt his temper rising. He ran out of the open porch doors and jumped off, taking on his dragon form as his feet left the ledge. His daughter was out there alone, with the dragon slayer lurking in the shadows.

Chapter 38

What he found was not what he had imagined. But it did make him, if possible, even more angry than he already was. Rionach was in the arms of the dragon slayer, but not as he first feared. This was potentially as dangerous and as lethal.

"Rionach! Put your clothes on and leave. Now!" he sent to her as he flew over the camp. She looked up and reacted instantly, grabbing her clothes and running off. The young dragon slayer shouted after her to stop. Bas circled down and landed between them, blocking the young man off from chasing after his daughter. He cried out in anger towards the man who had grabbed his sword, standing in the light of the fire wearing only his pants. The clearing was just big enough for him to circle the man. Their eyes locked as they sized each other up. Bas raised the spikes on his neck and roared at him.

"That's it, you dumb beast. Lose your temper," the young man said as he walked sideways with his sword pointing towards Bas. Could this be young Conri? He did not look much like the child Bas remembered him to be. He could smell the old blood of dragons not only on him but in him, surprisingly enough he smelled no fear. Conri lunged

LORE OF THE DRAGONS: ESSENCE OF A QUEEN

towards Bas who pounced and knocked him to the ground. Pinned down under the dragon's huge front paw he was incapacitated. His sword was too far away for him to reach, not that it would not have helped much in the situation he was in anyway. He found himself wondering if the dragon would burn him or just gulp him down. What followed was nothing he would ever have thought possible: the dragon spoke to him.

"Did you even for a moment stop to consider that we are not all mindless beasts?! Should I burn all humans because of what evil I see in a few? No? Well, you judge us in that manner, so why should I not pour out to you in the same measure?" The dragon shook his head. "I am not like the others. They are sick, and so far there is no cure. Nor am I like you, so blinded by hate that you don't even stop to consider that some of your targets are innocent. Never judge by the outside, because what lies within can be more than it first appears." Conri opened and closed his mouth repeatedly, not knowing if he should reply or not. "Close your mouth or speak, boy. You look like a fish on land."

Rionach's voice cut through as she came running.

"Don't hurt him. He doesn't know who you are to me." Bas glared at him.

"If I release you, will you stop with your futile attacks?" Conri nodded, and slowly, Bas removed his paw from his chest. Conri scrambled backwards before he got to his feet. "I will leave you your life if Rionach comes with me willingly." They both looked at her.

"Don't do it, Rionach. I can take him. He just caught me

off guard."

"No! I will go with you if you promise to do him no harm."

"Done." Bas replied, and in one quick move he had swung Rionach up on his back and flown off.

Conri stared after them until they disappeared behind the trees, then he quickly jumped on his horse and raced after them. A dragon had taken away his mother and father. He would not let one take away the woman he loved as well. Conri had only one thought in his head: to find Rionach. By the light of the moon, he made his way through the dense forest. They had flown this way, and wherever the dragon was, he knew he would find Rionach. He pushed on, and soon enough he heard agitated voices coming from a hillside close by.

"Don't you understand what you have done? This will be the death of you!" he heard a dark male voice say.

"I don't care! I love him and I want to be with him." Rionach's voice was angry, and he was glad he was not on the receiving end of her temper. As he crept closer he saw them standing on a hill. The moon lit up her long copper hair making it glow and the wind lifting it made it come alive. Facing her was the golden dragon that had snatched her up a short while ago. They stared at each other, his big golden eyes facing her green, locked in a mental battle. The dragon sighed and closed his eyes.

"You know I can not stay angry at you. But now the circle will begin all over and even if I know we will never lose you for good, it still pains me that you will have to take

LORE OF THE DRAGONS: ESSENCE OF A QUEEN

time to learn everything over again. I don't want to lose what we have, my beloved child." Rionach's temper was spent, too, and she threw her arms around the dragon's neck.

"I am sorry, father," she cried. Father? The dragon was her father? How could that be? He felt his legs give way under him. He had fallen in love with a dragon's daughter! It was hard enough for him just to get his head around the fact that some dragons actually were intelligent creatures. Now he was faced with another mind-blowing revelation: dragons and humans could breed! He was a dragon slayer, but everything he had once believed in was crumbling. The things he had once called certain were unraveling before his eyes. He felt torn between the love he had for Rionach and his hate for dragons.

"Are you prepared for what will come? I know you have the facts of the process, but you will die, and only your memories will be carried on along with the queen's powers and her memories." She turned away from the dragon and crossed her arms.

"My mother did it. I don't see how it could be harder for me." The dragon laid down on his belly.

"Oh Rionach, your mother is not like you. You have all the powers and memories of our queen. Your mother is mostly human. You, my darling, are not." Conri was about to pass out from all the new information he was trying to process. He stumbled and fell.

"I think the best thing is to take him with us, father. That way he will not be a threat to us, and you can keep an eye on him at all times. I think he will be more understanding than you think," Rionach said and turned back to Bas.

"If I die I want to spend my time... my last months... with him. But first we have to find him."

"That will not be necessary. He's already here," Bas said and turned towards where Conri was hiding. "You can come out now, young Conri. I will try not to kill you for what you have done." Conri sat still, his eyes darting back and forth in the darkness. Had the dragon truly sensed him? Or was that just a trick to get him to reveal himself? "Don't make me come down there and get you!" The voice left no room for discussion. Slowly, Conri got up and followed the trail leading up the hill to where they were standing. To his surprise, the horse did not seem afraid of the huge golden dragon as he led it behind him. Conri kept one eye on the dragon and still had his sword in his hand.

"You won't be needing that toothpick, so put it away, Conri." The dragon said and sat up. Conri stuck it in the ground in front of him, close by in case he needed it.

"How do you know my name? Did Rionach tell you?" he said and looked up at the huge dragon. "I know who you are, boy. And I know who your brother is. Little Garbhan..." Conri almost went for his sword again.

"You stay away from my brother!" he shouted. The dragon shot a flame out towards him that hit his sword, setting it aglow with pure heat.

"You stupid boy! Have you not understood yet? I know you well. And I know what happened to your mother and father. I am sorry that it left you and your brother orphans,

LORE OF THE DRAGONS: ESSENCE OF A QUEEN

but I had nothing to do with that." Conri just stared at him.

"You can't know me… I have never met you before." Conri was confused.

"But you have, young Conri. Several times actually. I came to care deeply for you and your brother. Where is he now?" The dragon spoke softly to him. Conri was so confused.

"I don't understand. I can't have met you. I think I would have remembered talking to a dragon…"

Bas got up and unfolded his wings, "There is a castle a few hours ride from here. Get your things and come there in the morning. I need to discuss with the others what to do with you before I show you any more. Rionach, climb on." Bas flapped his wings a few times.

"There will be someone to show you around when you get there, but speak nothing of what has happened here tonight. For now, young dragon slayer, I bid you a good night." And with that, the golden dragon jumped up in the air and flew off with Rionach on his back.

"Is she pregnant?" Bas asked, looking over Vig's shoulder as she examined Rionach.

"She is." Vig sighed and opened her eyes. Orelaith sobbed loudly and hugged her daughter tightly. "I could try to… remove it?" Vig said quietly.

"She would still die," Opulentia said and walked into the room. Rionach jumped out of the bed, and to everyone's surprise she ran over and embraced her.

"Opulentia! I had thought I would never see you again. I have such fond memories of you." She smiled at the young girl. "I was not sure you would have memories of me yet, child, but it warms my heart that you do. But what have you gotten yourself into?" Rionach looked at her feet.

"I know now what it means, but my heart would not listen when I met the young man." Opulentia kissed the top of her head.

"I understand, my dear, but surely you knew of the consequences? Vig…?" Vig looked a little like a mouse cornered by a cat.

"Well… I hadn't quite gotten to that part yet. She is still so young, and I thought…"

"Vigoratus, you did not think at all. This child is not a child in mind, even if she is in body. She has changed the very physicality of her own vessel so it would catch up with her intellect. Even if she did not realize it at the time, she only did what she had to so she would be able to tackle all the power that was flooding up to the surface in her mind. Her memories should have been locked away to prevent her mind from being overcharged with power she doesn't yet know how to handle." Vig got up.

"We tried that, but she was much too strong for me. Even with the help of two others, she unraveled the knots like it was nothing." Opulentia looked at her.

"That is because you waited too long. If it is to be done right, the web must be cast as soon as the child is born and not a day later. If you wait, the child will quickly become too powerful, even for me." She walked over and took Orelaith's hand. "I know you think you will be losing your child, but for her, you need to make your peace with what is to come. She will need you to take care of her daughter. And this time..." She turned and looked at the others who were gathered in the room. "I will be here to tie the knots so this does not happen again. The child who comes now will be the queen we have all waited for."

Conri did not sleep much that night. By first light he had packed everything up and set off in the direction of the castle. Once he got to the road, he let the horse find its way while he sunk into deep thought. Everything that had happened to him over the last couple of days seemed like a dream. His entire world turned upside down, and now he was following a dragon's instructions. How could he ever explain all these things to his uncle? And his brother... How did the dragon know about him? Or how his parents had died? Nothing made any sense. He looked up and saw the beautiful castle looming on the hillside. Did the dragon control the lord who lived here? He expected to see cowed farmers working the field, but saw only smiling faces and well fed children running around. Maybe the lord controlled the dragon then. He made his way to the inner bailey. A man came running over and took his horse while another told him to follow him to the inn. He was given a small bag of gold and told to wait there until he was summoned. Soon he realized how tired and hungry he was, and when the barmaid wrinkled her nose as she brought him his food, he knew he would need a bath too. But first, food...

"So he's coming here?" Vig asked. Bas nodded.

"At the time, I did not know what else to do. We need to keep him close. If he left, there would always be the danger of him returning after gathering an army of men."

"I highly doubt that, but I do get your point. All he needs to do is ask some questions about who is lord of this castle and he will put two and two together. No, I think it was wise to bring him here. If he shows any sign of hostility, I can wipe his mind clean of any memories about what has happened the last few days and send him on his merry way," Opulentia said and sipped her wine.

"You can do that? You have so much to teach me," Vig said with awe in her voice.

"These knots are only used as a last resort, Vig. Powerful knots like that are not to be trifled with," Opulentia said as she looked seriously at Vig.

"He's sitting in the inn as we speak. But there is another matter we need to consider: Saoirse. Opulentia, do you think she could handle the truth about us? You are after all the one who knows her best," Bas said and refilled his cup. She stared into her cup for a moment.

"Yes I think so. She is an open-hearted woman, and I believe that if it comes from Orelaith, she will take it best. She already thinks of her to be an angel, so everything that comes out of her mouth, she considers to be words from heaven. But of course, if she panics, I can always pluck the memories out of her brain again," she answered matter-of-factly.

"Orelaith, are you willing to go talk to her for us?" Bas asked and put his hand over hers. She nodded.

"Yes, I can do that. Do you want me to go find her right away?"

"The sooner the better," Bas said and she got up. "I will go with her and take care of the children while you talk. Rionach, would you like to come with me?" Luna said and looked at Rionach who nodded.

"So it is settled then. Orelaith will talk to Saoirse, and when Conri joins us for dinner, we tell him who we are. Do we all agree?" Bas said and looked at them. They nodded. "Good. Then I suggest we all get some rest before dinner. This may be a long evening…"

Chapter 39

Opulentia had gone with Orelaith to talk to Saoirse, and as they suspected, even though she was shocked she was as open minded as she was open-hearted. But there was one thing she had asked Orelaith to do for her.

"Bas, my dear. Can you come meet us in the counsell chamber? There is a little something you need to do for me," Orelaith sent to Bas as he was cleaning up for dinner.

"Of course, my love. Did everything go well with Saoirse?"

"Oh yes, but just come up here, would you please?" When he walked in, he found Orelaith and Saoirse waiting for him.

"What did you want, my love?" he said and smiled at them.

"It was not so much me, but Saoirse who had a request." He smiled at Saoirse.

"I know this must be much for you to take in. Anything I can do to help, just ask." Saoirse blushed a little and spoke almost shyly.

LORE OF THE DRAGONS: ESSENCE OF A QUEEN

"I have been told that you are all dragons, but I have yet to see one… and I guess seeing is believing…" Bas smiled.

"Of course. But promise me you will let me know if I scare you. The first time can be frightening." She giggled.

"That's what my husband said on our wedding night." Orelaith laughed as Bas blushed. Then he quickly walked to the porch and turned around, jumped up in the air and transformed. Saoirse gasped and backed into Orelaith. Bas laid down on his belly.

"It is still me, Saoirse," Bas said and tried not to smile, knowing well how his teeth had affected Orelaith the first time he smiled at her in dragon form. For a little while, Saoirse just stared at him, but soon she relaxed and took a few brave steps out on the porch.

"You are huge!" She said and walked a little closer.

"I am, even in dragon standards, pretty big." Bas laughed. Saoirse giggled again.

"Bas, take her for a short ride. I think she would really enjoy that." Orelaith smiled. Bas nodded and put his head down so Saoirse did not have to break her neck trying to look at him.

"I have an idea. How would you like to go for a short flight?" Saoirse turned to Orelaith with an expression of joyful over-excitement that made Orelaith laugh loudly.

"Can I? Can I really?" They both nodded at her. "I would love to! But you must promise not to drop me," she said as Bas helped her up on his back.

"We won't be long," he said and winked at Orelaith. "Are you ready?" he asked.

"Yes yes yes!" Saoirse answered excitedly.

"Then you better hold on, because here we goooo," Bas said and jumped off the edge. Saoirse squealed in joy and Orelaith watched on as they swooped down then back up.

It was dark by the time a man from the castle finally came to get Conri from the inn. He had taken a bath, cut his hair, shaved and even had his leather pants and coat cleaned. As he walked through the streets on his way to the castle, he tried to find out who lived there, but the man had been as tight-lipped as the people at the inn. He was a little annoyed, but he guessed he would find out soon enough what was going on. They walked into the keep itself and stopped outside the doors of what he suspected was the main hall. He was instructed to stay there until he was called in, then the man left him. A few servants walked past him, and it seemed like they were all leaving the keep. When he asked why, they just smiled and said their day was over and that the lord and lady of the castle had said that all servants needed to go home once dinner was served so they could spend the evening with their families. All the evidence said that these people were good to their subjects. How could it be that they were associated with dragons?

"Come!" a loud voice sounded from the other side of the big wooden doors. He took a deep breath and pushed them open. When he saw who was sitting at the long table, he just stared. Orelaith, Basilicus, Vigoratus, Luna, Aqua, Terra, Tempest, Solis, Serovita and, to his surprise, Saoirse and

Bridget. And sitting next to Bas was Rionach. They were all smiling at him.

"Conri, it is good to see you again." Orelaith smiled at him. "Please, take a seat." Conri looked from one to the other as he slowly walked over and sat down. What was Rionach doing with his old friends? Wait a minute, wasn't Rionach the name of Orelaith and Bas' child? But she was no older than Garbhan… No, it could not be her.

"I smell smoke," Luna said and winked at him.

"Conri, have you not figured it out yet?" Bas smiled at him.

"I…" Conri looked at him.

"Oh, have pity on the poor boy, Bas. Just tell him." Luna laughed. Bas walked around the table to where Conri was sitting.

"I see you brought your toothpick," Bas said and winked at him. Conri went pale as he stared at Bas.

"You? But you're humans, aren't you?" Conri looked around at the others.

"Never judge by the outside, because what lies within can be more than it first appears." Bas winked at him and returned to his seat.

"You too, Saoirse?" He looked at her wide-eyed. She shook her head.

"No, just plain old human here. But Bridget is one." She smiled widely. "I just found out myself. Isn't it amazing?" Again his world was turned upside down.

"Just take your time to let it sink in, sweetheart. You will soon get used to the idea," Saoirse added and sipped her wine. Bridget, frowned at Saoirse.

"You can't call a young man sweetheart, Saoirse. Really…"

"Saoirse is right. Let it sink in while we eat. Feel free to ask any questions if you want," Bas said. Conri watched as everyone helped themselves to the food set out on the table. They smiled and laughed, talked amongst themselves and paid him little attention. He did not have much of an appetite, but drank wine and glanced at them each in turn trying to find any sign of dragon-like behavior. Everyone was eating normally, except for the one called Aqua, who did not bother with cutlery and was filling her plate over and over, almost inhaling her food. Conri stared wide-eyed at her as she stuffed four potatoes in her mouth at once. Even if it was not exactly the sort of manners one would expect from a lady, it hardly qualified as dragon-like behavior.

"How are you holding up?" Conri looked towards Rionach and found her looking at him, but no one else seemed to notice that she had said anything. *"That's because I didn't say it out loud, Conri of the northern lands."* She smiled and winked at him. How did she do that? *"It is a way of thought sending. I can hear your thoughts and send mine back to you."* He tried to clear his mind by staring at her, not wanting her to read his thoughts, but a few rather vivid memories from the first time they met slipped through. She turned a bright red. *"Conri! Would you stop that? What if some of the others catch on to those thoughts?"* He grinned sheepishly. *"Sorry, I can't help it. It's all I can think about to keep me from going mad right now."*

"And what are you two talking about? And don't give me that fake astounded look, Rionach. I know very well that you are sending," Vig said, frowning at her.

"For god's sake, Vig, let the kids have a private conversation. What they are talking about is none of your business," Opulentia said and sighed. Vig huffed and leaned back in her chair.

"I just find it rude to exclude the rest of us from the conversation, that's all."

"If they are talking like me and Orelaith do, it is not a conversation your tender little ears can take." Bas grinned at Vig.

"No, she is too much of a stick in the mud," Luna said and grinned. Conri caught himself smiling at how they interacted with each other. They were so human it was hard to think of them as anything else.

"Well, I think it's cause to celebrate. We have a wedding to plan," Orelaith said and held up her cup in a toast.

"W-wedding…" Conri stuttered.

"Well, usually we don't marry like you humans do," Bas said as Conri took a large gulp of his wine. "But now that we live among you as humans, you will have to marry Rionach before she starts showing," Bas said and winked at him. Conri sprayed out the wine in his mouth.

"I am to be a father? But.. but.. we only… it only… I mean…" This sent the room into fits of laughter.

"Once is all it takes, boy." Luna winked at him.

"We dragons are a fertile breed. Passionate too. But I think after dinner, you and Bas need to have a man to man… or rather a man to dragon talk. He will teach you more about us. If you have any questions, you can ask him then," Opulentia said and smiled softly at him. Of course, all he saw was Bridget, the old housekeeper he knew from Saoirse's farm.

"I thought I would be teaching him about us..." Vig said, sounding almost insulted.

"Oh please, we don't have all night." Luna grinned. "You can go on for hours once you first get started." Vig blushed.

"I guess you are right, I do tend to go too much into details." Then she smiled at Opulentia.

"How about you shake off that old lady look and show young Conri what you really look like?" "I think that's a great idea," Saoirse said and clapped her hands almost simultaneously with Solis. The two looked at each other and giggled. Opulentia got up and shook off the knots as she transformed from plain old Bridget to the beautiful young looking woman with rainbow coloured hair. Conri stared at her.

"Wow... you don't look much like an old hag now," he said without thinking, sending the room bursting with laughter again.

After dinner, Conri had relaxed more and was actually starting to get used to the idea of them being dragons. And he had a lot of questions ready for Bas once the two of them walked up to the counseling chamber to have a talk. Bas told him the story of how they had first arrived on the isle and about how the infection made some dragons mad or evil. Conri listened intently and stopped Bas only to ask some questions. When Bas was finished, he gave Conri some time

LORE OF THE DRAGONS: ESSENCE OF A QUEEN

to think and ask a few questions of his own. However, when Conri went silent, Bas asked him the question he had known would come.

"I need to know, Conri: will you keep this to yourself? I don't need to tell you how devastating it could be to my family if this ever got out." Conri smiled at him.

"I won't tell anyone of what I have learned here, Basilicus. I mean, it's not like anyone would believe me anyway. You and the others have been almost like family to me and my brother Garbhan. Besides, I am to be part of this family as well soon. It would be like betraying myself." Bas smiled and gave him a big hug, then he held him out at arm's length, suddenly looking very serious.

"About your brother… there is one more thing that I need to tell you."

Conri's head was spinning and he needed some air. Out on the porch he leaned on the railing and after a few minutes Bas came out to him with a cup of wine.

"I know it is a lot to take in, but give it some time." Conri took the cup offered to him and drained it.

"Everything I believed, everything I knew to be true has been turned upside down in two days. I don't know if I can handle any more right now. I just can't think straight." Bas put his hand on Conri's shoulder and smiled at him.

"I have a suggestion; something I think would take your mind off this for a little while, at least." Conri looked at him questioningly. "How would you like to go for a ride?" Bas said and winked at him.

Over the next week Saoirse moved into the castle and Conri went back to his uncle's place to ask them if they would like to come live with him at the castle. Rionach, Luna and Tempest went with him, making the journey shorter as they all flew there together. The wedding was announced to the people living in and around the castle, much to the joy of the locals. Even the king sent his congratulations on the upcoming event, and other lords sent gifts and announced that they would be attending the wedding. This annoyed Vig immensely as they had never been invited, but this was more or less custom among the high-born. Conri and the others returned later that week with the news that his uncle and wife were coming, bringing all their belongings along with young Garbhan. Conri had taken the news that Rionach would not survive the birth of their child pretty hard, but as their wedding approached, he had more or less come to terms with it. Bas and Conri had become close during the time he had been there, and together they had created a special guard to take care of security around the family, especially the child that was to come. The dragon guards, Dracones custodia, would be led by him and Garbhan once he got old enough.

Chapter 40

The rider was pushing his horse to the breaking point, driving it on through the night. The animal was drenched in sweat and foaming around the mouth as he approached the castle perched on the cliffs overlooking the sea. The drawbridge lowered as he got close, not slowing down one second but charged through till he got into the inner bailey. The rider jumped off almost before the beast had stopped and ran in through the doors into the inner keep. The guards let him into the main hall and he stopped only a few feet short of the steps leading up to the throne.

"Your Highness Nex, I have news for you," Dougal said and fell to one knee.

"Yes, I was expecting your return. What has my cursed brother done this time? Has he built another castle? Or maybe crowned himself king?" Nex laughed. Dougal was glad Nex was in a good mood, because he had no idea how he would take the news of Rionach marrying a young dragon slayer. The last time he had been here he had barely escaped with his life. He did not like to hear how his brother's lands prospered or how all his people loved him. And when Dougal had told him of Rionach being a young woman, Nex had just about lost it. But now he just listened silently as Dougal gave his report about the upcoming wedding. When Dougal was finished, Nex sat quietly, tapping his long fingernails on the armrest of the chair. The situation was still not certain for Dougal as Nex could still lose his temper and tear him apart; but he didn't. Instead, he got up and walked slowly down the steps as he smiled.

"How wonderful. That is good news, Dougal."

"My Lord?" Dougal looked confused.

"Well, it can only mean one thing: the circle will start again. And this time we know where they are. I can take the child once it is born. I'll be able to raise it as my own and turn it to my will. Then when the child gets all its powers, I can harvest them for myself. All I have to figure out is how to deal with my brother." Dougal got up.

"Can't you just kill his woman? That should unbalance him enough to give you the upper hand." "What an excellent idea, even better than you think. Killing her would be the death of him. Yes, it may take some time, but I do believe you just solved my problem. Well done, Dougal." Nex smiled widely at him. They both turned as the doors opened. Inanis came walking into the room wearing a dark blue velvet dress which was cut so low it was threatening to reveal more than it hid. Dougal fell to his knees again.

"Lady Inanis. You look beautiful as always." She smiled vainly.

"Flattery will get you anywhere with me." She sniffed the air as she got close to him and frowned. "But not till you get scrubbed properly. You smell dreadful." She walked a half circle around him and kissed Nex on the cheek.

"I found what I was looking for." She spoke quietly and

grinned as she took Nex's hands. He threw his head back and laughed. "More good news. How wonderful. She is willing to join our cause?"

"More than willing, but she has some unfinished business to take care of before she joins us. She should be arriving some time at the end of this week." Dougal had never seen Nex this pleased and had to admit it actually scared him a little.

"What of Carliga? Any word from her?" Nex asked almost excitedly.

"She will be flying in sometime tonight." Nex threw his hands out to the sides and slowly turned as he laughed.

"Soon we will not be quite as outnumbered by my brother's little family. I can almost taste how sweet victory will be." He spun around and grinned at Inanis.

"And I have some news: we are going to crash a wedding. Bas and Orelaith's little spawn is marrying the young dragon slayer. I guess the invitation got lost on its way here."

"I guess so. When is this farce supposed to be played?" Inanis asked.

"In two weeks time, so we will have time to gather our own little family."

"I can't wait to see their stupid faces when we ride in through the gates to their castle." Inanis grinned evilly.

"And I know just who we will take with us. I feel like having a feast! What do you say, my dear Inanis? Do you want to go on a killing spree?" Nex smiled at her. She clapped her hands.

"Oh yes, that sounds like fun!"

As the last days before the wedding passed, Orelaith was feeling a little sad. It all just reminded her too much of the weeks before she lost her family. Bas found her standing on the porch outside the counsell chamber one evening and asked her why she was unhappy.

"I am not unhappy, my love. I am just thinking of my father and mother. You know that it was in preparation for my marriage that I lost them. I never went back to bury them, and it still pains me to this day." He turned her around.

"I understand, but all you had to do was ask, my love. I can take you there if that would give you peace. Do you want that?" She looked up at him with eyes brimming with tears and whispered,

"Really? Oh Bas, I would be so grateful."

"And I think it would be a good idea to take Rionach with you so she could see where you grew up. What do you think?" Smiling, she threw her arms around his neck. "I will take that as a yes." He laughed. "Why don't you go talk to her? I will ask Luna and Tempest if they want to come too." She kissed him and smiled.

"I will go right away." She almost ran out of the room. Luna came strolling in and looked after Orelaith as she ran down the stairs.

"Someone's in a hurry… What's going on, Bas?"

"Ah, Luna, just the dragon I wanted to see. I have a favor

LORE OF THE DRAGONS: ESSENCE OF A QUEEN

to ask of you. How would you like to go on a little trip?"

"Oh yeah, that sounds like fun. Where are we going?" Luna asked and leaned up against the bench as Bas poured himself a cup of wine.

"Orelaith never went back to the farm where she grew up, and is feeling guilty for not returning there to bury her family after they died. The upcoming wedding has woken some painful memories, so I suggested that we take her back so she can get some closure. What do you say, are you up for the trip?"

"Yes, most definitely. Anything to get me out of Vig's way. She is driving me crazy these days getting all worked up about the wedding and is worse than usual. I swear she is enjoying herself way too much, bossing everyone around." Bas laughed.

"So I am guessing Tempest won't mind joining us then."

"Oh, she will be overjoyed to get out of Vig's grasp. I will go talk to her right away. When do you want to leave?" Luna asked as she headed towards the door.

"As soon as it gets dark enough to fly without detection."

"Very well, but you get to tell Vig. I don't much feel like listening to her go on and on about how she needs us here and how dangerous it can be," Luna said and hurried out the door before Bas could object.

"Not fair!" he called after her and laughed.

As Luna suspected, Vig had given Bas a hard time, but in the end she had to agree that it was a good idea to go back to Orelaith's roots. She fussed a little, making them take warm clothes and food enough to feed a small army, but she joined the others on the porch to wave goodbye.

"We should be back again tomorrow night or the day after that. That should leave plenty of time before the wedding," Bas shouted over his shoulder as they lifted off from the porch and flew into the night.

Conri watched them go and shook his head and laughed.

"I know what you are thinking. I am just as amazed at this as you are," Saoirse said and leaned against the railing next to him. "But it is wonderful, and I feel so privileged to know them. They are truly amazing people... dragons, I mean." Conri nodded.

"Not in my wildest imagination had I ever thought that this would be my life; marrying a woman with a dragon for a father. Only a few months ago I would have sworn all dragons were evil monsters that needed to be eradicated. Just goes to show you never know what can happen. Not only that, I also have a dragon brother." Saoirse looked at him.

"Does that change the way you feel about him?" He shook his head.

"No, quite the opposite actually. He may not be my father's son, but he's my brother nonetheless. And now I think he's even more special to me."

"He is how old again?" Saoirse tapped her lip with her finger.

"He just turned five. Although, he acts and looks more like an eight year old." Conri said and grinned. "I think it's a dragon thing."

"It is." They turned and saw Opulentia walking out to them. "Dragons mature much faster than humans; we had to. In our home world, there were many dangers for a little whelp, so we needed to be strong and fast at an early age," she said and handed them each a cup of wine.

"How big will he get? Do you know?" Conri asked and took a sip. Opulentia smiled and said,

"As big as Bas, if not bigger. He was larger than Bas and Nex when they were whelps. And when he was appointed head of the elite guard, he was huge even among us. But as far as I know, he's mostly human now with no possibility to take on dragon form. He will however be very strong and unnaturally fast once the web that Vig cast on him fades." Conri nodded.

"Yes, Bas told me about that. And I do understand why he did it. I guess we'll just have to see how he turns out." Saoirse yawned,

"I think it's time I headed to bed. The kids will be up early and I don't want to be half asleep when Vig comes to ask me what color I think the flowers should be or how far I have gotten with the dresses for the wedding."

"I think we all should get some rest. Now that we are five less, she will be demanding that we step in and help with all the silly little details most of us could not give a rat's ass about." Opulentia rolled her eyes and they headed down to their chambers.

Chapter 41

As the morning light crept over the hillside, Orelaith saw her old home for the first time in five years. Her old home was nothing more than an old pile of overgrown rubble, and the other buildings likewise. As Bas landed gently in the middle of what had once been her father's pride and joy, she sat still for a moment just staring at the remains.

"How are you holding up, Orelaith?" Bas asked softly.

"I just… it feels strange to be here again," She said and slid off Bas' back. The dragons transformed and the five of them walked around in silence for a while just staring.

"Orelaith, over here!" Luna called out. They all walked over to where Luna was and saw she had found five graves. Her parents' names, her brother and his wife and her own name.

"It must have been old man O'Tool and his family who did this. They were invited to the wedding…" Orelaith started clearing away the grass around the graves but Rionach put her hand on her shoulder.

"Let me.." she said. She held up her right hand and her

nails grew so they more or less resembled her talons in dragon form, then she rammed her fist into the ground and closed her eyes. The grass that surrounded the graves slowly receded as they watched, and small white flowers grew out of the topsoil covering the mounds of earth. The weather-worn wooden crosses withered away, and in their place, five stones came out of the ground. Rionach frowned as she strained under the work she was doing, but soon the names appeared on the stones in clear letters. Once she was done, she opened her eyes and found the others staring at her.

"I had no idea you could do that," Bas said, smiling at her. Orelaith hugged her.

"Thank you, sweetheart. It looks wonderful." Rionach wiped a tear off her mother's cheek.

"I never knew them, but they are my family too and I wanted to do something special for them. Now they will always be remembered. " Tempest turned her head and looked around as if she had heard something.

"What is it, Tempest?" Bas asked and looked in the direction Tempest was staring.

"I felt something. I am not sure, but I think there is another dragon here." Luna and Bas closed their eyes and tried to sense what Tempest had felt.

"Yes, I also feel it now." Rionach got up and stared towards the trees.

"Well, what do you know, the royal prince! What a coincidence." They turned and saw a pale woman leaning up against the remains of the old house. "And with your little family too. Now that is a surprise" she said and walked slowly towards them.

"Ruina. I was hoping I had seen the last of you," Bas said through clenched teeth.

"You wound me, brother. All these years, and that is the welcome I get?"

"You have a sister?" Orelaith sent without taking her eyes off the slender woman who circled around them. Her yellow hair was long and straight reaching to her waist. But it was a flat, almost sickly yellow, not the vibrant golden color Solis had. Her almost red eyes darted from one to the other as she stopped on the other side of the graves.

"Yes, she is my sister. But I thought she was dead centuries ago. She was one of the first to get infected," Bas sent and placed himself between Orelaith and Ruina.

The sickly looking woman sniffed the air and looked at Rionach.

"What have we here? There is a familiar smell to you, child. No… it can't be? You are the thorn in my dear brother Nex's side?" She laughed coldly.

"I… I remember you. How you have faded… You were so lively and full of joy. Now I sense only death and decay. How sad…" Rionach said and cocked her head to one side as she looked at Ruina. Her words obviously struck a chord in the pale woman, but her bemusement was only apparent for a second. Then she laughed.

LORE OF THE DRAGONS: ESSENCE OF A QUEEN

"You mean weak and naive? But you do surprise me. I had come to believe you were still a whelp, but here I find a young woman already carrying her own destruction within. It was unintended, I suppose?"

"That is none of your business, Ruina. You are no longer a part of my family, and I think it is time for you to leave." Bas took a threatening step towards her. Black tendrils shot out towards them all, but they were thrown back so violently that they sent the woman staggering backwards. A flash of light emanated from Rionach. It slowly died away as she walked towards Ruina who stood on wobbly legs and stared wide-eyed at her.

"You foolish whelp! You forget who you are dealing with!" Rionach's eyes were still aglow with a green light. "Now be gone before I decide to finish you off." The woman jumped up in the air, transformed into a pale yellow dragon covered in broken scales and flew off. Rionach stared after her as the glow in her eyes died away.

When she looked around at the others, they were all looking at her with their mouths wide open.

"What? Why are you looking at me like that?" Bas was the first to regain his wits.

"You… you sounded just like my mother… and what you did. Amazing! How did you do that? That was no tendril casting…" Rionach just smiled at him.

"I don't really know. I just got angry at her for trying to hurt you and I reacted." Luna came over and gave her a hug.

"That my dear child, was pure dragon magic I have not seen since before the fiery rain on our home world. It fills me with so much joy I can't even begin to describe."

Tempest was looking around.

"I think we better head out of here, I don't like what I am feeling right now. If we stay low we can avoid being detected and we will be home not long after dark."

"Mama! Are you ok?" Rionach ran over to Orelaith who was sitting on the ground next to her father's grave.

"Oh yes darling. I just fell over when that dreadful woman tried to attack Bas."

"Are you sure?" Bas asked as he and Rionach helped her up on her feet.

"Yes, now stop worrying. I have done all I can for my family now, and more than ever I see that my life is with you." She smiled and put her arms around them both.

"Well, let's go then," Tempest said and grinned as she transformed. Soon they were airborne, and Orelaith looked over her shoulder down at the farm that had once been her home. Her life was not there any more but she was glad she had the chance to say her final goodbyes to her mother and father. A pain shot through her chest and she looked down. There was a small black spot on her dress, right over her heart. The snake-like tendril had hit her, but she didn't want any of the others to worry about that now. They had a wedding coming up and a baby that was on its way. The last thing she needed now was everyone worrying about her. It was probably nothing anyway…

LORE OF THE DRAGONS: ESSENCE OF A QUEEN

When they arrived back at the castle that night, they found the others in the dining hall. Conri's uncle and aunt had arrived and little Garbhan was sitting in his brother's lap as they came in.

"You have returned. Did you have a pleasant trip?" Vig said and called a maid to set out more plates.

"Yes, we did, but we can talk more about that later." Bas smiled and walked over to the newcomers. "You must be Conri's uncle and aunt. I am sorry, but Conri never mentioned your names." The big man got up and shook Bas' hand.

"Art, and this is my wife, Cara. It is truly an honor to meet you, Lord Basilicus; and under such happy circumstances as well." Bas smiled.

"Please just call me Bas. You are to be family after all."

Something was tugging at Bas' pants and he looked down to find little Garbhan smiling up at him.

"Well hello there young man. It is a pleasure to see you again." Bas crouched down.

"I remember you too." The boy grinned.

"You have grown so big since the last time we met. What have they been feeding you?"

"A lot of vegetables." Garbhan made a face. "And fish, lots of fish, but I like that." Bas picked him up and sat down in his chair next to Orelaith.

"You're pretty," Garbhan said and smiled at her.

"Why thank you, young man." Orelaith replied and

stroked his little chin.

"I will marry a woman just like you when I get older," he said, making them all laugh.

"I bet you will. But to win her heart you must be big and strong, so you will have to eat your food," Cara said and handed over his plate with his unfinished food. He sighed and picked at it.

"The things a boy has to do for love..."

"Now I think we all have to finish our plates. I heard that the cook has made her special apple pie, but no one gets any till she gets all the empty plates back to the kitchen," Solis said and winked at him.

The rest of the evening they all talked and got to know Conri's family. There were only two days left till the wedding, and the days would be full so they all turned in early. Bas did talk to them all in the counsell chamber about Ruina and of how Rionach had used true dragon magic to protect them. Solis had been her best friend once, and it was hard for her to hear of how she had changed. They all knew what the infection did to their kind. Opulentia had a theory about how Ruina had gotten to be here on earth. Nex and she had been very close, and she suspected that he had smuggled her into his own sphere, believing he could save her. That, of course, resulted in the entire unit being infected. They decided to leave the subject alone till after the wedding and concentrate on matters of more pressing nature, as Vig called it.

LORE OF THE DRAGONS: ESSENCE OF A QUEEN

The next day, a letter arrived that caused quite a stir among them. Nex had sent word that he wished a truce would be called between them and that he and three other dragons would be coming to the celebration. He also apologized for Ruina's behavior and promised it would not happen again. They discussed this at length before deciding that maybe they could find some way to interact with their family even despite the infection.

After lunch, Conri pulled Vig and Opulentia aside.

"I have a favour to ask you…" Opulentia smiled at him.

"Of course, young Conri. Ask away."

"As you both know, my uncle and aunt do not have any children of their own, and it is not for the lack of wanting one. Wanting many children even. But for some reason, they can not conceive any between them. I was hoping you would be able to help them," he said and looked hopefully at them. The two women looked at each other and smiled.

"Yes, I think that can be arranged. Where are they now?" Vig said and smiled at him. Conri brightened up in a big smile.

"They are in their room. I can take you to them right away. If now is a good time for you, of course."

"Lead the way," Opulentia followed behind him as he made his way to the room. He knocked gently on the door and entered.

"Uncle? Auntie? Vig and Opulentia said they might be able to help." The couple were sitting on the bed and Cara took her husband's hand.

"Really? Oh Art…" she said and looked at him.

"Now wait, we don't know what they will find yet, so don't get yourself all worked up," Art said and patted his wife's hand. Vig and Opulentia walked in.

"How do you want to do this, Opulentia?" Vig asked. Opulentia crossed her arms.

"Hmm… how about you take Art here to Conri's room, and I will take care of our lovely Cara here?" Vig nodded.

"Sounds like a plan to me. Conri, you can wait in the hallway." Vig took hold of Art's hand and led him out of the room. Opulentia sat down next to the little woman.

"Now then, let's see. Oh, before I start, I want you to close your eyes and relax. This may feel a little strange, but it will be worth it, I promise."

Conri walked back and forth for what seemed like hours, but after only a few minutes Art came bursting out of Conri's room with a wide smile on his face. Opulentia was holding the door open as he reached it and once he had passed she closed it behind her.

"That was easy." She smiled at Vig.

"Yes, only a minor correction and he was fine. Same with Cara?" Opulentia nodded.

"What did you do?" Conri asked as he walked down the hallway between the two women.

"Well you see, your aunt's–" Conri covered his ears.

"Lalalalaa! Never mind, I don't need to know!" Vig huffed

"You shouldn't have asked then." Opulentia laughed.

"He should have known better. But now we have other business to attend to that involves you, young Conri. You need to get your wedding clothes tailored," she said and hooked her arm in his before he managed to get away. The rest of the day, Conri was poked and prodded, pinched and stung by Saoirse's needles till he felt like screaming. Bas laughed at him when he came by. When he told Bas of what Vig and Opulentia had done for his uncle and aunt, Bas smiled warmly.

"I am glad to hear that. It may be the opening to get them on our side if we decide to tell them who we are."

"They have been praying for this for years. If my aunt becomes pregnant now, you will have an ally that you can trust with your life."

"Good to know. Now I will leave you to your torture…" he said and winked at Conri.

"Don't leave me here! Ouch! That was uncalled for," Bas heard as he walked out the door.

Chapter 42

The day had finally arrived and the entire castle was decorated with white flowers. A long table had been set in the main bailey for all the locals to share in the feast as well. A few hours before the wedding service, a large black coach pulled up in front of the keep's main doors. Bas and the others knew instantly who it was and stood ready at the top of the steps as Nex stepped out of the coach, followed by Inanis, Caliga, and Ruina.

"Brother." Bas nodded. Nex was dressed in all black with a red dragon embroidered onto the breast of his jacket. His long black hair hung loose and he had a snarky grin on his face as he walked slowly up the steps.

"Basilicus, you have not changed much, I see." Bas shook his hand and pulled him in.

"If you try anything, I will finish you off myself." Nex sent him a shocked look. "I would not dream of it…" he said, sounding almost offended. But they all knew this was just an act.

"That goes for you… ladies as well," Vig said and glared at Inanis who returned her look with an equal amount of contempt. Caliga was hanging behind, staring at them almost curiously.

"Who is that?" Orelaith asked Luna and nodded towards the dark skinned woman in the blue dress.

"Her name is Caliga. She was a noble at the court where Bas grew up. After Ruina she was the second to be infected. We thought she too was long dead, but I guess one can never know. She has great dark powers, literally." Bas took a step forward.

"I have prepared some rooms for you to dress and clean up in, but do not expect to stay over." "That is fine. We never planned on it," Nex said and followed him in through the big wooden doors. As Ruina passed by, Orelaith's hand went to her chest. A pain like a needle prick went through and she saw Ruina smiling as she glanced at her.

"Are you ok, Orelaith? You look a little pale." Tempest asked. "Thank you for your concern Tempest, my dear, but I am fine. That woman just unsettles me" she answered and smiled at her. She was unsure if Tempest believed her but she had bigger concerns right now, her daughter was getting married in an hour…

The big hall was completely silent despite being fully packed with people. Orelaith and the others from their family along with Nex and the three dragon women stood in the front of the hall as the doors opened and Rionach came walking in with Bas. There was a collective gasp as they saw her. The cream white lace dress flowed behind her and a matching veil covered her waist long copper curls. Conri watched them gliding up the center of the room with a rather sheepish grin on his face. The three dragon ladies never smiled and Inanis was actually picking uninterested at her nails. They had the local priest perform the actual ceremony. Solis, Vig and Serovita were constantly wiping their eyes with handkerchiefs. Once the ceremonial part was over, the couple turned and the gathered people cheered as Conri and Rionach walked out to the steps to greet the people who had gathered there. A little girl walked up and gave Rionach a handful of little white flowers she had picked. Rionach kissed her little cheeks and gave her a big hug, much to the joy of the child's mother.

"Thank you all for coming to this celebration. Eat and drink to your heart's delight." Servants carried out tray upon tray of food and wine for the people. Conri and Rionach waved as they walked back in, followed by their family and the other lords and ladies. Most of them went straight to the main hall, but Bas and the other dragons who lived there went up to the counsell chamber to have a private moment. Opulentia, who had been in her Bridget form all day shook it off and sat down.

"I must say Nex and his little troupe look dreadful. It is rather sad really. But I am looking forward to seeing the look on their faces when I walk in." She grinned.

"Yes, that may be a bit of a surprise to them," Vig stated and smiled smugly. "But I think it is good for them to see how outnumbered they are, not only in actual numbers, but also in power."

LORE OF THE DRAGONS: ESSENCE OF A QUEEN

"I suggest we all freshen up then join our guests," Bas said. "We will have to spend some time in the same room as Nex and the other three, but it will be worth it when they see Opulentia come walking into the room."

When they returned to the main hall, they saw that Nex and his companions had taken an entire table for themselves and the people they had brought with them . Orelaith gasped when she saw who was sitting next to Lady Ruina. Malum looked at her and winked.

"What is it, Orelaith? You look like you have seen a ghost." Bas said when he saw how pale she had become. Orelaith just stared towards Nex's table. Bas followed her gaze and she felt him tense up when he saw who it was.

"How dare he bring that man into my home?!" Bas was about to get up, but Orelaith grabbed his arm.

"I will not have a fuss on my daughter's wedding day. It was a long time ago, my love."

"I should have known he was one of Nex's men as he's almost as bad as his master," Bas said and shot Malum a toxic look. Malum cringed and looked away. Nex and his ladies laughed when they saw his reaction. Another surprise was when Dougal walked in and sat down next to Lady Inanis.

"I should have seen that one coming. His story had more holes in it than substance," Bas said and sipped his wine.

"It's time we give them a little surprise of our own now." Luna grinned and nodded towards the doors as Opulentia entered, adorned in a beautiful dress of different shades of green and blue. Nex stared at her as did the others at his table. To most it just seemed that he was only vaguely interested, but Bas saw how his knuckles whitened around his cup. Ruina pushed her food away and looked even more pallid than usual. Now it was Bas' turn to gloat. As Opulentia took her place next to Orelaith, Bas raised his cup and nodded to Nex.

"I must say the look on his face is priceless," Vig said and grinned.

"This charade is giving me a headache." Terra sighed. "I have never liked all these mind games the royal family's play with each other…"

"I will be glad when all these people go home again. I can't even fly down to the ocean to get a quick snack if I get hungry at night." Aqua said between bites. The rest of the dinner was a tense affair but somehow they got through it. When Rionach and Conri announced their honeymoon departure most of the nobles said their goodbyes and departed as well. Only Nex and his little pack stayed behind. Both groups dallied at their tables till the last of the humans left the room. Bas had dismissed the servants and as they closed the doors behind them, Bas got up and sat on the edge of the table facing Nex.

"Why did you come here, Nex? Surely you knew you would not be welcome." Nex leaned back in his chair.

"And miss a celebration like this? No, I had to come. We

are family after all, are we not?" Bas shook his head and sent him a sad smile.

"My brother died the moment he got infected. Family is more than just blood ties, Nex. Look around me, all around this table sits my family." Nex laughed.

"Blood is still thicker, brother. I have our sister here with me. You asked why I came; I have come to repeat my offer, the one I gave you when I attacked your sergeant-at-arms." He got up and walked around the table.

"Do you remember? Join us or die…" He said grinning at Bas.

"Enough of that!" Opulentia got up and stared at them. "I have had enough of you, you annoying little whelp. And Bas, do not let his mind games set you off. I am way too tired of this." Both men walked back to their seats.

"Bas, you should have known better than to let your brother and his band of merry men, or women in this case, take any part in the celebration. And you." Opulentia turned her eyes on Nex. "I know what you want and it will never be yours. Even before the infection hit you, I knew you wanted to be king, but you were last in line for the throne and you still are. You do not have the power to oust Bas because he was always superior to you. And as you can see we greatly outnumber you, not only because there are more of us, but we are more powerful than you are. Ruina, how stupid can you get trying to attack four of your own kind and one of them being the queen reborn?"

"Ladies, I think we have overstayed our welcome." Nex

glared.

"Overstayed? You were never invited in the first place," Tempest said and sat down in her chair.

"I thought that the invitation got lost before I received it. I mean, as the father's brother I would have thought I was on the guest list for sure." Nex displayed a fake shocked expression and got up slowly.

"Come ladies, I do believe that it is time for us to return to where we are more welcome..." As he passed Bas he stared into his eyes and said with a low threatening voice.

"You don't deserve to be king. You don't have the balls to do what it takes. I do. One day I will possess the power to undo what our mother did, and then I will breed an entire army of my kind and create a new world here." Bas stared back at him.

"The only way you can ever be king is if you kill me, and I am stronger than you, little brother." "There is more than one way to skin a cat..." Nex said and glanced at Orelaith with a nasty smile on his face. Bas growled at him.

"Don't ever come near my family. Ever!" Nex pulled back and looked around at the others,

"I would say it has been a pleasure, but that would be a lie." Then he left, followed by Ruina, Caliga and Inanis.

"Tempest, Luna, go and make sure they actually leave. Then come meet us in the counsell chamber. They may be a bigger threat than we first thought, but even if they are not, we do need to make sure we can protect our own if he should be stupid enough to attack." Tempest and Luna walked out as Opulentia walked over and placed her hand on Bas' shoulder.

"I must say you are starting to become the king I thought you would always be." Bas shook his head.

"A king is only as good as his family makes him. I would be nothing without all of you." Opulentia looked up at him and stroked his cheek.

"Your mother would have been proud of you, young prince. I know I am." He smiled at her and they all went to the counsell chamber to wait for Luna and Tempest to return.

Chapter 43

It had been a long night and Orelaith had fallen asleep in her chair as the others discussed how to best secure the castle and its people. Bas smiled as he looked at her.

"She must have been so anxious with everything that has been going on that it has tired her out. Maybe you should just carry her to bed and we can continue this tomorrow instead. It's not like Nex and the others will attack tonight," Opulentia said. Bas nodded and got up.

"Yes, I think that is a good idea. We already have found plenty of places where we can tighten security." Aqua got up and headed for the porch.

"I thought you would never call an end to the chit chat. I am starving…" Tempest stopped her.

"Not tonight, Aqua. Even though we made sure that Nex and the others left the castle, we can not be sure they left the area completely. However, there are plenty of leftovers in the kitchen that you can dig into." Aqua grinned widely.

"That sounds like an excellent idea. Kitchen it is."

LORE OF THE DRAGONS: ESSENCE OF A QUEEN

"I do believe I will join you. I had a hard time getting any food down with Lord tall, dark and toxic staring at us all evening," Luna said and put her arm around Aqua as they left the room. Bas gently picked up Orelaith and nodded to the others.

"Sleep well, tomorrow we have more to discuss."

"Anything besides the security issues?" Opulentia said as she poured herself a cup of wine.

"If and how to tell Conri's aunt and uncle about us for one. Then there is Garbhan, of course… Think of these things and let me know how you feel tomorrow. Now, I need to get this fair lady to bed…"

The next day was mostly spent saying goodbye to their overnight guests, some lords and ladies that had traveled far to come to the wedding. It seemed they were all quite keen to get to know more about Bas and the others. Some of them could become valued allies, but they all appeared to be rather shallow people who cared more about power and wealth than anything else. Once the last of them had left, the entire castle breathed a sigh of relief and things quickly got back to normal. Terra and Serovita helped get the main hall tidied and Solis and Tempest worked in the bailey taking down decorations and carrying in plates and dishes that had been set out for the people the night before. Servants and ladies alike enjoyed the shared co-operation, it appeared, and Solis more than Tempest as the young men flocked around them offering to help with every little thing. No one saw Rionach or Conri all morning, but they were excused for obvious reasons.

Around lunchtime, Art and Cara approached Vig and Opulentia as they sat in the castle garden. They were a little unsure of themselves and wondered if the ladies had a minute to spare.

"Of course, have a seat." Opulentia smiled.

"Have some tea with us and tell us what is troubling you," Vig said and set out a cup for each of them. Once they had been served, Cara looked at Art and nodded at him.

"We were kind of wondering about a few things," he said hesitantly.

"Yes?" Vig said and smiled at him. He floundered a little before he continued, as if he was trying to figure something out in his head.

"The thing is… what we wanted to know… How did you…? I mean… we felt so different after you…" Opulentia put her hand on his.

"You want to know what we did to you and how we did it. Am I right?" The couple nodded and looked at them expectantly. "It was magic. And a little secret remedy that has been in our family for a long time. But before I say anything more, I would like to see if it worked. Is that ok, Cara?" Opulentia said and smiled at her.

"Of course, milady," Cara said and bowed her head respectfully.

"Just give me your hands and sit still. This will only take a second." Cara stretched out her hands and Opulentia took them in hers as she closed her eyes. For a moment she said nothing... Then she smiled and opened her eyes.

"I am glad to say come spring you will be having not only one, but two little ones to bring you joy. Congratulations." Art smiled widely.

"Really? We are having a baby?" Cara's eyes were brimming with tears,

"Are you sure? I am afraid to get my hopes up." Opulentia nodded.

"I am sure. It's two little boys." Art looked serious for a second

"Are you witches? Is that how you do this? I mean, I don't really care if you are witches. We would never tell anyone if you are.." Vig laughed.

"No, my friend, we are not witches." She looked at Opulentia,

"What do you think? Should we gather the others so we can make a decision about what to tell them?"

"Yes, I believe we should." Opulentia nodded, then turned to Art."Come to the counsell chamber after lunch and we will have an answer for you." Art nodded and he and Cara left with smiles on their faces, holding hands as they walked away.

They all gathered after lunch. As Bas talked of who they were, Art's face went from white to gray, and from gray to red as he realized that he had been part of killing their kind. He apologized over and over for being involved in an extermination that could very well have been close friends or even family members of Bas or the others. Bas smiled.

"If I held it against you for killing dragons, do you really think I would have let your nephew marry my daughter? No, as I told you, they were all infected and it may even have been some kind of mercy to end their lives." Opulentia looked at Art and Cara. "So now you know how we were able to heal you and know that Cara is already pregnant. But for us, the big question is: can we trust you to keep our secret?" Art looked from one to the other then he got up and walked over to Bas. Then he fell to one knee and said, "I will serve you with honor till the day I die. And I will raise my sons to do the same when I get too old and stiff to fight for you." Cara knelt down next to Art.

"I swear that I will never betray the trust that you have shown us. And I too pledge my life to serve you in any way I can."

"Please.. get up." Bas smiled. "We are not like others you have served under. We promise if you stay here with us, we will do everything we can to keep you safe and well. And please, feel free to call me Bas, I am not really a lord…" Luna grinned.

"No that is true, but he's a crown prince…" Art looked at Bas.

"Really?" Bas nodded and sent Luna a glare.

"Yes, I was to be king, but as I see it one can not be king without a country. But enough of that. There is one more matter we need to address: what do we do with young Garbhan?"

"May I ask a question?" Cara asked almost timidly. They all turned and looked at her.

"Of course. What is it?" Bas smiled at the little woman. She glanced nervously at the others before she continued.

"What would happen if you remove the… spell? Will he still be Garbhan?" Bas looked at Vig.

"Do you know?" Vig looked thoughtful as she walked slowly over to Bas.

"To tell you the truth, I really don't know what would happen. It was different with Rionach. She carries a different type of magic and her memories are much stronger than Frater's would be, at least that is what I suspect. If we do decide to remove the spell, and I must say I don't even know if that is possible, I guess all we can do is wait and see what happens." Bas frowned.

"I think… we should hold off on this, and I believe he should remain with Art and Cara till he gets older. But he should go through training with Conri and with you, Art, as soon as you see fit. Do you all agree?" A collective yes sounded and the matter was settled.

In the weeks and months that followed, Conri and Art started gathering what soon turned out to be a formidable army of men. Tempest was set as the head of the army, something a few of the men found strange till she came up against them in combat. As they lay bleeding at her feet, not one of them objected to having a woman commanding them. Thirteen men were picked out to be the elite guard and they were given a mixture of herbs with one single drop of dragon's blood to enhance their senses. They were called the Dracones Custodia and were soon widely known to be men of unwavering loyalty.

Rionach spent a lot of time with her family and did not venture out in dragon form any more, much to Aqua and Luna's disappointment. But in her condition they took no chances because could maybe affect the child. Opulentia and Vig kept a close eye on the baby's growth and found it to be no more than an empty vessel to begin with. But slowly and surely it started pulling away the memories and powers from Rionach leaving her more or less forgetful of even the simplest spells. By the time deep winter came, she did not recall anything of her life as a dragon queen or of the powers she once possessed.

Chapter 44

"Mama!" Orelaith woke up with her heart racing and found Bas jumping out of bed. "Rionach…" Orelaith rushed to the door with Bas on her heels. Vig and Opulentia were coming down the hallway as Orelaith ran into Rionach and Conri's room.

"Rionach, are you ok?" Orelaith said as she sat down on the bed next to her wide eyed daughter. "Mama… something is wrong. The pain, it's too early. The baby is not due for another month," Rionach cried. Vig and Opulentia came quickly and lit up the candles in the room.

"Orelaith, we need to check and see what is going on," Vig said and put her hand on Orelaith's shoulder.

"I will be right here, sweetheart. But we need to let Vig and Opulentia examine you to see what is happening." Rionach took a deep breath and nodded.

"Now let's see…" Opulentia placed her hand on Rionach's belly as did Vig, then they closed their eyes and let their golden tendrils forth to find the cause of Rionach's pains.

"Do you see what I do?" Opulentia said quietly.

"Yes… the baby is coming now. Do you think you can stop it?" Opulentia shook her head.

"No, the child has already taken so much of Rionach's powers and has made her mind up that now is the time to be born. I couldn't stop it no matter how hard I tried." Vig sighed and opened her eyes.

"You'd better go wake the others, Conri. It will take all of us to do the binding and I think they want to say goodbye to Rionach before she slips away." Opulentia said quietly.

"I will go with him." Bas said and put his arm around Conri's shoulders as they walked out.

"I will take the edge off the pain, but that is all I can do, Rionach. Orelaith, come take her hand," Vig said and moved to the side so Orelaith could sit next to her daughter.

"Mama… I don't want to die without seeing her. And promise me you will give her the name we talked about."

"Shhh, my child, I gave you that promise and I will keep it." Orelaith said and Rionach put her head in her lap. "Can you stop the process long enough for her to see the child, Opulentia?" Tears were running down Orelaith's cheeks as she turned and looked at her.

"I do not think so, Orelaith. But I will try." Opulentia was visibly moved as she closed her eyes again. The strain of what she was doing showed on her face, but a few seconds later she opened her eyes. "I may have won her a few seconds, but that is all I can manage. Any longer and Rionach's memories will be lost forever." Orelaith nodded and stroked Rionach's hair. She seemed calmer now. The pain was not as strong once Vig had done what she could.

LORE OF THE DRAGONS: ESSENCE OF A QUEEN

"Mama… it's ok. I am not afraid anymore, so please don't cry." Rionach looked up into her mother's eyes. Orelaith kissed her hair and tried to hold back the tears.

"I know, my child. I will wait for the day when I can look into your daughter's eyes and see you there." Conri came running back into the room with Bas right behind him and he knelt down on the opposite side of Orelaith.

"My love." She took his hand and smiled weakly. "I need your word too; that you will protect her with your life… promise." Conri nodded and kissed her hand.

"I promise." Luna burst into the room.

"Kiddo… how dare you have a baby now? We had plans tomorrow…" she joked, but could not hold back the tears.

"Luna…" Rionach smiled at her as Luna knelt down next to Conri. Soon Tempest, Solis, Terra and Serovita came in. Aqua hesitated in the hallway but soon they were all gathered around the bed. Bas and Orelaith on the left with Rionach resting her head in her mother's lap. On her right Conri was now sitting holding his wife's hand and Luna sitting next to him. Tempest was standing behind Luna with her hand on her shoulder and next to Tempest stood Solis and Aqua. Beside Bas there were Terra and Serovita, while Vig, who was sitting on the bed, tried to take some of Rionach's pain away. Opulentia was standing at the end of the bed with her eyes closed. The contractions were getting more frequent and she was getting warmer and warmer till she was literally almost on fire.

As the first rays of sunlight came in through the window

Vig caught the little child as she came out.

"Quickly, give her to Rionach before she passes," Opulentia said as she cut the umbilical cord and tied it off. Vig handed the little girl to Orelaith and she placed her in Rionach's arms. Rionach looked at her daughter.

"She is perfect." Dark brown curls surrounded the little heart shaped face. She opened her emerald green eyes and looked at her mother. A fiery glow surrounded the two and Orelaith leaned back to avoid the heat.

"What is happening?"

"The transfer is almost complete. I could buy her no more time," Opulentia said quietly. Orelaith turned back and saw Rionach smiling softly down at the baby cradled in her arms with empty eyes.

"She has passed over, Orelaith," Bas said and put his arms around her shoulders.

"No. No…" Orelaith cried and buried her face in his chest. Vig picked up Rionach's daughter and wrapped her in a soft blanket.

"Here Conri, she needs to be with her father now," she said and handed the soft little bundle to him. He looked up with eyes full of tears.

"How can I take care of her? I know nothing about a baby and what it needs. What if I do something wrong? What if I hurt her?" Orelaith put her arm around him.

" I do. We all do… and we will do it together." Conri

LORE OF THE DRAGONS: ESSENCE OF A QUEEN

wiped his tears and smiled weakly at Orelaith.

"Thank you, but we need to give her a name. Did Rionach tell you what she was to be called?" Orelaith nodded.

"Yes, her name is Aednat. It means little fire."

"A very fitting name considering her entry into this world," Terra said and got up. "I need to go and write this down. Our history needs to be recorded." Bas was still staring at Rionach's lifeless body.

"This must never happen again. We need to do this now, Opulentia." He looked up at her. She nodded.

"You are right. Everyone gather around and hold hands. I will need to pull on all your powers to do this." Once everyone was in position, Opulentia closed her eyes and started casting a series of knots that grew and grew till it was an elaborate web.

"I think that is it. Are you all ready?"

"Yes." Opulentia took a deep breath.

"Here it goes…" As she cast the web over the child, the others felt their powers being drained as the knotwork folded around the child, almost melting into her skin. Opulentia tied off the ends and opened her eyes.

"It is done." Bas walked over to the bed and looked at Rionach's limp body.

"I will bury her in the cave under us. Terra, can you make a stone coffin to place her in?" Terra nodded. "Good. Let's wash her and put her in her blue dress; the one with the dragon on the chest. She loved that dress..." Bas said quietly. Orelaith, Luna, Tempest and Solis started washing and preparing the body.

"Conri, come with me. I think your uncle and aunt will want to hear what has happened," Vig said. Conri got up slowly, not taking his eyes off the little bundle in his arms.

"The people have a right to know. They have become so fond of her," Luna said softly.

"Maybe a statue in the bailey?" Solis looked around at the others. Terra nodded

"I can do that if we decide to make one." The door opened and a young maid came in, unaware what was going on. When she saw they were all gathered there, she apologized for disturbing them.

"No, its ok. Come here, child. We have something we want you to do for us." The maid came over and stared at Rionach lying on the bed.

"Oh no! Is she... But the baby?" The young girl looked at Orelaith and saw tears in her eyes.

"She did not survive the birth, but the baby is doing well. I need you to let the people know. Can you do that for me? For us? I don't think I could do it myself right now." The young girl curtsied.

"Milady, I would be honored to tell the people, but I am so very sad to hear this news. She was one of the kindest people I have ever met."

LORE OF THE DRAGONS: ESSENCE OF A QUEEN

"Thank you, child. I am grateful, we all are." The girl turned and walked to the door. But then she stopped and looked back at Orelaith.

"Milady, would you like me to find a nursemaid for the baby?" Orelaith looked up.

"Thank you, that would be wonderful. We had not even thought of that yet." The girl curtsied again

"I will have her come to the keep once I have found one." With that she left the room.

By noon, the steps were covered in flowers the people had left in memory of Rionach. Some spent the day crying in the bailey while others left flowers and quickly walked away. Terra made an additional room in the cave in which she sculptured a stone coffin for Rionach. Bas carried her body down followed by Orelaith and the rest of the family. Solis had put a big pillow in the coffin and Bas gently laid his daughter's head down upon it. Each of them walked over and said their own goodbyes and as they did so they walked out. Finally, only Bas and Orelaith remained.

"I can't ever do this again," Bas said and pulled his wife close.

"I know. I feel the same way." Orelaith looked down on Rionach's face which was covered with a transparent cloth. Her pale lips, still curled up in a soft smile. Bas dried his eyes and looked into Orelaith's tear filled eyes.

"But we need to remember one thing. Rionach the person may be gone, but her memories live on in her child. A child that will need us. So say your goodbyes and let us go find our granddaughter." Orelaith nodded and leaned into the coffin and kissed Rionach's forehead. "Sleep well, my child, till we see eachother again," she whispered.

"I have already said my goodbye." He put his arm around Orelaith's shoulders and together they walked out of the dark cave into the afternoon sun shining in through the window of their chamber.

Chapter 45

"Grandma! The twins are picking on me again. Make them stop!" The little girl came running over and right into her arms. Orelaith smiled down at the girl.

"What did they do this time?" With dark brown curls reaching down her back and wearing a bright yellow dress, the six year old girl looked up at her with big emerald green eyes.

"They told me I couldn't go fishing with them because I was a girl. It's not fair! They said I wouldn't want to get my little girly hands dirty, but I don't mind that. I am not afraid to dig for worms or to clean fish." Aednat was growing slower than her mother had, one could almost say at a normal rate.

"Don't you bother with them. How about we ask Luna to take you fishing instead?" Aednat lit up in a bright smile.

"Oh yes! Do you think she will, grandma?" Orelaith laughed.

"I think she would love to. Come, let's go see if we can find out where she is hiding." Orelaith got up and took her little hand just as Bas came walking towards them.

"Hello there. Where are you two off to in such a hurry?" He smiled down at them.

"We are looking for Luna," Aednat said. "I wanted to go fishing with the twins, but they said I couldn't come because I'm a girl, so I'm going to ask Luna if she will take me instead." She looked up at Bas with a smug grin on her face. He laughed.

"I think Luna is very, very busy now. But I know just who you can ask." She frowned.

"If you are thinking of daddy, you might as well forget it. He always has something else to do." Bas knelt down.

"I know, but he's trying to keep the bad man away, remember? Anyway, that was not who I had in mind. Someone just got home from a trip." Aednat lit up.

"Garbhan is back?" Bas laughed.

"Yes he is, and he told me he was looking for you." Aednat gave Bas a big kiss on the cheek. "Thank you, grandpa." Then she ran off looking for Garbhan.

"Was he really looking for her, Bas?" Orelaith asked.

"Yes, he takes his task very seriously. Appointing him to be her guardian is the best thing we ever did. Do you remember the look on his face when we asked him the week Aednat was born?" Orelaith smiled thinking back.

"Yes, he could not have been more proud." She looked up at him,

"But what brings you down here? I thought you would be

in war meetings all day?" Bas nodded. "I was. But we needed a break and I wanted to see you." She smiled up at him.

"It is good to see your face every once in a while. I just wish this could all be over soon."

"Me too, but Nex is constantly trying to find a way to take the dragon crown." Bas said as they strolled along. Summer had finally taken hold and the flowers were blooming in the castle gardens.

"Do you think he will ever give up?" Orelaith asked, looking up at Bas' serious face.

"No, I don't believe he ever will," he said and shook his head.

"There is one thing I could never understand. Why is he so desperate to be king?" Orelaith asked. "It's not like there is a kingdom to go with the title."

"He wants to harness the powers that come with it. As king he would possess the power to undo the spell that was cast on us to prevent us from overrunning this planet." Orelaith frowned.

"I don't understand. We do want the curse lifted, right?" Bas stopped and looked at her.

"Not like that. He wants to spread the infection again."

"But how? I thought you could no longer be infected. I mean, didn't Rionach change that?"

"Yes, she did, but Nex wants the power to change it back. He wants to turn this planet into his own personal kingdom no matter the consequences it will bring with it for humankind." They walked up the steps to the keep and found their way into the dining room. The others were gathered already and Garbhan sat next to Aednat and told her about his trip to the king's castle.

"Tempest, good to see you back. How was the trip?" Orelaith gave her a quick hug.

"We had a little run-in with some of Nex's men, but nothing I couldn't handle. He really is a pain in the –"

"Tempest! Little ears…" Vig sent her a cross look. Tempest leaned towards her.

"…butt. Anyway, it was only a handful of men and they were poorly trained in combat. I swear Nex is running out of men to send against us," Tempest said and took a big bite out of an apple.

"I don't think you are right, Tempest. I think he's sending the worst of what he has just to make us think just that. Nex is not stupid, you know. He was a very bright… child. I should know, I was in charge of schooling the little rascals, Bas included," Opulentia said and winked at her.

"So what do you think is going on?" Bas asked as he refilled his cup.

"I think he's gathering an army and I think he has been doing that since the day he came here for Rionach and Conri's wedding." Opulentia passed the bread to Aqua.

LORE OF THE DRAGONS: ESSENCE OF A QUEEN

"But surely he knows that an army will do him little good against us?" Bas said as he passed the cheese down to Aqua.

"He knows very well that we can't just fly out against his troops and burn them. Few know our secret, and he's counting on us wanting to keep it that way," Opulentia said.

"I don't know, I would burn him to a cinder in a heartbeat if I thought for just a second it would do any good. But Opulentia has a point. If he's gathering an army, it would make sense. Not that I thought I would ever hear myself say that, but if he is, it would be a smart move from his side." Tempest frowned and passed the bowl of fruit to Aqua.

"Over the last years, he has attacked us more than a hundred times, always to no avail. What if he has simply been testing us to see if we would shift or to see where our weaknesses are?" Bas said and sent Aqua the pitcher of milk.

"My thoughts exactly. We need to find a way to… oh for god's sake, Aqua, what is it you want now?" Tempest said as Aqua tapped her on the shoulder.

"The fish," she said and pointed at the plate of fish that was just out of reach.

"Do you ever get full?" Tempest asked and passed the plate.

"Sorry, but all this war talk is making me hungry…" Orelaith smiled.

"I think we've had enough war talk for now. That is what your war counsel is for. Here we eat." Tempest looked around the table.

"Or you mean we should, if Aqua hadn't eaten it all." Aqua stuck her tongue out at Tempest.

"It's not my fault you are too busy talking." Bas smiled,

"Orelaith is right, enough war talk. We need to grab what we can before Aqua finishes it all."

Orelaith watched them eating and smiled. She loved her family so dearly. The pain shot through her chest again. It was happening almost daily now, from once a month, maybe, when Aednat was born. She still hadn't told anyone about it, not even Bas. She thought he suspected something, but when she smiled and said everything was fine, he let it go. She concealed the pain by taking another sip of her tea. It lasted longer now too. She'd had these pains for so many years. At first she had not said anything because she didn't want to worry Rionach before her wedding. Thereafter she kept it to herself to avoid upsetting her daughter when she was carrying Aednat. And after that… so much time had passed that she was embarrassed that she had not spoken of it earlier. But she was still alive six years later, so it was probably nothing. She almost felt as if she needed this pain to remind her that she was, after all, human. So the charade went on. She looked at the others gathered around the table with her. They all looked the same, but some minor changes had occurred in some of them. Solis and Aqua were pretty much the same. Vig had become more humble, probably from spending time with Opulentia. Tempest hardly wore a dress at all anymore. She had traded them in for leather armor. It was probably hard to fight with a dress constricting her movements and that was mostly what she did these days. Luna spent a lot of her time with Aednat and if she was not with her she was helping Tempest train the men together

LORE OF THE DRAGONS: ESSENCE OF A QUEEN

with Conri and Art. Terra had been writing book after book about the history of the dragons and how they came to be who they were now. She recorded everything and spent many hours in her room writing down their history for the future generations. Serovita helped craft anything the people needed made in wood. No one knew how she did it, of course, and when she was not busy making spoons and cups, she could be found in the castle gardens tending to the plants and flowers that grew there. Orelaith herself spent at least one hour a day in the cave just sitting next to Rionach's coffin. She missed her so much, even if she did see so much of her in Aednat. Her granddaughter had the same green eyes and the same smile. Orelaith looked over and saw how Garbhan was focused on her granddaughter. The two of them had developed a remarkable bond over the past six years and it warmed her heart to see how he cared for little Aednat.

"He truly is remarkable. I don't know of any other boy his age that would rather spend his time with a six year old than out with boys his own age." Saoirse said and sat down next to her. Orelaith smiled.

"My dear friend, you must remember he's not like most other children; he's dragonkin. And like most dragonkin, his loyalty runs stronger and deeper than it ever could with us humans." Saoirse nodded.

"True and you could not have picked a better guardian for her. But are they not actually related somehow? I mean she is the dragon queen, in a way. And he's the queen's son reborn, yes?" Opulentia leaned in.

"Not really. It's only the memories and power that passed

on to her. One could say she is only Orelaith's granddaughter."

"But she is Bas' granddaughter too, right?" Opulentia shook her head.

"Not really. You see, Orelaith and Bas did not really have Rionach together. But when I examined her I could not find any of his essence in her. Yes, I did find dragon essence, but not his. It is still a puzzle Vig and I are trying to figure out. But one thing is certain, they are not related, at least not in blood." Orelaith saw the smile on Opulentia's lips and frowned.

"Am I right to think you have some kind of plan going on here?" Opulentia put up an innocent look.

"Whatever do you mean?" Orelaith squinted at her. "It's a little early to play matchmaker, don't you think? I do not want to lose another child like I lost her mother." Opulentia smiled.

"Oh no, I don't think so. This way we can be certain that she will not run off with a man behind our backs once she gets old enough. We can keep a close eye on the situation this way." Orelaith looked at Garbhan and Aednat. His deep bronze eyes smiling down at Aednat's emerald green. They did have the same dark curls, but his were not visible now that he had cut it so close to the scalp. He still had his little boy face, but he was getting really tall, and all the weapons training he had with Conri and Tempest was showing in the way he moved. She knew they had done the right thing when they gave him the task of being Aednat's honor guard. It still scared her… thinking of Aednat becoming a teenager. She knew she could not take another loss like that. What if

Aednat became pregnant before they removed the spell? No, she could not think that way.

"Why the serious face, my love?" Bas sent.

"Oh, it's nothing. I was just thinking of Rionach…" Orelaith smiled at him as another sharp pain shot through her chest.

Chapter 46

Dougal rolled over in the big bed and stretched his arm out. He searched for the warm body but found the spot next to him empty. He sat up and looked around. Lady Inanis stood by the window and looked out over the bailey. Her long red hair covered most of her back and she only had a sheet wrapped around her body.

"Get up." She turned around and looked at him with an almost expressionless face.

"Why don't you come back here instead?" Dougal grinned.

"Because the bailey is filling up with men that you need to pick through again. I see a few tasty ones down there." Dougal sighed and put his feet on the floor.

"The army is almost 7000 men strong now. How many more does Nex need? It's not like our target has even half that amount of soldiers…" Inanis shrugged her shoulders and watched him as he picked up his clothes that lay scattered around the room.

"Nex wants what Nex wants. If he says more men, we will find him more men," Inanis said matter-of-factly.

LORE OF THE DRAGONS: ESSENCE OF A QUEEN

"You are right, of course," Dougal said as he pulled on his pants. She walked over to the bed and laid down.

"I will take whatever leftovers you discard, but make sure they get cleaned up first. I do hate when my food reeks of sweat and manure." He leaned over and kissed her hips, belly and breasts.

"Your wish is my command, milady." Her eyes followed him as he left the room, then she rolled over hoping Nex would not send for her again.

"Dougal, there you are. I was just about to send for you." Nex said as Dougal came out on the steps next to him. "I see Inanis has left a mark on you again," he said. Dougal's hand went to his neck.

"Yes, she does like to snack while she is indulging in her new found pleasures." Dougal replied with a wolfish grin. "So let's see…" He looked out over the crowd then glanced over at Nex.

"How many more do you need?"

"I think we have just about enough. However, these critters turned up anyway, so I guess I could use them. I am sure you will think of something…" Nex picked at his nails appearing almost uninterested. Dougal nodded.

"Very well. I will pick out the ones that have actual

fighting skills and store the rest?"

"Yes, that sounds like a plan." Nex said as he turned and walked back into the castle. Dougal stared at approximately three hundred men gathered before him, talking amongst themselves. "Alright, listen up! This is what is going to happen…"

Nex sat down on his throne and picked up his silver goblet.

"So how long are we going to wait? You have enough men, you have us. Why are you not charging into the attack?" Ruina's pale face had an almost ghostly glow to it in the dark room.

"You have so little patience, my dear Ruina. But I can say it will be soon. Just give Dougal a little time to sort through the last flock that wandered in here. I will start making the final preparations in which you play a vital role, my dear…"

"And what is that?" she asked and crossed her pale arms.

"Oh, all in due time, Ruina. All in due time." He grinned at her in a most unsettling way.

Nex was finishing his meal as Caliga entered his room.

LORE OF THE DRAGONS: ESSENCE OF A QUEEN

"Care to join me? There is a heart and a liver left."

"No, thank you, Nex. I have already had my meal," Caliga said and sat down next to him.

"Have you acquired all you need for the spell?" Nex said, picking his teeth with a long nail.

"All besides the obvious…" she replied and took the goblet that Nex offered her.

"We will have the right conditions with the arrival of the full moon tomorrow, but how are you going to do this? I doubt she will come willingly." Nex grinned.

"That is already taken care of. Tomorrow, I will give her a little gift, one I know she can not resist. Soon after that she will be fast asleep. Then all we have to do is make sure we gather up all the blood once I slit her throat." Caliga leaned back in her chair.

"You do remember that she needs to be in dragon form for the blood to have the wanted effect?" "Yes, yes, I know that and it's all taken care of. Frankly, I am glad it is almost time to do this. She has been extremely aggravating lately. Always complaining, always whining that something is not the way she wants it. You haven't noticed much of it because you have been spending most of your time in your chambers…" Caliga raised one eyebrow.

"And why do you think I have kept to myself? Ruina was never my kind of dragon before or after she got infected. She used to be so annoying before, now she is just a pain that won't go away."

"Yes... but tomorrow it will. Then all that stands in my way is Basilicus and Frater. Frater should be easy, just another casualty in the war and Basilicus is already being worn down and he doesn't even know it." Nex grinned evilly.

"So Ruina's little dot is actually working... Not bad, not bad at all." Caliga raised her cup.

"She will be useful twice, it seems. I was hoping it would not take as long as it has. She should be sicker by now. Irritating." Nex frowned.

"At least the timing is right. Tomorrow we will finally be moving things along." Caliga said and drained her cup.

"Yes, and about time. I have waited so long for this. Now... I can almost taste the power on my lips." Nex grinned and filled Caliga's cup again.

⁂

"Ah, there you are, my love." Bas said and gave Orelaith a kiss.

"What was it you wanted, my love?" Orelaith asked and sat down in the chair next to him.

"I need you to find some place you and Aednat can go if Nex decides to attack us in full force." Bas said.

"You really think there is a chance he will actually do that?" Orelaith asked and poured herself a cup of tea. Bas leaned back in his chair.

LORE OF THE DRAGONS: ESSENCE OF A QUEEN

"Yes. Tempest has two men on the inside who are gathering information for us. The word is that Nex's army is growing large. They are no longer actively looking for more soldiers, which tells me they will soon move towards us. I can not risk you and Aednat. If anything should happen to you…" Bas took her hand and she saw how he trembled at the thought.

"But my place is at your side, not hiding away somewhere." Bas shook his head.

"I cannot fight a war while worrying about your safety. I need to know you are safe so that I can focus on what I am doing. And I want you to take Garbhan with you. Your task is to keep them both safe." She knew there was no point in arguing with him on this.

"Very well. I will find somewhere we can be protected." She sighed. "But for how long?"

"For as long as it takes. The war is coming to us and there is no avoiding it. But please, be quick about finding a place. Nex is almost ready to march and I want you nowhere near us when he attacks." She put her arms around his neck.

"I wish he would just go away and leave us alone." Bas smiled weakly.

"Me too, but it doesn't look like he's going to give up easily. Let me know when you have picked a place and I will send someone there to prepare things for you and the children." She nodded and said,

"I may have a place already. There is a church out by the coast that could house us for a while. Nex's men would have to go past the king's castle to get to it, so there will be a second line of defense should he discover where we are." Bas looked at her.

"Why not the king's castle instead?" She shook her head.

"There are too many people that could be a threat to us. If you have planted a man in Nex's castle, think how easy it would be for Nex to plant a man in the king's castle. No, the risk is too high." He smiled at her.

"You amaze me, my carus. I had not thought of that…" She smiled back at him.

"I have learned a bit by sitting in on some of the war-meetings you know." He laughed.

"I will send some men there to make the arrangements. And I will fly you there myself when I have word back." She walked to the door, then stopped and turned around.

"What should I tell the children? They will know what is going on."

"Just tell them it's a learning trip and that you are going there to study the church and the scriptures. Tell them it will be the journey of their lives."

Chapter 47

The full moon lit up the big field and shone in the faces of the men gathered there. Nex's army was over seven thousand strong now and tonight he would make them even more powerful. A platform had been raised facing the castle he called home and now he sat looking at the crowd from a big chair. Dougal and Malum stood just at the bottom of the steps leading up. On Nex's right side was Caliga and to his left was Inanis.

"Dougal!" Nex shouted from his seat.

"Yes, my Lord?" He ran up the steps and knelt down at Nex's feet.

"Is my little surprise ready for Ruina?" He leaned forward in his chair.

"Yes, my Lord. As soon as you want them, I will send for them."

"Good, good. I will give you a sign," Nex said and got up. He walked to the edge of the platform and looked out at the men.

"You have all been chosen to be a part of my new order. And tonight I will give you two things; a warning and a gift…" He looked up at the sky,

"Ruina, we are ready for you." A terrifying roar sounded from above. They all looked up as a pale yellow dragon flew in and landed gracefully in the field.

"Behold my powers!" Nex shouted out as Ruina walked over to the platform and sent a flame up into the night sky. There was a collective gasp as Ruina knelt down in front of Nex.

"Even dragons bow before me!" he said. "As promised, I will give you two things tonight. First, a warning." He nodded to Dougal who brought forth three men, stripped down and tied up with their hands behind their backs. "Two of these men were planning to leave. To desert." Dougal pulled one of the men to the side, leaving two standing in front of yellow dragon. "Burn them!" Nex shouted. Ruina sent white-hot flame towards the men. Only a short moment they screamed in agony, then fell silent. Where the two men had stood, only a pile of ashes remained. A sea of faces stared at Nex in awestruck terror.

"And this man. A spy! A loyal subject of the pathetic Basilicus himself." Dougal dragged the man in front of Ruina and threw him to the ground. "What do you say, my dear? Are you feeling a little hungry?" Nex said. He patted Ruina's neck and grinned evilly at the man screaming through the gag in his mouth. Ruina roared and threw her head back before she started ripping the man apart. It took longer for the screams to stop this time. The men stared with horrified fascination as she devoured the spy piece by piece.

"You see, I am always looking for a reason to feed one of my wonderful dragons." Ruina laid down on her belly as

LORE OF THE DRAGONS: ESSENCE OF A QUEEN

Nex walked back up to the platform. "So therein lies my first gift... I will grant you life if you stay loyal to me," he glanced over at Ruina who was shaking her head and trying to stand up. But her feet would not carry her and she fell over.

"What... what have you done to... me?" Ruina sent, shocked as she strained to lift her head.

"Only what you would have done to me if given half the chance." The moonlight caught his face as he grinned evilly at her. Dougal led a handful of men rolling several large barrels over to what would be Ruina's final resting place.

"This brings me to your second gift," Nex said and looked out over the crowd. "A chance at being more than pathetic little pests. A chance to taste a small portion of true greatness. You will be faster, stronger and your very senses will be sharpened to the point of divinity! You will be invincible!" The crowd roared excitedly. "No ordinary man will be able to stand against you when you fight for me. We will be victorious!" Again the crowd roared and Nex pulled out a long silver blade. "Tonight you will become more than you thought you ever could, and you have me to thank for it." Nex spoke almost softly as he walked over to Ruina's head. She was totally paralyzed now and her eyes stared fearfully at him as he raised the blade.

"Nex! Don't do it! I am still of use to you. I am more valuable to you alive than dead!"

"For the Lord Nex! For King Nex!" Dougal shouted as Nex drove the blade into Ruina's eye. As he pulled it out, the blood started flowing and was caught in barrel after barrel. The men were intoxicated with bloodlust. They cheered and shouted. Nex handed the blade to Dougal and walked back up to the platform and sat down. Soon all the barrels were full and Caliga walked to the front of the platform. The black dress with red inlays and the silver jewelry made her look like a priestess of the old religion. In one hand she held a big brush of horsehair, while the other was raised towards the moon.

"Hac nocte Deos eris! Sanguis effusus et luna ad ligandum te!" she shouted. Then she dipped the brush in one of the blood barrels and started swinging it at the closest men, spraying them with dragon blood. The men who had filled the barrels started moving through the crowd, repeating what Caliga had done, making sure every last one had blood on them. Then she started chanting. It was mostly for show, but also helped her concentrate while she created a huge web of knots. Black tendrils seemed to stretch up to the moon as well and with Nex on one side and Inanis on the other side resting their hands on her shoulders she flung the net over the army. For a short while, not one of the men moved but stood completely still like an army of statues.

"Is it working?" Nex asked impatiently.

"Wait for it… wait for it…" she replied, not taking her eyes off the men. Then came a crackling sound and a black wave flowed over the crowd from Caliga. A collective gasp followed and several of the men fell to their knees.

"It is done." Caliga sighed.

"Yes!" Nex grinned widely. "Tomorrow, we march!"

Chapter 48

The three riders that came trotting into the bailey were all part of the Dracones Custodia. They all wore the same black leather armor adorned with intricate silver patterns on the arms and shoulders. A silver dragon with its wings spread covered their backs. Bas came out to meet them as they dismounted.

"Good to see you back. How was the trip?"

"Uneventful," the man called Castiel answered.

"Any problems getting the convent to accommodate them?" Bas asked as they walked up the steps to the keep.

"A little hesitant at first, but they came around when they saw the generous gifts we brought." He grinned. "Everything is prepared for their arrival. Two rooms have been made ready; one for the lady Orelaith and little Aednat and one for lord Garbhan." he glanced at Bas.

"However, they would only accept the three of them, so no soldiers or guards of any kind. Don't think they liked us much. Good thing I didn't take it personally." Bas laughed.

"What is there not to like about you, Castiel?"

"You got a week?" Certus said, which caused Fidelis to snicker behind them.

"Very funny…" Castiel said and punched Certus in the shoulder. Bas gave Castiel a friendly slap on the back,

"I will let you go and get cleaned up. I will have some food sent to your rooms. Later we can meet in the counsell chamber. There are things we need to prepare should Nex decide to hit us with a full attack." The Dracones Custodia nodded in reply. He left them to go in search of Orelaith and give her the news.

"Bas! Wait up!" Tempest came up behind him. He stopped and turned around.

"Tempest, what is it?"

"I have received some disturbing news. We need to gather everyone in the council chamber immediately." Bas put his hand on her shoulder.

"What has happened?"

"Just gather the others and meet me in the tower," she said and hurried down the hallway. The dragons were soon gathered in the council chamber at the top of the tower. The twelve Dracones Custodia were also there, one behind each chair.

"I just had word from one of my men inside Nex's camp. The news is not good," Tempest said as she let her eyes wander around the room. "They killed one of my spies. How they found out who he was is still unclear. One thing is

LORE OF THE DRAGONS: ESSENCE OF A QUEEN

certain: Nex has an army of over seven thousand men. Last night he fed one of my inside men to Ruina in front of the entire army. What followed is still puzzling me, but I hope you can shed some light on this, Opulentia."

"Not sure what it is that you need my help with, but if I can, I will." Tempest explained what her contact had seen, about how Nex had killed Ruina and doused the men with her blood before casting a web. Opulentia was visibly shaken when Tempest had finished the story. They all seemed equally disturbed by Nex killing one of their own. Opulentia closed her eyes and covered her face in her hands but said nothing.

"Opulentia? Have you heard of anything like this before?" Bas asked. She sighed, opening her eyes,

"I am afraid I have. Binding the power of the moon and the magical powers of our blood in a lesser creature is dangerous to say the least. The outcome is very unpredictable." Tempest folded her hands on the table in front of her.

"What kind of possible outcomes are we talking about here?" Opulentia raised her eyebrows.

"A number of things come to mind, such as mutations, madness, sickness and even death."

"Isn't that the same symptoms the infection has?" Orelaith asked. Opulentia nodded.

"It is. You see, by using infected dragon blood, Caliga has not only given them the abilities we see in the Dracones Custodia, but she has also infected them." Tempest frowned.

"This could be really bad for us." One of the Dracones

Custodia refilled their cups.

"By using the moon to bind it, she has made them stronger, faster and fearless. There is however a flaw in this spell that may be to our advantage. Because she has bound the knots to the moon, it will only last until the moon goes dark."

"I would think we can keep them at bay for that long," Tempest said, sounding almost relieved. "What will happen once the web dissolves?" Vig asked.

"The very moment the moon goes dark, they will die where they stand," Opulentia answered quietly.

"Nex knew that before he had Caliga cast the web?" Bas asked. Opulentia nodded.

"Yes, but you can be sure he has not told the affected men about that unfortunate side effect." They all went silent for a little while, pondering how easily Nex wasted over seven thousand lives.

"Do you know what Nex plans to do next?" Bas asked and looked at Tempest.

"He's coming here. It would take him seven days to march the men here, but if he decides to fly them in…" Castiel said, crossing his arms.

"No." Tempest shook her head, "His men do not know he's a dragon. He would not risk it."

"So we have a week then?" Luna asked.

"Something like that," Tempest said and got up,

LORE OF THE DRAGONS: ESSENCE OF A QUEEN

"I will start getting the army prepared for war."

"And I will prepare the people," Vig said. Bas turned to Orelaith.

"We will need to get you out of here as soon as possible. Let Aednat and Garbhan know you are leaving tomorrow evening. I will fly you out there myself."

"I will cast a small web of sleep so that they don't remember the trip," Opulentia added. Bas finished his wine and with a solemn look on his face he spoke the word.

"It is settled then. Let us prepare for war!"

The castle was like an ant hill the next morning. People bustled back and forth, bringing food and provisions inside the walls. Bas had not yet talked to the people of the small community, but news of the coming war had spread through word of mouth. Tempest and Luna were training the new recruits that had joined them last week. At noon, Bas sent word he would talk to the people and soon enough the main bailey filled up. Bas stood on the top of the steps with Tempest at his right and Art on his left. The rest of the family gathered behind him as he raised his hand to speak.

"As you already know, an army is coming. We have about seven days till it reaches us and we believe we can hold them off for as long as it takes. I will not lie to you, the army is about seven thousand men strong and the soldiers in it are ruthless. I have come to an agreement with the king that any of you who do not wish to take part in this can seek refuge with him till this is over. Your homes will be waiting for you when you return." He looked out over the men, women and children who stood before him and realized it was his task to keep them safe. Their trusting faces stared up at him expectantly as he continued. "For those of you who choose to stay, I will do all I can to keep you and your families safe. I know this is my war, and trust me when I say I would never expect you to fight this war for me, but I am grateful for all who will stay. Let my men know if there is anything I can do for you. If it is within my power, I will do my best to help you." A young woman stepped forward.

"Before my family and I came here, we had nothing. But you have given us a home, a place to feel safe, and our future is brighter than it has ever been. I would willingly lay down my life to defend that which you have brought to us: peace and harmony in a land otherwise devastated by war. I, for one, will stay." The crowd cheered at her words and the family at the top of the steps was moved by how loyal the people were to them.

"I don't think we will see a rush of families leaving before Nex attacks," Tempest said quietly to Bas and smiled. A man stepped out of the crowd and asked,

"What do you need us to do?" Bas answered,

"Make sure you and your family have everything you need for the siege. When you have taken care of them, report to Tempest or any of the Dracones Custodia and they will tell you what is needed. For those of you who will not be fighting, Vig and Opulentia are the ones who will be in charge of food and taking care of anyone injured. Terra and Serovita will be strengthening the castle to withstand any attacks on the outer walls. I just want to thank you all for being a part of making this castle such a wonderful place to live. I believe that it will be again once we defeat this enemy that is determined to take what we have built here." The crowd cheered, then eagerly went to the task at hand. Bas put his arm around Orelaith.

"Did you tell the children you will be leaving tonight?" She looked up at him hopefully.

"Do we have to leave tonight? Nex is not going to be here for another seven days."

"I don't want you anywhere near this castle when he attacks. I could not bear to lose you. It would be the death of me." He looked into her eyes. "I can not risk losing Aednat or Frater either, so I need you to do as I ask this time. Please…" She sighed and nodded.

"I will let the children know that we are leaving as soon as it gets dark. Who is going with us?" "Both Luna and Vig insisted on coming along."

Orelaith looked down at Aednat sleeping in her arms.

"She should be asleep till morning." Vig said and got up. Orelaith looked up at her.

"And she will not remember a thing?" Vig shook her head.

"No, but she will be hungry and maybe have a little bit of a headache, so make sure she gets a big breakfast."

Opulentia entered the counseling chamber followed by Luna.

"Garbhan is asleep too. We placed the wagon and the horses in the field beyond the trees." "So we are all ready?" Luna smiled and looked at Bas.

"Yes. I will be carrying Aednat, Orelaith and Garbhan and, Luna will take two horses and Vig will be taking the wagon." Orelaith gave Opulentia a big hug.

"Keep safe. We will see you again in two weeks time." A pain shot through Orelaith's chest as Opulentia released her from the hug and Orelaith saw that Opulentia noticed something was wrong.

"Please don't tell Bas now, Opulentia. Everyone has enough to think about as it is. Don't worry, it's probably nothing." Opulentia frowned but nodded. Whatever it was, it would have to wait.

Opulentia was standing on the porch outside the counsell chamber after they had left. She could rid herself of the feeling that whatever Orelaith was hiding, it was something serious. Yes, she had noticed that Orelaith had kept to herself a lot these past years, but she had assumed it was somehow related to Rionach's death. Grief was a powerful emotion that could last for a lifetime, and Orelaith had gone to her daughter's grave every day since her death. She had gotten a little thinner and her complexion was a little pale, but like the others she thought it was just because of

Rionach's passing. Now, however, she suspected it was something other than just the grief of losing a child. How long had this been going on, and why had neither she nor Vig noticed it before? No, she needed to discuss this with Vig when she returned.

"Opulentia? May I have a word?" She turned around and found Tempest standing behind her in her leather armor.

"Yes, of course, child. What can I do for you?" she said and smiled at her.

"We need a plan of action for when it becomes necessary to tend the wounded, an out of the way place? We cannot keep our secret if you and Vig go in and heal the injured with your powers, but we can't let people die simply because we are afraid to expose that we can. What do you suggest?" Tempest looked at her expectantly.

"I will need to talk with Vig about that when she returns. Just find somewhere suitable." Opulentia walked over and put her hand on Tempest's shoulder. "But for now we should just leave this matter alone. I am sure there are plenty of other things that need our attention, like the wonderful meal our sweet cook has prepared for us in the dining room."

Just as morning approached and the first light bathed the landscape in an eerie grey radiance, Bas landed in a big field not far from a road. Orelaith climbed off with Aednat in her arms. Vig transformed and started to wake the horses. Bas gently put Garbhan in the wagon, then transformed quickly, as did Luna.

"We will need to leave before the children wake up," Luna said and looked around.

"The monastery is only a short way up this road. You should be there in no time," Bas said as Orelaith laid Aednat down next to Garbhan and pulled the soft blankets over them.

"I will be fine, so don't worry about me or the children," Orelaith said quietly and climbed down from the wagon. Luna hitched the horses up and Vig pulled Orelaith aside.

"If anything happens here or at home, you can use your mind to reach out to Bas. I am not sure how well it works over such a long distance but the two of you are bonded to each other which strengthens the connection you have. Orelaith… what is wrong?" Vig asked and frowned at her. Orelaith smiled bravely at Vig.

"It's nothing. Just that we have never been apart for this long before. It feels wrong somehow…" Vig still frowned.

"Are you sure that is all that is going on? I have this feeling it's more than that."

"Really, I am fine, Vig. Stop worrying about me. There are enough things you need to think about besides a girl's heartache from being away from the ones she loves." She glanced over at Bas who was helping Luna finish up with the horses.

"Very well… but I better not find out later that you are hiding something. I care too deeply for you, child."

"Ok you are all set," Luna smiled and walked over to Orelaith to give her a big hug.

"You take good care of the little ones and we will see you as soon as we get rid of Nex. He will regret the day he was born by the time we are done with him." Orelaith laughed.

"He should know better than to go up against you all, but I guess some men are thicker than others." Vig and Luna gave Orelaith and Bas some space to say goodbye.

"I hate leaving you here, my carus. But your safety is more important to me than having you close by, and it will only be for two weeks, at the most."

"I know my love, but it doesn't make it any easier to say goodbye." She looked into his eyes and smiled sadly.

"I hate goodbyes…" Bas said as he pulled her close.

"You must go before someone sees you." Orelaith gave him a quick kiss and stepped away from him. "Go now… while I still have a smile on my face."

"I will come back for you as soon as I can." Bas sent. Then he jumped up in the air and transformed, followed by Luna and Vig. Orelaith watched them till they disappeared over the trees, then she climbed up into the driver's seat and cracked the reins. The horses moved forward out onto the road, still a little groggy from the unnatural sleep. Maybe it would not be so bad once they got to the monastery. Maybe time would go by quickly. She just had to believe it would. Anything else was unbearable.

Chapter 49

About an hour later, she spotted the convent on a hill close by. The stone walls were old and worn with green climbing vines that covered most of the outer walls. She reigned in the horses in front of the gates as they slowly opened.

"You must be the Lady Orelaith. I am Sister Maria," the old nun said with a smile.

"I would have thought you would have had an escort as you traveled here."

"I did, but they turned back. As I came to understand, you do not allow men within your walls." The nun nodded,

"Yes, that is true, but we do have five monks who stay in a separate part of the monastery." Orelaith signaled the horse to move, and the wagon rolled in through the big gates.

"Grandma?" Aednat sat up and rubbed her eyes. "Where are we?" Orelaith smiled at her granddaughter.

"We have arrived at the monastery we talked about." Garbhan yawned and sat up.

LORE OF THE DRAGONS: ESSENCE OF A QUEEN

"Last thing I remember was sitting on the bed while Opulentia checked my neck after I got hurt during practice. She gave me a drink to help with the pain, or so I thought. She must have slipped me a sleeping potion." He frowned for a second, then grinned.

"So I missed the long, boring trip here?" Orelaith laughed.

"Yes, you both did."

"This must be the young Lady Aednat and Lord Garbhan. I am Sister Maria." Aednat crossed her arms and stared suspiciously at the nun.

"I don't know whose sister you are, but I don't have any." The old nun smiled.

"No, you are quite right. We are not sisters in blood but in spirit." Aednat cocked her head.

"Spirit?" Orelaith helped Aednat down from the wagon.

"That is one of the things we are here to learn about, sweetheart." As the horses were led away to the stable, Sister Maria walked towards the main door to the convent.

"This way. I will show you to your rooms." Orelaith took Aednat's hand and with Garbhan trailing behind them, they followed Sister Maria into the building.

Over the next couple of days, they met the other nuns and

the children attended classes to learn more about life there and about the scriptures. Orelaith was feeling worse every day and spent longer periods in her room resting. Garbhan followed Aednat like a shadow, taking care of her every need and helping her with her studies. When they were not in classes with Sister Maria, Aednat and Garbhan explored the building and helped out in the garden. Soon the sisters got used to seeing the two children walking down corridors or playing in the garden. Orelaith would sit in the sun some days watching them play or help out with the vegetable garden. She missed home, she missed Bas and the others, she missed her soft bed, but most of all she missed being able to visit her daughter's grave. She longed for Bas to return saying it was all over and that he would take them home. She would stand by her window looking out over the fields surrounding the monastery hoping to see him coming. But he didn't come and she felt so selfish for thinking only of herself and what she wanted and needed. Bas would come as soon as it was safe, she knew that. This was the last place anyone would think of looking for her or the children. No harm would come to them here.

"They are only two days away," Tempest said. "Just about here." She pointed on the big map spread out on the table in the counsell chamber. Bas frowned and crossed his arms.

"How could they possibly have gotten that close already? We were not expecting them to arrive for another two days."

Opulentia leaned forward.

"It's the web Caliga cast on them. They don't need to rest as long. They will march from morning till dusk without so much as a shortstop to drink. They will keep going at the same strength till the moon has gone black. Then all the strain they have put on their bodies will come crashing down on them in a split second." Vig shook her head and added,

"And they will die where they stand."

"I can't help but feel sorry for them," Solis said, letting out a sad sigh.

"They are evil men that care nothing for their fellow man, woman or child. They have no respect for life and think only of riches and glory. Trust me, they do not deserve any compassion," Tempest said bitterly.

"Is there anything we can do to slow them down?" Castiel asked as he studied the map. Bas didn't take his eyes off the map as he asked,

"Maybe… Tempest? Do you think you could whip up a storm for them?" Tempest looked up from the map and rubbed her chin thoughtfully.

"Yes… that might work. I would need to get very close and it would be risky." Luna grinned.

"Risky? I'm in." Tempest crossed her arms and looked at Bas.

"If I do this, you may have a little more time to get all the people into the castle and gather the last of the provisions we need to last through the siege." Aqua's belly rumbled loudly,

"We have been sitting in this war-meeting all morning. Isn't it about time we have some lunch? I am practically wasting away here."

"Yes, I think that's a good idea. We can meet back here after we have eaten," Bas said and got up. "Try not to spend any more time there than necessary. Nex is getting closer as we speak."

After lunch they came to the conclusion that any extra time Tempest could give them by slowing the army was indeed needed. That night, Tempest and Luna set off in the direction of the army's last known location. The pale blue moonlight guided their way as they flew close to the treetops. They soon spotted the lights from the camp fires.

"I need to get as close as possible. That way it's easier for me to control the area of downfall." Tempest sent to Luna as they closed in on the huge camp.

"This will have to be close enough, if we get any closer Nex will sense us." Luna answered as she searched for a suitable place to land. "There." Luna nodded at a hillside overlooking the entire army. As soon as they touched ground, Tempest closed her eyes and released her tendrils. They were not golden like the others but more like the color of lightning and just as bright. Out of nothing, clouds started appearing in the night sky and within a few seconds the moon was no longer visible.

"Tempest... we need to go." Luna said quietly.

"Just a little longer or it will be a waste of time. If I can just finish the web, I can make it follow us all the way home." Tempest's voice was strained as she struggled to control her tendrils. "Usually I just let the tendrils do as they please. Having to try controlling where they go is harder than I imagined." Luna put her hand on her shoulder.

"Here, draw on my strength. Nex has sensed us, so we need to finish this now." Tempest nodded but did not open her eyes.

"Almost there... just a few more seconds.. Done!" As she opened her eyes, thunder boomed overhead.

"Nice one. Now let's go home," Luna said and flapped her wings. "It should be quite the show. Let's just hope it works the way we want it to." As they left the camp, heavy rain started to pour down on the unsuspecting men.

"This is not a natural storm, Nex. I believe it is the work of the dragon, Tempest." Caliga said as she looked out of the tent opening. Nex leaned back in his chair and smiled.

"I think it's wonderful."

"How can you think this dreadful downpour is wonderful?" Inanis asked.

"Because it tells me that they are actually worried enough to try to slow us down. And that again tells me we can beat them. So yes, it is wonderful."

"It will slow us down quite a bit. Even though the men do not tire, the mud will make it harder for the wagons to move at a satisfying pace." Caliga said, still staring out into the night. Nex poured himself a cup of thick, red blood.

"Be that as it may, we will still get there in a day or two, and then we will crush him like the spineless whelp that he is."

"Do not underestimate your brother, Nex. You have threatened his family and that is enough to make any dragon dangerous." Caliga added and glanced at him over her shoulder. Nex waved his free hand dismissively.

"Yes, yes, I know. But we have seven thousand men that do not tire, are stronger and faster and have no fear even in the face of certain death. What does Basilicus have? A handful of farmers with pitchforks?" He laughed. "No, Caliga. You will see that we can deal with any resistance swiftly. And then I will take what should have been mine in the first place: the dragon crown and all the powers that come with it." Nex sighed and closed his eyes with a smile on his lips. "It's so close, I can almost taste it. I will not be denied my rightful place any longer. The powers will be mine, and anyone who stands in my way will burn."

The storm had slowed the army enough to make them reach the castle a day later. By then all the farmers that lived outside the walls had moved their belongings inside along with all their livestock. The town overflowed with people, animals and wagons loaded with personal belongings. As morning came on the third day, the army was visible from the castle walls. It flowed towards them like a wave of darkness. It was enough to make even the most hardened men feel a little shaky at the knees. Bas, Tempest and Luna stood on the allure looking at the approaching men.

"Are we all ready for this?" Bas said without taking his eyes off of Nex's army.

"As ready as we'll ever be. We are outnumbered and out-equipped but not outwitted. I believe we will survive this with only a small amount of losses." Tempest replied.

"Terra has fortified the outer walls and we have men posted all along it. If they try to come over we will be ready for them," Luna said and grinned. Despite her and Tempest's reassurances, Bas was still worried,

"Make sure all the women and children who do not wish to fight are taken to a safe place. I do not think Nex will wait long before he attacks. Time is running out for his men."

Chapter 50

Aednat closed the door quietly behind her and sighed.

"She is sleeping again. I don't know why she's always so tired when all she does is sleep." Garbhan smiled at her.

"She will be fine, don't you worry. Anyway, you have me to keep you company. What does Lady Aednat want to do today?" He bowed and winked at her. She giggled.

"The Lady Aednat wants to go fishing."

"Ah, an excellent choice, but alas we are out of fishing poles. How about a stroll in the garden? I hear the strawberries are ripe." She clapped little her hands and looked up at him with a bright smile,

"Oh yes, I love strawberries!"

"Well then, let's go," he said. She placed her small hand on his offered arm and together they found their way out into the morning sun.

LORE OF THE DRAGONS: ESSENCE OF A QUEEN

The sleek longboats were gliding through the calm sea. Sigvald, their leader, was standing at the railing on the largest of the ships. He was a monster of a man, as tall as he was broad and his long straggly hair clung to his battle-scarred face as he stared at his men. They had raided a few villages on their way to their final destination, but this was supposed to be the grand prize; gold and women all in the same place. His men would be high on mushrooms and drunk on mead, as they were every time they went ashore. It probably made the killing easier for some of them. Sigvald never touched the stuff. He liked the killing and the brutality that came with raiding, the look of horror as he forced his way into both buildings and women alike… He didn't care what he killed as long as he got a profit out of it, be it gold or slaves.

"In a few days we will reach the prize for this trip. We go in after dark. Take only the men or women that have some years left as slaves. Any weak or sick, we kill. We don't need to be taking any with us that won't last the trip home. Then burn the rest." He grinned as his men cheered. "When we are done, we set sail and go home with our riches!" Again they cheered and raised their weapons. He looked around at his men. They were tall and strong, every single one of them. Their clothing was made of leather and most of them had thick furs to keep the cold wind of the north sea out. Iron helmets and long beards covered their hardened features and the parts exposed to the elements were covered in battlescars. These were men he could count on, at least most of them. Bjørn had brought his youngest son along for his first raid. He could be about sixteen-seventeen summers old, usually a full grown man in every way, but this one had been sheltered by his mother. He had not shown much interest in the killing so far and Bjørn appeared almost ashamed of his boy. This last landing would be his final chance to prove himself a man and they all knew it.

Aqua paced restlessly back and forth on the battlements. She occasionally cast a glance at Nex's army in the field outside the castle walls.

"Why aren't they attacking? They have already set up the camp and the siege machines. What are they waiting for?" Bas answered,

"They are probably resting. It's been quite the march for them. They do not tire in the same manner as normal men, but they will still need to rest a little before they attack. It probably won't be until morning. Did we get everyone inside, Luna?" he asked and turned to her. Luna was wearing black leather armor like the Dracones Custodia. Her hair was gathered in a thick braid which for the time being was resting on her left shoulder.

"As many as would come. Only a few decided to go to the king's castle for protection. I am pretty sure we checked every farm in the area. If anyone is left out there, it's too late now."

"Good," Bas said and looked at Solis.

LORE OF THE DRAGONS: ESSENCE OF A QUEEN

"I want you to get the children, women and old people set up in Aednat's chamber. If we are breached, I want them to hide in the cave below, but only as a last resort."

"I will make sure we have food stored there for at least a week. We already have water in Orelaith's old chamber." Solis said solemnly, quite unlike her usual cheery self.

"And blankets for all." Aqua added.

"We will get it done right away." Solis said. She grabbed Aqua's hand and pulled her along.

"Can we find some food for ourselves too? I need to keep up my strength, you know." Opulentia walked out to them and put her hand on Bas' shoulder.

"You need to get some rest." He turned and managed a strained smile.

"I am fine. I just want this to be over so I can bring Orelaith and the children back home. It is tearing me apart that we have to be separated like this."

"I know. Can you feel her when you are this far apart?" Opulentia asked. Bas closed his eyes and sighed.

"No. If I am to be truthful with you, I would not be able to sense her even if she was here in the castle."

"But that is not right. You are bonded and should be able to reach out to each other from miles apart. What is going on?" Bas sighed again and spoke quietly.

"She has found a way to shut me out. I don't know how she has done it, but I can not sense how she is feeling or where she is. She says it's a human thing, that she needs to keep some part of herself." Opulentia frowned.

"But she still cares deeply for you? And does not regret being bonded to you?" Bas smiled.

"There is no doubt in my mind. It was hard at first, but I have come to accept it over the years."

"Years?!" Opulentia stared at him with wide open eyes.

"How long has it been this way?" Bas looked out over the army below.

"It started not long before Rionach's wedding." Opulentia looked thoughtful and took a few steps away from him as she pondered.

"I believe I know what is going on, but I need to talk to Vig first to be sure," she said as she turned and looked at him.

"What do you mean? Do you think something is wrong?" Bas' voice had a tinge of panic in it. Opulentia took his hands in hers.

"Do not worry. I am sure it is nothing. You have a war to fight, so let me take care of this." Then she walked off leaving him standing there with one more thing to worry about. He was not left to ponder for long, Tempest and Luna came over and started going over placements of men and strategies should the walls be breached. So he turned and dealt with things he could do something about… well, in one way, at least.

LORE OF THE DRAGONS: ESSENCE OF A QUEEN

Over the next few days the army below did nothing in the way of attacking. It was unsettling, but it bought them some time to get everyone ready for what would most certainly come. Some people started relaxing, saying that the army must be discouraged by the massive walls and that they would probably just leave. The night time was full of screams from the camp below as Nex and the other dragons fed on the men that showed any sign of weakness. As darkness fell on the third day of the siege, there was a change in the waiting army. Shouts and cheers from below brought Bas to the outer walls. Tempest was already there with most of the Dracones Custodia.

"What is happening down there?" Bas asked as he came up next to her.

"They are getting ready to attack," she answered without taking her eyes off the shouting men below. "Let them come, I am more than ready for them." she said almost grinning.

"And the men lining the walls up here? Are they ready?" Bas asked and glanced along the walkway at the soldiers with their swords drawn.

"As ready as they'll ever be." She looked at him. "Are you ready to take on Nex should he decide to take on his true form?" Bas nodded.

"Yes, I am. But I doubt he will try that. I was always stronger than him, even when we were just whelps, and he knows that very well." Luna came up behind them.

"Oh, good. I was worried you had started without me." She peeked over the wall.

"Seems I got here just in time, because here they come." They heard the wooden ladders being propped up against the stone walls and archers started picking men off before they reached the top. But the stream of men scaling the walls was greater than the arrows the archers could send flying from their bows, and soon the first men started to reach the top. Tempest swung her huge sword with ease, splintering bone and sending men crashing to the ground below with their guts spilling out. Luna cut down her share of men as well. Agile and sleek like a cat, she pounced on the men that dared set their feet on her side of the wall. For a long while the men coming up the ladders appeared to have no end, but eventually they stopped coming. Tempest leaned on her sword next to Bas, his foot resting on the huge battle axe he had been swinging.

"I believe we evened things out a little, don't you think?" Luna said as she came walking over with her thin blade resting on her shoulder.

"We have taken some hits too, Luna. But yes, we gave them a good fight," Bas said and slapped her on the back. Conri came running with Art right behind him.

"Are you all in one piece?"

"We lost some soldiers and some were wounded. Let's get them to Vig as quickly as possible." Luna said and picked up a young man with a deep cut to his leg. He stared at her as she lifted him, amazed how easily she carried his weight.

"Bas, this attack was only to get our attention away from the gate. Some of Nex's men threw oil at it. I think they will try to set it on fire," Conri said and looked down over the wall.

LORE OF THE DRAGONS: ESSENCE OF A QUEEN

"They know they will never get the army over the wall, and the only other way in is the gate. Let me take a look at it. Tempest, can you go find Aqua? If Conri is right, we will need her abilities to take care of it." Bas followed Conri and Art to take a closer look at the gate. Tempest helped up a wounded soldier and took him to the main hall to get him patched up.

Orelaith was feeling a little better that morning and decided to go outside after breakfast to get some fresh air. Aednat and Garbhan came with her and were playing tag, chasing each other around the garden. The pain was not so bad today, but with the pain gone for a little while, she started thinking that maybe she should have told Vig or Bas about what really happened the day they ran into Ruina. Reaching out to Bas now was out of the question, as he had more than enough to worry. No, it would just have to wait. She did feel a little bad about not spending more time with Aednat, though. Thankfully Garbhan was keeping her company.

"Grandma?" Aednat came running over.

"Yes, my darling?" Orelaith smiled at Aednat. She looked so much like her mother it was almost painful.

"Garbhan has made some fishing rods for us. Can we go down to the sea and fish for a little? Please?" Orelaith sighed.

"I don't think that is such a good idea, at least not for me. Grandma is still not feeling well, and I don't want you two going off alone."

"I will take good care of her, Lady Orelaith. And we will be back before dinner, I promise," Garbhan said and put his arm around Aednat's shoulders. They both looked at her with big smiles and Orelaith could not deny her.

"Very well, but take the big black horse and go get some lunch to take with you." Aednat threw her arms around Orelaith's neck.

"Thank you, Grandma. I will be a good girl and listen to everything Garbhan says." She smiled widely.

"Go get a cloak. It may get chilly down there," Orelaith shouted after them as they ran off to get their things.

"Yes, Grandma. I will." Orelaith smiled to herself as she saw the two of them together. She was not sure if she did the right thing letting them go off on their own, but Nex's army was far away and there weren't that many dangers in a small village by the sea.

"Two more days and Nex will find himself without an army." Tempest said and poured herself a cup of wine.

"Can we hold them back that long?" Vig leaned forward resting her hands on the big round table in the counsell chamber.

"If we can keep his soldiers out, yes. Aqua poured so much water into the gate that it will take a miracle to get it burning," Bas replied.

"How many injured and dead on our side so far?" he asked, turning to Opulentia.

LORE OF THE DRAGONS: ESSENCE OF A QUEEN

"About fifty dead and one hundred and fifty injured. We can heal them or just bandage them up, that is your decision. If we do heal them, we will have some explaining to do." Bas sighed.

"Just do what you can for them without being too obvious about it. Bandage up the ones that are not too seriously hurt. We will need every man we have by nightfall. I expect he will attack again then. Ok, you all get some rest and I will send someone for you if he decides to make a move before then," Bas said and got up. As the others left, Opulentia followed Bas out onto the porch.

"Have you heard anything from Orelaith?" she asked as she came up next to him. He shook his head.

"No. Did you talk to Vig yet?"

"No, I have not had the chance. She has been so busy with the injured men."

"Can you at least tell me what it is you suspect?" Bas asked and turned to her. She looked away,

"I am not sure that is such a good idea, Bas. You have a war to fight and need all your focus here."

"At least tell me if it is serious. Opulentia, I need to know," he pleaded with her. She sighed.

"It may be and it could all be just fine. I really don't know. But it is not as pressing as our situation here."

"How serious are you talking about here? Life threatening?" he asked and placed his hands on her shoulders. She just stared back at him, her face not revealing any emotions.

"Just let me talk to Vig first. And if need be we will go to her, ok?" She looked into his eyes. For a moment he just stared back at her, then he nodded.

"Very well. But you must promise me you will let me know what you find out."

"I will. Now you need to take your own advice and get some rest. The Dracones Custodia will come for you if anything changes down there."

"Aednat! We have to go. It's getting dark and I promised Lady Orelaith we would be home by dinner." Garbhan shouted.

"Coming! I just have to gather up the fish I caught. Will you come help me?" she replied as she pulled in the line. Garbhan came walking over, but a few feet short of her he stopped and stared out to sea.

"Grandma is going to be so surprised when she sees how many fish I have caught. Are you going to help me or not?" she asked and looked up at him. He was squinting against the setting sun, then his eyes widened.

"Leave the fish. We have to go, now!" He grabbed hold of her arm and threw her up on the horse.

"But we can't just leave the fish…" she complained. He stuffed a few in his bag and looked up at her.

"Aednat, I don't have time to explain right now. Some bad men are coming and we need to warn the people in the village and the nuns in the monastery." He jumped up behind her and drove his heels into the animal's sides, setting them off at a breakneck pace. She looked back and saw the ships with their big sails silhouetted against the setting sun. There were more ships than she could count, but then again, she could not count very far yet. As they raced up the hill from the dock, Garbhan shouted at the people they passed.

"Vikings! The Vikings are coming! Get to the monastery!" Soon the warning bell sounded and people raced behind them on their way up to the monastery. As the ships pulled up on the shore, hordes of ruthless men jumped over the railings. Garbhan did not stop till he was inside the stone walls, then he jumped off and caught Aednat as she jumped down.

"Go find Lady Orelaith and stay with her. Once I have warned the nuns I will come and find you. Now run!"

"You promise?" she asked and looked up at him.

"I will find you, no matter what happens," he said and kissed her forehead. She was afraid now. Her little heart racing as she ran down the dark hallway to their room

"Grandma! Grandma! Some bad men are coming!" Aednat shouted as she swung the door to their chamber open. A nun was sitting next to the bed where Orelaith lay. She turned and stared wide-eyed at the little girl who had come crashing into the room.

"Vikings?! The Vikings are coming? Oh lord!" The nun crossed herself and got up.

"Stay with your grandmother, child. She fell down earlier and is really sick now. You need to be with her. I will return as soon as I can." Aednat stared after her as she walked out and closed the door behind her. She stood there for a second then turned, climbed into the bed and curled up next to Orelaith.

Chapter 51

Sigvald roared in anger as they searched through the houses and found nothing but a few old people and worthless goods. They had been spotted too early by a boy on the docks. Bjørn and some of the men pulled the old people out of the houses before setting the buildings on fire in pure spite.

"What do you want me to do with these bags of bones?" Bjørn called over to Sigvald. "Kill them and bring the heads with you up to the monastery walls." The old men and women begged for mercy, but mercy was for the weak, not for Vikings. Cries of horror came from the small village and their cries reached the stone building at the top of the hill as his men slaughtered the old ones. A trail of blood followed them as they made their way up the hill.

"Toss the heads over the walls. That should scare them good." Sigvald laughed. The walls were not that tall, so they used some ladders they found around the village to climb over. These people deserved to be killed. They did not even try to defend themselves. Pathetic! They met little resistance in the courtyard. A handful of the town's men went to their gods quickly. Sigvald set his eyes on the large wooden doors to the people's holy house.

LORE OF THE DRAGONS: ESSENCE OF A QUEEN

"To the main doors! Break them down!" It did not take long for the men to get through, and inside they found what they had been looking for: gold and women.

Garbhan and two of the older boys from the village had gotten a few of the women and all the children out through a side door and over the wall. "Get as far away as you can and do not look back till you know you are safe." One of the boys stared at him.

"You're not coming?"

"I have to go back for the girl I am the guardian of, and her grandmother too. Just go!" he said and climbed back down into the shadows behind the stable. He had to get to the sleeping quarters before the men were done in the chapel. His training came to good use as he made his way silently through the kitchens and down the dark narrow hallway to Lady Orelaith's and Aednat's room. He was just about to open the door to their chamber when a young Viking came running at him, screaming at the top of his lungs. Garbhan jumped to the side just in time and he felt the draft of the man's mace at the back of his neck. He sent his sword into the barbarian's leg causing him to cry out in pain. He saw the shadow behind him too late and a blinding pain sent him to the ground, then everything went black.

"Damn it, Brage! He almost got the better of you. If I had not followed you here, you would have been killed. Your mother would have ended me if I came home without you," Bjørn shouted at his son.

"I am sorry, father. I could have taken him, but he

wouldn't stop moving around." The young man sobbed.

"You better wipe away those tears before any of the others come this way. I will not have you shame me with that kind of weakness," Bjørn said and pulled his son to his feet. Brage dried his cheeks.

"He was going into that chamber, so there must be something of value in that room."

"Let's see what he was hiding," Bjørn said and tore the door open. The small chamber was dark and only contained two small beds, a chest and a chair.

"Go through the chest, there may be gold in it and…" A soft whimper made Bjørn turn to the bed. He tore the covers back and found a beautiful woman asleep wearing a white dress and a little girl curled up next to her. Big green eyes stared at him fearfully and he backed away for a second. This small child looked so much like the daughter that he had lost to the fever it was almost like seeing a ghost.

"Do you see what I see?" he almost whispered to his son. The boy limped over. As he looked down at the little girl, he gasped.

"She looks like Ragnhild!" Bjørn straightened up.

"Take her and put this woman out of her misery." When he headed out the door, he casually added, "She looks half dead anyway." Brage looked at the woman. He had killed before, but only in a fair fight. He pulled the girl out of the bed and raised his sword, ready to plunge it into the woman's heart. But as he was standing like that, she opened her eyes and looked at him. Her hand shot out and grabbed hold of his leg, which for some reason made him feel so weak he almost stumbled. Then she looked over at the girl and smiled weakly. He dropped his sword, he could not kill her.

"I will give you your life." She closed her eyes slowly, still with a soft smile quivering on her pale lips. Then he heard a voice resonating in his head.

"Do not harm her, she is chosen and more powerful than she looks. If you take her, know that powerful creatures will come looking for her." He stared at her in horror as he backed away. She had to be some kind of witch! He grabbed the girl and ran out of the room before she could cast a spell on him. The girl cried and kicked him but she was too small to cause him much trouble. He came out into the courtyard with the crying girl tucked under his arm as the other men came out from the church dragging the other women behind them.

"What have you got there, Brage?" Sigvald laughed. "Finally found someone you could actually beat?" He blushed,

"I had to kill a few men to get her. And she will fetch a good price should I decide to sell her." His father came over.

"Take her to the ship and stay there with her. We will be right behind you with the other thralls. And then we will sail home." He nodded to his father, then glared at the other men before walking out the gate with the struggling girl in his arms.

Orelaith could not move but she smelled the smoke. Would this be the end of her? The young Viking had not killed her, but there was no way she could stop him from taking Aednat. She started unraveling the web that kept her shielded from Bas, but it was a long and painstaking process because of her weakened state. It took her quite a while, but finally she broke the last binding. She could sense the direction of where he was, but they were too far apart for her to feel his emotions. Hopefully he would notice and come to her, but all she could do now was wait and hope the building did not collapse around her.

Nex had thrown all he had at them this night. Maybe he realized that time was running out for his men. One more day, then they would be no more than carrion, falling wherever they stood. The bulk of the men were concentrated on the gates, repeatedly throwing oil on it and shooting flaming arrows in an attempt to burn it down. Aqua was constantly flooding the wood with water and Serovita used her powers to spread the very grain of the wood to allow more water in. On the outer walls men were fighting the ones trying to come in that way. Blood was making the footing slippery and it was wearing on the defenders. Luna, Tempest and Bas, along with the soldiers, were fighting the endless stream of men climbing up the ladders. When one fell to his death, another took his place immediately.

"I don't know how long our men can keep this up!" Tempest shouted over to Bas when the stream of men died down a little.

"I know. But the night is almost over and—" Bas stopped mid sentence and stared off into the night.

"Bas!" Tempest screamed as an attacker jumped over the wall with his sword raised. It came down inches from Bas' head. He swung his big axe sending the man who attacked him flying over the wall in a shower of blood. Then Bas leaned over the wall and pushed the ladder away. The men on it cried out as they fell to the ground.

"What the hell is going on, Bas? That man almost cleaved you in two."

"Orelaith... I can feel her again," Bas said and closed his eyes.

Dawn was coming. As they expected, Nex's men pulled back, which gave them a chance to get some much needed rest. Word was sent to the others and they all gathered in the counseling chamber. Bas was pacing back and forth while the others collapsed in the chairs.

"What is going on?" Opulentia asked as she strode in through the big doors.

"Orelaith. I can feel her again!" Bas said as he walked over and took her hands.

"You can?" she said looking at him. "Can you feel her emotions?" Bas shook his head,

"No, just her presence." They sat down with the others.

"It is good news, I think..." Opulentia said thoughtfully.

"But why now? Why would she let me in now?" Bas asked, his voice unsure.

"I... I don't know. Once we have all rested, there is a

spell I can cast that can intensify the bond you two have, but I will need all of you. It may be enough to communicate with her briefly."

"Can't we do it now?" Bas asked impatiently. Opulentia shook her head.

"We can't, unfortunately. We will need to be fully rested, as it is a very draining spell." Tempest folded her hands on the table

"I am sorry to interrupt, but we have a more pressing matter to attend to here and now. The few soldiers we have left are exhausted, and most of them have minor injuries of some kind."

"Tempest! Bas is worried about Orelaith. It is hard for him to concentrate when he is worried about his one true love. Solis said and gave Bas a compassionate smile. Tempest looked at him,

"Forgive me, Bas. It was not my intention to be inconsiderate. However, if we do not think of something soon, there will be nothing for Orelaith to come back to."

"Don't worry about it, Tempest. You are of course right. We need to plan out what to do here. Nex still has a large number of men left, but time's running out for him." Luna picked at the fruit on the table.

"It still puzzles me that he has not taken on his true form." Bas smiled bitterly.

"He has a bigger army and still thinks he can beat us that way. However, winning this battle is not enough for him. He wants me and Garbhan to submit to him. If he can't have that, he wants us both dead. As for Aednat, he wants her power, one way or the other..." Opulentia sighed.

"He needs to be stopped. Are you willing to do what it takes, Bas? If he should throw all caution to the wind and take on dragon form, are you willing to do the same?" Bas just looked at her for a moment, then he nodded.

"If it will keep these people safe, yes."

"Should his men die before he has achieved his goal, he just might become that desperate." Vig got up, "But for now, I do believe we all need some rest. As time runs out for Nex's army he will become increasingly unpredictable."

And sure enough, Bas was woken from his sleep not long after he had put his head down.

"Bas! They are attacking again." Castiel shouted as he burst into his room.

"Already?!" Bas jumped up and started pulling on the leather armor. Castiel helped him tighten some of the straps.

"He's throwing everything he has at us. Not one man is left in the camp down there. They are all concentrating on the gate. Nex himself is making his way there now." Bas turned and stared at him.

"To the gate??" Castiel nodded. "He's probably already there." Bas grabbed his sword and ran for the door with Castiel at his heels.

"Let's finish this."

Chapter 52

 Garbhan tried to open his eyes. A sharp pain shot through his head and he felt sick to his stomach. Smoke was stinging his nostrils as he tried to remember where he was and what had happened. Fire! The building was burning. His brain was working overtime as he crawled over to the wall and leaned up against it. There was something he was supposed to do, someone he needed to get to. But who? He looked around. The stone hallway was sparsely lit, the only light came from a handful of torches along the walls. Smoke was billowing in from the far end of it. He could make out the wooden doors that lined the narrow space and blinked as he tried to remember. Then it all came back to him, Aednat and Orelaith! He scrambled to his feet and stumbled over to their room. When he reached the open door, he noticed a trail of blood leading from the room and his heart started racing. How long had he been unconscious? He leaned a hand on the door frame and gazed into the overturned room.

 "Aednat? Are you here?" he whispered. The afternoon sun shone in through the small windows and he realized he must have been senseless for hours. A low cough came from the bed and he hurried over.

LORE OF THE DRAGONS: ESSENCE OF A QUEEN

"Lady Orelaith? Oh lady Orelaith… where is Aednat?" He knelt down next to the bed and took her hand. Her breath was strained and she was very weak, but she managed to turn her head towards him and opened her eyes.

"The Vikings have her. I could not stop them from taking her." A tear fell from her eye and trickled down onto the pillow. Garbhan hung his head and cried. His shoulders shook with emotion and he clung to her hand as if it were a lifeline.

"I let her down… I let you all down. I should never have left her." She managed to lift her hand and stroked his dark curls.

"Garbhan, you did not fail. We put too big a burden on your young shoulders. There was no way any of us could have known that something like this would happen. I am proud of you, no matter what." He dried his eyes and looked at her.

"I will find her, I swear to you with all that I know. I will bring her back to you no matter how long it takes." He got to his feet. "I need to get you to safety. The monastery is burning and we need to get out. Can you walk?" Orelaith nodded but was unsure if she actually could. Garbhan helped her sit up and lifted her feet out of the bed. With her arm around his shoulders she strained to get up and take a few stumbling steps. Garbhan frowned and said,

"This is not going to work. You are too weak to walk on your own." She was about to protest when he picked her up and started to walk down the hallway at a fast pace. She stared at him, amazed at his strength. He smiled at her.

"I have always been strong for my age, Lady Orelaith. And I must say you are as light as a feather." The sun was bright as Garbhan stepped into the courtyard. The few that he had helped escape the night before had returned and came running towards him. One of the women put down her cloak and he laid Orelaith gently on it.

"Word must be sent to Lord Basilicus at once." Garbhan said and looked at the young novice. She nodded.

"I will find a runner." She started to walk away. Garbhan called after her, "I need some food and water as soon as that is taken care of."

"I will see to it at once. And if you don't mind me saying, you need someone to take a look at the wound." His hand went up to the back of his head. It was sticky with blood. He had taken a hard blow, good thing his skull was thicker than most. He nodded and the novice ran off.

As the last rays of sun disappeared behind the surrounding hills, a smothering darkness fell on them. By then Nex's men had almost broken through the gate. It was becoming more of an effort for Aqua to put the flames out every time it caught fire.

"I can't keep this up much longer! It's as if the water I am pouring into the wood is being drawn right back out again!" she shouted over the sound of the fighting.

LORE OF THE DRAGONS: ESSENCE OF A QUEEN

"I will see if I can find out what is going on," Luna shouted back and ran off. A little while later she returned with a handful of men. "Nex is still shooting flames at the gate while Caliga and Inanis are both casting some kind of tendril spell towards the door." Bas shook his head.

"I should have known. What is going on up there? Are his men still scaling the walls?" he asked as the two of them walked away from the worst of the noise.

"They only have a few ladders up. Tempest and the Dracones Custodia can hold them back. Most of his forces are concentrated on the gate. We need to –" A loud crash sounded behind them and they turned just as the last pieces of the gate burst inwards in an inferno of flames. Through the shredded opening they saw Nex standing just beyond the splintered remains of the gate. He stared at them with an arrogant grin on his face. A split second later, hordes of men came running through the opening like a black wave.

"The gate has been breached! Pull back to the inner bailey!" Bas shouted. They fell back to a position that was easier to defend and from there, slowly backed up further and further until they reached the steps leading up to the keep itself.

"Get the men inside, now! Only the Dracones Custodia and us should be left outside." Bas shouted at Tempest between swings. He and Castiel pushed forward to create enough space to enable Tempest and Luna to get the few remaining soldiers inside. Luna pushed Aqua inside as well,

"You are no good to us out here. You have drained yourself too much. Besides, I need you to make sure this door stays closed. Can you do that?"

"Of course I can do that. I could fly circles around you right now if I wanted to," she replied.

"Good. You can do that later," Luna said and winked at her before pushing the big doors shut. Then she turned and charged into the fight. Aqua heard the battle raging through the thick doors. Soon the men out there would die, she only prayed that Bas, Tempest and Luna could hold out that long. Vig came running down the hallway.

"Aqua my dear, are you hurt?" She shook her head.

"No, I am fine. But I am rather hungry. Do you think maybe you could..." Vig crossed her arms and looked at her.

"Here? Now?" Aqua nodded and smiled.

"Just something to keep me going. A couple of pies, or maybe a leg of lamb?" Vig stroked her cheek.

"I would ask how you can think of food at a time like this, but I know better. The constant casting you did at the gate must have drained you completely and with the metabolism you water dragons have... well, I should have thought of that before you did. I will have some food sent down right away." Then Vig turned and walked off.

"Wait! Have you seen Conri or Art? They were not among the men I sent inside," Aqua called after her.

"Art is up in the room for the wounded with Cara and the twins, but I have not seen Conri." Aqua turned towards the doors. She could still hear the fighting in the bailey.

LORE OF THE DRAGONS: ESSENCE OF A QUEEN

"Luna, is Conri out there with you?" she sent, pressing her ear against the door. It took a while before she got a reply.

"No, he's not with us on the steps. Maybe he's with Art?"

"No. Vig already checked, and he's not there. We need to find him!" The screams outside the door reached a crescendo. Fear for her friends squeezed Aquas chest, making it hard for her to breathe. Then the door shook as something on the other side hit it with great force. Aqua backed away and noticed that the world outside had gone completely silent.

"Bas?" she anxiously sent out beyond the battered, wooden door. It swung open and Bas' huge figure blocked the opening as he walked in. His tangled and bloody hair clung to his face, his arms colored red and his eyes glowed.

"It is over. The men just collapsed, dead," he said. He should have been happy it was over but there was a sadness in his eyes as he looked back out of the door.

"Such a waste of life… and for what? One dragon's greed for power?" He shook his head and let out a long drawn sigh.

"No! This is unacceptable!" They turned and saw Nex standing in the archway leading to the inner bailey. He was furiously mad and erratic. He transformed and charged towards Bas, roaring madly. Without hesitation, Bas also transformed and met Nex's charge. The two giants crashed into each other and lifted off the ground. The golden and the black dragon locked together in an aerial battle, spinning up into the night sky. Balls of flame could be seen from the ground as the royal brothers fought over who would be king of the dragons. Even from the ground, it was easy to see that Bas was tired. His movements were strained and Nex was winning. In a burst of flames Bas came crashing down into the bailey, making the whole castle tremble at the impact. Nex followed him down and landed next to him.

"I win, brother. Just bring me the girl and I just might spare your life." Nex gloated as he circled Bas. Halfway across the courtyard stood Caliga and Inanis, blocking their path and preventing Tempest and Luna from coming to Bas' aid. Nex said, grinning madly. "You always thought you were better than me. But you were never willing to kill to gain your power. I am." Bas got up, slowly and painfully.

"I am not dead yet, brother, and I have no intentions of letting you take Aednat away so you can corrupt or end her."

"Fool! Then you will die for your stupidity," Nex shouted and pounced on Bas. Just as he landed, a small shadow with the speed of an arrow shot across the yard. Conri landed on Nex's head and drove a dagger into the black dragon's eye. He screamed out in pain and anger, swatting Conri aside like an insect. Caliga and Inanis glanced back, taking their eyes off Tempest and Luna long enough for them to charge forward. Nex jumped up into the air and when the two females saw what was happening they transformed and followed him.

"I will return, brother! And I will take what is mine!" Luna ran over to where Conri had landed.

"He's still breathing!" Bas turned back into his human form and limped over.

"Take him to Opulentia, quickly!"

"What about you? Are you ok?" Tempest asked as she came over.

"I am fine, don't worry about me. Just get the others inside and start assessing the damage." The sound of a galloping horse made them turn around. It was the white horse that they had sent with Orelaith and the children. Bas felt fear squeezing his heart as it came to a stop next to him. The rider was a young novice. When Bas helped her down, she collapsed in his arms.

"Lady Orelaith… is dying. Vikings…" This was all she said before passing out. Without a word he ran up the steps and found his way to the room where Opulentia was treating the wounded. "This girl needs care, now! She comes from the monastery where Orelaith and Aednat are. You need to come with me, now." Vig heard what was being said and nodded.

"Go, I can take care of everyone here. Bring them home." Bas and Opulentia hurried off followed by Tempest and Luna. From the window, Vig saw the four of them fly off and prayed they would all return safely.

Chapter 53

Orelaith heard Bas whisper softly to her and she smiled. She did not want to wake up from this dream, it was so lifelike. She could feel his presence as if he was truly there.

"Orelaith. Orelaith, you must wake up, my carus. Come back to me." She opened her eyes and saw his tear stained face.

"Bas? Am I dreaming, or are you actually here?" Her voice was weak, and speaking made her throat hurt. She touched his face and smiled. "You came. I tried calling for you, but I didn't think you could hear me." Tears welled up in his eyes.

"I will never leave you again. I almost lost you…" She saw Opulentia, Tempest and Luna standing next to them. Their faces grave with concern.

"We need to get you home. But first Opulentia will do what she can for you." Bas said,

"I will not go far." Garbhan came running.

"Lord Basilicus! We need to go after them. They took

her. I tried to protect her, but I failed." Bas embraced him.

"Garbhan, I am so glad to see you are still alive. But what are you talking about? Where is Aednat?" The young boy hung his head and started telling him what had happened that night. Bas closed his eyes as Garbhan told him how the barbarians had taken his granddaughter away. When he finished, Bas knelt down in front of him and looked into his eyes.

"You are not to blame, Garbhan. You did everything in your power to protect her and more. We will find her again, don't you worry." Bas pulled him close again and looked up at Tempest and Luna. "Gather all the information you can about these men. We will go after her as soon as we can." Opulentia put her hand on his shoulder.

"I have done what I can for her here, but it is worse than I thought. We need to get her back home again as soon as possible." He nodded.

"Garbhan, show me to their room. Luna, get someone to hitch the horse up to the wagon. We will be leaving shortly." Bas followed Garbhan into the smoking ruins. He noticed how the roof was burned away everywhere but over Orelaith's chamber.

"Remarkable. She seems to have conjured a protective field around her room." Tempest came in behind them.

"What on earth…" she said as she saw the state of the room. The chests were emptied out on the floor, the small table and chair were overturned and the window was stained black with soot from the fire.

"See if you can find anything that may have belonged to the barbarian who took Aednat. We will need it to be able to track the men who took her." Bas spoke softly as he picked up his granddaughter's doll where it lay halfway under the overturned table. Garbhan gently picked up the things from the floor and put them in the chests.

"Blood... Didn't you say you cut him, Garbhan?" Tempest asked as she knelt down.

"Yes, I did. A rather good hit to the leg," Garbhan said almost proudly.

"Blood we can use. Hand me that scarf." she said and pointed at a yellow piece of cloth on the floor. "It's almost completely dried up, but we only need a few drops." Tempest soaked up as much as she could.

"That should do it." She tucked the scarf into her pocket and helped Garbhan and Bas pick up the last of Orelaith and Aednat's belongings.

When they got back home, the people had started to clean up. Outside the walls several big fires had been lit and the bodies of Nex's men were being burned on them. When they saw Bas and the others returning, they cheered. But when they saw how grave his expression was they stopped.

"The people will need to be told. They love Aednat and maybe some of them have information that can be useful to us." Tempest said quietly to Bas.

"I agree, but make sure they know she is not dead. I will have no mourning over her," Bas replied as they came to a halt outside the stables. Solis and Terra were waiting for them at the top of the steps. Before they even had the chance to ask about the situation, Bas cut them off by saying

"I want everyone gathered in the counsell chamber immediately, except Vig and Opulentia, of course. Garbhan, Conri is in his room. He will want to see you. Stay with him till I send for you both." He gently lifted Orelaith out of the wagon and carried her past the worried faces of Solis and Terra. Opulentia came up behind him and stopped in front of them.

"Terra, go find Vig. Tell her I need her in Bas and Orelaith's chamber right away. Solis, go find the others and get them to the meeting. Oh, and have a maid bring us food and drink. None of us have eaten in quite a while." With those words she walked off. They stared at each other for a moment, then Solis ran off and Terra followed quickly.

Vig hurried down the hallway and in through the open door to Bas and Orelaith's chamber. Opulentia looked up and came to meet her.

"Let us talk in the hallway," she whispered. Once outside she closed the door behind her and looked at Vig. "Orelaith has been keeping something from us for quite a while. The day they met Ruina at Orelaith's old home, she got hit by a spell. It has withered her body and soul away for years."

"Can we remove it?" Vig asked anxiously. Opulentia shook her head,

"I don't think we can, but we will have to try. First we will need to see how it has been set up and take it from there. I am surprised how a dragon like Ruina could possibly make a web so complicated."

"Does Bas know?" Vig asked and glanced at the closed door.

"Not how serious it is, but he knows I was not able to heal her when we first found her."

"Let's see what we can do." Vig said and opened the door.

Bas entered the counsell chamber and found the others waiting for him there. He walked to his seat as they stared expectantly at him.

"You are probably all wondering what has happened and I will tell you all that I know. After that I will try to answer any questions you may have, but I want to leave as soon as I can to be with Orelaith." He looked around at them. When they nodded, he explained the series of events that had transpired and what had caused Orelaith's weakened condition. When he was done, several of them were crying and the Dracones Custodia all stood with their heads bowed in respect.

"As you can understand, I wish to go to Orelaith, but I know we need to find these men that took Aednat and go after –" Vig and Opulentia entered the room, their faces clearly showing the emotional strain they were under. Bas stared at them for a moment before he managed to speak.

"Can you… tell us what you found?" Vig looked at Opulentia as they found their seats.

"I think Opulentia should tell you." Every eye in the room was on Opulentia as she opened her mouth to speak.

"As you know, Orelaith is extremely sick. Vig and I have just done an examination of her condition to see if there is anything we can do about it."

"And is there?" Bas asked as he leaned forward, resting his elbows on the table. Opulentia shook her head.

"I am afraid this is beyond us. The only one who could possibly heal her is Aednat, but not until she comes into her full power. The problem is, I don't think we can find her in time." There was an outcry from those gathered in the room and the Dracones Custodia fell to their knees.

"There is one more thing to consider: should she die, it may only be a matter of time before Bas follows her." The room was silent now and Bas folded his hands on the table.

"Is there nothing you can do? I can not lose her."

"And we do not want to lose you, Bas," Tempest said and

put her hand on his shoulder. Opulentia looked thoughtful.

"There is one thing... but it is risky. I honestly don't even know if it is possible." Bas stared at her hopefully.

"What? Anything that might save her..." She looked up at him.

"The crystal, do you still have it?"

"I do. But what do you want with it?" Bas asked with a frown.

"Orelaith is not dead yet, but she soon will be unless we find Aednat. The crystal will buy us some time to bring her back home." Vig looked at her with a skeptical frown on her face.

"What exactly are you talking about doing here?" Opulentia leaned back in her chair.

"I want to put Orelaith's soul into the crystal. That way, Bas can keep her close till we are able to cure her body. I know how it is done. After all, I was the one who helped your mother get into it before." Bas rubbed his chin.

"But what about her body? Without her soul in it... won't it just decompose?" Opulentia shook her head.

"Not if we encase it in stone. But it has to be completely sealed. Nothing must touch it or it will fall apart. I have a spell that will let it draw on the powers of the earth to sustain itself." Vig nodded slowly.

"Yes... that may actually work." Luna squinted at

Opulentia.

"What is the catch? What would happen if it went wrong?"

"The same thing that is going to happen should we do nothing, she will die. But I will need Orelaith to agree to this. I can not do this without her help." Opulentia said and took a sip of her wine.

"Will she be able to communicate with us after she is put into the crystal?" Bas asked.

"I am unsure of that. Your mother could not, and she was the most powerful dragon I have known. But she had already lost your father at the time. You alone should be able to reach her. However, I am unsure if it is even possible. "

"I say we do this. I believe it is the only way for us to save her. Bas, you and Opulentia will need to talk to her. Get her consent and send for us if she agrees to this," Vig said and got up. Bas nodded slowly.

"I will do it now. There is no time to lose. We need to find a way to track the men who took Aednat. But first I need to talk to Orelaith." He got up and sighed.

"Tempest, you are in charge of the search team. Find out what you can." Tempest nodded and Bas left the room with Opulentia trailing behind.

Chapter 54

Orelaith opened her eyes and looked up into Bas' face. She smiled weakly,

"Bas..."

"Orelaith, my carus. How are you feeling?" Bas asked softly.

"I have been better. I... I am sorry, Bas. I should have told you about this earlier." A tear rolled down the side of her face.

"Hush, my love. It is not important now that you are back home again." Bas stroked her hair.

"But I will not get any better, Bas. I told Vig and Opulentia to be truthful with me and I know I am dying." Bas glanced at Opulentia.

"We won't let you die. I will do anything in my power to..." Orelaith touched his lips.

"Bas, I know you would do whatever it takes, but I know there is nothing you can do. I will fight this, but I feel my strength leaving me as we speak. If there was anything, anything at all, I would do it without question." Opulentia took a step towards the bed.

"There is something, but it is risky and I am not even sure if it will work. But if it does, it may be a way to stop you from getting any worse. At least till we can get Aednat back so she can heal you." Orelaith looked from Opulentia to Bas and back.

"What is it? If it will save Bas, I will do it."

"It's not about saving Bas. It is about saving you, my dear. But it may not work." Opulentia said and took Orelaith's hand.

"If we do nothing, we will both die. I want to try this. For both of us."

"Before you decide, I need to explain exactly what we are suggesting," Opulentia said seriously.

"If you agree, we can proceed in the morning." Orelaith nodded and Opulentia started to explain the process. Orelaith listened intently as all the details were laid out. She interrupted Opulentia to ask some questions, but when all the points were made clear for her, she seemed thoughtful.

"If it does not work, I want to be able to say goodbye to everyone." Orelaith spoke the words with grim determination.

"Of course. Do you feel up to it tonight or do you want to do it tomorrow?" Opulentia asked and squeezed her hand.

"Tomorrow. I am still pretty tired from traveling back

here," Orelaith replied and closed her eyes.

"I think you need to rest now. As I said, you will need to take part in the spell if we are going to succeed, so you need as much strength as you can muster," Opulentia said and got up.

"I will be back later to check on you." Once she had left, Orelaith looked at Bas,

"I need you to promise me something."

"Anything," he said and kissed her hand.

"If this does not work… I want you to live on for me. And find Aednat and bring her back home."

"Don't worry, it is going to work. It has to…" Bas said and smiled as bravely as he could. Orelaith looked at him and frowned.

"Promise." Bas got up and walked to the window.

"I wish I could, my carus. But I can't and I don't want to think about it. So please, don't make me give you a promise I can't possibly keep." Orelaith sighed.

"Then at least promise me you will try. I can not make this decision only in regards to my own life when I know your life is as much at risk as mine." He closed his eyes.

"I will try." He sat back down at her side and stroked her hair. "As for finding Aednat, I will never give up. I will find her and I will bring her back home." Orelaith smiled up at him and closed her eyes.

LORE OF THE DRAGONS: ESSENCE OF A QUEEN

"That is all I can ask of you, my love. Now I think I will sleep for a while. I am so very tired…"

As Bas left the room, Garbhan came running down the hallway.

"Lord Basilicus."

"Garbhan, how are you doing?" Bas smiled weakly at him. Garbhan was losing his boyish features, becoming a man. He stopped in front of Bas.

"My brother was wondering if you could come to his chamber? He would come to you, but is still too weak to walk. I am afraid that the news of Aednat's kidnapping has hit him pretty hard. Would you come with me?" Garbhan asked. Bas put his arm around his shoulder and smiled.

"Of course. I will go to him now. Would you go ask the cook to send some food to his chamber? I have not eaten in a while, and even though I am not very hungry, I do need to eat something." Garbhan nodded.

"Right away, my Lord." Bas stopped and turned Garbhan towards him. With one hand on each shoulder he looked into the boy's face.

"Garbhan, my boy. You do not need to call me lord. You are like a son to me and I think of you as part of the family. You can just call me Bas like everyone else does. Can you do that?" Garbhan looked up at him and smiled.

"Yes, I can do that… Bas."

"Good. Now run along to the kitchen and see what the cook can whip up for us. Then come join us in your brother's room," Bas said and walked down the hallway.

Nex was laughing. At first, just a low rumbling, bubbling up into a full blown roar.

"Viking raiders? Really?" he finally managed to say after a little while. Dougal was smiling widely.

"Yes, indeed. They came the day before we attacked the castle. No one has seen the family since they came back with Orelaith." Nex burst out laughing again.

"Now, that is like music to my ears. Have someone sent after her as soon as possible. We need to find her before they do." Caliga was smiling too.

"She will be alone and unprotected. What a wonderful turn of events." Nex leaned back on his throne and smiled.

"My brother has failed and I can not begin to tell you how much I enjoy this. And the woman, Orelaith? Is she dead yet?"

"Not yet, but the word is that she is dying," Dougal said and grinned. Nex clapped his hands. "That is good news. All I have to do is wait for it to be over, then the power will be all mine."

Inanis took the cup Dougal offered her.

"Any leads on where the child has been taken?" Dougal grinned.

"A few… But I would be lying if I said it would be easy to find her. The Vikings in question come from across the big sea. That much at least is certain." Nex took a sip from his cup and frowned.

"Just get it taken care of. A chance like this must be seized. Whatever you need, it is yours. But find the girl before my cursed brother does." Dougal bowed.

"I will start at once, your highness." As he walked out, Caliga's eyes followed on him. "How long will you give him?" she asked as the door closed behind him. "Oh, I don't know. A month, maybe. If he comes back with bad news…well, let us just say it will be rather unpleasant for him if he does." "How is your eye?" Caliga asked. "I was unable to heal it properly I'm afraid." "I can not see it, if that is what you wanted to know. But take a look and see what you think," Nex said and removed the bandage so Caliga could examine it. The skin around the eye was untouched but where the pupil had once been a dark hazel, it was now all white with a red streak through it. "This is as good as it is going to get. You will carry this mark for the rest of your life," Caliga said and leaned back. "The human that did this, did you kill him?" Inanis asked. Nex shook his head and put his cup down on the table. "Dougal says he is still alive. But I will find him and end him for what he has done, slowly and painfully." Caliga frowned. "Do you even know his name?" Nex leaned forward and grinned. "Yes, his name is Conri. He is the young dragon slayer."

Chapter 55

Morning came too soon and Bas knew he would have to let go of Orelaith. He looked down on her face as she lay sleeping in his arms. How could he possibly manage to live on without her, even for the time it took them to find Aednat and bring her back home? The long talk he had with Conri last night had soothed him a little. It had taken his mind off what was going to happen in a short while. As the time grew near, it was painfully apparent that it was not just a bad dream or that Orelaith would miraculously recover. She stirred in his arms and opened her eyes. She smiled weakly as she looked up at him.

"Bas, my love…" He kissed her forehead and smiled back at her.

"My carus, did you sleep well?" Orelaith sat up and stretched her arms over her head.

"Yes, my love. I feel better than I have in years. Opulentia said that I would. The web she cast on me before I fell asleep has stopped the poison from spreading further. It is only temporary, so I can be strong enough to help her in what we are about to attempt." She stroked his chin and frowned at him. "But what about you? Did you get any sleep, my love?" Bas looked away but smiled.

"I can sleep later, my love. We don't know how long it is going to be before I get Aednat back home again, so sleeping seemed like a waste of our time together." Orelaith frowned.

"Bas... I love you with all my heart. Promise me you will take care of yourself until we are reunited... Promise." Bas took her hand and kissed it.

"I promise. Now, are you ready for some breakfast?" Orelaith nodded.

"Oh yes, I seem to have worked up quite an appetite." Bas smiled and walked over to the table where the food had been set out.

"I had the cook bring some food here earlier. Fresh bread, cheese and even some strawberries. I believe there is some honey too," he said while he set the tray on the bed. She smiled at him and picked up a big red strawberry.

"Thank you. Come and sit with me so we can spend this last hour together." They had always enjoyed each other's company. They talked of what had been and how they first met. The sadness Bas felt was now forgotten and for the first time since Rionach had died, he thought he saw true happiness in her eyes.

This soon turned to worry as someone knocked on the door and Opulentia entered followed by the others. She sat down next to Orelaith and took her hands.

"It is good to see you looking so well, but I am afraid it is time. We have to do this now while you are still feeling strong. Are you ready, my dear?" Orelaith glanced at Bas, then nodded.

"I do believe I am. However, I would like you to go over my part again. I want to be absolutely sure of what you need me to do." Opulentia and Vig went over the details with her yet again, while the others gathered around the bed.

"You really think this is going to work?" Bas asked concerned. Vig put her arm around his shoulders.

"Yes, Bas, I do. Now then, are you ready?" Reluctantly he nodded and handed the crystal to Opulentia.

"I have to be, I guess." So with Bas sitting behind Orelaith, Vig and Opulentia sitting on each side and the others forming a physical circle around them the web weaving started. Vig was the first to place her spell on Orelaith.

"This will keep your body alive once your soul goes into the crystal. Now, my child, it is yours and Opulentia's turn…" Vig said and Opulentia took over.

"Follow my lead, child, and do as we talked about." Orelaith closed her eyes and let her tendrils reach into the crystal. A green light filled the room as more and more of her essence flowed into it. Suddenly she opened her eyes and looked up at Bas.

LORE OF THE DRAGONS: ESSENCE OF A QUEEN

"I will see you soon, my love, but for now you have to let me go. He pulled her close and kissed her forehead, then sighed deeply. Orelaith closed her eyes and let her soul follow the tendrils into the crystal. A blinding flash of light filled the room, then she was gone. After a moment of silence Opulentia handed the crystal to Bas who immediately mind sent into the crystal.

"My carus… can you hear me?" For what seemed like an eternity to him, there was no reply and he felt his heart sink. He put his hands over his eyes and sighed. Opulentia sat down next to him.

"Is she not replying?" Bas shook his head.

"No. How do we know it really worked? How do we know she is really in there if she does not answer?" Opulentia put her hand on his shoulder.

"Give her some time. Let her get used to being in spirit form. It must be strange for her to not have a physical body any more." Then she turned to Terra,

"Are you ready for your part, my dear friend?" Terra nodded,

"I am. I made an altar next to Rionach's resting place. Once her body is in place I will finish it."

"Good. And you, Serovita, are you ready too?" Opulentia asked.

"As ready as I'll ever be. Both Vig and Opulentia will assist me with the part I am to play in this." Bas got up and picked up Orelaith's limp body. Then he looked around the room.

"Then let us waste no more time." As he walked into the dark hallway, the others followed him silently. Torches lit the cave below and the flickering light shone on Orelaith's copper red curls as Bas carried her to the chamber where their daughter was buried. As he stood at the stone altar Terra had made, he hesitated for a second, not wanting to let go of her body.

"It is ok, Bas. You will be reunited with her again very soon. But for now, we need to make sure her physical body does not die." Vig spoke softly as she came up next to him. He looked at her with eyes brimming with tears.

"It feels like I have lost her... like we lost Rionach." Vig stroked his chin and smiled softly.

"But you haven't, Bas. This is only temporary, until we can get Aednat back home again." He sighed and kissed Orelaith's forehead.

"I will find Aednat and bring her back home, I promise." He whispered before gently laying her body down on the cold stone. Terra stood at her feet, Serovita at her head and Vig and Opulentia on either side of the altar. The others positioned themselves between them so they all formed a circle. Terra placed her hands on the stone and nodded to Serovita, who put her hands on either side of Orelaith's head. Vig took Orelaith's left hand and Opulentia the right one. The others rested their hands on each other's shoulders so they were all physically connected. As they started weaving the complicated web, the whole chamber hummed. Slowly the web was lowered over Orelaith's body, melting

LORE OF THE DRAGONS: ESSENCE OF A QUEEN

into her very skin. Serovita opened her eyes and nodded to Terra who sent her own tendrils forth into the stone itself. A crystal casing soon covered Orelaith's body and the humming stopped. Vig sent her tendrils into the empty shell.

"The spell is working. Her body should be able to sustain itself indefinitely." Bas let out a sigh of relief. After a little while, the chamber slowly emptied, but Bas did not budge. Luna walked up next to him and put her head on his shoulder.

"She will be returned to us soon and everything will be back to normal. Well… normal for us anyway." Bas smiled softly and put his arm around Luna's shoulders.

"Yes… I must believe it will be so. But before that can happen we need to get Aednat back home. So let's get the others gathered in the counseling chamber as soon as possible. Can you let them all know? I want to stay a little longer, if you don't mind."

"Of course, I will take care of it." Luna nodded and walked out leaving Bas standing in the dark chamber with the body of his wife on one side and the shell of his daughter in a stone coffin on the other side. His heart was heavy in his chest and he felt like the walls were closing in on him. But he did not want to leave. The last time he was in this chamber was the day Rionach passed away, and it somehow felt like Orelaith was gone too, even though he knew it was not so. He turned around and walked out quickly, knowing that if he stayed there much longer he would not be able to leave at all. So for the second time he walked out into the afternoon sunlight in their chamber, leaving someone he loved deeply behind in the darkness below.

When he entered the counsell chamber, the others were already there waiting for him. The room was heavy with sadness and everyone around the table seemed to be struggling with emotions they were not accustomed to. Bas knew he had to shift their focus as much as he needed to shift his own.

"We need to bring Aednat home. What have you come up with so far?" he asked and sat down.

"The men that took her do not belong to the settlement to the east. They come from across the big sea, so we will need to find a way of passage. I have sent out men to the coastal town to look into it. I will let you know as soon as I have word back from them," Tempest said. Bas nodded.

"Good. And the blood you found, were you able to find a way to track the men who took her?" Tempest shook her head.

"No, but it may be because she is so far away. We'll take it with us and see if we can use it once we get closer."

"That brings me to the next question; who is going?" They looked at eachother, then they all raised their hands. Bas shook his head.

"We can not all go. Nex is not going to rest for long and we have a responsibility to the people who live here." Tempest got up.

LORE OF THE DRAGONS: ESSENCE OF A QUEEN

"I have a suggestion. We set up four teams. Luna and Certus, Bas and Castiel, Conri and Garbhan and Fidelis and I. Every group will be accompanied by two of the Dracones Custodia."

"And what of the rest of us? We are just to stay here and do nothing?" Vig said, sounding very flustered. Bas smiled warmly at her.

"No, I do not intend to have you sit and do nothing. I agree to a certain point with Tempest's choice of who to send, but you will be going in her place, Vig. Tempest is needed here."

"What?! You can't be serious?!" Tempest said, sounding rather outraged. Bas put his hand on her shoulder.

"Now listen before you get yourself all worked up. You are the head of what is left of our army. You need to stay here and make sure that Nex does not try anything. Serovita and Aqua will be lending a helping hand in the harvest and Terra will be busy with repairs to the castle. Solis, I need you to be out there with the people, taking up Orelaith's role. Opulentia, I don't need to ask you to check on Orelaith's body every day, just to make sure she is doing well." She nodded in reply, as did the others. Tempest was sulking, but when Bas looked at her, she nodded too.

"Good, it is settled then. I want us to leave within the next week. And make sure…" Bas stopped and stared into the air in front of him.

"Bas? Are you ok?" Vig asked. For a while they all stared at him.

"Orelaith... I can feel her presence again." He spoke softly as tears filled his eyes.

"Try to reach her, Bas." Opulentia smiled warmly at him.

"Orelaith... my carus. Can you hear me?" Bas mind sent into the crystal he carried around his neck.

"Bas? Oh, my love, I can hear you." she sent back. Bas sighed in relief. When he looked around, he saw all their faces staring expectantly at him.

"I can hear her and she can hear me!" He smiled at them and they all looked as relieved as he was.

"Are you ok, my dear?" he sent into the crystal again.

"Yes, my love, I am. But my love, there is something else..."

"What, my love?" It took a while before she replied, but what she said sent shivers down his spine.

"I am not alone in here".

Her big hazel eyes stared out over the dark sea. Aednat wanted to go home, but the man who had

taken her away from Grandma Orelaith did not seem to care. She was scared, wet and tired. How

would grandpa and grandma know where she was going?

LORE OF THE DRAGONS: ESSENCE OF A QUEEN

She sat down on the hard deck of the ship and cried.

"Lady Aednat?" a voice whispered close by. Aednat looked up and saw one of the young nuns from the monastery sitting with the other people in the front of the boat.

"Sister Ruth? What are you doing here?" Aednat asked, sounding very surprised.

"Hush, don't let them hear you. Come here, child." The nun waved her over. Aednat dried her cheeks with the sleeve of her dress and crawled over. "Poor child. I can not believe they took you away from your grandmother," Sister Ruth said and put her arms around her. "

Why did they take us away?" Aednat asked. "I told the boy who took me I wanted to go home, but he just laughed at me and walked away." She looked up at Sister Ruth.

"They are evil men, Aednat. They do not care about what is right or wrong, about who they hurt or if we belong to someone else. To them we are no more than animals that can be kept for work or sold to others," Sister Ruth replied and rocked back and forth. Aednat still didn't understand.

"When are they going to take us home again?" The nun kissed her head and held her tight.

"We will not be going home again, child. You do best to forget about your family and those left behind. Forget who you were. They will probably give you a new name and you will have to work hard every day," Sister Ruth said and started crying. Aednat found herself getting angry.

"I will not forget who I am and I know that papa and

grandpa will come looking for me. They will punish the bad men and take me home again. Just wait and see." She looked around and saw about five other women sitting with them. "Garbhan promised he would find me, no matter what. He always keeps his promises, always!" Sister Ruth did not reply, but continued rocking back and forth with Aednat in her arms. Soon Aednat fell into a restless sleep.

Names and meanings

Basilicus – From Latin meaning regal, royal, princely. Golden dragon and heir to the throne. Son of Primoris.

Vigoratus – From Latin meaning healer, stout, hale, heal, hearty. White dragon, the healer and sort of a mother henn for all the others.

Serovita – Combination of the two Latin words Sero which means to sow or plant and Vita that means life. Green dragon. Kind and gentle.

Solis – From the Latin Sol Solis that means sun. Yellow dragon. A bit "blond". Usually the last to get the joke.

Aqua – From Latin meaning water. Blue dragon. A bit of a big child with a huge appetite.

Luna – From Latin meaning moon. The dark blue dragon. Rule breaker.

Terra – From Latin meaning earth. The Brown dragon. Royal historian who always has her nose in a book.

Tempest – From Latin meaning storm. Gray dragon with

lightning blue eyes. Was once the head of the royal army. Strong sense of honor. Wants to be more like Luna but is a stickler for order.

Frater – From Latin meaning brother. Basilicus youngest brother. Se Garbhan.

Opulentia - From Latin meaning wealth, riches, power, might, opulence, splendor. Rainbow dragon who has lived by herself in hiding.

Primoris – From Latin meaning first, foremost, at the top, uppermost, most distinguished. Queen and Basilicus mother. Her essence was in the crystal Orelaith had.

Nex - From Latin meaning violent death, slaughter. Black dragon. Infected and brother of Basilicus and Frater.

Inanis - From Latin meaning empty, vain, inane, useless. Red dragon with almost white eyes. Arrogant, stuck up and completely useless.

Caliga - From Latin meaning darkness, gloom, mist. Infected dragon. Is staying with Nex.

Ruina - From Latin meaning downfall, destruction. Yellow dragon. Sister of Nex and Bas.

Orelaith - "or + la" Orelaith means "golden princess." Farmers daughter that becomes the link between dragons and humans.

Bronagh -"bro + nah" Though rooted in bronach "sad, sorrowful" Woman sitting at the gate with her two children. Orelaith gives her gold and a new start.

Saoirse - "sear + sha" Irish word saoirse "freedom, liberty. She has changed her name as part of her new life from Bronagh. Becoming Orelaiths best human friend.

Conri – Means wolf king in Irish Gaelic. The young boy who is left orphaned after a dragon kills his mum and dad. His brother is Garbhan.

Garbhan - "Gahr-vawn " Means "little rough one" from Irish garbh "rough" combined with a diminutive suffix. This was the name of a 7th-century Irish saint. Is Conri's brother and a dragon reborn.

Cara "car + a" In Irish cara simply means a "friend." Conri's Aunt

Art - In Ireland a separate name from Arthur, it comes from an ancient word for "a bear," used in the sense of "outstanding warrior" or "champion." Conri's uncle.

Dougal - Anglicized form of the Gaelic name Dubhghall, which meant "dark stranger" from dubh "dark" and gall "stranger". Nex's henchman.

Rionach - "ree + in + ock" From rionach meaning "queenly." Orelaiths and Bas daughter. Has the Dragon queens memories and powers.

Aednat - "ey + nit" Enat, Ena The feminine of the name Aidan meaning "little fire." Rionach reborn as a result of Conri and Rionach falling in love. They did not know the curse.

Bridget - "bridge + id" Brigit The name Brigid from bright meaning "power, vigor, virtue" epitomizes the Irish genius for layering old and new. The dragon Opulentia

Blathnaid, Blanaid - "blaw + nid" blath means "flower, blossom." Saoirse's daughter.

Faolan - "fwail + awn" Phelan Comes from the word faol "wolf." Saoirse's son.

Is nox noctis vos ero Deus - This night you will be God sanguis effusus et luna ad ligandum te - Blood shed and moon to bind you